Conway Moncure

The Life of Thomas Paine Vol. 2

With a History of His Literary, Political, and Religious Career in America

Conway Moncure

The Life of Thomas Paine Vol. 2
With a History of His Literary, Political, and Religious Career in America

ISBN/EAN: 9783337202507

Printed in Europe, USA, Canada, Australia, Japan

Cover: Foto ©Raphael Reischuk / pixelio.de

More available books at **www.hansebooks.com**

T Paine

FROM THE SEAL AT LEWES

PROBABLE AGE, 35

THE

LIFE OF THOMAS PAINE

WITH A HISTORY OF HIS LITERARY, POLITICAL AND RELIGIOUS CAREER IN AMERICA FRANCE, AND ENGLAND

BY

MONCURE DANIEL CONWAY

AUTHOR OF "OMITTED CHAPTERS OF HISTORY DISCLOSED IN THE LIFE AND PAPERS OF EDMUND RANDOLPH," "GEORGE WASHINGTON AND MOUNT VERNON," "WASHINGTON'S 'RULES OF CIVILITY,'" ETC.

TO WHICH IS ADDED A SKETCH OF PAINE

BY WILLIAM COBBETT

(HITHERTO UNPUBLISHED)

VOL. II.

G. P. PUTNAM'S SONS

NEW YORK   LONDON
27 WEST TWENTY-THIRD STREET   24 BEDFORD STREET, STRAND

The Knickerbocker Press

1892

Electrotyped, Printed, and Bound by
The Knickerbocker Press, New York
G. P. Putnam's Sons

CONTENTS OF VOLUME II.

THE LIFE OF THOMAS PAINE.

CHAPTER I.

"KILL THE KING, BUT NOT THE MAN."

DUMAS' hero, Dr. Gilbert (in "Ange Pitou"), an idealization of Paine, interprets his hopes and horrors on the opening of the fateful year 1793. Dr. Gilbert's pamphlets had helped to found liberty in the New World, but sees that it may prove the germ of total ruin to the Old World.

"A new world," repeated Gilbert; "that is to say, a vast open space, a clear table to work upon,—no laws, but no abuses ; no ideas, but no prejudices. In France, thirty thousand square leagues of territory for thirty millions of people ; that is to say, should the space be equally divided, scarcely room for a cradle or a grave for each. Out yonder, in America, two hundred thousand square leagues for three millions of people ; frontiers which are ideal, for they border on the desert, which is to say, immensity. In those two hundred thousand leagues, navigable rivers, having a course of a thousand leagues ; virgin forests, of which God alone knows the limits,—that is to say, all the elements of life, of civilization, and of a brilliant future. Oh, how easy it is, Billot, when a man is called Lafayette, and is accustomed to wield a sword ; when a man is called Washington, and is accustomed to reflect deeply,—how easy is it to combat against walls of wood, of earth, of stone, of human flesh ! But when, instead of founding, it is necessary to destroy ; when we see in the old order things that we are obliged to attack,— walls of bygone, crumbling ideas ; and that behind the ruins even of these walls crowds of people and of interests still take refuge ; when, after having found the idea, we find that in order to make the people adopt it, it will be necessary perhaps to decimate that people, from the old who remember to the child who has still to learn ; from the recollection which is the monument to the instinct that is its germ—then, oh then, Billot, it is a task that will make all shudder who can see beneath the horizon. . . . I shall, however, persevere, for although I see obstacles, I can perceive the end ; and that end is splendid, Billot. It is not the liberty of France alone that I dream of ; it is the liberty of the whole world. It is not the physical equality ; it is equality before the law,—equality of rights. It is not only the fraternity of our own citizens, but of all nations. . . . Forward, then, and over the heaps of our dead bodies may one day march the generations of which this boy here is in the advanced guard ! "

Though Dr. Gilbert has been in the Bastille, though he barely escapes the bullet of a revolutionist, he tries to unite the throne and the people. So, as we have seen, did Paine struggle until the King took flight, and, over his own signature, branded all his pledges as extorted lies. Henceforth for the King personally he has no respect ; yet the whole purpose of his life is now to save that of the prisoner. Besides his humane horror of capital punishment, especially in a case which involves the heads of thousands, Paine foresees Nemesis fashioning her wheels in every part of Europe, and her rudder across the ocean,—where America beholds in Louis XVI. her deliverer.

Paine's outlawry, announced by Kersaint in Convention, January 1st, was more eloquent for wrath than he for clemency. Under such menaces the majority for sparing Louis shrank with the New Year; French pride arose, and with Danton was eager to defy despots by tossing to them the head of a king. Poor Paine found his comrades retreating. What would a knowledge of the French tongue have been worth to this leading republican of the world, just then the one man sleeplessly seeking to save a King's life! He could not plead with his enraged republicans, who at length overpowered even Brissot, so far as to draw him into the fatal plan of voting for the King's death, coupled with submission to the verdict of the people. Paine saw that there was at the moment no people, but only an infuriated clan. He was now defending a forlorn hope, but he struggled with a heroism that would have commanded the homage of Europe had not its courts been also clans. He hit on a scheme which he hoped might, in that last extremity, save the real revolution from a suicidal inhumanity. It was the one statesmanlike proposal of the time: that the King should be held as a hostage for the peaceful behavior of other kings, and, when their war on France had ceased, banished to the United States.

On January 15th, before the vote on the King's punishment was put, Paine gave his manuscript address to the president: debate closed before it could be read, and it was printed. He argued that the Assembly, in bringing back Louis when he had abdicated and fled, was the more guilty; and against his transgressions it should be remembered that by his aid the shackles of America were broken.

"Let then those United States be the guard and the asylum of Louis Capet. There, in the future, remote from the miseries and crimes of royalty, he may learn, from the constant presence of public prosperity, that the true system of government consists not in monarchs, but in fair, equal, and honorable representation.   In recalling this circumstance, and submitting this proposal, I consider myself a citizen of both countries. I submit it as an American who feels the debt of gratitude he owes to every Frenchman.   I submit it as a man, who, albeit an adversary of kings, forgets not that they are subject to human frailties.   I support my proposal as a citizen of the French Republic, because it appears to me the best and most politic measure that can be adopted.   As far as my experience in public life extends, I have ever observed that the great mass of people are always just, both in their intentions and their object ; but the true method of attaining such purpose does not always appear at once.   The English nation had groaned under the Stuart despotism.   Hence Charles I. was executed ; but Charles II. was restored to all the powers his father had lost.   Forty years later the same family tried to re-establish their oppression ; the nation banished the whole race from its territories.   The remedy was effectual ;   the Stuart family sank into obscurity, merged itself in the masses, and is now extinct."

He reminds the Convention that the king had two brothers out of the country who might naturally desire his death : the execution of the king might make them presently plausible pretenders to the throne, around whom their foreign enemies would rally : while the man recognized by foreign powers as the rightful monarch of France was living there could be no such pretender.

"It has already been proposed to abolish the penalty of death, and it is with infinite satisfaction that I recollect the humane and excellent oration pronounced by Robespierre on the subject, in the constituent Assembly.   Monarchical gov-

ernments have trained the human race to sanguinary punishments, but the people should not follow the examples of their
oppressors in such vengeance. As France has been the first
of European nations to abolish royalty, let her also be the
first to abolish the punishment of death, and to find out a
milder and more effectual substitute."

This was admirable art. Under shelter of
Robespierre's appeal against the death penalty,
the "Mountain"[1] could not at the moment break
the force of Paine's plea by reminding the Convention of his Quaker sentiments. It will be
borne in mind that up to this time Robespierre
was not impressed, nor Marat possessed, by the
homicidal demon. Marat had felt for Paine a
sort of contemptuous kindness, and one day privately said to him: "It is you, then, who believe in a republic; you have too much sense to
believe in such a dream." Robespierre, according
to Lamartine, "affected for the cosmopolitan radicalism of Paine the respect of a neophite for ideas
not understood." Both leaders now suspected that
Paine had gone over to the "Brissotins," as the
Girondists were beginning to be called. However,
the Brissotins, though a majority, had quailed before
the ferocity with which the Jacobins had determined
on the king's death. M. Taine declares that the
victory of the minority in this case was the familiar
one of reckless violence over the more civilized—
the wild beast over the tame. Louis Blanc denies
that the Convention voted, as one of them said,
under poignards; but the signs of fear are unmis-

[1] So called from the high benches on which these members sat. The seats
of the Girondists on the floor were called the "Plain," and after their overthrow the "Marsh."

takable. Vergniaud had declared it an insult for any
one to suppose he would vote for the king's death,
but he voted for it. Villette was threatened with
death if he did not vote for that of the king. Sieyès,
who had attacked Paine for republicanism, voted
death. "What," he afterward said—"what were
the tribute of my glass of wine in that torrent of
brandy?" But Paine did not withhold his cup
of cold water. When his name was called he cried
out: "I vote for the detention of Louis till the
end of the war, and after that his perpetual banishment." He spoke his well prepared vote in French,
and may have given courage to others. For even
under poignards—the most formidable being liability to a charge of royalism—the vote had barely
gone in favor of death.[1]

The fire-breathing Mountain felt now that its
supremacy was settled. It had learned its deadly
art of conquering a thinking majority by recklessness. But suddenly another question was sprung
upon the Convention : Shall the execution be immediate, or shall there be delay? The Mountain
groans and hisses as the question is raised, but the
dictation had not extended to this point, and
the question must be discussed. Here is one more
small chance for Paine's poor royal client. Can
the execution only be postponed it will probably
never be executed. Unfortunately Marat, whose

---

[1] Upwards of three hundred voted with Paine, who says that the majority
by which death was carried, unconditionally, was twenty-five. As a witness
who had watched the case, his testimony may correct the estimate of Carlyle :
"Death by a small majority of Fifty-three. Nay, if we deduct from the
one side, and add to the other, a certain Twenty-six who said Death but
coupled some faintest ineffectual surmise of mercy with it, the majority will
be but *One*." See also Paine's "Mémoire, etc.. à Monroe."

thirst for the King's blood is almost cannibalistic, can read on Paine's face his elation. He realizes that this American, with Washington behind him, has laid before the Convention a clear and consistent scheme for utilizing the royal prisoner. The king's neck under a suspended knife, it will rest with the foreign enemies of France whether it shall fall or not ; while the magnanimity of France and its respect for American gratitude will prevail. Paine, then, must be dealt with somehow in this new debate about delay.

He might, indeed, have been dealt with summarily had not the *Moniteur* done him an opportune service ; on January 17th and 18th it printed Paine's unspoken argument for mercy, along with Erskine's speech at his trial in London, and the verdict. So on the 19th, when Paine entered the Convention, it was with the prestige not only of one outlawed by Great Britain for advocating the Rights of Man, but of a representative of the best Englishmen and their principles. It would be vain to assail the author's loyalty to the republic. That he would speak that day was certain, for on the morrow (20th) the final vote was to be taken. The Mountain could not use on Paine their weapon against Girondins ; they could not accuse the author of the " Rights of Man " of being royalist. When he had mounted the tribune, and the clerk (Bancal, Franklin's friend) was beginning to read his speech, Marat cried, " I submit that Thomas Paine is incompetent to vote on this question ; being a Quaker his religious principles are opposed to the death-penalty." There was

great confusion for a time. The anger of the
Jacobins was extreme, says Guizot, and "they refused to listen to the speech of Paine, the American,
till respect for his courage gained him a hearing."[1]
Demands for freedom of speech gradually subdued
the interruptions, and the secretary proceeded :

"Very sincerely do I regret the Convention's vote of yesterday for death. I have the advantage of some experience ; it
is near twenty years that I have been engaged in the cause of
liberty, having contributed something to it in the revolution
of the United States of America. My language has always
been that of liberty *and* humanity, and I know by experience
that nothing so exalts a nation as the union of these two
principles, under all circumstances. I know that the public
mind of France, and particularly that of Paris, has been heated
and irritated by the dangers to which they have been exposed ;
but could we carry our thoughts into the future, when the
dangers are ended, and the irritations forgotten, what to-day
seems an act of justice may then appear an act of vengeance.
[*Murmurs.*] My anxiety for the cause of France has become
for the moment concern for its honor. If, on my return to
America, I should employ myself on a history of the French
Revolution, I had rather record a thousand errors dictated by
humanity, than one inspired by a justice too severe. I voted
against an appeal to the people, because it appeared to me
that the Convention was needlessly wearied on that point ; but
I so voted in the hope that this Assembly would pronounce
against death, and for the same punishment that the nation
would have voted, at least in my opinion, that is, for reclusion
during the war and banishment thereafter. That is the punishment most efficacious, because it includes the whole family
at once, and none other can so operate. I am still against the
appeal to the primary assemblies, because there is a better
method. This Convention has been elected to form a Constitution, which will be submitted to the primary assemblies.
After its acceptance a necessary consequence will be an election, and another Assembly. We cannot suppose that the

[1] "History of France," vi., p. 136.

present Convention will last more than five or six months. The choice of new deputies will express the national opinion on the propriety or impropriety of your sentence, with as much efficacy as if those primary assemblies had been consulted on it. As the duration of our functions here cannot be long, it is a part of our duty to consider the interests of those who shall replace us. If by any act of ours the number of the nation's enemies shall be needlessly increased, and that of its friends diminished,—at a time when the finances may be more strained than to-day,—we should not be justifiable for having thus unnecessarily heaped obstacles in the path of our successors. Let us therefore not be precipitate in our decisions.

"France has but one ally—the United States of America. That is the only nation that can furnish France with naval provisions, for the kingdoms of northern Europe are, or soon will be, at war with her. It happens, unfortunately, that the person now under discussion is regarded in America as a deliverer of their country. I can assure you that his execution will there spread universal sorrow, and it is in your power not thus to wound the feelings of your ally. Could I speak the French language I would descend to your bar, and in their name become your petitioner to respite the execution of the sentence on Louis."

Here were loud murmurs from the "Mountain," answered with demands for liberty of opinion. Thuriot sprang to his feet crying, " This is not the language of Thomas Paine." Marat mounted the tribune and asked Paine some questions, apparently in English, then descending he said to the Assembly in French : " I denounce the interpreter, and I maintain that such is not the opinion of Thomas Paine. It is a wicked and faithless translation."[1] These words, audacious as mendacious,

[1] "Venant d'un démocrate tel que Thomas Paine, d'un homme qui avait vécu parmi les Américains, d'un penseur, cette déclaration parut si dangereuse à Marat que, pour en détruire l'effet, il n'hésita pas à s'écrier : 'Je dénonce le truchement. Je soutiens que ce n'est point là l'opinion de Thomas Paine. C'est une traduction infidèle.' "—Louis Blanc. See also " Histoire Parliamentaire," xxiii., p. 250.

caused a tremendous uproar. Garran came to the
rescue of the frightened clerk, declaring that he
had read the original, and the translation was correct. Paine stood silent and calm during the storm.
The clerk proceeded :

"Your Executive Committee will nominate an ambassador
to Philadelphia ; my sincere wish is that he may announce to
America that the National Convention of France, out of pure
friendship to America, has consented to respite Louis. That
people, your only ally, have asked you by my vote to delay
the execution.

"Ah, citizens, give not the tyrant of England the triumph
of seeing the man perish on a scaffold who helped my dear
brothers of America to break his chains ! "

At the conclusion of this speech Marat "launched
himself into the middle of the hall " and cried out
that Paine had "voted against the punishment
of death because he was a preacher." Paine replied, "I voted against it both morally and politically."

Had the vote been taken that day perhaps Louis
might have escaped. Brissot, shielded from charges
of royalism by Paine's republican fame, now strongly
supported his cause. "A cruel precipitation," he
cried, "may alienate our friends in England, Ireland, America. Take care ! The opinion of European peoples is worth to you armies !" But all
this only brought out the Mountain's particular
kind of courage ; they were ready to defy the
world—Washington included—in order to prove
that a King's neck was no more than any other
man's. Marat's clan—the " Nihilists " of the time,
whose strength was that they stopped at nothing

—had twenty-four hours to work in ; they surrounded the Convention next day with a mob
howling for "justice !" Fifty-five members were
absent ; of the 690 present a majority of seventy
decided that Louis XVI. should die within twenty-
four hours.

A hundred years have passed since that tragedy
of poor Louis ; graves have given up their dead ;
secrets of the hearts that then played their part are
known. The world can now judge between England's Outlaw and England's King of that day. For
it is established, as we have seen, both by English
and French archives, that while Thomas Paine was
toiling night and day to save the life of Louis that
life lay in the hand of the British Ministry. Some
writers question the historic truth of the offer made
by Danton, but none can question the refusal of
intercession, urged by Fox and others at a time
when (as Count d'Estaing told Morris) the Convention was ready to give Pitt the whole French
West Indies to keep him quiet. It was no doubt
with this knowledge that Paine declared from the
tribune that George III. would triumph in the execution of the King who helped America to break
England's chains. Brissot also knew it when with
weighed words he reported for his Committee
(January 12th) : "The grievance of the British
Cabinet against France is not that Louis is in
judgment, but that Thomas Paine wrote 'The
Rights of Man.'"   "The militia were armed," says
Louis Blanc, "in the south-east of England troops
received order to march to London, the meeting of
Parliament was advanced forty days, the Tower

was reinforced by a new garrison, in fine there was unrolled a formidable preparation of war against —Thomas Paine's book on the Rights of Man!"[1]

Incredible as this may appear the debates in the House of Commons, on which it is fairly founded, would be more incredible were they not duly reported in the "Parliamentary History."[2]   In the debates on the Alien Bill, permitting the King to order any foreigner out of the country at will, on making representations to the French Convention in behalf of the life of Louis, on augmenting the military forces with direct reference to France, the recent trial of Paine was rehearsed, and it was plainly shown that the object of the government was to suppress freedom of the press by Terror. Erskine was denounced for defending Paine and for afterwards attending a meeting of the "Society of Friends of the Liberty of the Press," to whose resolutions on Paine's case his name was attached. Erskine found gallant defenders in the House, among them Fox, who demanded of Pitt: "Can you not prosecute Paine without an army?" Burke at this time enacted a dramatic scene. Having stated that three thousand daggers had been ordered at Birmingham by an Englishman, he drew from his pocket a dagger, cast it on the floor of the House of Commons, and cried : "That is what we are to get from an alliance with France!" Paine—Paine—Paine—was the burden laid on Pitt, who had said to Lady Hester Stanhope : "Tom Paine is quite right."   That Thomas Paine and his

---

[1] " Histoire de la Révolution," vol. viii., p. 96.
[2] Vol. xxv.

"Rights of Man" were the actual cause of the English insults to which their declaration of war replied was so well understood in the French Convention that its first answer to the menaces was to appoint Paine and Condorcet to write an address to the English people.[1]

It is noticeable that on the question whether the judgment on the King's fate should be submitted to the people, Paine voted " No." His belief in the right of all to representation implied distrust of the immediate voice of the masses. The King had said that if his case were referred to the people "he should be massacred." Gouverneur Morris had heard this, and no doubt communicated it to Paine, who was in consultation with him on his plan of sending Louis to America.[2] Indeed, it is probable that popular suffrage would have ratified the decree. Nevertheless, it was a fair " appeal to the people" which Paine made, after the fatal verdict, in expressing to the Convention his belief that the people would not have done so. For after the decree the helplessness of the prisoner appealed to popular compassion, and on the fatal day the tide had turned. Four days after the execution the American Minister writes to Jefferson : " The greatest care was taken to prevent a concourse of people. This proves a conviction that the majority was not favorable to that severe measure. In fact the great mass of the people mourned the fate of their unhappy prince."

[1] " Le Département des Affaires Étrangères pendant la Révolution, 1787–1804." Par Frédéric Masson, Bibliothécaire du Ministère des Affaires Étrangères. Paris, 1877, p. 273.

[2] Morris' " Diary," ii., pp. 19, 27, 32.

To Paine the death of an "unhappy prince" was no more a subject for mourning than that of the humblest criminal—for, with whatever extenuating circumstances, a criminal he was to the republic he had sworn to administer. But the impolicy of the execution, the resentment uselessly incurred, the loss of prestige in America, were felt by Paine as a heavy blow to his cause—always the international republic. He was, however, behind the scenes enough to know that the blame rested mainly on America's old enemy and his league of foreign courts against liberated France. The man who, when Franklin said "Where liberty is, there is my country," answered "Where liberty is not, there is mine," would not despair of the infant republic because of its blunders. Attributing these outbursts to maddening conspiracies around and within the new-born nation, he did not believe there could be peace in Europe so long as it was ruled by George III. He therefore set himself to the struggle, as he had done in 1776. Moreover, Paine has faith in Providence.[1]

At this time, it should be remembered, opposition to capital punishment was confined to very

---

[1] "The same spirit of fortitude that insured success to America will insure it to France, for it is impossible to conquer a nation determined to be free. . . . Man is ever a stranger to the ways by which Providence regulates the order of things. The interference of foreign despots may serve to introduce into their own enslaved countries the principles they come to oppose. Liberty and equality are blessings too great to be the inheritance of France alone. It is honour to her to be their first champion ; and she may now say to her enemies, with a mighty voice, ' O, ye Austrians, ye Prussians ! ye who now turn your bayonets against us, it is for you, it is for all Europe, it is for all mankind, and not for France alone, that she raises the standard of Liberty and Equality ! ' "—Paine's address to the Convention (September 25, 1792) after taking his seat.

few outside of the despised sect of Quakers. In
the debate three, besides Paine, gave emphatic
expression to that sentiment, Manuel, Condorcet,
—Robespierre! The former, in giving his vote
against death, said : "To Nature belongs the right
of death. Despotism has taken it from her ;
Liberty will return it." As for Robespierre, his
argument was a very powerful reply to Paine, who
had reminded him of the bill he had introduced
into the old National Assembly for the abolition
of capital punishment. He did, indeed, abhor it,
he said ; it was not his fault if his views had been
disregarded. But why should men who then opposed him suddenly revive the claims of humanity
when the penalty happened to fall upon a King?
Was the penalty good enough for the people, but
not for a King? If there were any exception in
favor of such a punishment, it should be for a royal
criminal.

The opinion of Robespierre is held by some
humane men. The present writer heard from
Professor Francis W. Newman—second to none in
philanthropy and compassionateness—a suggestion
that the death penalty should be reserved for those
placed at the head of affairs who betray their trust,
or set their own above the public interests to the
injury of a Commonwealth.

The real reasons for the execution of the King
closely resemble those of Washington for the
execution of Major André, notwithstanding the
sorrow of the country, with which the Commander
sympathized. The equal nationality of the United
States, repudiated by Great Britain, was in ques-

tion.   To hang spies was, however illogically, a
conventional usage among nations.   Major André
must die, therefore, and must be refused the
soldier's death for which he petitioned.   For a like
reason Europe must be shown that the French
Convention is peer of their scornful Parliaments;
and its fundamental principle, the equality of men,
could not admit a King's escape from the penalty
which would be unhesitatingly inflicted on a " Citizen."   The King had assumed the title of Citizen,
had worn the republican cockade ;   the apparent
concession of royal inviolability, in the moment of
his betrayal of the compromise made with him,
could be justified only on the grounds stated by
Paine,—impolicy of slaying their hostage, creating
pretenders, alienating America ; and the honor of
exhibiting to the world, by a salient example, the
Republic's magnanimity in contrast with the cruelty
of Kings.

CHAPTER II.

AN OUTLAWED ENGLISH AMBASSADOR.

Soon after Paine had taken his seat in the Convention, Lord Fortescue wrote to Miles, an English agent in Paris, a letter fairly expressive of the feelings, fears, and hopes of his class.

" Tom Paine is just where he ought to be—a member of the Convention of Cannibals. One would have thought it impossible that any society upon the face of the globe should have been fit for the reception of such a being until the late deeds of the National Convention have shown them to be most fully qualified. His vocation will not be complete, nor theirs either, till his head finds its way to the top of a pike, which will probably not be long first." [1]

[1] This letter, dated September 26, 1792, appears in the Miles Correspondence (London, 1890). There are indications that Miles was favorably disposed towards Paine, and on that account, perhaps, was subjected to influence by his superiors. As an example of the way in which just minds were poisoned towards Paine, a note of Miles may be mentioned. He says he was "told by Col. Bosville, a declared friend of Paine, that his manners and conversation were coarse, and he loved the brandy bottle." But just as this Miles Correspondence was appearing in London, Dr. Grece found the manuscript diary of Rickman, who had discovered (as two entries show) that this " declared friend of Paine," Col. Bosville, and professed friend of himself, was going about uttering injurious falsehoods concerning him (Rickman), seeking to alienate his friends at the moment when he most needed them. Rickman was a bookseller engaged in circulating Paine's works. There is little doubt that this wealthy Col. Bosville was at the time unfriendly to the radicals. He was staying in Paris on Paine's political credit, while depreciating him.

But if Paine was so fit for such a Convention, why should they behead him? The letter betrays a real perception that Paine possesses humane principles, and an English courage, which would bring him into danger. This undertone of Fortescue's invective represented the profound confidence of Paine's adherents in England. When tidings came of the King's trial and execution, whatever glimpses they gained of their outlawed leader showed him steadfast as a star caught in one wave and another of that turbid tide. Many, alas, needed apologies, but Paine required none. That one Englishman, standing on the tribune for justice and humanity, amid three hundred angry Frenchmen in uproar, was as sublime a sight as Europe witnessed in those days. To the English radical the outlawry of Paine was as the tax on light, which was presently walling up London windows, or extorting from them the means of war against ideas.[1] The trial of Paine had elucidated nothing, except that, like Jupiter, John Bull had the thunderbolts, and Paine the arguments. Indeed, it is difficult to discover any other Englishman who at the moment pre-eminently stood for principles now proudly called English.

But Paine too presently held thunderbolts. Although his efforts to save Louis had offended the

---

[1] In a copy of the first edition of " The Rights of Man," which I bought in London, I found, as a sort of book-mark, a bill for 1*l.* 6*s.* 8*d.*, two quarters' window-tax, due from Mr. Williamson, Upper Fitzroy Place. Windows closed with bricks are still seen in some of the gloomiest parts of London. I have in manuscript a bitter anathema of the time :

> " God made the Light, and saw that it was good :
> Pitt laid a tax on it.—G— d— his blood ! "

"Mountain," and momentarily brought him into
the danger Lord Fortescue predicted, that party
was not yet in the ascendant. The Girondists were
still in power, and though some of their leaders
had bent before the storm, that they might not be
broken, they had been impressed both by the courage and the tactics of Paine. "The Girondists
consulted Paine," says Lamartine, "and placed him
on the Committee of Surveillance." At this moment many Englishmen were in France, and at a
word from Paine some of their heads might have
mounted on the pike which Lord Fortescue had
imaginatively prepared for the head that wrote "The
Rights of Man." There remained, for instance,
Mr. Munro, already mentioned. This gentleman,
in a note preserved in the English Archives, had
written to Lord Grenville (September 8, 1792)
concerning Paine : "What must a nation come to
that has so little discernment in the election of their
representatives, as to elect such a fellow ?" But
having lingered in Paris after England's formal
declaration of war (February 11th), Munro was
cast into prison. He owed his release to that
"fellow" Paine, and must be duly credited with
having acknowledged it, and changed his tone for
the rest of his life,—which he probably owed to the
English committeeman. Had Paine met with the
fate which Lords Gower and Fortescue hoped, it
would have gone hard with another eminent countryman of theirs,—Captain Grimstone, R.A. This
personage, during a dinner party at the Palais
Égalité, got into a controversy with Paine, and,
forgetting that the English Jove could not in Paris

safely answer argument with thunder, called Paine
a traitor to his country and struck him a violent
blow.   Death was the penalty of striking a deputy,
and Paine's friends were not unwilling to see
the penalty inflicted on this stout young Captain
who had struck a man of fifty-six.   Paine had
much trouble in obtaining from Barrère, of the
Committee of Public Safety, a passport out of the
country for Captain Grimstone, whose travelling
expenses were supplied by the man he had struck.

In a later instance, related by Walter Savage
Landor, Paine's generosity amounted to quixotism.
The story is finely told by Landor, who says in a
note : "This anecdote was communicated to me at
Florence by Mr. Evans, a painter of merit, who
studied under Lawrence, and who knew personally
(Zachariah) Wilkes and Watt.   In religion and
politics he differed widely from Paine."

"Sir," said he, "let me tell you what he did for me.   My
name is Zachariah Wilkes.   I was arrested in Paris and condemned to die.   I had no friend here ; and it was a time when
no friend would have served me : Robespierre ruled.   'I am
innocent !' I cried in desperation.   'I am innocent, so help
me God ! I am condemned for the offence of another.'   I
wrote a statement of my case with a pencil ; thinking at first
of addressing it to my judge, then of directing it to the president of the Convention.   The jailer, who had been kind to me,
gave me a gazette, and told me not to mind seeing my name,
so many were there before it.

"'O !' said I 'though you would not lend me your ink, do
transmit this paper to the president.'

"'No, my friend !' answered he gaily.   'My head is as good
as yours, and looks as well between the shoulders, to my
liking.   Why not send it (if you send it anywhere) to the
deputy Paine here ?' pointing to a column in the paper.

"'O God! he must hate and detest the name of Englishman : pelted, insulted, persecuted, plundered . . .'

"'I could give it to him,' said the jailer.

"'Do then!' said I wildly. 'One man more shall know my innocence.' He came within the half hour. I told him my name, that my employers were Watt and Boulton of Birmingham, that I had papers of the greatest consequence, that if I failed to transmit them, not only my life was in question, but my reputation. He replied : 'I know your employers by report only ; there are no two men less favourable to the principles I profess, but no two upon earth are honester. You have only one great man among you : it is Watt ; for Priestley is gone to America. The church-and-king men would have japanned him. He left to these philosophers of the rival school his house to try experiments on ; and you may know, better than I do, how much they found in it of carbon and calx, of silex and argilla.'

"He examined me closer than my judge had done ; he required my proofs. After a long time I satisfied him. He then said, 'The leaders of the Convention would rather have my life than yours. If by any means I can obtain your release on my own security, will you promise me to return within twenty days ?' I answered, 'Sir, the security I can at present give you, is trifling . . . I should say a mere nothing.'

"'Then you do not give me your word ?' said he.

"'I give it and will redeem it.'

"He went away, and told me I should see him again when he could inform me whether he had succeeded. He returned in the earlier part of the evening, looked fixedly upon me, and said, 'Zachariah Wilkes ! if you do not return in twenty-four days (four are added) you will be the most unhappy of men ; for had you not been an honest one, you could not be the agent of Watt and Boulton. I do not think I have hazarded much in offering to take your place on your failure : such is the condition.' I was speechless ; he was unmoved. Silence was first broken by the jailer. 'He seems to get fond of the spot now he must leave it.' I had thrown my arms upon the table towards my liberator, who sat opposite, and I rested my head and breast upon it too, for my temples ached and tears

had not yet relieved them. He said, 'Zachariah! follow me
to the carriage.' The soldiers paid the respect due to his
scarf, presenting arms, and drawing up in file as we went
along. The jailer called for a glass of wine, gave it me,
poured out another, and drank to our next meeting."[1]

Another instance may be related in Paine's own
words, written (March 20, 1806) to a gentleman in
New York.

"SIR,—I will inform you of what I know respecting General
Miranda, with whom I first became acquainted at New York,
about the year 1783. He is a man of talents and enterprise,
and the whole of his life has been a life of adventures.

"I went to Europe from New York in April, 1787. Mr. Jefferson was then Minister from America to France, and Mr. Littlepage, a Virginian (whom Mr. Jay knows), was agent for the
king of Poland, at Paris. Mr. Littlepage was a young man of
extraordinary talents, and I first met with him at Mr. Jefferson's house at dinner. By his intimacy with the king of
Poland, to whom also he was chamberlain, he became well
acquainted with the plans and projects of the Northern
Powers of Europe. He told me of Miranda's getting himself
introduced to the Empress Catharine of Russia, and obtaining
a sum of money from her, four thousand pounds sterling; but
it did not appear to me what the object was for which the
money was given; it appeared a kind of retaining fee.

"After I had published the first part of the 'Rights of
Man' in England, in the year 1791, I met Miranda at the house
of Turnbull and Forbes, merchants, Devonshire Square, London. He had been a little before this in the employ of Mr. Pitt,
with respect to the affair of Nootka Sound, but I did not at
that time know it; and I will, in the course of this letter,
inform you how this connection between Pitt and Miranda
ended; for I know it of my own knowledge.

---

[1] Zachariah Wilkes did not fail to return, or Paine to greet him with
safety, and the words, "There is yet English blood in England." But here
Landor passes off into an imaginative picture of villages rejoicing at the fall
of Robespierre. Paine himself had then been in prison seven months; so
we can only conjecture the means by which Zachariah was liberated.—Landor's Works, London, 1853, i., p. 296.

":I published the second part of the 'Rights of Man' in London, in February, 1792, and I continued in London till I was elected a member of the French Convention, in September of that year ; and went from London to Paris to take my seat in the Convention, which was to meet the 20th of that month. I arrived in Paris on the 19th. After the Convention met, Miranda came to Paris, and was appointed general of the French army, under General Dumouriez. But as the affairs of that army went wrong in the beginning of the year 1793, Miranda was suspected, and was brought under arrest to Paris to take his trial. He summoned me to appear to his charac-ter, and also a Mr. Thomas Christie, connected with the house of Turnbull and Forbes. I gave my testimony as I believed, which was, that his leading object was and had been the eman-cipation of his country, Mexico, from the bondage of Spain ; for I did not at that time know of his engagements with Pitt. Mr. Christie's evidence went to show that Miranda did not come to France as a necessitous adventurer ; but believed he came from public-spirited motives, and that he had a large sum of money in the hands of Turnbull and Forbes. The house of Turnbull and Forbes was then in a contract to sup-ply Paris with flour. Miranda was acquitted.

"A few days after his acquittal he came to see me, and in a few days afterwards I returned his visit. He seemed desirous of satisfying me that he was independent, and that he had money in the hands of Turnbull and Forbes. He did not tell me of his affair with old Catharine of Russia, nor did I tell him that I knew of it. But he entered into conversation with respect to Nootka Sound, and put into my hands several let-ters of Mr. Pitt's to him on that subject ; amongst which was one which I believe he gave me by mistake, for when I had opened it, and was beginning to read it, he put forth his hand and said, ' O, that is not the letter I intended ' ; but as the letter was short I soon got through with it, and then returned it to him without making any remarks upon it. The dispute with Spain was then compromised ; and Pitt compromised with Miranda for his services by giving him twelve hundred pounds sterling, for this was the contents of the letter.

"Now if it be true that Miranda brought with him a credit upon certain persons in New York for sixty thousand pounds sterling, it is not difficult to suppose from what quarter the money came ; for the opening of any proposals between Pitt and Miranda was already made by the affair of Nootka Sound. Miranda was in Paris when Mr. Monroe arrived there as Minister ; and as Miranda wanted to get acquainted with him, I cautioned Mr. Monroe against him, and told him of the affair of Nootka Sound, and the twelve hundred pounds.

"You are at liberty to make what use you please of this letter, and with my name to it."

Here we find a paid agent of Pitt calling on outlawed Paine for aid, by his help liberated from prison ; and, when his true character is accidentally discovered, and he is at the outlaw's mercy, spared, —no doubt because this true English ambassador, who could not enter England, saw that at the moment passionate vengeance had taken the place of justice in Paris. Lord Gower had departed, and Paine must try and shield even his English enemies and their agents, where, as in Miranda's case, the agency did not appear to affect France. This was while his friends in England were hunted down with ferocity.

In the earlier stages of the French Revolution there was much sympathy with it among literary men and in the universities. Coleridge, Southey, Wordsworth, were leaders in the revolutionary cult at Oxford and Cambridge. By 1792, and especially after the institution of Paine's prosecution, the repression became determined. The memoir of Thomas Poole, already referred to, gives the experiences of a Somerset gentleman, a friend of Coleridge. After the publication of Paine's "Rights of Man" (1791) he became a "political Ishmaelite." "He made his appearance amongst the wigs and powdered locks of his kinsfolk and acquaintance, male and female, without any of the customary powder in his hair, which innocent novelty was a scandal to all beholders, seeing that it was the outward and visible sign of a love of innovation, a well-known badge of sympathy with democratic ideas."

Among Poole's friends, at Stowey, was an attorney named Symes, who lent him Paine's " Rights of Man." After Paine's outlawry Symes met a cabinet-maker with a copy of the book, snatched it out of his hand, tore it up, and, having learned that it was lent him by Poole, propagated about the country that he (Poole) was distributing seditious literature about the country. Being an influential man, Poole prevented the burning of Paine in effigy at Stowey. As time goes on this country-gentleman and scholar finds the government opening his letters, and warning his friends that he is in danger.

" It was," he writes to a friend, " the boast an Englishman was wont to make that he could think, speak, and write whatever he thought proper, provided he violated no law, nor injured any individual. But now an absolute controul exists, not indeed over the imperceptible operations of the mind, for those no power of man can controul ; but, what is the same thing, over the effects of those operations, and if among these effects, that of speaking is to be checked, the soul is as much enslaved as the body in a cell of the Bastille. The man who once feels, nay fancies, this, is a slave. It shows as if the suspicious secret government of an Italian Republic had replaced the open, candid government of the English laws."

As Thomas Poole well represents the serious and cultured thought of young England in that time, it is interesting to read his judgment on the king's execution and the imminent war.

"Many thousands of human beings will be sacrificed in the ensuing contest, and for what? To support three or four individuals, called arbitrary kings, in the situation which they have usurped. I consider every Briton who loses his life in the war us much murdered as the King of France, and every one who approves the war, as signing the death-warrant of each soldier or sailor that falls. . . . The excesses in France are great; but who are the authors of them? The Emperor of Germany, the King of Prussia, and Mr. Burke. Had it not been for their impertinent interference, I firmly believe the King of France would be at this moment a happy monarch, and that people would be enjoying every advantage of political liberty. . . . The slave-trade, you will see, will not be abolished, because to be humane and honest now is to be a traitor to the constitution, a lover of sedition and licentiousness! But this universal depression of the human mind cannot last long."

It was in this spirit that the defence of a free press was undertaken in England. That thirty years' war was fought and won on the works of Paine. There were some "Lost Leaders": the king's execution, the reign of terror, caused reaction in many a fine spirit; but the rank and file followed their Thomas Paine with a faith that crowned heads might envy. The London men knew Paine thoroughly. The treasures of the world would not draw him, nor any terrors drive him, to the side of cruelty and inhumanity. Their eye was upon him. Had Paine, after the king's execution, despaired of the republic there might have ensued some demoralization among his followers in London. But they saw him by the side

of the delivered prisoner of the Bastille, Brissot,
an author well known in England, by the side of
Condorcet and others of Franklin's honored circle,
engaged in death-struggle with the fire-breathing
dragon called " The Mountain." That was the
same unswerving man they had been following,
and to all accusations against the revolution their
answer was—Paine is still there !

A reign of terror in England followed the outlawry of Paine. Twenty-four men, at one time or
another, were imprisoned, fined, or transported for
uttering words concerning abuses such as now
every Englishman would use concerning the same.
Some who sold Paine's works were imprisoned before Paine's trial, while the seditious character of
the books was not yet legally settled. Many were
punished after the trial, by both fine and imprisonment. Newspapers were punished for printing extracts, and for having printed them before the trial.[1]
For this kind of work old statutes passed for other
purposes were impressed, new statutes framed, until
Fox declared the Bill of Rights repealed, the con-

---

[1] The first trial after Paine's, that of Thomas Spence (February 26, 1793),
for selling " The Rights of Man," failed through a flaw in the indictment,
but the mistake did not occur again. At the same time William Holland
was awarded a year's imprisonment and £100 fine for selling " Letter to the
Addressers." H. D. Symonds, for publishing " Rights of Man," £20 fine and
two years ; for " Letter to the Addressers," one year, £100 fine, with sureties in £1,000 for three years, and imprisonment till the fine be paid and
sureties given. April 17, 1793, Richard Phillips, printer, Leicester, eighteen months. May 8th, J. Ridgway, London, selling " Rights of Man,"
£100 and one year ; " Letter to the Addressers," one year, £100 fine ; in
each case sureties in £1,000, with imprisonment until fines paid and
sureties given. Richard Peart, " Rights " and " Letter," three months.
William Belcher, " Rights " and " Letter," three months. Daniel
Holt, £50, four years. Messrs. Robinson, £200. Eaton and Thompson,
the latter in Birmingham, were acquitted. Clio Rickman escaped punish-

stitution cut up by the roots, and the obedience of the people to such "despotism" no longer "a question of moral obligation and duty, but of prudence." [1]

From his safe retreat in Paris bookseller Rickman wrote his impromptu :

> "Hail Briton's land !   Hail freedom's shore !
>   Far happier than of old ;
> For in thy blessed realms no more
>   The Rights of Man are sold ! "

The famous town-crier of Bolton, who reported to his masters that he had been round that place "and found in it neither the rights of man nor common sense," made a statement characteristic of the time. The aristocracy and gentry had indeed lost their humanity and their sense under a disgraceful panic. Their serfs, unable to read, were fairly represented by those who, having burned Paine in effigy, asked their employer if there was "any other gemman he would like burnt, for a

---

ment by running over to Paris. Dr. Currie (1793) writes : " The prosecutions that are commenced all over England against printers, publishers, etc., would astonish you ; and most of these are for offences committed many months ago. The printer of the *Manchester Herald* has had seven different indictments preferred against him for paragraphs in his paper ; and six *different* indictments for selling or disposing of six different copies of Paine,—all previous to the *trial* of Paine. The man was opulent, supposed worth 20,000 *l.* ; but these different actions will ruin him, as they were intended to do."—" Currie's Life," i., p. 185. See Buckle's " History of Civilization," etc., American ed., p. 352. In the cases where " gentlemen " were found distributing the works the penalties were ferocious. Fische Palmer was sentenced to seven years' transportation. Thomas Muir, for advising persons to read " the works of that wretched outcast Paine " (the Lord Advocate's words) was sentenced to fourteen years' transportation. This sentence was hissed. The tipstaff being ordered to take those who hissed into custody, replied : " My lord, they 're all hissing."

[1] " Parl. Hist.," xxxii., p. 383.

glass o' beer."   The White Bear (now replaced by the Criterion Restaurant) no longer knew its little circle of radicals.   A symbol of how they were trampled out is discoverable in the " T. P." shoe-nails.   These nails, with heads so lettered, were in great request among the gentry, who had only to hold up their boot-soles to show how they were trampling on Tom Paine and his principles.   This at any rate was accurate.   Manufacturers of vases also devised ceramic anathemas.[1]

In all of this may be read the frantic fears of the King and aristocracy which were driving the Ministry to make good Paine's aphorism, " There is no English Constitution."   An English Constitution was, however, in process of formation,—in prisons, in secret conclaves, in lands of exile, and chiefly in Paine's small room in Paris.   Even in that time of Parisian turbulence and peril the hunted liberals of

---

[1] There are two Paine pitchers in the Museum at Brighton, England. Both were made at Leeds, one probably before Paine's trial, since it presents a respectable full-length portrait, holding in his hand a book, and beneath, the words : " Mr. Thomas Paine, Author of The Rights of Man." The other shows a serpent with Paine's head, two sides being adorned with the following lines :

> " God save the King, and all his subjects too,
> Likewise his forces and commanders true,
> May he their rights forever hence Maintain
> Against all strife occasioned by Tom Paine."

> " Prithee Tom Paine why wilt thou meddling be
> In others' business which concerns not thee ;
> For while thereon thou dost extend thy cares
> Thou dost at home neglect thine own affairs."

> " God save the King ! "

> " Observe the wicked and malicious man
> Projecting all the mischief that he can."

England found more security in France than in
their native land.[1] For the eyes of the English
reformer of that period, seeing events from prison
or exile, there was a perspective such as time has
now supplied to the historian.   It is still difficult to
distribute the burden of shame fairly.   Pitt was
unquestionably at first anxious to avoid war.   That
the King was determined on the war is certain ; he
refused to notice Wilberforce when he appeared at
court after his separation from Pitt on that point.

[1] When William Pitt died in 1806,—crushed under disclosures in the impeachment of Lord Melville,—the verdict of many sufferers was expressed
in an " Epitaph Impromptu " (MS.) found among the papers of Thomas
Rickman.   It has some historic interest.

> " Reader ! with eye indignant view this bier ;
>   The foe of all the human race lies here.
>   With talents small, and those directed, too,
>   Virtue and truth and wisdom to subdue,
>   He lived to every noble motive blind,
>   And died, the execration of mankind.

> " Millions were butchered by his damnéd plan
>   To violate each sacred right of man ;
>   Exulting he o'er earth each misery hurled,
>   And joyed to drench in tears and blood, the world.

> " Myriads of beings wretched he has made
>   By desolating war, his favourite trade,
>   Who, robbed of friends and dearest ties, are left
>   Of every hope and happiness bereft.

> " In private life made up of fuss and pride,
>   Not e'en his vices leaned to virtue's side ;
>   Unsound, corrupt, and rotten at the core,
>   His cold and scoundrel heart was black all o'er ;
>   Nor did one passion ever move his mind
>   That bent towards the tender, warm, and kind.

> " Tyrant, and friend to war ! we hail the day
>   When Death, to bless mankind, made thee his prey,
>   And rid the earth of all could earth disgrace,—
>   The foulest, bloodiest scourge of man's oppresséd race."

But the three attempts on his life, and his mental
infirmity, may be pleaded for George III.   Paine,
in his letter to Dundas, wrote " Madjesty " ; when
Rickman objected, he said : " Let it stand."   And it
stands now as the best apology for the King, while
it rolls on Pitt's memory the guilt of a twenty-two
years' war for the subjugation of thought and freedom.   In that last struggle of the barbarism sur-
viving in civilization, it was shown that the madness
of a populace was easily distanced by the cruelty
of courts.   Robespierre and Marat were humanitarian beside George and his Ministers ; the Reign
of Terror, and all the massacres of the French
Revolution put together, were child's-play compared with the anguish and horrors spread through
Europe by a war whose pretext was an execution
England might have prevented.

CHAPTER III.

REVOLUTION *VS.* CONSTITUTION.

THE French revolutionists have long borne responsibility for the first declaration of war in 1793. But from December 13, 1792, when the Painophobia Parliament began its debates, to February 1st, when France proclaimed itself at war with England, the British government had done little else than declare war—and prepare war—against France. Pitt, having to be re-elected, managed to keep away from Parliament for several days at its opening, and the onslaught was assumed by Burke. He began by heaping insults on France. On December 15th he boasted that he had not been cajoled by promise of promotion or pension, though he presently, on the same evening, took his seat for the first time on the Treasury bench. In the "Parliamentary History" (vols. xxx. and xxxi.) may be found Burke's epithets on France,—the "republic of assassins," "Cannibal Castle," "nation of murderers," "gang of plunderers," "murderous atheists," "miscreants," "scum of the earth." His vocabulary grew in grossness, of course, after the King's execution and the declaration of war, but from the first it was ribaldry and abuse. And this did not come from a private

32

member, but from the Treasury bench. He was supported by a furious majority which stopped at no injustice. Thus the Convention was burdened with guilt of the September massacres, though it was not then in existence. Paine's works being denounced, Erskine reminded the House of the illegality of so influencing a trial not yet begun. He was not listened to. Fox and fifty other earnest men had a serious purpose of trying to save the King's life, and proposed to negotiate with the Convention. Burke fairly foamed at the motions to that end, made by Fox and Lord Lansdowne. What, negotiate with such villains ! To whom is our agent to be accredited ? Burke draws a comic picture of the English ambassador entering the Convention, and, when he announces himself as from " George Third, by the grace of God," denounced by Paine. " Are we to humble ourselves before Judge Paine ? " At this point Whetstone made a disturbance and was named. There were some who found Burke's trifling intolerable. Mr. W. Smith reminded the House that Cromwell's ambassadors had been received by Louis XIV. Fox drew a parallel between the contemptuous terms used toward the French, and others about " Hancock and his crew," with whom Burke advised treaty, and with whom His Majesty did treat. All this was answered by further insults to France, these corresponding with a series of practical injuries. Lord Gower had been recalled August 17th, after the formation of a republic, and all intercourse with the French Minister in London, Chauvelin, was terminated. In violation of the treaty of 1786, the agents of France were refused permission to purchase grain and arms in England, and their vessels loaded with provisions seized. The circulation of French bonds, issued in 1790, was prohibited in England. A coalition had been formed with the enemies of France, the Emperor of Austria and the King of Prussia. Finally, on the execution of Louis XVI., Chauvelin was ordered (January 24th) to leave England in eight days. Talleyrand remained, but Chauvelin was kicked out of the country, so to say, simply because the Convention had recognized him. This appeared a plain *casus belli*, and was answered by the declaration of the Convention in that sense (February 1st), which England answered ten days later.[1]

In all this Paine recognized the hand of Burke. While his adherents in England, as we have seen, were finding in Pitt a successor to Satan, there is a notable absence from Paine's writings and letters of any such animosity towards that Minister. He

[1] " It was stipulated in the treaty of commerce between France and England, concluded at Paris [1786] that the sending away an ambassador by either party, should be taken as an act of hostility by the other party. The declaration of war (February, 1793) by the Convention . . . was made in exact conformity to this article in the treaty ; for it was not a declaration of war against England, but a declaration that the French republic is *in* war with England ; the first act of hostility having been committed by England. The declaration was made on Chauvelin's return to France, and in consequence of it."—Paine's " Address to the People of France " (1797). The words of the declaration of war, following the list of injuries, are : " La Convention Nationale déclaré, au nom de la nation Française, qu'attendu les actes multipliés et d'agressions ci-dessus mentionnés, la république Française est en guerre avec le roi d'Angleterre." The solemn protest of Lords Lauderdale, Lansdowne, and Derby, February 1st, against the address in answer to the royal message, before France had spoken, regards that address as a demonstration of universal war. The facts and the situation are carefully set forth by Louis Blanc, " Histoire de la Révolution," tome viii., p. 93 *seq.*

regarded Pitt as a victim.   " The father of Pitt,"
he once wrote, "when a member of the House of
Commons, exclaiming one day, during a former
war, against the enormous and ruinous expense of
German connections, as the offspring of the Hanover succession, and borrowing a metaphor from
the story of Prometheus, cried out : ' Thus, like
Prometheus, is Britain chained to the barren rock
of Hanover, whilst the imperial eagle preys upon
her vitals.'"   It is probable that on the intimations from Pitt, at the close of 1792, of his desire
for private consultations with friendly Frenchmen,
Paine entered into the honorable though unauthor-
ized conspiracy for peace which was terminated by
the expulsion of Chauvelin.   In the light of later
events, and the desertion of Dumouriez, these
overtures of Pitt made through Talleyrand (then in
London) were regarded by the French leaders, and
are still regarded by French writers, as treacherous.
But no sufficient reason is given for doubting
Pitt's good faith in that matter.   Writing to the
President (Washington), December 28, 1792, the
American Minister, Gouverneur Morris, states the
British proposal to be :

" France shall deliver the royal family to such branch of
the Bourbons as the King may choose, and shall recall her
troops from the countries they now occupy.   In this event
Britain will send hither a Minister and acknowledge the Republic, and mediate a peace with the Emperor and King of
Prussia.   I have several reasons to believe that this information is not far from the truth."

It is true that Pitt had no agent in France whom
he might not have disavowed, and that after the

fury with which the Painophobia Parliament, under
lead of Burke, inspired by the King, had opened,
could hardly have maintained any peaceful terms.
Nevertheless, the friends of peace in France secretly acted on this information, which Gouverneur
Morris no doubt received from Paine. A grand
dinner was given by Paine, at the Hôtel de Ville,
to Dumouriez, where this brilliant General met
Brissot, Condorcet, Santerre, and several eminent
English radicals, among them Sampson Perry. At
this time it was proposed to send Dumouriez secretly to London, to negotiate with Pitt, but this
was abandoned. Maret went, and he found Pitt
gracious and pacific. Chauvelin, however, advised
the French government of this illicit negotiation,
and Maret was ordered to return. Such was the
situation when Louis was executed. That execution, as we have seen, might have been prevented
had Pitt provided the money; but it need not be
supposed that, with Burke now on the Treasury
bench, the refusal is to be ascribed to anything
more than his inability to cope with his own majority, whom the King was patronizing. So completely convinced of Pitt's pacific disposition were
Maret and his allies in France that the clandestine
ambassador again departed for London. But on
arriving at Dover, he learned that Chauvelin had
been expelled, and at once returned to France.[1]

Paine now held more firmly than ever the first
article of his faith as to practical politics : the chief

[1] See Louis Blanc's " Histoire," etc., tome viii., p. 100, for the principal
authorities concerning this incident.—*Annual Register,* 1793, ch. vi. ;
" Mémoires tirés des papiers d'un homme d'État.," ii., p. 157 ; " Mémoires
de Dumouriez," t. iii., p. 384.

task of republicanism is to break the Anglo-German sceptre. France is now committed to war; it must be elevated to that European aim. Lord North and America reappear in Burke and France.

Meanwhile what is said of Britain in his " Rights of Man " was now more terribly true of France—it had no Constitution. The Committee on the Constitution had declared themselves ready to report early in the winter, but the Mountaineers managed that the matter should be postponed until after the King's trial. As an American who prized his citizenship, Paine felt chagrined and compromised at being compelled to act as a legislator and a judge because of his connection with a Convention elected for the purpose of framing a legislative and judicial machinery. He and Condorcet continued to add touches to this Constitution, the Committee approving, and on the first opportunity it was reported again. This was February 15, 1793. But, says the *Moniteur*, " the struggles between the Girondins and the Mountain caused the examination and discussion to be postponed." It was, however, distributed.

Gouverneur Morris, in a letter to Jefferson (March 7th), says this Constitution "was read to the Convention, but I learnt the next morning that a Council had been held on it overnight, by which it was condemned." Here is evidence in our American archives of a meeting or " Council" condemning the Constitution on the night of its submission. It must have been secret, for it does not appear in French histories, so far as I can discover. Durand de Maillane says that " the exclu-

sion of Robespierre and Couthon from this eminent
task [framing a Constitution] was a new matter for
discontent and jealousy against the party of Pétion "—a leading Girondin,—and that Robespierre
and his men desired " to render their work useless." [1]   No indication of this secret condemnation
of the Paine-Condorcet Constitution, by a con-
clave appeared on March 1st, when the document was again submitted.   The Convention now
set April 15th for its discussion, and the Mountaineers fixed that day for the opening of their
attack on the Girondins.   The Mayor of Paris appeared with a petition, adopted by the Communal
Council of the thirty-five sections of Paris, for the
arrest of twenty-two members of the Convention,
as slanderers of Paris,—" presenting the Parisians
to Europe as men of blood,"—friends of Roland,
accomplices of the traitor Dumouriez, enemies of
the clubs.   The deputies named were : Brissot,
Guadet, Vergniaud, Gensonné, Grangeneuve, Buzot,
Barbaroux, Salles, Biroteau, Pontécoulant, Pétion,
Lanjuinais, Valaze, Hardy, Louvet, Lehardy, Gor-
sas, Abbé Fauchet, Lanthenas, Lasource, Valady,
Chambon.   Of this list five were members of the
Committee on the Constitution, and two supple-
mentary members.[2]   Besides this, two of the
arraigned—Louvet and Lasource—had been especially active in pressing forward the Constitution.
The Mountaineers turned the discord they thus

---

[1] " Histoire de la Convention Nationale," p. 50. Durand-Maillane was
"the silent member" of the Convention, but a careful observer and well-
informed witness. I follow him and Louis Blanc in relating the fate of the
Paine-Condorcet Constitution.

[2] See vol. i., p. 357.

caused into a reason for deferring discussion of the Constitution. They declared also that important members were absent, levying troops, and especially that Marat's trial had been ordered. The discussion on the petition against the Girondins, and whether the Constitution should be considered, proceeded together for two days, when the Mountaineers were routed on both issues. The Convention returned the petition to the Mayor, pronouncing it " calumnious," and it made the Constitution the order of the day. Robespierre, according to Durand-Maillane, showed much spite at this defeat. He adroitly secured a decision that the preliminary " Declaration of Rights " should be discussed first, as there could be endless talk on those generalities.[1]

[1] This Declaration, submitted by Condorcet, April 17th, being largely the work of Paine, is here translated : The end of all union of men in society being maintenance of their natural rights, civil and political, these rights should be the basis of the social pact : their recognition and their declaration ought to precede the Constitution which secures and guarantees them. 1. The natural rights, civil and political, of men are liberty, equality, security, property, social protection, and resistance to oppression. 2. Liberty consists in the power to do whatever is not contrary to the rights of others ; thus, the natural rights of each man has no limits other than those which secure to other members of society enjoyment of the same rights. 3. The preservation of liberty depends on the sovereignty of the Law, which is the expression of the general will. Nothing unforbidden by law can be impeached, and none may be constrained to do what it does not command. 4. Every man is free to make known his thought and his opinions. 5. Freedom of the press (and every other means of publishing one's thoughts) cannot be prohibited, suspended, or limited. 6. Every citizen shall be free in the exercise of his worship [*culte*]. 7. Equality consists in the power of each to enjoy the same rights. 8. The Law should be equal for all, whether in recompense, punishment, or restraint. 9. All citizens are admissible to all public positions, employments, and functions. Free peoples can recognise no grounds of preference except talents and virtues. 10. Security consists in the protection accorded by society to each citizen for the preservation of his person, property, and rights. 11. None should be sued, accused, arrested, or detained, save in cases determined by the law, and in accordance with forms prescribed by it. Every other act against a

It now appears plain that Robespierre, Marat, and the Mountaineers generally were resolved that there should be no new government. The difference between them and their opponents was fundamental : to them the Revolution was an end, to the others a means. The Convention was a purely revolutionary body. It had arbitrarily absorbed all legislative and judicial functions, exercising them without responsibility to any code or constitution. For instance, in State Trials French law required three fourths of the voices for condemnation ; had the rule been followed Louis XVI. would not have perished. Lanjuinais had pressed the point, and it was answered that the sentence on Louis was political, for the interest of the State ; *salus populi suprema lex.* This implied that the Convention,

citizen is arbitrary and null. 12. Those who solicit, promote, sign, execute or cause to be executed such arbitrary acts are culpable, and should be punished. 13. Citizens against whom the execution of such acts is attempted have the right of resistance by force. Every citizen summoned or arrested by the authority of law, and in the forms prescribed by it, should instantly obey ; he renders himself guilty by resistance. 14. Every man being presumed innocent until declared guilty, should his arrest be judged indispensable, all rigor not necessary to secure his person should be severely repressed by law. 15. None should be punished save in virtue of a law established and promulgated previous to the offence, and legally applied. 16. A law that should punish offences committed before its existence would be an arbitrary Act. Retroactive effect given to any law is a crime. 17. Law should award only penalties strictly and evidently necessary to the general security ; they should be proportioned to the offence and useful to society. 18. The right of property consists in a man's being master in the disposal, at his will, of his goods, capital, income, and industry. 19. No kind of work, commerce, or culture can be interdicted for any one ; he may make, sell, and transport every species of production. 20. Every man may engage his services, and his time ; but he cannot sell himself ; his person is not an alienable property. 21. No one may be deprived of the least portion of his property without his consent, unless because of public necessity, legally determined, exacted openly, and under the condition of a just indemnity in advance. 22. No tax shall be established except for the general utility, and to relieve public needs. All citizens have the right to co-operate.

turning aside from its appointed functions, had, in anticipation of the judicial forms it meant to estab-lish, constituted itself into a Vigilance Committee to save the State in an emergency. But it never turned back again to its proper work. Now when the Constitution was framed, every possible ob-struction was placed in the way of its adoption, which would have relegated most of the Mountain-eers to private life.

Robespierre and Marat were in luck. The Paine-Condorcet Constitution omitted all mention of a Deity. Here was the immemorial and infallible recipe for discord, of which Robespierre made the most. He took the "Supreme Being" under his protection ; he also took morality under his protec-tion, insisting that the Paine-Condorcet Constitution

personally or by their representatives, in the establishment of public con-tributions. 23. Instruction is the need of all, and society owes it equally to all its members. 24. Public succors are a sacred debt of society, and it is for the law to determine their extent and application. 25. The social guarantee of the rights of man rests on the national sovereignty. 26. This sovereignty is one, indivisible, imprescriptible, and inalienable. 27. It resides essentially in the whole people, and each citizen has an equal right to co-operate in its exercise. 28. No partial assemblage of citizens, and no individual may attribute to themselves sovereignty, to exercise authority and fill any public function, without a formal delegation by the law. 29. Social security cannot exist where the limits of public administra-tion are not clearly determined by law, and where the responsibility of all public functionaries is not assured. 30. All citizens are bound to co-ope-rate in this guarantee, and to enforce the law when summoned in its name. 31. Men united in society should have legal means of resisting oppression. In every free government the mode of resisting different acts of oppression should be regulated by the Constitution. 32. It is oppression when a law violates the natural rights, civil and political, which it should ensure. It is oppression when the law is violated by public offi-cials in its application to individual cases. It is oppression when arbi-trary acts violate the rights of citizens against the terms of the law. 33. A people has always the right to revise, reform, and change its Constitu-tion. One generation has no right to bind future generations, and all heredity in offices is absurd and tyrannical.

gave liberty even to illicit traffic. While these dis-
cussions were going on Marat gained his triumphant
acquittal from the charges made against him by the
Girondins. This damaging blow further demoral-
ized the majority which was eager for the Constitution. By violence, by appeals against atheism, by
all crafty tactics, the Mountaineers secured recom-
mitment of the Constitution. To the Committee
were added Hérault de Séchelles, Ramel, Mathieu,
Couthon, Saint-Just,—all from the Committee of
Public Safety. The Constitution as committed
was the most republican document of the kind ever
drafted, as remade it was a revolutionary instrument ; but its preamble read : " In the presence
and under the guidance (*auspices*) of the Supreme
Being, the French People declare," etc.

God was in the Constitution ; but when it was
reported (June 10th) the Mountaineers had their
opponents *en route* for the scaffold. The arraignment of the twenty-two, declared by the Convention " calumnious " six weeks before, was approved
on June 2d. It was therefore easy to pass such a
constitution as the victors desired. Some had
suggested, during the theological debate, that
" many crimes had been sanctioned by this
King of kings,"—no doubt with emphasis on the
discredited royal name. Robespierre identified
his " Supreme Being " with NATURE, of whose
ferocities the poor Girondins soon had tragical
evidence.[1]

[1] " Les rois, les aristocrates, les tyrants qu'ils soient, sont des esclaves
révoltés contre le souverain de la terre, qui est le *genre humain*, et contre
le législateur de l'univers, qui est la *nature*."—Robespierre's final article of
" ' Rights," adopted by the Jacobins, April 21, 1793. Should not slaves revolt ?

The Constitution was adopted by the Convention on June 25th; it was ratified by the Communes August 10th. When it was proposed to organize a government under it, and dissolve the Convention, Robespierre remarked: *That sounds like a suggestion of Pitt!* Thereupon the Constitution was suspended until universal peace, and the Revolution superseded the Republic as end and aim of France.[1]

Some have ascribed to Robespierre a phrase he borrowed, on one occasion, from Voltaire, *Si Dieu n'existait pas, il faudrait l'inventer.* Robespierre's originality was that he did invent a god, made in his own image, and to that idol offered human sacrifices,—beginning with his own humanity. That he was genuinely superstitious is suggested by the plausibility with which his enemies connected him

---

[1] " I observed in the french revolutions that they always proceeded by stages, and made each stage a stepping stone to another. The Convention, to amuse the people, voted a constitution, and then voted to suspend the practical establishment of it till after the war, and in the meantime to carry on a revolutionary government. When Robespierre fell they proposed bringing forward the *suspended* Constitution, and apparently for this purpose appointed a committee to frame what they called *organic laws*, and these organic laws turned out to be a new Constitution (the Directory Constitution which was in general a good one). When Bonaparte overthrew this Constitution he got himself appointed first *Consul* for ten years, then for life, and now Emperor with an hereditary succession."—Paine to Jefferson. MS. (Dec. 27, 1804). The Paine-Condorcet Constitution is printed in *Œuvres Complètes de Condorcet*, vol. xviii. That which superseded it may be read (the Declaration of Rights omitted) in the "Constitutional History of France. By Henry C. Lockwood." (New York, 1890). It is, *inter alia*, a sufficient reason for describing the latter as revolutionary, that it provides that a Convention, elected by a majority of the departments, and a tenth part of the primaries, to revise or alter the Constitution, shall be "formed in like manner as the legislatures, and unite in itself the highest power." In other words, instead of being limited to constitutional revision, may exercise all legislative and other functions, just as the existing Convention was doing.

with the "prophetess," Catharine Théot, who pronounced him the reincarnate "Word of God." Certain it is that he revived the old forces of fanaticism, and largely by their aid crushed the Girondins, who were rationalists. Condorcet had said that in preparing a Constitution for France they had not consulted Numa's nymph or the pigeon of Mahomet; they had found human reason sufficient.

Corruption of best is worst. In the proportion that a humane deity would be a potent sanction for righteous laws, an inhuman deity is the sanction of inhuman laws. He who summoned a nature-god to the French Convention let loose the scourge on France. Nature inflicts on mankind, every day, a hundred-fold the agonies of the Reign of Terror. Robespierre had projected into nature a sentimental conception of his own, but he had no power to master the force he had evoked. That had to take the shape of the nature-gods of all time, and straightway dragged the Convention down to the savage plane where discussion becomes an exchange of thunder-stones. Such relapses are not very difficult to effect in revolutionary times. By killing off sceptical variations, and cultivating conformity, a cerebral evolution proceeded for ages by which kind-hearted people were led to worship jealous and cruel gods, who, should they appear in human form, would be dealt with as criminals. Unfortunately, however, the nature-god does not so appear; it is represented in euphemisms, while at the same time it coerces the social and human standard. Since the nature-god punishes hereditarily, kills every man at last,

and so tortures millions that the suggestion of hell
seems only too probable to those sufferers, a political system formed under the legitimacy of such a
superstition must subordinate crimes to sins, regard
atheism as worse than theft, acknowledge the arbitrary principle, and confuse retaliation with justice.
From the time that the shekinah of the nature-god
settled on the Mountain, offences were measured,
not by their injury to man, but as insults to the
Mountain-god, or to his anointed.   In the mysterious counsels of the Committee of Public Safety
the rewards are as little harmonious with the
human standard as in the ages when sabbath-
breaking and murder met the same doom.   Under
the paralyzing splendor of a divine authority, any
such considerations as the suffering or death of
men become petty.   The average Mountaineer was
unable to imagine that those who tried to save
Louis had other than royalist motives.   In this
Armageddon the Girondins were far above their
opponents in humanity and intelligence, but the
conditions did not admit of an entire adherence to
their honorable weapons of argument and eloquence.   They too often used deadly threats,
without meaning them ; the Mountaineers, who
did mean them, took such phrases seriously, and
believed the struggle to be one of life and death.
Such phenomena of bloodshed, connected with
absurdly inadequate causes, are known in history
only where gods mingle in the fray.   Reign of
Terror ?   What is the ancient reign of the god of
battles, jealous, angry every day, with everlasting
tortures of fire prepared for the unorthodox, how-

ever upright, even more than for the immoral? In France too it was a suspicion of unorthodoxy in the revolutionary creed that plunged most of the sufferers into the lake of fire and brimstone.

From the time of Paine's speeches on the King's fate he was conscious that Marat's evil eye was on him. The American's inflexible republicanism had inspired the vigilance of the powerful journals of Brissot and Bonneville, which barred the way to any dictatorship. Paine was even propagating a doctrine against presidency, thus marring the example of the United States, on which ambitious Frenchmen, from Marat to the Napoleons, have depended for their stepping-stone to despotism. Marat could not have any doubt of Paine's devotion to the Republic, but knew well his weariness of the Revolution. In the simplicity of his republican faith Paine had made a great point of the near adoption of the Constitution, and dissolution of the Convention in five or six months, little dreaming that the Mountaineers were concentrating themselves on the aim of becoming masters of the existing Convention and then rendering it permanent. Marat regarded Paine's influence as dangerous to revolutionary government, and, as he afterwards admitted, desired to crush him. The proposed victim had several vulnerable points : he had been intimate with Gouverneur Morris, whose hostility to France was known ; he had been intimate with Dumouriez, declared a traitor ; and he had no connection with any of the Clubs, in which so many found asylum. He might have joined one of them had he known the French language, and perhaps it would have been prudent to unite himself with the "Cordeliers," in whose *esprit de corps* some of his friends found refuge.

However, the time of intimidation did not come for two months after the King's death, and Paine was busy with Condorcet on the task assigned them, of preparing an Address to the People of England concerning the war of their government against France. This work, if ever completed, does not appear to have been published. It was entrusted (February 1st) to Barrère, Paine, Condorcet, and M. Faber. As Frédéric Masson, the learned librarian and historian of the Office of Foreign Affairs, has found some trace of its being assigned to Paine and Condorcet, it may be that further research will bring to light the Address. It could hardly have been completed before the warfare broke out between the Mountain and the Girondins, when anything emanating from Condorcet and Paine would have been delayed, if not suppressed. There are one or two brief essays in Condorcet's works—notably "The French Republic to Free Men"—which suggest collaboration with Paine, and may be fragments of their Address.[1]

[1] "Œuvres Complètes de Condorcet," Paris, 1804, t. xvi., p. 16: "La République Française aux hommes libres." In 1794, when Paine was in prison, a pamphlet was issued by the revolutionary government, entitled: "An Answer to the Declaration of the King of England, respecting his Motives for Carrying on the Present War, and his Conduct towards France." This anonymous pamphlet, which is in English, replies to the royal proclamation of October 29th, and bears evidence of being written while the English still occupied Toulon or early in November, 1793. There are passages in it that suggest the hand of Paine, along with others which he could not have written. It is possible that some composition of his, in pursuance of the task assigned him and Condorcet, was utilized by the Committee of Public Safety in its answer to George III.

At this time the long friendship between Paine
and Condorcet, and the Marchioness too, had
become very intimate. The two men had acted
together on the King's trial at every step, and
their speeches on bringing Louis to trial suggest
previous consultations between them.

Early in April Paine was made aware of Marat's
hostility to him. General Thomas Ward reported
to him a conversation in which Marat had said:
"Frenchmen are mad to allow foreigners to live
among them. They should cut off their ears, let
them bleed a few days, and then cut off their
heads." "But you yourself are a foreigner,"
Ward had replied, in allusion to Marat's Swiss
birth.[1] The answer is not reported. At length a
tragical incident occurred, just before the trial of
Marat (April 13th), which brought Paine face to
face with this enemy. A wealthy young Englishman, named Johnson, with whom Paine had been
intimate in London, had followed him to Paris,
where he lived in the same house with his friend.
His love of Paine amounted to worship. Having
heard of Marat's intention to have Paine's life
taken, such was the young enthusiast's despair, and
so terrible the wreck of his republican dreams, that
he resolved on suicide. He made a will bequeath-
ing his property to Paine, and stabbed himself.
Fortunately he was saved by some one who entered
just as he was about to give himself the third blow.
It may have been Paine himself who then saved
his friend's life ; at any rate, he did so eventually.

[1] "Englishmen in the French Revolution." By John G. Alger. London,
1889, p. 176. (A book of many blunders.)

The decree for Marat's trial was made amid galleries crowded with his adherents, male and female ("Dames de la Fraternité"), who hurled cries of wrath on every one who said a word against him. All were armed, the women ostentatious of their poignards. The trial before the Revolutionary Tribunal was already going in Marat's favor, when it was determined by the Girondins to bring forward this affair of Johnson. Paine was not, apparently, a party to this move, though he had enjoined no secrecy in telling his friend Brissot of the incident, which occurred before Marat was accused. On April 16th there appeared in Brissot's journal *Le Patriote Français*, the following paragraph :

"A sad incident has occurred to apprise the anarchists of the mournful fruits of their frightful teaching. An Englishman, whose name I reserve, had abjured his country because of his detestation of kings ; he came to France hoping to find there liberty ; he saw only its mask on the hideous visage of anarchy. Heart-broken by this spectacle, he determined on self-destruction. Before dying, he wrote the following words, which we have read, as written by his own trembling hand, on a paper which is in the possession of a distinguished foreigner :—'I had come to France to enjoy Liberty, but Marat has assassinated it. Anarchy is even more cruel than despotism. I am unable to endure this grievous sight, of the triumph of imbecility and inhumanity over talent and virtue.'"

The acting editor of *Le Patriote Français*, Girey-Dupré, was summoned before the Tribunal, where Marat was on trial, and testified that the note published had been handed to him by Brissot, who assured him that it was from the original, in the hands of Thomas Paine. Paine deposed that he had been unacquainted with Marat before the Convention assembled; that he had not supposed Johnson's note to have any connection with the accusations against Marat.

> *President.*—Did you give a copy of the note to Brissot?
> *Paine.*—I showed him the original.
> *President.*—Did you send it to him as it is printed?
> *Paine.*—Brissot could only have written this note after what I read to him, and told him. I would observe to the tribunal that Johnson gave himself two blows with the knife after he had understood that Marat would denounce him.
> *Marat.*—Not because I would denounce the youth who stabbed himself, but because I wish to denounce Thomas Paine.[1]
> *Paine (continuing).*—Johnson had for some time suffered mental anguish. As for Marat, I never spoke to him but once. In the lobby of the Convention he said to me that the English people are free and happy; I replied, they groan under a double despotism.[2]

No doubt it had been resolved to keep secret the fact that young Johnson was still alive. The moment was critical; a discovery that Brissot had written or printed "avant de mourir" of one still alive might have precipitated matters.

It came out in the trial that Marat, addressing a club ("Friends of Liberty and Equality"), had asked them to register a vow to recall from the Convention "all of those faithless members who had betrayed their duties in trying to save a tyrant's life," such deputies being "traitors, royalists, or fools."

Meanwhile the Constitution was undergoing discussion in the Convention, and to that Paine now

---

[1] It would appear that Paine had not been informed until Marat declared it, and was confirmed by the testimony of Choppin, that the attempted suicide was on his account.

[2] *Moniteur*, April 24, 1793.

gave his entire attention.   On April 20th the Convention, about midnight, when the Moderates had
retired and the Mountaineers found themselves
masters of the field, voted to entertain the petition
of the Parisian sections against the Girondins.
Paine saw the star of the Republic sinking.   On
"April 20th, 2d year of the Republic," he wrote as
follows to Jefferson :

" My dear Friend,—The gentleman (Dr. Romer) to whom
I entrust this letter is an intimate acquaintance of Lavater ;
but I have not had the opportunity of seeing him, as he had
sett off for Havre prior to my writing this letter, which I forward to him under cover from one of his friends, who is also
an acquaintance of mine.

" We are now in an extraordinary crisis, and it is not altogether without some considerable faults here.   Dumouriez,
partly from having no fixed principles of his own, and partly
from the continual persecution of the Jacobins, who act without either prudence or morality, has gone off to the Enemy,
and taken a considerable part of the Army with him.   The
expedition to Holland has totally failed and all Brabant is
again in the hands of the Austrians.

" You may suppose the consternation which such a sudden
reverse of fortune has occasioned, but it has been without
commotion.   Dumouriez threatened to be in Paris in three
weeks.   It is now three weeks ago ; he is still on the frontier
near to Mons with the Enemy, who do not make any progress.
Dumouriez has proposed to re-establish the former Constitution, in which plan the Austrians act with him.   But if France
and the National Convention act prudently this project will
not succeed.   In the first place there is a popular disposition
against it, and there is force sufficient to prevent it.   In the
next place, a great deal is to be taken into the calculation with
respect to the Enemy.   There are now so many powers accidentally jumbled together as to render it exceedingly difficult
to them to agree upon any common object.

" The first object, that of restoring the old Monarchy, is

evidently given up by the proposal to re-establish the late Constitution. The object of England and Prussia was to preserve Holland, and the object of Austria was to recover Brabant; while those separate objects lasted, each party having one, the Confederation could hold together, each helping the other; but after this I see not how a common object is to be formed. To all this is to be added the probable disputes about opportunity, the expense, and the projects of reimbursements. The Enemy has once adventured into France, and they had the permission or the good fortune to get back again. On every military calculation it is a hazardous adventure, and armies are not much disposed to try a second time the ground upon which they have been defeated.

"Had this revolution been conducted consistently with its principles, there was once a good prospect of extending liberty through the greatest part of Europe; but I now relinquish that hope. Should the Enemy by venturing into France put themselves again in a condition of being captured, the hope will revive; but this is a risk that I do not wish to see tried, lest it should fail.

"As the prospect of a general freedom is now much shortened, I begin to contemplate returning home. I shall await the event of the proposed Constitution, and then take my final leave of Europe. I have not written to the President, as I have nothing to communicate more than in this letter. Please to present to him my affection and compliments, and remember me among the circle of my friends. Your sincere and affectionate friend,

"THOMAS PAINE.

"P. S. I just now received a letter from General Lewis Morris, who tells me that the house and Barn on my farm at N. Rochelle are burnt down. I assure you I shall not bring money enough to build another."

Four days after this letter was written Marat, triumphant, was crowned with oak leaves. Foufrede in his speech (April 16th) had said: "Marat has formally demanded dictatorship." This was the mob's reply: *Bos locutus est.*

With Danton, Paine had been on friendly terms, though he described as "rose water" the author's pleadings against the guillotine.   On May 6th, Paine wrote to Danton a letter brought to light by Taine, who says: "Compared with the speeches and writings of the time, it produces the strangest effect by its practical good sense." [1]   Dr. Robinet also finds here evidence of " a lucid and wise intellect." [2]

"PARIS, May 6th, 2nd year of the Republic (1793).

" CITOYEN DANTON : .

" As you read English, I write this letter to you without passing it through the hands of a translator.   I am exceedingly disturbed at the distractions, jealousies, discontents and uneasiness that reign among us, and which, if they continue, will bring ruin and disgrace on the Republic.   When I left America in the year 1787, it was my intention to return the year following, but the French Revolution, and the prospect it afforded of extending the principles of liberty and fraternity through the greater part of Europe, have induced me to prolong my stay upwards of six years.   I now despair of seeing the great object of European liberty accomplished, and my despair arises not from the combined foreign powers, not from the intrigues of aristocracy and priestcraft, but from the tumultuous misconduct with which the internal affairs of the present revolution is conducted.

" All that now can be hoped for is limited to France only, and I agree with your motion of not interfering in the government of any foreign country, nor permitting any foreign country to interfere in the government of France.   This decree was necessary as a preliminary toward terminating the war.   But while these internal contentions continue, while the hope remains to the enemy of seeing the Republic fall to pieces, while not only the representatives of the departments but representation itself is publicly insulted, as it has lately

[1] " La Révolution," ii., pp. 382, 413, 414.
[2] " Danton Emigré," p. 177.

been and now is by the people of Paris, or at least by the tribunes, the enemy will be encouraged to hang about the frontiers and await the issue of circumstances.

"I observe that the confederated powers have not yet recognised Monsieur, or D'Artois, as regent, nor made any proclamation in favour of any of the Bourbons ; but this negative conduct admits of two different conclusions. The one is that of abandoning the Bourbons and the war together ; the other is that of changing the object of the war and substituting a partition scheme in the place of their first object, as they have done by Poland. If this should be their object, the internal contentions that now rage will favour that object far more than it favoured their former object. The danger every day increases of a rupture between Paris and the departments. The departments did not send their deputies to Paris to be insulted, and every insult shown to them is an insult to the departments that elected and sent them. I see but one effectual plan to prevent this rupture taking place, and that is to fix the residence of the Convention, and of the future assemblies, at a distance from Paris.

"I saw, during the American Revolution, the exceeding inconvenience that arose by having the government of Congress within the limits of any Municipal Jurisdiction. Congress first resided in Philadelphia, and after a residence of four years it found it necessary to leave it. It then adjourned to the State of Jersey. It afterwards removed to New York ; it again removed from New York to Philadelphia, and after experiencing in every one of these places the great inconvenience of a government, it formed the project of building a Town, not within the limits of any municipal jurisdiction, for the future residence of Congress. In any one of the places where Congress resided, the municipal authority privately or openly opposed itself to the authority of Congress, and the people of each of those places expected more attention from Congress than their equal share with the other States amounted to. The same thing now takes place in France, but in a far greater excess.

"I see also another embarrassing circumstance arising in Paris of which we have had full experience in America. I mean that of fixing the price of provisions. But if this measure is to be attempted it ought to be done by the Municipality. The Convention has nothing to do with regulations of this kind ; neither can they be carried into practice. The people of Paris may say they will not give more than a certain price for provisions, but as they cannot compel the country people to bring provisions to market the consequence will be directly contrary to their expectations, and they will find dearness and famine instead of plenty and cheapness. They may force the price down upon the stock in hand, but after that the market will be empty.

"I will give you an example. In Philadelphia we undertook, among other regulations of this kind, to regulate the price of Salt ; the consequence was that no Salt was brought to market, and the price rose to thirty-six shillings sterling per Bushel. The price before the war was only one shilling and sixpence per Bushel ; and we regulated the price of flour (farine) till there was none in the market, and the people were glad to procure it at any price.

"There is also a circumstance to be taken into the account which is not much attended to. The assignats are not of the same value they were a year ago, and as the quantity increases the value of them will diminish. This gives the appearance of things being dear when they are not so in fact, for in the same proportion that any kind of money falls in value articles rise in price. If it were not for this the quantity of assignats would be too great to be circulated. Paper money in America fell so much in value from this excessive quantity of it, that in the year 1781 I gave three hundred paper dollars for one pair of worsted stockings. What I write you upon this subject is experience, and not merely opinion.

"I have no personal interest in any of these matters, nor in any party disputes. I attend only to general principles.

"As soon as a constitution shall be established I shall return to America ; and be the future prosperity of France ever so great, I shall enjoy no other part of it than the happiness of knowing it. In the mean time I am distressed to see matters so badly conducted, and so little attention paid to moral principles. It is these things that injure the character of the Revolution and discourage the progress of liberty all over the world.

"When I began this letter I did not intend making it so lengthy, but since I have gone thus far I will fill up the remainder of the sheet with such matters as occur to me.

"There ought to be some regulation with respect to the spirit of denunciation that now prevails. If every individual is to indulge his private malignacy or his private ambition, to denounce at random and without any kind of proof, all confidence will be undermined and all authority be destroyed. Calumny is a species of Treachery that ought to be punished as well as any other kind of Treachery. It is a private vice productive of public evils ; because it is possible to irritate men into disaffection by continual calumny who never intended to be disaffected. It is therefore, equally as necessary to guard against the evils of unfounded or malignant suspicion as against the evils of blind confidence. It is equally as necessary to protect the characters of public officers from calumny as it is to punish them for treachery or misconduct. For my own part I shall hold it a matter of doubt, until better evidence arises than is known at present, whether Dumouriez has been a traitor from policy or from resentment. There was certainly a time when he acted well, but it is not every man whose mind is strong enough to bear up against ingratitude, and I think he experienced a great deal of this before he revolted. Calumny becomes harmless and defeats itself when it attempts to act upon too large a scale. Thus the denunciation of the Sections [of Paris] against the twenty-two deputies falls to the ground. The departments that elected them are better judges of their moral and political characters than those who have denounced them. This denunciation will injure Paris in the opinion of the departments because it has the appearance of dictating to them what sort of deputies they shall elect. Most of the acquaintances that I have in the convention are among those who are in that list, and I know there are not better men nor better patriots than what they are.

"I have written a letter to Marat of the same date as this but not on the same subject. He may show it to you if he chuse.

"Votre Ami,

"Thomas Paine.

"Citoyen Danton."

It is to be hoped that Paine's letter to Marat may
be discovered in France ; it is shown by the Cobbett papers, printed in the Appendix, that he kept
a copy, which there is reason to fear perished with
General Bonneville's library in St. Louis.   Whatever may be the letter's contents, there is no indication that thereafter Marat troubled Paine.   Possibly Danton and Marat compared their letters, and
the latter got it into his head that hostility to this
American, anxious only to cross the ocean, could
be of no advantage to him.   Or perhaps he remembered that if a hue and cry were raised against
"foreigners" it could not stop short of his own
leaf-crowned Neufchatel head.   He had shown
some sensitiveness about that at his trial.   Samson-
Pegnet had testified that, at conversations in Paine's
house, Marat had been reported as saying that it
was necessary to massacre all the foreigners, especially the English.   This Marat pronounced an
"atrocious calumny, a device of the statesmen [his
epithet for Girondins] to render me odious."   Whatever his motives, there is reason to believe that
Marat no longer included Paine in his proscribed
list.   Had it been otherwise a fair opportunity of
striking down Paine presented itself on the occasion, already alluded to, when Paine gave his testimony in favor of General Miranda.   Miranda was
tried before the Revolutionary Tribunal on May
12th, and three days following. He had served under
Dumouriez, was defeated, and was suspected of
connivance with his treacherous commander.   Paine
was known to have been friendly with Dumouriez,
and his testimony in favor of Miranda might natu-

rally have been used against both men. Miranda
was, however, acquitted, and that did not make Marat better disposed towards that adventurer's friends,
all Girondins, or, like Paine, who belonged to no
party, hostile to Jacobinism. Yet when, on June
2d, the doomed Girondins were arrested, there
were surprising exceptions : Paine and his literary
collaborateur, Condorcet. Moreover, though the
translator of Paine's works, Lanthenas, was among
the proscribed, his name was erased on Marat's
motion.

On June 7th Robespierre demanded a more
stringent law against foreigners, and one was soon
after passed ordering their imprisonment. It was
understood that this could not apply to the two foreigners in the Convention—Paine and Anacharsis
Clootz,—though it was regarded as a kind of warning to them. I have seen it stated, but without
authority, that Paine had been admonished by Danton to stay away from the Convention on June 2d,
and from that day there could not be the slightest
utility in his attendance. The Mountaineers had it
all their own way. For simply criticising the Constitution they brought forward in place of that of the
first committee, Condorcet had to fly from prosecution. Others also fled, among them Brissot and
Duchatel. What with the arrestations and flights
Paine found himself, in June, almost alone. In the
Convention he was sometimes the solitary figure left
on the Plain, where but now sat the brilliant statesmen of France. They, his beloved friends, have
started in procession towards the guillotine, for even
flight must end there ; daily others are pressed into

their ranks ; his own summons, he feels, is only a
question of a few weeks or days. How Paine loved
those men—Brissot, Condorcet, Lasource, Duchatel, Vergniaud, Gensonné ! Never was man more
devoted to his intellectual comrades. Even across
a century one may realize what it meant to him,
that march of some of his best friends to the scaffold, while others were hunted through France, and
the agony of their families, most of whom he well
knew.

Alas, even this is not the worst ! For what were
the personal fate of himself or any compared with
the fearful fact that the harvest is past and the
republic not saved ! Thus had ended all his labors,
and his visions of the Commonwealth of Man. The
time had come when many besides poor Johnson
sought peace in annihilation. Paine, heartbroken,
sought oblivion in brandy. Recourse to such
anæsthetic, of which any affectionate man might
fairly avail himself under such incredible agony as
the ruin of his hopes and the approaching murder
of his dearest friends, was hitherto unknown in
Paine's life. He drank freely, as was the custom
of his time ; but with the exception of the evidence
of an enemy at his trial in England, that he once
saw him under the influence of wine after a dinner
party (1792), which he admitted was " unusual,"
no intimation of excess is discoverable in any contemporary record of Paine until this his fifty-seventh
year. He afterwards told his friend Rickman that,
" borne down by public and private affliction, he had
been driven to excesses in Paris" ; and, as it was
about this time that Gouverneur Morris and Colonel

Bosville, who had reasons for disparaging Paine, reported stories of his drunkenness (growing ever since), we may assign the excesses mainly to June. It will be seen by comparison of the dates of events and documents presently mentioned that Paine could not have remained long in this pardonable refuge of mental misery. Charlotte Corday's poignard cut a rift in the black cloud. After that tremendous July 13th there is positive evidence not only of sobriety, but of life and work on Paine's part that make the year memorable.

Marat dead, hope springs up for the arrested Girondins. They are not yet in prison, but under "arrestation in their homes"; death seemed inevitable while Marat lived, but Charlotte Corday has summoned a new leader. Why may Paine's imperilled comrades not come forth again? Certainly they will if the new chieftain is Danton, who under his radical rage hides a heart. Or if Marat's mantle falls on Robespierre, would not that scholarly lawyer, who would have abolished capital punishment, reverse Marat's cruel decrees? Robespierre had agreed to the new Constitution (reported by Paine's friend, Hérault de Séchelles) and when even that dubious instrument returns with the popular sanction, all may be well. The Convention, which is doing everything except what it was elected to do, will then dissolve, and the happy Republic remember it only as a nightmare. So Paine takes heart again, abandons the bowl of forgetfulness, and becomes a republican Socrates instructing disciples in an old French garden.

CHAPTER IV.

A GARDEN IN THE FAUBOURG ST. DENIS.

SIR GEORGE TREVELYAN has written a pregnant passage, reminding the world of the moral burden which radicals in England had to bear a hundred years ago.

· " When to speak or write one's mind on politics is to obtain the reputation, and render one's self liable to the punishment of a criminal, social discredit, with all its attendant moral dangers, soon attaches itself to the more humble opponents of a ministry. To be outside the law as a publisher or a pamphleteer is only less trying to conscience and conduct than to be outside the law as a smuggler or a poacher ; and those who, ninety years ago, placed themselves within the grasp of the penal statutes as they were administered in England and barbarously perverted in Scotland were certain to be very bold men, and pretty sure to be unconventional up to the uttermost verge of respectability. As an Italian Liberal was sometimes half a bravo, and a Spanish patriot often more than half a brigand, so a British Radical under George the Third had generally, it must be confessed, a dash of the Bohemian. Such, in a more or less mitigated form, were Paine and Cobbett, Hunt, Hone, and Holcroft ; while the same causes in part account for the elfish vagaries of Shelley and the grim improprieties of Godwin. But when we recollect how these, and the like of these, gave up every hope of worldly prosperity, and set their life and liberty in continual hazard for the sake of that personal and political freedom which we now exercise as unconsciously as we breathe the air, it would be too exacting

to require that each and all of them should have lived as deco-
rously as Perceval, and died as solvent as Bishop Tomline." [1]

To this right verdict it may be added that, even
at the earlier period when it was most applicable,
the radicals could only produce one rival in profli-
gacy (John Wilkes) to their aristocratic oppressors.
It may also be noted as a species of homage that
the slightest failings of eminent reformers become
historic.   The vices of Burke and Fox are forgotten.   Who remembers that the younger Pitt was
brought to an early grave by the bottle ?   But every
fault of those who resisted his oppression is placed
under a solar microscope.   Although, as Sir George
affirms, the oppressors largely caused the faults,
this homage to the higher moral standard of the
reformers may be accepted. [2]

It was, indeed, a hard time for reformers in England.   Among them were many refined gentlemen
who felt that it was no country for a thinker and
scholar to live in.   Among the pathetic pictures of
the time was that of the twelve scholars, headed by
Coleridge and Southey, and twelve ladies, who
found the atmosphere of England too impure for

[1] " Early History of Charles James Fox," American ed., p. 440.
[2] The following document was found among the papers of Mr. John Hall,
originally of Leicester, England, and has been forwarded to me by his
descendant, J. Dutton Steele, Jr., of Philadelphia.

" A Copy of a Letter from the chairman of a meeting of the Gentry and
Clergy at Atherstone, written in consequence of an envious schoolmaster and
two or three others who informed the meeting that the Excise Officers of
Polesworth were employed in distributing the Rights of Man ; but which was
very false.

" Sir : I should think it unnecessary to inform you, that the purport of his
Majesty's proclamation in the Month of May last, and the numerous meetings
which are daily taking place both in Town and Country, are for the avowed
purpose of suppressing treasonable and seditious writings amongst which

any but slaves to breathe, and proposed to seek in America some retreat where their pastoral " pantisocrasy " might be realized. Lack of funds prevented the fulfilment of this dream, but that it should have been an object of concert and endeavor, in that refined circle at Bristol, is a memorable sign of that dreadful time. In the absence of means to form such communities, preserving the culture and charm of a society evolved out of barbarism, apart from the walls of a remaining political barbarism threatening it with their ruins, some scholars were compelled, like Coleridge, to rejoin the feudalists, and help them to buttress the crumbling castle. They secured themselves from the social deterioration of living on wild "honey-dew" in a wilderness, at cost of wearing intellectual masks. Some fled to America, like Cobbett. But others fixed their abode in Paris, where radicalism was fashionable and invested with the charm of the *salon* and the theatre.

Before the declaration of war Paine had been on friendly terms with some eminent Englishmen in Paris : he dined every week with Lord Lauder-

Mr. Payne's Rights of Man ranks most conspicuous. Were I not informed you have taken some pains in spreading that publication, I write to say If you don't from this time adopt a different kind of conduct you will be taken notice of in such way as may prove very disagreeable.

"The Eyes of the Country are upon you and you will do well in future to shew yourself faithful to the Master who employs you.

"I remain,
"Your IIble servant,
"(Signed) Jos. Boultbee.

"Baxterby, 15th Decr., '92.

"N. B. The letter was written the next morning after the Meeting where most of the Loyal souls got drunk to an uncommon degree. They drank his Majesty's health so often the reckoning amounted to 7s. 6d. each. One of the informers threw down a shilling and ran away."

dale, Dr. John Moore, an author, and others in
some restaurant. After most of these had followed
Lord Gower to England he had to be more guarded.
A British agent, Major Semple, approached him
under the name of Major Lisle. He professed to
be an Irish patriot, wore the green cockade, and
desired introduction to the Minister of War. Paine
fortunately knew too many Irishmen to fall into
this snare.[1] But General Miranda, as we have
seen, fared better. Paine was, indeed, so overrun
with visitors and adventurers that he appropriated
two mornings of each week at the Philadelphia
House for levees. These, however, became insufficient to stem the constant stream of visitors, including spies and lion-hunters, so that he had little
time for consultation with the men and women
whose co-operation he needed in public affairs. He
therefore leased an out-of-the-way house, reserving
knowledge of it for particular friends, while still
retaining his address at the Philadelphia Hotel,
where the levees were continued.

The irony of fate had brought an old mansion of
Madame de Pompadour to become the residence
of Thomas Paine and his half dozen English disciples. It was then, and still is, No. 63 Faubourg
St. Denis. Here, where a King's mistress held her
merry fêtes, and issued the decrees of her reign—
sometimes of terror,—the little band of English
humanitarians read and conversed, and sported in
the garden. In a little essay on " Forgetfulness,"
addressed to his friend, Lady Smith, Paine described
these lodgings.

[1] Rickman, p. 129.

"They were the most agreeable, for situation, of any I ever had in Paris, except that they were too remote from the Convention, of which I was then a member. But this was recompensed by their being also remote from the alarms and confusion into which the interior of Paris was then often thrown. The news of those things used to arrive to us, as if we were in a state of tranquillity in the country. The house, which was enclosed by a wall and gateway from the street, was a good deal like an old mansion farm-house, and the court-yard was like a farm yard, stocked with fowls,—ducks, turkies, and geese ; which, for amusement, we used to feed out of the parlor window on the ground floor. There were some hutches for rabbits, and a sty with two pigs. Beyond was a garden of more than an acre of ground, well laid out, and stocked with excellent fruit trees. The orange, apricot, and greengage plum were the best I ever tasted ; and it is the only place where I saw the wild cucumber. The place had formerly been occupied by some curious person.

"My apartments consisted of three rooms ; the first for wood, water, etc.; the next was the bedroom ; and beyond it the sitting room, which looked into the garden through a glass door ; and on the outside there was a small landing place railed in, and a flight of narrow stairs almost hidden by the vines that grew over it, by which I could descend into the garden without going down stairs through the house. . . . I used to find some relief by walking alone in the garden, after dark, and cursing with hearty good will the authors of that terrible system that had turned the character of the Revolution I had been proud to defend. I went but little to the Convention, and then only to make my appearance, because I found it impossible to join in their tremendous decrees, and useless and dangerous to oppose them. My having voted and spoken extensively, more so than any other member, against the execution of the king, had already fixed a mark upon me ; neither dared any of my associates in the Convention to translate and speak in French for me anything I might have dared to have written. . . . Pen and ink were then of no use to me ; no good could be done by writing, and no printer dared to print ; and whatever I might have written, for my private amusement, as

anecdotes of the times, would have been continually exposed
to be examined, and tortured into any meaning that the rage
of party might fix upon it.   And as to softer subjects, my
heart was in distress at the fate of my friends, and my harp
hung upon the weeping willows.

"As it was summer, we spent most of our time in the
garden, and passed it away in those childish amusements
that serve to keep reflection from the mind,—such as
marbles, Scotch hops, battledores, etc., at which we were all
pretty expert.   In this retired manner we remained about six
or seven weeks, and our landlord went every evening into the
city to bring us the news of the day and the evening journal."

The "we" included young Johnson, Mr. and
Mrs. Christie, Mr. Choppin, probably Mr. Shapworth, an American, and M. Laborde, a scientific
friend of Paine.   These appear to have entered
with Paine into co-operative housekeeping, though
taking their chief meals at the restaurants.   In the
evenings they were joined by others,—the Brissots
(before the arrest), Nicholas Bonneville, Joel Barlow, Captain Imlay, Mary Wollstonecraft, the
Rolands.   Mystical Madame Roland dreaded
Paine's power, which she considered more adapted
to pull down than to build, but has left a vivid impression of "the boldness of his conceptions, the
originality of his style, the striking truths he throws
out bravely among those whom they offend."   The
Mr. Shapworth alluded to is mentioned in a manuscript journal of Daniel Constable, sent me by his
nephew, Clair J. Grece, LL.D.   This English
gentleman visited Baton Rouge and Shapworth's
plantation in 1822.   "Mr. S.," he says, "has
a daughter married to the Governor [Robin-
son], has travelled in Europe, married a French

lady.   He is a warm friend of Thomas Paine, as
is his son-in-law.   He lived with Paine many
months at Paris.   He [Paine] was then a sober,
correct gentleman in appearance and manner."
The English refugees, persecuted for selling the
" Rights of Man," were, of course, always welcomed
by Paine, and poor Rickman was his guest during
this summer of 1793.[1]   The following reminiscence
of Paine, at a time when Gouverneur Morris was
(for reasons that presently appear) reporting him
to his American friends as generally drunk, was
written by Rickman :

" He usually rose about seven.   After breakfast he usually
strayed an hour or two in the garden, where he one morning
pointed out the kind of spider whose web furnished him with the
first idea of constructing his iron bridge ; a fine model of which,
in mahogany, is preserved in Paris.   The little happy circle
who lived with him will ever remember those days with delight:
with these select friends he would talk of his boyish days,
played at chess, whist, piquet, or cribbage, and enliven the
moments by many interesting anecdotes : with these he would

[1] Rickman appears to have escaped from England in 1792, according to
the following sonnet sent me by Dr. Grece.   It is headed : " Sonnet to my
Little Girl, 1792.   Written at Calais, on being pursued by cruel prosecution
and persecution."

> " Farewell, sweet babe ! and mayst thou never know,
>   Like me, the pressure of exceeding woe.
> Some griefs (for they are human nature's right)
>   On life's eventful stage will be thy lot ;
> Some generous cares to clear thy mental sight,
>   Some pains, in happiest hours, perhaps, begot ;
> But mayst thou ne'er be, like thy father, driven
>   From a loved partner, family, and home,
> Snatched from each heart-felt bliss, domestic heaven !
>   From native shores, and all that 's valued, roam.
> Oh, may bad governments, the source of human woe,
> Ere thou becom'st mature, receive their deadly blow ;
> Then mankind's greatest curse thou ne'er wilt know."

play at marbles, scotch hops, battledores, etc.: on the broad
and fine gravel walk at the upper end of the garden, and then
retire to his boudoir, where he was up to his knees in letters
and papers of various descriptions. Here he remained till
dinner time ; and unless he visited Brissot's family, or some
particular friend, in the evening, which was his frequent custom, he joined again the society of his favorites and fellow-
boarders, with whom his conversation was often witty and
cheerful, always acute and improving, but never frivolous.
Incorrupt, straightforward, and sincere, he pursued his political course in France, as everywhere else, let the government
or clamor or faction of the day be what it might, with firmness, with clearness, and without a shadow of turning."

In the spring of 1890 the present writer visited
the spot. The lower front of the old mansion is
divided into shops,—a Fruiterer being appropriately next the gateway, which now opens into a
wide thoroughfare. Above the rooms once occupied by Paine was the sign "Ecrivain Publique,"—
placed there by a Mademoiselle who wrote letters
and advertisements for humble neighbors not expert
in penmanship. At the end of what was once the
garden is a Printer's office, in which was a large
lithograph portrait of Victor Hugo. The printer,
his wife, and little daughter were folding publications of the "Extreme Left." Near the door remains a veritable survival of the garden and its
living tenants which amused Paine and his friends.
There were two ancient fruit trees, of which one
was dying, but the other budding in the spring sunshine. There were ancient coops with ducks, and
pigeon-houses with pigeons, also rabbits, and some
flowers. This little nook, of perhaps forty square
feet, and its animals, had been there—so an old

inhabitant told me—time out of mind. They belonged to nobody in particular; the pigeons were fed by the people around ; the fowls were probably kept there by some poultryman. There were eager groups attending every stage of the investigation. The exceptional antiquity of the mansion had been recognized by its occupants,—several families,— but without curiosity, and perhaps with regret. Comparatively few had heard of Paine.

Shortly before I had visited the garden near Florence which Boccaccio's immortal tales have kept in perennial beauty through five centuries. It may be that in the far future some brother of Boccace will bequeath to Paris as sweet a legend of the garden where beside the plague of blood the prophet of the universal Republic realized his dream in microcosm. Here gathered sympathetic spirits from America, England, France, Germany, Holland, Switzerland, freed from prejudices of race, rank, or nationality, striving to be mutually helpful, amusing themselves with Arcadian sports, studying nature, enriching each other by exchange of experiences. It is certain that in all the world there was no group of men and women more disinterestedly absorbed in the work of benefiting their fellowbeings. They could not, however, like Boccaccio's ladies and gentlemen "kill Death" by their witty tales; for presently beloved faces disappeared from their circle, and the cruel axe was gleaming over them.

And now the old hotel became the republican capitol of Europe. There sat an international Premier with his Cabinet, concentrated on the work of saving the Girondins. He was indeed treated by the Executive government as a Minister. It was supposed by Paine and believed by his adherents that Robespierre had for him some dislike. Paine in later years wrote of Robespierre as a " hypocrite," and the epithet may have a significance not recognized by his readers. It is to me probable that Paine considered himself deceived by Robespierre with professions of respect, if not of friendliness before being cast into prison ; a conclusion naturally based on requests from the Ministers for opinions on public affairs. The archives of the Revolution contain various evidences of this, and several papers by Paine evidently in reply to questions. We may feel certain that every subject propounded was carefully discussed in Paine's little cosmopolitan Cabinet before his opinion was transmitted to the revolutionary Cabinet of Committees. In reading the subjoined documents it must be borne in mind that Robespierre had not yet been suspected of the cruelty presently associated with his name. The Queen and the Girondist leaders were yet alive. Of these leaders Paine was known to be the friend, and it was of the utmost importance that he should be suavely loyal to the government that had inherited these prisoners from Marat's time.

The first of these papers is erroneously endorsed " January 1793. Thom. Payne. Copie," in the French State Archives.[1] Its reference to the defeat of the Duke of York at Dunkirk assigns its date to the late summer. It is headed, " Observa-

---

[1] États Unis. Vol. 37. Document 39.

tions on the situation of the Powers joined against France."

" It is always useful to know the position and the designs of one's enemies. It is much easier to do so by combining and comparing the events, and by examining the consequences which result from them, than by forming one's judgment by letters found or intercepted. These letters could be fabricated with the intention of deceiving, but events or circumstances have a character which is proper to them. If in the course of our political operations we mistake the designs of our enemy, it leads us to do precisely that which he desired we should do, and it happens, by the fact, but against our intentions, that we work for him.

" It appears at first sight that the coalition against France is not of the nature of those which form themselves by a treaty. It has been the work of circumstances. It is a heterogeneous mass, the parts of which dash against each other, and often neutralise themselves. They have but one single point of reunion, the re-establishment of the monarchical government in France. Two means can conduct them to the execution of this plan. The first is, to re-establish the Bourbons, and with them the Monarchy ; the second, to make a division similar to that which they have made in Poland, and to reign themselves in France. The political questions to be solved are, then, to know on which of these two plans it is most probable, the united Powers will act ; and which are the points of these plans on which they will agree or disagree.

" Supposing their aim to be the re-establishment of the Bourbons, the difficulty which will present itself, will be, to know who will be their Allies ?

" Will England consent to the re-establishment of the compact of family in the person of the Bourbons, against whom she has machinated and fought since her existence ? Will Prussia consent to re-establish the alliance which subsisted between France and Austria, or will Austria wish to re-establish the ancient alliance between France and Prussia, which was directed against her ? Will Spain, or any other maritime Power, allow France and her Marine to ally themselves to

England? In fine, will any of these Powers consent to furnish forces which could be directed against herself? However, all these cases present themselves in the hypothesis of the restoration of the Bourbons.

"If we suppose that their plan be the dismemberment of France, difficulties will present themselves under another form, but not of the same nature. It will no longer be question, in this case, of the Bourbons, as their position will be worse; for if their preservation is a part of their first plan, their destruction ought to enter in the second; because it is necessary for the success of the dismembering that not a single pretendant to the Crown of France should exist.

"As one must think of all the probabilities in political calculations, it is not unlikely that some of the united Powers, having in view the first of these plans, and others the second, —that this may be one of the causes of their disagreement. It is to be remembered that Russia recognised a Regency from the beginning of Spring; not one of the other Powers followed her example. The distance of Russia from France, and the different countries by which she is separated from her, leave no doubt as to her dispositions with regard to the plan of division; and as much as one can form an opinion on the circumstances, it is not her scheme.

"The coalition directed against France, is composed of two kinds of Powers. The Maritime Powers, not having the same interest as the others, will be divided, as to the execution of the project of division.

"I do not hesitate to believe that the politic of the English Government is to foment the scheme of dismembering, and the entire destruction of the Bourbon family.

"The difficulty which must arise, in this last hypothesis, between the united Maritime Powers proceeds from their views being entirely opposed.

"The trading vessels of the Northern Nations, from Holland to Russia, must pass through the narrow Channel, which lies between Dunkirk and the coasts of England; and consequently not one of them, will allow this latter Power to have forts on both sides of this Strait. The audacity with which she has seized the neutral vessels ought to demonstrate to all Nations how much her schemes increase their danger, and menace the security of their present and future commerce.

"Supposing then that the other Nations oppose the plans of England, she will be forced to cease the war with us; or, if she continues it, the Northern Nations will become interested in the safety of France.

"There are three distinct parties in England at this moment: the Government party, the Revolutionary party, and an intermedial party,—which is only opposed to the war on account of the expense it entails, and the harm it does commerce and manufacture. I am speaking of the People, and not of the Parliament. The latter is divided into two parties : the Ministerial, and the Anti-Ministerial. The Revolutionary party, the intermedial party and the Anti-Ministerial party will all rejoice, publicly or privately, at the defeat of the Duke of York's army, at Dunkirk. The intermedial party, because they hope that this defeat will finish the war. The Antiministerial party, because they hope it will overthrow the Ministry. And all the three because they hate the Duke of York. Such is the state of the different parties in England.

"Signed :   THOMAS PAINE."

In the same volume of the State Archives (Paris) is the following note by Paine, with its translation :

"You mentioned to me that saltpetre was becoming scarce. I communicate to you a project of the late Captain Paul Jones, which, if successfully put in practice, will furnish you with that article.

"All the English East India ships put into St. Helena, off the coast of Africa, on their return from India to England. A great part of their ballast is saltpetre. Captain Jones, who had been at St. Helena, says that the place can be very easily taken. His proposal was to send off a small squadron for that purpose, to keep the English flag flying at port. The English vessels will continue coming in as usual. By this means it will be a long time before the Government of England can have any knowledge of what has happened. The success of this depends so much upon secrecy that I wish you would translate this yourself, and give it to Barrère."

In the next volume (38) of the French Archives, marked "États Unis, 1793," is a remarkable document (No. 39), entitled "A Citizen of America to the Citizens of Europe." The name of Paine is only pencilled on it, and it was probably written by him ; but it purports to have been written in America, and is dated "Philadelphia, July 28, 1793; 18th Year of Independence." It is a clerk's copy, so that it cannot now be known whether the ruse of its origin in Philadelphia was due to Paine or to the government. It is an extended paper, and repeats to some extent, though not literally, what is said in the "Observations" quoted above. Possibly the government, on receiving that paper (Document 39 also), desired Paine to write it out as an address to the "Citizens of Europe." It does not appear to have been published. The first four paragraphs of this paper, combined with the "Observations," will suffice to show its character.

"Understanding that a proposal is intended to be made at the ensuing meeting of the Congress of the United States of America, to send Commissioners to Europe to confer with the Ministers of all the Neutral Powers, for the purpose of negociating preliminaries of Peace, I address this letter to you on that subject, and on the several matters connected therewith.

"In order to discuss this subject through all its circumstances, it will be necessary to take a review of the state of Europe, prior to the French revolution. It will from thence appear, that the powers leagued against France are fighting to attain an object, which, were it possible to be attained, would be injurious to themselves.

"This is not an uncommon error in the history of wars and governments, of which the conduct of the English government in the war against America is a striking instance. She com-

menced that war for the avowed purpose of subjugating
America ; and after wasting upwards of one hundred millions
sterling, and then abandoning the object, she discovered in the
course of three or four years, that the prosperity of England
was increased, instead of being diminished, by the independence of America.   In short, every circumstance is pregnant
with some natural effect, upon which intentions and opinions
have no influence ; and the political error lies in misjudging
what the effect will be.   England misjudged it in the American
war, and the reasons I shall now offer will shew, that she mis-
judges it in the present war.—In discussing this subject, I
leave out of the question every thing respecting forms and
systems of government ; for as all the governments of Europe
differ from each other, there is no reason that the government
of France should not differ from the rest.

"The clamours continually raised in all the countries of
Europe were, that the family of the Bourbons was become too
powerful ; that the intrigues of the court of France endangered
the peace of Europe.   Austria saw with a jealous eye the connection of France with Prussia ; and Prussia, in her turn
became jealous of the connection of France with Austria ;
England had wasted millions unsuccessfully in attempting to
prevent the family compact with Spain ; Russia disliked the
alliance between France and Turkey ; and Turkey became
apprehensive of the inclination of France towards an alliance
with Russia.   Sometimes the quadruple alliance alarmed some
of the powers, and at other times a contrary system alarmed
others, and in all those cases the charge was always made
against the intrigues of the Bourbons."

In each of these papers a plea for the imperilled
Girondins is audible.   Each is a reminder that he,
Thomas Paine, friend of the Brissotins, is continuing their anxious and loyal vigilance for the Republic.   And during all this summer Paine had
good reason to believe that his friends were safe.
Robespierre was eloquently deprecating useless
effusion of blood.   As for Paine himself, he was

not only consulted on public questions, but trusted in practical affairs. He was still able to help Americans and Englishmen who invoked his aid. Writing to Lady Smith concerning two applications of that kind, he says :

"I went into my chamber to write and sign a certificate for them, which I intended to take to the guard house to obtain their release. Just as I had finished it, a man came into my room, dressed in the Parisian uniform of a captain, and spoke to me in good English, and with a good address. He told me that two young men, Englishmen, were arrested and detained in the guard house, and that the section (meaning those who represented and acted for the section) had sent him to ask me if I knew them, in which case they would be liberated. This matter being soon settled between us, he talked to me about the Revolution, and something about the 'Rights of Man,' which he had read in English ; and at parting offered me, in a polite and civil manner, his services. And who do you think the man was who offered me his services ? It was no other than the public executioner, Samson, who guillotined the King and all who were guillotined in Paris, and who lived in the same street with me."

There appeared no reason to suppose this a domiciliary visit, or that it had any relation to anything except the two Englishmen. Samson was not a detective. It soon turned out, however, that there was a serpent creeping into Paine's little garden in the Faubourg St. Denis. He and his guests knew it not, however, until all their hopes fell with the leaves and blossoms amid which they had passed a summer to which Paine, from his prison, looked back with fond recollection.

CHAPTER V.

A CONSPIRACY.

"HE suffered under Pontius Pilate." Pilate's gallant struggle to save Jesus from lynchers survives in no kindly memorial save among the peasants of Oberammergau. It is said that the impression once made in England by the Miracle Play has left its relic in the miserable puppet-play Punch and Judy (*Pontius cum Judæis*); but meanwhile the Church repeats, throughout Christendom, "He suffered under Pontius Pilate." It is almost normal in history that the brand of infamy falls on the wrong man. This is the penalty of personal eminence, and especially of eloquence. In the opening years of the French Revolution the two men in Europe who seemed omnipotent were Pitt and Robespierre. By reason of their eloquence, their ingenious defences, their fame, the columns of credit and discredit were begun in their names, and have so continued. English liberalism, remembering the imprisoned and flying writers, still repeats, "They suffered under William Pitt." French republics transmit their legend of Condorcet, Camille Desmoulins, Brissot, Malesherbes, "They suffered under Robespierre." The friends, disciples, biographers, of Thomas Paine have it

in their creed that he suffered under both Pitt and
Robespierre. It is certain that neither Pitt nor
Robespierre was so strong as he appeared. Their
hands cannot be cleansed, but they are historic
scapegoats of innumerable sins they never committed.

Unfortunately for Robespierre's memory, in
England and America especially, those who for
a century might have been the most ready to
vindicate a slandered revolutionist have been confronted by the long imprisonment of the author
of the " Rights of Man," and by the discovery
of his virtual death-sentence in Robespierre's handwriting. Louis Blanc, Robespierre's great vindi-
cator, could not, we may assume, explain this
ugly fact, which he passes by in silence. He has
proved, conclusively as I think, that Robespierre
was among the revolutionists least guilty of the
Terror; that he was murdered by a conspiracy
of those whose cruelties he was trying to restrain ;
that, when no longer alive to answer, they burdened him with their crimes, as the only means of
saving their heads. Robespierre's doom was
sealed when he had real power, and used it to prevent any organization of the constitutional government which might have checked revolutionary
excesses. He then, because of a superstitious faith
in the auspices of the Supreme Being, threw the
reins upon the neck of the revolution he afterwards vainly tried to curb. Others, who did not
wish to restrain it, seized the reins and when the
precipice was reached took care that Robespierre
should be hurled over it.

Many allegations against Robespierre have been disproved. He tried to save Danton and Camille Desmoulins, and did save seventy-three deputies whose death the potentates of the Committee of Public Safety had planned. But against him still lies that terrible sentence found in his Note Book, and reported by a Committee to the Convention : " Demand that Thomas Payne be decreed of accusation for the interests of America as much as of France."[1]

The Committee on Robespierre's papers, and especially Courtois its Chairman, suppressed some things favorable to him (published long after), and it can never be known whether they found anything further about Paine. They made a strong point of the sentence found, and added : " Why Thomas Payne more than another? Because he helped to establish the liberty of both worlds."

An essay by Paine on Robespierre has been lost, and his opinion of the man can be gathered only from occasional remarks. After the Courtois report he had to accept the theory of Robespierre's malevolence and hypocrisy. He then, for the first time, suspected the same hand in a previous act of hostility towards him. In August, 1793, an address had been sent to the Convention from Arras, a town in his constituency, saying that they had lost confidence in Paine. This failed of success because a counter-address came from St. Omer. Robespierre being a native of Arras, it now seemed clear that he had instigated the address. It was,

---

[1] " Demander que Thomas Payne soit décréte d'accusation pour les intérêts de l'Amerique autant que de la France."

however, almost certainly the work of Joseph Lebon, who, as Paine once wrote, "made the streets of Arras run with blood." Lebon was his *suppléant,* and could not sit in the Convention until Paine left it.

But although Paine would appear to have ascribed his misfortunes to Robespierre at the time, he was evidently mystified by the whole thing. No word against him had ever fallen from Robespierre's lips, and if that leader had been hostile to him why should he have excepted him from the accusations of his associates, have consulted him through the summer, and even after imprisonment, kept him unharmed for months? There is a notable sentence in Paine's letter (from prison) to Monroe, elsewhere considered, showing that while there he had connected his trouble rather with the Committee of Public Safety than with Robespierre.

"However discordant the late American Minister Gouverneur Morris, and the late French Committee of Public Safety, were, it suited the purposes of both that I should be continued in arrestation. The former wished to prevent my return to America, that I should not expose his misconduct; and the latter lest I should publish to the world the history of its wickedness. Whilst that Minister and that Committee continued, I had no expectation of liberty. I speak here of the Committee of which Robespierre was a member."

Paine wrote this letter on September 10, 1794. Robespierre, three months before that, had ceased to attend the Committee, disavowing responsibility for its actions: Paine was not released. Robespierre, when the letter to Monroe was written, had been dead more than six months: Paine was not released. The prisoner had therefore good reason to look behind Robespierre for his enemies; and although the fatal sentence found in the Note Book, and a private assurance of Barrère, caused him to ascribe his wrongs to Robespierre, farther reflection convinced him that hands more hidden had also been at work. He knew that Robespierre was a man of measured words, and pondered the sentence that he should "be decreed of accusation for the interests of America as much as of France." In a letter written in 1802, Paine said: "There must have been a coalition in sentiment, if not in fact, between the terrorists of America and the terrorists of France, and Robespierre must have known it, or he could not have had the idea of putting America into the bill of accusation against me." Robespierre, he remarks, assigned no reason for his imprisonment.

The secret for which Paine groped has remained hidden for a hundred years. It is painful to reveal it now, but historic justice, not only to the memory of Paine, but to that of some eminent contemporaries of his, demands that the facts be brought to light.

The appointment of Gouverneur Morris to be Minister to France, in 1792, passed the Senate by 16 to 11 votes. The President did not fail to advise him of this reluctance, and admonish him to be more cautious in his conduct. In the same year Paine took his seat in the Convention. Thus the royalist and republican tendencies, whose struggles made chronic war in Washington's Cabinet, had their counterpart in Paris, where our Minister

Morris wrote royalist, and Paine republican, mani-
festoes. It will have been seen, by quotations
from his diary already given, that Gouverneur
Morris harbored a secret hostility towards Paine ;
and it is here assumed that those entries and incidents are borne in mind. The Diary shows an appearance of friendly terms between the two ;
Morris dines Paine and receives information from
him. The royalism of Morris and humanity of
Paine brought them into a common desire to save
the life of Louis.

But about the same time the American Minister's
own position became a subject of anxiety to him.
He informs Washington (December 28, 1792) that
Genêt's appointment as Minister to the United
States had not been announced to him (Morris).
" Perhaps the Ministry think it is a trait of republicanism to omit those forms which were anciently
used to express good will." His disposition
towards Paine was not improved by finding that it
was to him Genêt had reported. " I have not yet
seen M. Genêt," writes Morris again, " but Mr.
Paine is to introduce him to me." Soon after this
Morris became aware that the French Ministry had
asked his recall, and had Paine also known this the
event might have been different. The Minister's
suspicion that Paine had instigated the recall gave
deadliness to his resentment when the inevitable
break came between them.

The occasion of this arose early in the spring.
When war had broken out between England and
France, Morris, whose sympathies were with Eng-
land, was eager to rid America of its treaty obli-

gations to France. He so wrote repeatedly to
Jefferson, Secretary of State. An opportunity
presently occurred. for acting on this idea. In re-
prisal for the seizure by British cruisers of American
ships conveying provisions to France, French
cruisers were ordered to do the like, and there
were presently ninety-two captured American vessels at Bordeaux. They were not allowed to re-
load and go to sea lest their cargoes should be captured by England. Morris pointed out to the
French Government this violation of the treaty
with America, but wrote to Jefferson that he would
leave it to them in Philadelphia to insist on the
treaty's observance, or to accept the "unfettered"
condition in which its violation by France left
them. Consultation with Philadelphia was a slow
business, however, and the troubles of the American
vessels were urgent. The captains, not suspecting
that the American Minister was satisfied with the
treaty's violation, were angry at his indifference
about their relief, and applied to Paine. Unable to
move Morris, Paine asked him " if he did not feel
ashamed to take the money of the country and do
nothing for it." It was, of course, a part of Morris'
scheme for ending the treaty to point out its violation and the hardships resulting, and this he did;
but it would defeat his scheme to obtain the
practical relief from those hardships which the un-
theoretical captains demanded. On August 20th,
the captains were angrily repulsed by the American
Minister, who, however, after they had gone, must
have reflected that he had gone too far, and was in
an untenable position ; for on the same day he

wrote to the French Minister a statement of the complaint.

"I do not [he adds] pretend to interfere in the internal concerns of the French Republic, and I am persuaded that the Convention has had weighty reasons for laying upon Americans the restriction of which the American captains complain. The result will nevertheless be that this prohibition will severely aggrieve the parties interested, and put an end to the commerce between France and the United States."

The note is half-hearted, but had the captains known it was written they might have been more patient. Morris owed his subsequent humiliation partly to his bad manners. The captains went off to Paine, and proposed to draw up a public protest against the American Minister. Paine advised against this, and recommended a petition to the Convention. This was offered on August 22d. In this the captains said : "We, who know your political situation, do not come to you to demand the rigorous execution of the treaties of alliance which unite us to you. We confine ourselves to asking for the present, to carry provisions to your colonies." To this the Convention promptly and favorably responded.

It was a double humiliation to Morris that the first important benefit gained by Americans since his appointment should be secured without his help, and that it should come through Paine. And it was a damaging blow to his scheme of transferring to England our alliance with France. A "violation" of the treaty excused by the only sufferers could not be cited as "releasing" the United States. A cruel circumstance for Morris was that

the French Minister wrote (October 14th) : " You
must be satisfied, sir, with the manner in which the
request presented by the American captains from
Bordeaux, has been received "—and so forth. Four
days before, Morris had written to Jefferson, speaking of the thing as mere " mischief," and belittling
the success, which " only served an ambition so
contemptible that I shall draw over it the veil of
oblivion."

The " contemptible ambition " thus veiled from
Paine's friend, Jefferson, was revealed by Morris to
others. Some time before (June 25th), he had
written to Robert Morris :

> " I suspected that Paine was intriguing against me, although
> he put on a face of attachment. Since that period I am con-
> firmed in the idea, for he came to my house with Col. Oswald,
> and being a little more drunk than usual, behaved extremely
> ill, and through his insolence I discovered clearly his vain
> ambition."

This was probably written after Paine's rebuke already quoted. It is not likely that Colonel Oswald
would have taken a tipsy man eight leagues out to
Morris' retreat, Sainport, on business, or that the
tipsy man would remember the words of his rebuke
two years after, when Paine records them in his
letter to Washington. At any rate, if Morris
saw no deeper into Paine's physical than into his
mental condition, the " insolent " words were those
of soberness. For Paine's private letters prove
him ignorant of any intrigue against Morris, and
under an impression that the Minister had himself
asked for recall ; also that, instead of being ambi-

tious to succeed Morris, he was eager to get out of
France and back to America.   The first expression
of French dissatisfaction with Morris had been
made through De Ternant, (February 20th, 1793,)
whom he had himself been the means of sending
as Minister to the United States.   The positive
recall was made through Genêt.[1]   It would appear
that Morris must have had sore need of a scapegoat to fix on poor Paine, when his intrigues with
the King's agents, his trust of the King's money,
his plot for a second attempt of the King to escape,
his concealment of royalist leaders in his house,
had been his main ministerial performances for
some time after his appointment.   Had the French
known half as much as is now revealed in Morris'
Diary, not even his office could have shielded him
from arrest.   That the executive there knew much
of it, appears in the revolutionary archives.   There
is reason to believe that Paine, instead of intriguing
against Morris, had, in ignorance of his intrigues,
brought suspicion on himself by continuing his intercourse with the Minister.   The following letter

[1] On September 1, 1792, Morris answered a request of the executive of the
republic that he could not comply until he had received "orders from his
Court," (*les ordres de ma cour*).   The representatives of the new-born republic were scandalized by such an expression from an American Minister, and
also by his intimacy with Lord and Lady Gower.   They may have suspected
what Morris' "Diary" now suggests, that he (Morris) owed his appointment
to this English Ambassador and his wife.   On August 17, 1792, Lord Gower
was recalled, in hostility to the republic, but during the further weeks of his
stay in Paris the American Minister frequented their house.   From the recall
Morris was saved for a year by the intervention of Edmund Randolph.   (See
my "Omitted Chapters of History," etc, p. 149.)   Randolph met with a
Morrisian reward.   Morris ("Diary," ii., p. 98) records an accusation of
Randolph, to which he listened in the office of Lord Grenville, Secretary of
State, which plainly meant his (Randolph's) ruin, which followed.   He
knew it to be untrue, but no defence is mentioned.

of Paine to Barrère, chief Committeeman of Public Safety, dated September 5th, shows him protecting Morris while he is trying to do something for the American captains.

"I send you the papers you asked me for.

"The idea you have to send Commissioners to Congress, and of which you spoke to me yesterday, is excellent, and very necessary at this moment. Mr. Jefferson, formerly Minister of the United States in France, and actually Minister for Foreign Affairs at Congress, is an ardent defender of the interests of France. Gouverneur Morris, who is here now, is badly disposed towards you. I believe he has expressed the wish to be recalled. The reports which he will make on his arrival will not be to the advantage of France. This event necessitates the sending direct of Commissioners from the Convention. Morris is not popular in America. He has set the Americans who are here against him, as also the Captains of that Nation who have come from Bordeaux, by his negligence with regard to the affair they had to treat about with the Convention. *Between us* [*sic*] he told them: 'That they had thrown themselves into the lion's mouth, and it was for them to get out of it as best they could.' I shall return to America on one of the vessels which will start from Bordeaux in the month of October. This was the project I had formed, should the rupture not take place between America and England; but now it is necessary for me to be there as soon as possible. The Congress will require a great deal of information, independently of this. It will soon be seven years that I have been absent from America, and my affairs in that country have suffered considerably through my absence. My house and farm buildings have been entirely destroyed through an accidental fire.

"Morris has many relations in America, who are excellent patriots. I enclose you a letter which I received from his brother, General Louis Morris, who was a member of the Congress at the time of the Declaration of Independence. You will see by it that he writes like a good patriot. I only mention this so that you may know the true state of things. It will be fit to have respect for Gouverneur Morris, on account of his relations, who, as I said above, are excellent patriots.

" There are about 45 American vessels at Bordeaux, at the present moment. If the English Government wished to take revenge on the Americans, these vessels would be very much exposed during their passage. The American Captains left Paris yesterday. I advised them, on leaving, to demand a convoy of the Convention, in case they heard it said that the English had begun reprisals against the Americans, if only to conduct as far as the Bay of Biscay, at the expense of the American Government. But if the Convention determines to send Commissioners to Congress, they will be sent in a ship of the line. But it would be better for the Commissioners to go in one of the best American sailing vessels, and for the ship of the line to serve as a convoy ; it could also serve to convoy the ships that will return to France charged with flour. I am sorry that we cannot converse together, but if you could give me a rendezvous, where I could see Mr. Otto, I shall be happy and ready to be there. If events force the American captains to demand a convoy, it will be to me that they will write on the subject, and not to Morris, against whom they have grave reasons of complaint. Your friend, etc.

THOMAS PAINE."[1]

This is the only letter written by Paine to any one in France about Gouverneur Morris, so far as I can discover, and not knowing French he could only communicate in writing. The American Archives are equally without anything to justify the Minister's suspicion that Paine was intriguing against him, even after his outrageous conduct about the captains. Morris had laid aside the functions of a Minister to exercise those of a treaty-making government. During this excursion into

[1] State Archives, Paris. États Unis, Vol. 38, No. 93. Endorsed : " No. 6. Translation of a letter from Thomas Payne to Citizen Barrère." It may be noted that Paine and Barrère, though they could read each other's language, could converse only in their own tongue.

presidential and senatorial power, for the injury of
the country to which he was commissioned, his own
countrymen in France were without an official
Minister, and in their distress imposed ministerial
duties on Paine. But so far from wishing to supersede Morris, Paine, in the above letter to Barrère, gives an argument for his retention, namely,
that if he goes home he will make reports disadvan-
tageous to France. He also asks respect for Morris on account of his relations, "excellent patriots."

Barrère, to whom Paine's letter is written, was
chief of the Committee of Public Safety, and had
held that powerful position since its establishment,
April 6, 1793. To this all-powerful Committee
of Nine Robespierre was added July 27th. On
the day that Paine wrote the letter, September 5th,
Barrère opened the Terror by presenting a report
in which it is said, "Let us make terror the order
of the day!" This Barrère was a sensualist, a
crafty orator, a sort of eel which in danger turned
into a snake. His "supple genius," as Louis Blanc
expresses it, was probably appreciated by Morris,
who was kept well informed as to the secrets of the
Committee of Public Safety. This omnipotent
Committee had supervision of foreign affairs and
appointments. At this time the Minister of Foreign Affairs was Deforgues, whose secretary was
the M. Otto alluded to in Paine's letter to Barrère.
Otto spoke English fluently ; he had been in the
American Legation. Deforgues became Minister
June 5th, on the arrest of his predecessor (Lebrun),
and was anxious lest he should follow Lebrun to
prison also,—as he ultimately did. Deforgues and

his secretary, Otto, confided to Morris their strong desire to be appointed to America, Genêt having been recalled. [1]

Despite the fact that Morris' hostility to France was well known, he had become an object of awe. So long as his removal was daily expected in reply to a request twice sent for his recall, Morris was weak, and even insulted. But when ship after ship came in without such recall, and at length even with the news that the President had refused the Senate's demand for Morris' entire correspondence, everything was changed. [2] " So long," writes Morris to Washington, " as they believed in the success of their demand, they treated my representations with indifference and contempt ; but at last, hearing nothing from their minister on that subject, or, indeed, on any other, they took it into their heads that I was immovable, and made overtures for conciliation." It must be borne in mind that at this time America was the only ally of France ; that already there were fears that Washington was feeling his way towards a treaty with England. Soon after the overthrow of the monarchy Morris had hinted that the treaty between the United States and France, having been made with the King, might be represented by the English Ministry in America as void under the revolution ; and that " it would be well to evince a degree of good will to America." When Robespierre first became a leader he had particular charge of diplo-

---

[1] Morris' letter to Washington, Oct. 18, 1793. The passage is omitted from the letter as quoted in his " Diary and Letters," ii., p. 53.
[2] See my " Life of Edmund Randolph," p. 214.

matic affairs. It is stated by Frédéric Masson that Robespierre was very anxious to recover for the republic the initiative of the alliance with the United States, which was credited to the King; and "although their Minister Gouverneur Morris was justly suspected, and the American republic was at that time aiming only to utilize the condition of its ally, the French republic cleared it at a cheap rate of its debts contracted with the King." [1] Such were the circumstances which, when Washington seemed determined to force Morris on France, made this Minister a power. Lebrun, the ministerial predecessor of Deforgues, may indeed have been immolated to placate Morris, who having been, under his administration, subjected to a domiciliary visit, had gone to reside in the country. That was when Morris' removal was supposed near; but now his turn came for a little reign of terror on his own account. In addition to Deforgues' fear of Lebrun's fate, should he anger Washington's immovable representative, he knew that his hope of succeeding Genêt in America must depend on Morris. The terrors and schemes of Deforgues and Otto brought them to the feet of Morris.

About the time when the chief of the Committee of Public Safety, Barrère, was consulting Paine about sending Commissioners to America, Deforgues was consulting Morris on the same point. The interview was held shortly after the humiliation which Morris had suffered, in the matter of the captains, and the defeat of his scheme for utilizing

[1] "Le Département des Affaires Étrangères pendant la Révolution," p. 295.

their grievance to release the United States from their alliance. The American captains had appointed Paine their Minister, and he had been successful. Paine and his clients had not stood in awe of Morris ; but he now had the strength of a giant, and proceeded to use it like a giant.

The interview with Deforgues was not reported by Morris to the Secretary of State (Paine's friend, Jefferson), but in a confidential letter to Washington,—so far as was prudent.

" I have insinuated [he writes] the advantages which might result from an early declaration on the part of the new minister that, as France has announced the determination not to meddle with the interior affairs of other nations, he can know only the *government* of America. In union with this idea, I told the minister that I had observed an overruling influence in their affairs which seemed to come from the other side of the channel, and at the same time had traced the intention to excite a seditious spirit in America ; that it was impossible to be on a friendly footing with such persons, but that at present a different spirit seemed to prevail, etc. This declaration produced the effect I intended."[1]

In thus requiring that the new minister to America shall recognize only the "government" (and not negotiate with Kentucky, as Genêt had done), notice is also served on Deforgues that the Convention must in future deal only with the American Minister, and not with Paine or sea-captains in matters affecting his countrymen. The reference to an influence from the other side of the channel could only refer to Paine, as there were then no Englishmen in Paris outside his gar-

---

[1] Letter to Washington, Oct. 18, 1793.

den in the Faubourg St. Denis. By this ingenious phrase Morris already disclaims jurisdiction over Paine, and suggests that he is an Englishman worrying Washington through Genêt. This was a clever hint in another way. Genêt, now recalled, evidently for the guillotine, had been introduced to Morris by Paine, who no doubt had given him letters to eminent Americans. Paine had sympathized warmly with the project of the Kentuckians to expel the Spanish from the Mississippi, and this was patriotic American doctrine even after Kentucky was admitted into the Union (June 1, 1792). He had corresponded with Dr. O'Fallon, a leading Kentuckian on the subject. But things had changed, and when Genêt went out with his blank commissions he found himself confronted with a proclamation of neutrality which turned his use of them to sedition. Paine's acquaintance with Genêt, and his introductions, could now be plausibly used by Morris to involve him. The French Minister is shown an easy way of relieving his country from responsibility for Genêt, by placing it on the deputy from "the other side of the channel."

"This declaration produced the effect I intended," wrote Morris. The effect was indeed swift. On October 3d, Amar, after the doors of the Convention were locked, read the memorable accusation against the Girondins, four weeks before their execution. In that paper he denounced Brissot for his effort to save the King, for his intimacy with the English, for injuring the colonies by his labors for negro emancipation! In this denunciation Paine had the honor to be included.

"At that same time the Englishman Thomas Paine, called by the faction [Girondin] to the honor of representing the French nation, dishonored himself by supporting the opinion of Brissot, and by promising us in his fable the dissatisfaction of the United States of America, our natural allies, which he did not blush to depict for us as full of veneration and gratitude for the tyrant of France."

On October 19th the Minister of Foreign Affairs, Deforgues, writes to Morris :

" I shall give the Council an account of the punishable conduct of their agent in the United States [Genêt], and I can assure you beforehand that they will regard the strange abuse of their confidence by this agent, as I do, with the liveliest indignation.   The President of the United States has done justice to our sentiments in attributing the deviations of the citizen Genêt to causes entirely foreign to his instructions, and we hope that the measures to be taken will more and more convince the head and members of your Government that so far from having authorized the proceedings and manœuvres of Citizen Genêt our only aim has been to maintain between the two nations the most perfect harmony."

One of "the measures to be taken" was the imprisonment of Paine, for which Amar's denunciation had prepared the way.   But this was not so easy.   For Robespierre had successfully attacked Amar's report for extending its accusations beyond the Girondins.   How then could an accusation be made against Paine, against whom no charge could be brought, except that he had introduced a French minister to his friends in America !   A deputy must be formally accused by the Convention before he could be tried by the Revolutionary Tribunal.   An indirect route must be taken to reach the deputy secretly accused by the American Minister, and the latter had pointed it out by alluding to Paine as an influence "from across the channel." There was a law passed in June for the imprisonment of foreigners belonging to countries at war with France. This was administered by the Committees. Paine had not been liable to this law, being a deputy, and never suspected of citizenship in the country which had outlawed him, until Morris suggested it. Could he be got out of the Convention the law might be applied to him without necessitating any public accusation and trial, or anything more than an announcement to the Deputies.

Such was the course pursued. Christmas day was celebrated by the terrorist Bourdon de l'Oise with a denunciation of Paine: "They have boasted the patriotism of Thomas Paine. *Eh bien!* Since the Brissotins disappeared from the bosom of this Convention he has not set foot in it. And I know that he has intrigued with a former agent of the bureau of Foreign Affairs." This accusation could only have come from the American Minister and the Minister of Foreign Affairs—from Gouverneur Morris and Deforgues. Genêt was the only agent of Deforgues' office with whom Paine could possibly have been connected; and what that connection was the reader knows. That accusation is associated with the terrorist's charge that Paine had declined to unite with the murderous decrees of the Convention.

After the speech of Bourdon de l'Oise, Bentabole moved the "exclusion of foreigners from every public function during the war." Bentabole was a leading member of the Committee of General

Surety.   " The Assembly," adds *The Moniteur*,
" decreed that no foreigner should be admitted to
represent the French people."   The Committee of
General Surety assumed the right to regard Paine
as an Englishman ; and as such out of the Convention, and consequently under the law of June
against aliens of hostile nations.   He was arrested
next day, and on December 28th committed to the
Luxembourg prison.

CHAPTER VI.

A TESTIMONY UNDER THE GUILLOTINE.

WHILE Paine was in prison the English gentry were gladdened by a rumor that he had been guillotined, and a libellous leaflet of " The Last Dying Words of Thomas Paine" appeared in London. Paine was no less confident than his enemies that his execution was certain—after the denunciation in Amar's report, October 3d—and did indeed utter what may be regarded as his dying words—"The Age of Reason." This was the task which he had from year to year adjourned to his maturest powers, and to it he dedicates what brief remnant of life may await him. That completed, it will be time to die with his comrades, awakened by his pen to a dawn now red with their blood.

The last letter I find written from the old Pompadour mansion is to Jefferson, under date of October 20th :

" DEAR SIR,—I wrote you by Captain Dominick who was to sail from Havre about the 20th of this month. This will probably be brought you by Mr. Barlow or Col. Oswald. Since my letter by Dominick I am every day more convinced and impressed with the propriety of Congress sending Commissioners to Europe to confer with the Ministers of the Jesuitical Powers on the means of terminating the war. The enclosed printed paper will shew there are a variety of subjects to be taken into consideration which did not appear at first, all of which have some tendency to put an end to the war. I see not how this war is to terminate if some intermediate power does not step forward. There is now no prospect that France can carry revolutions thro' Europe on the one hand, or that the combined powers can conquer France on the other hand. It is a sort of defensive War on both sides. This being the case how is the War to close? Neither side will ask for peace though each may wish it. I believe that England and Holland are tired of the war. Their Commerce and Manufactures have suffered most exceedingly—and besides this it is to them a war without an object. Russia keeps herself at a distance. I cannot help repeating my wish that Congress would send Commissioners, and I wish also that yourself would venture once more across the Ocean as one of them. If the Commissioners rendezvous at Holland they would then know what steps to take. They could call Mr. Pinckney to their Councils, and it would be of use, on many accounts, that one of them should come over from Holland to France. Perhaps a long truce, were it proposed by the neutral Powers, would have all the effects of a Peace, without the difficulties attending the adjustment of all the forms of Peace.—Yours affectionately   THOMAS PAINE."[1]

Thus has finally faded the dream of Paine's life —an international republic.

It is notable that in this letter Paine makes no mention of his own danger. He may have done so in the previous letter, unfound, to which he alludes. Why he made no attempt to escape after Amar's report seems a mystery, especially as he was assisting others to leave the country. Two of his friends, Johnson and Choppin—the last to part from him in the old garden,—escaped to Switzerland. John-

[1] I am indebted for this letter to Dr. John S. H. Fogg, of Boston. The letter is endorsed by Jefferson, "Rec'd Mar. 3." [1794.]

son will be remembered as the young man who
attempted suicide on hearing of Marat's menaces
against Paine. Writing to Lady Smith of these
two friends, he says :

" He [Johnson] recovered, and being anxious to get out of
France, a passport was obtained for him and Mr. Choppin ;
they received it late in the evening, and set off the next morning for Basle, before four, from which place I had a letter
from them, highly pleased with their escape from France,
into which they had entered with an enthusiasm of patriotic
devotion. Ah, France ! thou hast ruined the character of a
revolution virtuously begun, and destroyed those who produced it. I might also say like Job's servant, ' and I only am
escaped.'

" Two days after they were gone I heard a rapping at the
gate, and looking out of the window of the bedroom I saw the
landlord going with the candle to the gate, which he opened ;
and a guard with muskets and fixed bayonets entered. I went
to bed again and made up my mind for prison, for I was the
only lodger. It was a guard to take up Johnson and Choppin,
but, I thank God, they were out of their reach.

" The guard came about a month after, in the night, and
took away the landlord, Georgeit. And the scene in the house
finished with the arrestation of myself. This was soon after
you called on me, and sorry I was that it was not in my
power to render to Sir [Robert Smith] the service that you
asked."

All then had fled. Even the old landlord
had been arrested. In the wintry garden this lone
man—in whose brain and heart the republic and
the religion of humanity have their abode—moves
companionless. In the great mansion, where once
Madame de Pompadour glittered amid her cour-
tiers, where in the past summer gathered the Round
Table of great-hearted gentlemen and ladies,

Thomas Paine sits through the watches of the night at his devout task.[1]

" My friends were falling as fast as the guillotine could cut their heads off, and as I expected, every day, the same fate, I resolved to begin my work. I appeared to myself to be on my death bed, for death was on every side of me, and I had no time to lose. This accounts for my writing at the time I did, and so nicely did the time and intention meet, that I had not finished the first part of the work more than six hours before I was arrested and taken to prison. The people of France were running headlong into atheism, and I had the work translated in their own language, to stop them in that career, and fix them to the first article of every man's creed, who has any creed at all—*I believe in God.*" [2]

The second Christmas of the new republican era dawns. Where is the vision that has led this way-worn pilgrim ? Where the star he has followed so long, to find it hovering over the new birth of humanity ? It may have been on that day that, amid the shades of his slain friends, he wrote, as with

[1] It was a resumed task. Early in the year Paine had brought to his colleague Lanthenas a manuscript on religion, probably entitled " The Age of Reason." Lanthenas translated it, and had it printed in French, though no trace of its circulation appears. At that time Lanthenas may have apprehended the proscription which fell on him, with the other Girondins, in May, and took the precaution to show Paine's essay to Couthon, who, with Robespierre, had religious matters particularly in charge. Couthon frowned on the work and on Paine, and reproached Lanthenas for translating it. There was no frown more formidable than that of Couthon, and the essay (printed only in French) seems to have been suppressed. At the close of the year Paine wrote the whole work *de novo.* The first edition in English, now before me, was printed in Paris, by Barrois, 1794. In his preface to Part II., Paine implies a previous draft in saying: " I had not finished it more than six hours, *in the state it has since appeared*, before a guard came," etc. (The italics are mine.) The fact of the early translation appears in a letter of Lanthenas to Merlin de Thionville.

[2] Letter to Samuel Adams. The execution of the Girondins took place on October 31st.

blood about to be shed, the tribute to one that was pierced in trying to benefit mankind.

"Nothing that is here said can apply, even with the most distant disrespect, to the real character of Jesus Christ. He was a virtuous and amiable man. The morality that he preached and practised was of the most benevolent kind ; and though similar systems of morality had been preached by Confucius, and by some of the Greek philosophers, many years before, by the Quakers since, and by good men in all ages, it has not been exceeded by any. . . . He preached most excellent morality, and the equality of man ; but he preached also against the corruption and avarice of the Jewish priests, and this brought upon him the hatred and vengeance of the whole order of priesthood. The accusation which those priests brought against him was that of sedition and conspiracy against the Roman government, to which the Jews were then subject and tributary ; and it is not improbable that the Roman government might have some secret apprehension of the effect of his doctrine, as well as the Jewish priests ; neither is it improbable that Jesus Christ had in contemplation the delivery of the Jewish nation from the bondage of the Romans. Between the two, however, this virtuous reformer and religionist lost his life. . . . He was the son of God in like manner that every other person is—for the Creator is the Father of All. . . . Jesus Christ founded no new system. He called men to the practice of moral virtues, and the belief of one God. The great trait in his character is philanthropy."

Many Christmas sermons were preached in 1793, but probably all of them together do not contain so much recognition of the humanity of Jesus as these paragraphs of Paine. The Christmas bells ring in the false, but shall also ring in the true. While he is writing, on that Christmas night, word comes that he has been denounced by Bourdon de l'Oise, and expelled from the Convention. He now enters the Dark Valley. "Conceiving, after this, that I had but a few days of liberty I sat down, and brought the work to a close as speedily as possible."

In the "Age of Reason" there is a page of personal recollections. I have a feeling that this little episode marks the hour when Paine was told of his doom. From this overshadowed Christmas, likely to be his last, the lonely heart—as loving a heart as ever beat—here wanders across tempestuous years to his early Norfolkshire home. There is a grateful remembrance of the Quaker meeting, the parental care, the Grammar School; of his pious aunt who read him a printed sermon, and the garden steps where he pondered what he had just heard,—a Father demanding his Son's death for the sake of making mankind happier and better. He "perfectly recollects the spot" in the garden where, even then, but seven or eight years of age, he felt sure a man would be executed for doing such a thing, and that God was too good to act in that way. So clearly come out the scenes of childhood under the shadow of death.

He probably had an intimation on December 27th that he would be arrested that night. The place of his abode, though well known to the authorities, was not in the Convention's Almanach. Officially, therefore, his residence was still in the Passage des Petits Pères. There the officers would seek him, and there he should be found. "For that night only he sought a lodging there," reported the officers afterwards. He may have feared, too, that his manuscript would be destroyed if he were taken in his residence.

His hours are here traceable. On the evening
of December 27th, in the old mansion, Paine
reaches the last page of the "Age of Reason." They
who have supposed him an atheist, may search as far
as Job, who said " Though He slay me I will trust in
Him," before finding an author who, caught in the
cruel machinery of destructive nature, could write
that last page.

"The creation we behold is the real and ever existing
word of God, in which we cannot be deceived. It proclaim-
eth his power, it demonstrates his wisdom, it manifests his
goodness and beneficence. The moral duty of man consists
in imitating the moral goodness and beneficence of God manifested in the creation towards all his creatures. That seeing,
as we daily do, the goodness of God to all men, it is an example calling upon all men to practise the same towards each
other, and consequently that everything of persecution and
revenge between man and man, and everything of cruelty to
animals, is a violation of moral duty."

In what " Israel " is greater faith found? Having written these words, the pen drops from our
· world-wanderer's hand. It is nine o'clock of the
night. He will now go and bend his neck under
the decree of the Convention—provided by " the
goodness of God to all men." Through the Faubourg, past Porte St. Martin, to the Rue Richelieu,
to the Passage des Petits Pères, he walks in the
wintry night. In the house where he wrote his
appeal that the Convention would slay not the man
in destroying the monarch, he asks a lodging " for
that night only."

As he lays his head on the pillow, it is no doubt
with a grateful feeling that the good God has prolonged his freedom long enough to finish a defence

of true religion from its degradation by superstition or destruction by atheism,—these, as he declares, being the two purposes of his work. It was providently if not providentially timed. "I had not finished it more than six hours, in the state it has since appeared, before a guard came, about three in the morning, with an order, signed by the two Committees of Public Safety and Surety General, for putting me in arrestation as a foreigner, and conveying me to the prison of the Luxembourg."

The following documents are translated for this work from the originals in the National Archives of France.

"NATIONAL CONVENTION.

"Committee of General Surety and Surveillance of the National Convention.

"On the 7th Nivose [December 27th] of the 2d year of the French Republic, one and indivisible.

"TO THE DEPUTIES:

"The Committee resolves, that the persons named Thomas Paine and Anacharsis Clootz, formerly Deputies to the National Convention, be arrested and imprisoned, as a measure of General Surety; that an examination be made of their papers, and those found suspicious put under seal and brought to the Committee of General Surety.

"Citizens Jean Baptiste Martin and Lamy, bearers of the present decree are empowered to execute it,—for which they ask the help of the Civil authorities and, if need be, of the army.

"The representatives of the nation, members of the Committee of General Surety—Signed: M. Bayle, Voulland, Jagot, Amar, Vadier, Élie Lacoste, Guffroy, Louis (du bas Rhin) La Vicomterie, Panis."

"This day, the 8th Nivose of the 2d year of the French Republic, one and indivisible, to execute and fulfil the order

given us, we have gone to the residence of Citizen Thomas
Paine, Passage des Petits Pères, number seven, Philadelphia
House. Having requested the Commander of the [Police]
post, William Tell Section, to have us escorted, according to
the order we showed him, he obeyed by assigning us four
privates and a corporal, to search the above-said lodging ;
where we requested the porter to open the door, and asked
him whether he knew all who lodged there ; and as he did not
affirm it, we desired him to take us to the principal agent,
which he did ; having come to the said agent, we asked him
if he knew by name all the persons to whom he rented lodgings ; after having repeated to him the name mentioned in
our order, he replied to us, that he had come to ask him a
lodging for that night only ; which being ascertained, we asked
him to conduct us to the bedroom of Citizen Thomas Paine,
where we arrived ; then seeing we could not be understood by
him, an American, we begged the manager of the house, who
knows his language, to kindly interpret for him, giving him
notice of the order of which we were bearers ; whereupon
the said Citizen Thomas Paine submitted to be taken to Rue
Jacob, Great Britain Hotel, which he declared through his
interpreter to be the place where he had his papers ; having
recognized that his lodging contained none of them, we
accompanied the said Thomas Paine and his interpreter to
Great Britain Hotel, Rue Jacob, Unity Section ; the present
minutes closed, after being read before the undersigned.

"(Signed) :

THOMAS PAINE.   J. B. MARTIN.

DORLÉ, Commissary.

GILLET, Commissary.

F. DELLANAY.

ACHILLE AUDIBERT, Witness.[1]

LAMY."

"And as it was about seven or eight o'clock in the morning of
this day 8th Nivose, being worn out with fatigue, and forced to
take some food, we postponed the end of our proceeding till
eleven o'clock of the same day, when, desiring to finish it, we

---

[1] It will be remembered that Audibert had carried to London Paine's invitation to the Convention.

went with Citizen Thomas Paine to Britain House, where we
found Citizen Barlow, whom Citizen Thomas Paine informed
that we, the Commissaries, were come to look into the papers,
which he said were at his house, as announced in our preceding paragraph through Citizen Dellanay, his interpreter ; We,
Commissary of the Section of the Unity, undersigned, with
the Citizens order-bearers, requested Citizen Barlow to declare
whether there were in his house, any papers or correspondence
belonging to Citizen Thomas Paine ; on which, complying with
our request, he declared there did not exist any ; but wishing
to leave no doubt on our way of conducting the matter, we did
not think it right to rely on what he said ; resolving, on the
contrary, to ascertain by all legal ways that there did not exist
any, we requested Citizen Barlow to open for us all his cup-
boards ; which he did, and after having visited them, we, the
abovesaid Commissary, always in the presence of Citizen Thomas
Paine, recognized that there existed no papers belonging to him;
we also perceived that it was a subterfuge on the part of Citizen Thomas Paine who wished only to transfer himself to the
house of Citizen Barlow, his native friend *(son ami natal)* whom
we invited to ask of Citizen Thomas Paine his usual place of
abode ; and the latter seemed to wish that his friend might
accompany him and be present at the examination of his
papers.   Which we, the said Commissary granted him, as
Citizen Barlow could be of help to us, together with Citizen
Etienne Thomas Dessous, interpreter for the English language,
and Deputy Secretary to the Committee of General Surety of
the National Convention, whom we called, in passing by the
said Committee, to accompany us to the true lodging of the
said Paine, Faubourg du Nord, Nro. 63.   At which place we
entered his rooms, and gathered in the Sitting-room all the
papers found in the other rooms of the said apartment.   The
said Sitting-room receives light from three windows, looking,
one on the Garden and the two others on the Courtyard ; and
after the most scrupulous examination of all the papers, that
we had there gathered, none of them has been found suspicious, neither in French nor in English, according to what was
affirmed to us by Citizen Dessous our interpreter who signed
with us, and Citizen Thomas Paine ; and we, the undersigned
Commissary, resolved that no seal should be placed, after the

examination mentioned, and closed the said minutes, which we declare to contain the truth.   Drawn up at the residence, and closed at 4 p.m. in the day and year abovenamed ; and we have all signed after having read the minutes.

" (Signed) :

> THOMAS PAINE.   JOEL BARLOW.
> DORLÉ, Commissary.   GILLET, Commissary.
> DESSOUS.   J. B. MARTIN.   LAMY.

" And after having signed we have requested, according to the order of the Committee of General Surety of the National Convention, Citizen Thomas Paine to follow us, to be led to jail ; to which he complied without any difficulty, and he has signed with us :

> THOMAS PAINE.   J. B. MARTIN.
> DORLÉ, Commissary.   LAMY.
> GILLETT, Commissary."

" I have received from the Citizens Martin and Lamy, Deputy-Secretaries to the Committee of General Surety of the National Convention, the Citizens Thomas Paine and Anacharsis Clootz, formerly Deputies ; by order of the said Committee.

" At the Luxembourg, this day 8th Nivose, 2nd year of the French Republic, One and Indivisible.

> " Signed :   BENOIT, *Concierge.*"

" FOREIGN OFFICE—Received the 12th Ventose [March 2d]. Sent to the Committees of General Surety and Public Safety the 8th Pluviose [January 27th] this 2d year of the French Republic, One and indivisible.

> " Signed :   BASSOL, *Secretary.*"

" CITIZENS LEGISLATORS !—The French nation has, by a universal decree, invited to France one of our countrymen, most worthy of honor, namely, Thomas Paine, one of the political founders of the independence and of the Republic of America.

" Our experience of twenty years has taught America to know and esteem his public virtues and the invaluable services he rendered her.

" Persuaded that his character of foreigner and ex-Deputy is the only cause of his provisional imprisonment, we come in the name of our country (and we feel sure she will be grateful to us for it), we come to you, Legislators, to reclaim our friend, our countryman, that he may sail with us for America, where he will be received with open arms.

"If it were necessary to say more in support of the Petition which, as friends and allies of the French Republic, we submit to her representatives, to obtain the liberation of one of the most earnest and faithful apostles of liberty, we would beseech the National Convention, for the sake of all that is dear to the glory and to the heart of freemen, not to give a cause of joy and triumph to the allied tyrants of Europe, and above all to the despotism of Great Britain, which did not blush to outlaw this courageous and virtuous defender of Liberty.

"But their insolent joy will be of short duration; for we have the intimate persuasion that you will not keep longer in the bonds of painful captivity the man whose courageous and energetic pen did so much to free the Americans, and whose intentions we have no doubt whatever were to render the same services to the French Republic. Yes, we feel convinced that his principles and views were pure, and in that regard he is entitled to the indulgence due to human fallibility, and to the respect due to rectitude of heart; and we hold all the more firmly our opinion of his innocence, inasmuch as we are informed that after a scrupulous examination of his papers, made by order of the Committee of General Surety, instead of anything to his charge, enough has been found rather to corroborate the purity of his principles in politics and morals.

"As a countryman of ours, as a man above all so dear to the Americans, who like yourselves are earnest friends of Liberty, we ask you, in the name of that goddess cherished of the only two Republics of the World, to give back Thomas Paine to his brethren and permit us to take him to his country which is also ours.

"If you require it, Citizens Representatives, we shall make ourselves warrant and security for his conduct in France during the short stay he may make in this land.

"Signed:

W. JACKSON, of Philadelphia. J. RUSSELL, of Boston. PETER WHITESIDE, of Philadelphia. HENRY JOHNSON, of Boston. THOMAS CARTER, of Newbury Port. JAMES COOPER of Phila-

delphia. JOHN WILLERT BILLOPP, of New York. THOMAS
WATERS GRIFFITH, of Baltimore. TH. RAMSDEN, of Boston.
SAMUEL P. BROOME, of New York. A. MEADENWORTH, of Con-
necticut. JOEL BARLOW, of Connecticut. MICHAEL ALCORN, of
Philadelphia. M. ONEALY, of Baltimore. JOHN McPHERSON, of
Alexandria [Va.]. WILLIAM HASKINS, of Boston. J. GREGORY,
of Petersburg, Virginia. JAMES INGRAHAM, of Boston." [1]

The following answer to the petitioning Americans was given by Vadier, then president of the
Convention.

" CITIZENS : The brave Americans are our brothers in liberty ;
like us they have broken the chains of despotism ; like us they
have sworn the destruction of kings and vowed an eternal
hatred to tyrants and their instruments. From this identity of
principles should result a union of the two nations forever un-
alterable. If the tree of liberty already flourishes in the two
hemispheres, that of commerce should, by this happy alliance,
cover the poles with its fruitful branches. It is for France, it
is for the United States, to combat and lay low, in concert,
these proud islanders, these insolent dominators of the sea and
the commerce of nations. When the sceptre of despotism is
falling from the criminal hand of the tyrants of the earth, it is
necessary also to break the trident which emboldens the insolence of these corsairs of Albion, these modern Carthaginians.
It is time to repress the audacity and mercantile avarice of
these pirate tyrants of the sea, and of the commerce of nations.

" You demand of us, citizens, the liberty of Thomas Paine ;
you wish to restore to your hearths this defender of the rights
of man. One can only applaud this generous movement.
Thomas Paine is a native of England ; this is undoubtedly
enough to apply to him the measures of security prescribed by
the revolutionary laws. It may be added, citizens, that if
Thomas Paine has been the apostle of liberty, if he has powerfully co-operated with the American Revolution, his genius
has not understood that which has regenerated France ; he has
regarded the system only in accordance with the illusions with

[1] The preceding documents connected with the arrest are in the Archives
Nationales, F. 4641.

which the false friends of our revolution have invested it. You must with us deplore an error little reconcilable with the principles admired in the justly esteemed works of this republican author.

"The National Convention will take into consideration the object of your petition, and invites you to its sessions."

A memorandum adds : " Reference of this petition is decreed to the Committees of Public Safety and General Surety, united."

It is said that Paine sent an appeal for intervention to the Cordeliers Club, and that their only reply was to return to him a copy of his speech in favor of preserving the life of Louis XVI. This I have not been able to verify.

On leaving his house for prison, Paine entrusted to Joel Barlow the manuscript of the " Age of Reason," to be conveyed to the printer. This was with the knowledge of the guard, whose kindness is mentioned by Paine.

CHAPTER VII.

A MINISTER AND HIS PRISONER.

BEFORE resuming the history of the conspiracy against Paine it is necessary to return a little on our steps. For a year after the fall of monarchy in France (August 10, 1792), the real American Minister there was Paine, whether for Americans or for the French Executive. The Ministry would not confer with a hostile and presumably decapitated agent, like Morris. The reader has (Chaps. IV. and V., Vol. II.) evidence of their consultations with Paine. Those communications of Paine were utilized in Robespierre's report to the Convention, November 17, 1793, on the foreign relations of France. It was inspired by the humiliating tidings that Genêt in America had reinforced the European intrigues to detach Washington from France. The President had demanded Genêt's recall, had issued a proclamation of "impartiality" between France and her foes, and had not yet decided whether the treaty formed with Louis XVI. should survive his death. And Morris was not recalled !

In his report Robespierre makes a solemn appeal to the "brave Americans." Was it "that crowned automaton called Louis XVI." who helped to rescue them from the oppressor's yoke, or our arm.

and armies ?   Was it his money sent over or the
taxes of French labor ?   He declares that the
Republic has been treacherously compromised in
America.

> "By a strange fatality the Republic finds itself still repre-
> sented among their allies by agents of the traitors she has
> punished : Brissot's brother-in-law is Consul-General there ;
> another man, named Genêt, sent by Lebrun and Brissot to
> Philadelphia as plenipotentiary agent, has faithfully fulfilled
> the views and instructions of the faction that appointed
> him."

The result is that " parallel intrigues " are ob-
servable—one aiming to bring France under the
league, the other to break up the American
republic into parts.[1]

In this idea of " parallel intrigues " the irre-
movable Morris is discoverable.   It is the reappearance of what he had said to Deforgues about
the simultaneous sedition in America (Genêt's) and
" influence in their affairs from the other side of
the channel " (Paine's).   There was not, however,
in Robespierre's report any word that might be con-
strued into a suspicion of Paine ; on the contrary,
he declares the Convention now pure.   The Convention instructed the Committee of Public Safety
to provide for strictest fulfilment of its treaties with
America, and caution to its agents to respect the
government and territory of its allies.   The first
necessary step was to respect the President's Minister, Gouverneur Morris, however odious he might
be, since it would be on his representations that the
continuance of France's one important alliance

---

[1] " Hist. Parl.," xxx., p. 224.

might depend. Morris played cleverly on that string ; he hinted dangers that did not exist, and dangled promises never to be fulfilled. He was master of the situation. The unofficial Minister who had practically superseded him for a year was now easily locked up in the Luxembourg.

But why was not Paine executed? The historic paradox must be ventured that he owed his re-prieve—his life—to Robespierre. Robespierre had Morris' intercepted letters and other evidences of his treachery, yet as Washington insisted on him, and the alliance was at stake, he must be obeyed. On the other hand were evidences of Washington's friendship for Paine, and of Jefferson's intimacy with him. Time must therefore be allowed for the prisoner to communicate with the President and Secretary of State. They must decide between Paine and Morris. It was only after ample time had passed, and no word about Paine came from Washington or Jefferson, while Morris still held his position, that Robespierre entered his memorandum that Paine should be tried before the revolutionary tribunal.

Meanwhile a great deal happened, some of which, as Paine's experiences in the Luxembourg, must be deferred to a further chapter. The American Minister had his triumph. The Americans in Paris, including the remaining sea-captains, who had been looking to Paine as their Minister, were now to discover where the power was lodged. Know-ing Morris' hatred for Paine, they repaired to the Convention with their petition. Major Jackson, a well known officer of the American Revolution, who headed the deputation (which included every unofficial American in Paris), utilized a letter of introduction he had brought from Secretary Jefferson to Morris by giving it to the Committee of General Surety, as an evidence of his right to act in the emergency.

Action was delayed by excitement over the celebration of the first anniversary of the King's execution. On that occasion (January 21st) the Convention joined the Jacobin Club in marching to the "Place de la Révolution," with music and banners; there the portraits of kings were burned, an act of accusation against all the kings of the earth adopted, and a fearfully realistic drama enacted. By a prearrangement unknown to the Convention four condemned men were guillotined before them. The Convention recoiled, and instituted an inquisition as to the responsibility for this scene. It was credited to the Committee of General Surety, justly no doubt, but its chief, Vadier, managed to relieve it of the odium. This Vadier was then president of the Convention. He was appropriately selected to give the first anniversary oration on the King's execution. A few days later it fell to Vadier to address the eighteen Americans at the bar of the Convention on their petition for Paine's release. The petition and petitioners being referred to the Committees of Public Safety and General Surety in joint session, the Americans were there answered, by Billaud-Varennes it was said, "that their reclamation was only the act of individuals, without any authority from the American government.".

This was a plain direction.   The American government, whether in Paris or Philadelphia, had
Paine's fate in its hands.

At this time it was of course not known that
Jefferson had retired from the Cabinet.   To him
Paine might have written, but—sinister coincidence !—immediately after the committees had referred the matter to the American government an
order was issued cutting off all communication
between prisoners and the outside world.   That
Morris had something to do with this is suggested
by the fact that he was allowed to correspond with
Paine in prison, though this was not allowed to
his successor, Monroe.   However, there is, unfortunately, no need to repair to suspicions for the
part of Gouverneur Morris in this affair.   His first
ministerial mention of the matter to Secretary Jefferson is dated on the tragical anniversary, January
21st.   " Lest I should forget it," he says of this
small incident, the imprisonment of one whom
Congress and the President had honored—

" Lest I should forget it, I must mention that Thomas Paine
is in prison, where he amuses himself with publishing a pamphlet
against Jesus Christ.   I do not recollect whether I mentioned
to you that he would have been executed along with the rest
of the Brissotins if the advance party had not viewed him with
contempt.   I incline to think that if he is quiet in prison he
may have the good luck to be forgotten, whereas, should he be
brought much into notice, the long suspended axe might fall
on him.   I believe he thinks that I ought to claim him as an
American citizen ; but considering his birth, his naturalization
in this country, and the place he filled, I doubt much the right,
and I am sure that the claim would be, for the present at least,
inexpedient and ineffectual."

Although this paragraph is introduced in such a casual way, there is calculation in every word. First of all, however, be it observed, Morris knows precisely how the authorities will act several days before they have been appealed to. It also appears that if Paine was not executed with the Brissotins on October 31st, it was not due to any interference on his part. The "contempt" which saved Paine may be estimated by a reference to the executive consultations with him, and to Amar's bitter denunciation of him (October 3d) after Morris had secretly accused this contemptible man of influencing the Convention and helping to excite sedition in the United States. In the next place, Jefferson is admonished that if he would save his friend's head he must not bring the matter into notice. The government at Philadelphia must, in mercy to Paine, remain silent. As to the "pamphlet against Jesus Christ," my reader has already perused what Paine wrote on that theme in the "Age of Reason." But as that may not be so likely to affect freethinking Jefferson, Morris adds the falsehood that Paine had been naturalized in France. The reader need hardly be reminded that if an application by the American Minister for the release would be "ineffectual," it must be because the said Minister would have it so. Morris had already found, as he tells Washington, that the Ministry, supposing him immovable, were making overtures of conciliation; and none can read the obsequious letter of the Foreign Minister, Deforgues (October 19, 1793), without knowing that a word from Morris would release Paine. The

American petitioners had indeed been referred to their own government—that is, to Morris.

The American Minister's version of what had occurred is given in a letter to Secretary Jefferson, dated March 6th :

"I have mentioned Mr. Paine's confinement. Major Jackson—who, by the by, has not given me a letter from you which he says was merely introductory, but left it with the Comité de Sûreté Générale, as a kind of letter of credence—Major Jackson, relying on his great influence with the leaders here, stepped forward to get Mr. Paine out of jail, and with several other Americans, has presented a petition to that effect, which was referred to that Committee and the Comité de Salut Public. This last, I understand, slighted the application as totally irregular ; and some time afterwards Mr. Paine wrote me a note desiring I would claim him as an American, which I accordingly did, though contrary to my judgment, for reasons mentioned in my last. The Minister's letter to me of the 1st Ventose, of which I enclose a copy, contains the answer to my reclamation. I sent a copy to Mr. Paine, who prepared a long answer, and sent it to me by an Englishman, whom I did not know. I told him, as Mr. Paine's friend, that my present opinion was similar to that of the Minister, but I might, perhaps, see occasion to change it, and in that case, if Mr. Paine wished it, I would go on with the claim, but that it would be well for him to consider the result ; that, if the Government meant to release him, they had already a sufficient ground ; but if not, I could only push them to bring on his trial for the crimes imputed to him ; seeing that whether he be considered as a Frenchman, or as an American, he must be amenable to the tribunals of France for his conduct while he was a Frenchman, and he may see in the fate of the Brissotins, that to which he is exposed. I have heard no more of the affair since ; but it is not impossible that he may force on a decision, which, as far as I can judge, would be fatal to him : for in the best of times he had a larger share of every other sense than common sense, and lately the intemperate use of ardent spirits has, I am told, considerably impaired the small stock he originally possessed."

In this letter the following incidental points suggest comment :

1. "Several other Americans." The petitioners for Paine's release were eighteen in number, and seem to have comprised all the Americans then left in Paris, some of them eminent.

2. "The crimes imputed to him." There were none. Paine was imprisoned under a law against "foreigners." Those charged with his arrest reported that his papers were entirely innocent. The archives of France, now open to exploration, prove that no offence was ever imputed to him, showing his arrest due only to Morris' insinuation of his being objectionable to the United States. By this insinuation ("crimes imputed to him") Paine was asserted to be amenable to French laws for matters with which the United States would of course have nothing to do, and of which nothing could be known in Philadelphia.

3. "While he was a Frenchman." Had Paine ever been a Frenchman, he was one when Morris pretended that he had claimed him as an American. But Paine had been excluded from the Convention and imprisoned expressly because he was not a Frenchman. No word of the Convention's published action was transmitted by Morris.

4. "The fate of the Brissotins," etc. This of course would frighten Paine's friends by its hint of a French hostility to him which did not exist, and might restrain them from applying to America for interference. Paine was already restrained by the new order preventing him from

communicating with any one except the American Minister.

5. " Intemperate," etc.   This is mere calumny. Since the brief lapse in June, 1793, when over-whelmed by the arrest of his friends, Paine's daily life is known from those who dwelt with him. During the months preceding his arrest he wrote the " Age of Reason " ; its power, if alcoholic, might have recommended his cellar to Morris, or to any man living.

So much for the insinuations and *suggestiones falsi* in Morris' letter.   The suppressions of fact are more deadly.   There is nothing of what had really happened ; nothing of the eulogy of Paine by the President of the Convention, which would have been a commentary on what Morris had said of the contempt in which he was held ; not a word of the fact that the petitioners were reminded by the Committee that their application was unofficial,—in other words, that the determination on Paine's fate rested with Morris himself.   This Morris hides under the phrase : " slighted the application as totally irregular."

But the fatal far-reaching falsehood of Morris' letter to Jefferson was his assertion that he had claimed Paine as an American.   This falsehood, told to Washington, Jefferson, Edmund Randolph, paralyzed all action in America in Paine's behalf ; told to the Americans in Paris, it paralyzed further effort of their own.

The actual correspondence between Morris and Deforgues is now for the first time brought to light.

"PARIS, 14th February 1794.

"SIR,—Thomas Paine has just applied to me to claim him as a Citizen of the United States. These (I believe) are the facts which relate to him. He was born in England. Having become a citizen of the United States, he acquired great celebrity there through his revolutionary writings. In consequence he was adopted as French Citizen, and then elected Member of the Convention. His behaviour since that epoch is out of my jurisdiction. I am ignorant of the reason for his present detention in the Luxembourg prison, but I beg you, Sir, if there be reasons which prevent his liberation, and which are unknown to me, be so good as to inform me of them, so that I may communicate them to the Government of the United States.—I have the honour to be, Sir, Your very humble servant,

"GOUV. MORRIS."[1]

DEFORGUES TO MORRIS.

"PARIS, 1st Ventose, 2nd year of the Republic.
[February 19, 1794.]

"The Minister of Foreign Affairs to the Minister of the United
    States.

"In your letter of the 26th of last month you reclaim the liberty of Thomas Payne, as an American Citizen. Born in England, this co-deputy has become successively an American and a French Citizen. In accepting this last title, and in occupying a place in the Legislative Corps, he submitted himself to the laws of the Republic, and has renounced the protection which the right of the people and treaties concluded with the United States could have assured him.

"I am ignorant of the motives of his detention, but I must presume they are well founded. I shall nevertheless submit the demand you have addressed me to the Committee of Public Safety, and I shall lose no time in letting you know its decision.

"DEFORGUES."

[1] "États Unis," vol. xl., Doc. 54. Endorsed: "Received the 28th of same [Pluviose, i. e., Feb. 16th]. To declare reception and to tell him that the Minister will take the necessary steps." The French Minister's reply is Doc. 61 of the same volume.

The opening assertion of the French Minister's note reveals the collusion. Careful examination of the American Minister's letter, to find where he " reclaims the liberty of Thomas Payne as an American citizen," forces me to the conclusion that the Frenchman only discovered such reclamation there by the assistance of Morris.

The American Minister distinctly declares Paine to be a French citizen, and disclaims official recognition of him.

It will be borne in mind that this French Minister is the same Deforgues who had confided to Morris his longing to succeed Genêt in America, and to whom Morris had whispered his design against Paine. Morris resided at Sainport, twenty-seven miles away, but his note is written in Paris. Four days elapse before the reply. Consultation is further proved by the French Minister's speaking of Paine as " occupying a place in the Legislative Corps." No uninspired Frenchman could have so described the Convention, any more than an American would have described the Convention of 1787 as " Congress." Deforgues' phrase is calculated for Philadelphia, where it might be supposed that the recently adopted Constitution had been followed by the organization of a legislature, whose members must of course take an oath of allegiance, which the Convention had not required.[1] Deforgues also makes bold to declare—as far away as Philadelphia—that Paine is a French citizen, though he

---

[1] Deforgues' phrase " laws of the Republic " is also a deception. The Constitution had been totally suspended by the Convention ; no government or law had been or ever was established under or by it. There was as yet no Republic, and only revolutionary or martial laws.

was excluded from the Convention and imprisoned because he was a "foreigner." The extreme ingenuity of the letter was certainly not original with this Frenchman. The American Minister, in response to his note declaring Paine a French citizen, and disclaiming jurisdiction over him, returns to Sainport with his official opiate for Paine's friends in America and Paris—a certificate that he has "reclaimed the liberty of Thomas Paine as an American citizen." The alleged reclamation suppressed, the certificate sent to Secretary Jefferson and to Paine, the American Minister is credited with having done his duty. In Washington's Cabinet, where the technicalities of citizenship had become of paramount importance, especially as regarded France, Deforgues' claim that Paine was not an American must be accepted—Morris consenting—as final.

It may be wondered that Morris should venture on so dangerous a game. But he had secured himself in anything he might choose to do. So soon as he discovered, in the previous summer, that he was not to be removed, and had fresh thunderbolts to wield, he veiled himself from the inspection of Jefferson. This he did in a letter of September 22, 1793. In the quasi-casual way characteristic of him when he is particularly deep, Morris then wrote : "*By the bye, I shall cease to send you copies of my various applications in particular cases, for they will cost you more in postage than they are worth.*" I put in italics this sentence, as one which merits memorable record in the annals of diplomacy.

The French Foreign Office being secret as the
grave, Jefferson facile, and Washington confiding,
there was no danger that Morris' letter to Deforgues would ever appear. Although the letter
of Deforgues,—his certificate that Morris had reclaimed Paine as an American,—was a little longer
than · the pretended reclamation, postal economy
did not prevent the American Minister from sending *that*, but his own was never sent to his government, and to this day is unknown to its archives.

It cannot be denied that Morris' letter to Deforgues is masterly in its way. He asks the
Minister to give him such reasons for Paine's detention as may not be known to him (Morris),
there being no such reasons. He sets at rest any
timidity the Frenchman might have, lest Morris
should be ensnaring him also, by begging—not
demanding—such knowledge as he may communicate to his government. Philadelphia is at a safe
distance in time and space. Deforgues is com-
placent enough, Morris being at hand, to describe
it as a "demand," and to promise speedy action on
the matter—which was then straightway buried, for
a century's slumber.

Paine was no doubt right in his subsequent belief that Morris was alarmed at his intention of
returning to America. Should Paine ever reach
Jefferson and his adherents, Gouverneur Morris
must instantly lose a position which, sustained
by Washington, made him a power throughout
Europe. Moreover, there was a Nemesis lurking
near him. The revolutionists, aware of his relations with their enemies, were only withheld from

laying hands on him by awe of Washington and anxiety about the alliance. The moment of his repudiation by his government would have been a perilous one. It so proved, indeed, when Monroe supplanted him. For the present, however, he is powerful. As the French Executive could have no interest merely to keep Paine, for six months, without suggestion of trial, it is difficult to imagine any reason, save the wish of Morris, why he was not allowed to depart with the Americans, in accordance with their petition.

Thus Thomas Paine, recognized by every American statesman and by Congress as a founder of their Republic, found himself a prisoner, and a man without a country. Outlawed by the rulers of his native land—though the people bore his defender, Erskine, from the court on their shoulders —imprisoned by France as a foreigner, disowned by America as a foreigner, and prevented by its Minister from returning to the country whose President had declared his services to it pre-eminent!

Never dreaming that his situation was the work of Morris, Paine (February 24th) appealed to him for help.

"I received your letter enclosing a copy of a letter from the Minister of foreign affairs. You must not leave me in the situation in which this letter places me. You know I do not deserve it, and you see the unpleasant situation in which I am thrown. I have made an essay in answer to the Minister's letter, which I wish you to make ground of a reply to him. They have nothing against me—except that they do not choose I should be in a state of freedom to write my mind freely upon things I have seen. Though you and I are not on terms of the best harmony, I apply to you as the Minister of America,

and you may add to that service whatever you think my integrity deserves.   At any rate I expect you to make Congress
acquainted with my situation, and to send to them copies of
the letters that have passed on the subject.   A reply to the
Minister's letter is absolutely necessary, were it only to continue the reclamation.   Otherwise your silence will be a sort
of consent to his observations."

Supposing, from the French Minister's opening
assertion, that a reclamation had really been made,
Paine's simplicity led him into a trap.   He sent
his argument to be used by the Minister in an
answer of his own, so that Minister was able to do
as he pleased with it, the result being that it
was buried among his private papers, to be partly
brought to light by Jared Sparks, who is candid
enough to remark on the Minister's indifference
and the force of Paine's argument.   Not a word to
Congress was ever said on the subject.

Jefferson, without the knowledge or expectation
of Morris, had resigned the State Secretaryship
at the close of 1793.   Morris' letter of March 6th
reached the hands of Edmund Randolph, Jefferson's successor, late in June.   On June 25th Randolph writes Washington, at Mount Vernon, that
he has received a letter from Morris, of March 6th,
saying "that he has demanded Paine as an American citizen, but that the Minister holds him to be
amenable to the French laws."   Randolph was a
just man and an exact lawyer ; it is certain that if
he had received a copy of the fictitious "reclamation" the imprisonment would have been curtailed.
Under the false information before him, nothing
could be done but await the statement of the causes
of Paine's detention, which Deforgues would "lose

no time " in transmitting. It was impossible to
deny, without further knowledge, the rights over
Paine apparently claimed by the French government.

And what could be done by the Americans in
Paris, whom Paine alone had befriended? Joel
Barlow, who had best opportunities of knowing
the facts, says : " He [Paine] was always charitable
to the poor beyond his means, a sure friend and
protector to all Americans in distress that he found
in foreign countries ; and he had frequent occasions
to exert his influence in protecting them during
the Revolution in France." They were grateful and
deeply moved, these Americans, but thoroughly
deceived about the situation. Told that they must
await the action of a distant government, which
itself was waiting for action in Paris, alarmed by
the American Minister's hints of danger that might
ensue on any misstep or agitation, assured that
he was proceeding with the case, forbidden to communicate with Paine, they were reduced to helplessness. Meanwhile, between silent America and
these Americans, all so cunningly disabled, stood
the remorseless French Committee, ready to strike
or to release in obedience to any sign from the
alienated ally, to soothe whom no sacrifice would
be too great. Genêt had been demanded for the
altar of sacred Alliance, but (to Morris' regret) refused by the American government. The Revolution would have preferred Morris as a victim, but
was quite ready to offer Paine.

Six or seven months elapsed without bringing
from President or Cabinet a word of sympathy

for Paine.   But they brought increasing indications
that America was in treaty with England, and
Washington disaffected towards France.   Under
these circumstances Robespierre resolved on the
accusation and trial of Paine.   It does not necessarily follow that Paine would have been condemned ; but there were some who did not mean
that he should escape, among whom Robespierre
may or may not have been included.   The probabilities, to my mind, are against that theory.
Robespierre having ceased to attend the Committee of Public Safety when the order issued for
Paine's death.

CHAPTER VIII.

SICK AND IN PRISON.

IT was a strange world into which misfortune had introduced Paine. There was in prison a select and rather philosophical society, mainly persons of refinement, more or less released from conventional habit by the strange conditions under which they found themselves. There were gentlemen and ladies, no attempt being made to separate them until some scandal was reported. The Luxembourg was a special prison for the French nobility and the English, who had a good opportunity for cultivating democratic ideas. The gaoler, Benoit, was good-natured, and cherished his unwilling guests as his children, according to a witness. Paine might even have been happy there but for the ever recurring tragedies—the cries of those led forth to death. He was now and then in strange juxtapositions. One day Deforgues came to join him, he who had conspired with Morris. Instead of receiving for his crime diplomatic security in America he found himself beside his victim. Perhaps if Deforgues and Paine had known each other's language a confession might have passed. There were horrors on horrors. Paine's old friend, Hérault de Séchelles, was imprisoned for having humanely concealed in his house a poor officer who was hunted by the police; he parted from Paine for the scaffold. So also he parted from the brilliant Camille Desmoulins, and the fine dreamer, Anacharsis Clootz. One day came Danton, who, taking Paine's hand, said: "That which you did for the happiness and liberty of your country, I tried in vain to do for mine. I have been less fortunate, but not less innocent. They will send me to the scaffold; very well, my friends, I shall go gaily." Even so did Danton meet his doom.[1]

All of the English prisoners became Paine's friends. Among these was General O'Hara,—that same general who had fired the American heart at Yorktown by offering the surrendered sword of Cornwallis to Rochambeau instead of Washington. O'Hara's captured suite included two physicians— Bond and Graham—who attended Paine during an illness, as he gratefully records. What money Paine had when arrested does not appear to have been taken from him, and he was able to assist General O'Hara with £200 to return to his country; though by this and similar charities he was left without means when his own unexpected deliverance came.[2]

The first part of "The Age of Reason" was sent out with final revision at the close of January.

[1] " Mémoires sur les prisons," t. ii., p. 153.

[2] Among the anecdotes told of O'Hara in prison, one is related of an argument he held with a Frenchman, on the relative degrees of liberty in England and France. "In England," he said, "we are perfectly free to write and print, *George is a good King;* but you—why you are not even permitted to write, *Robespierre is a tiger !*"

In the second edition appeared the following inscription :

"To my fellow citizens of the United States of America.—I put the following work under your protection. It contains my opinion upon Religion. You will do me the justice to remember, that I have always strenuously supported the Right of every man to his opinion, however different that opinion might be to mine. He who denies to another this right, makes a slave of himself to his present opinion, because he precludes himself the right of changing it. The most formidable weapon against errors of every kind is Reason. I have never used any other, and I trust I never shall.—Your affectionate friend and fellow citizen,

"Thomas Paine."

This dedication is dated, " Luxembourg (Paris), 8th Pluviose, Second year of the French Republic, one and indivisible. January 27, O. S. 1794." Paine now addressed himself to the second part of "The Age of Reason," concerning which the following anecdote is told in the manuscript memoranda of Thomas Rickman :

"Paine, while in the Luxembourg prison and expecting to die hourly, read to Mr. Bond (surgeon of Brighton, from whom this anecdote came) parts of his *Age of Reason ;* and every night, when Mr. Bond left him, to be separately locked up, and expecting not to see Paine alive in the morning, he [Paine] always expressed his firm belief in the principles of that book, and begged Mr. Bond should tell the world such were his dying sentiments. Paine further said, if he lived he should further prosecute the work and print it. Bond added, Paine was the most conscientious man he ever knew."

In after years, when Paine was undergoing persecution for "infidelity," he reminded the zealots that they would have to "accuse Providence of

infidelity," for having " protected him in all his
dangers." Incidentally he gives reminiscences of
his imprisonment.

" I was one of the nine members that composed the first
Committee of Constitution. Six of them have been destroyed.
Sieyès and myself have survived—he by bending with the
times, and I by not bending. The other survivor [Barrère]
joined Robespierre ; he was seized and imprisoned in his turn,
and sentenced to transportation. He has since apologized to
me for having signed the warrant, by saying he felt himself in
danger and was obliged to do it. Hérault Séchelles, an acquaintance of Mr. Jefferson, and a good patriot, was my *suppleant* as member of the Committee of Constitution. . . . He
was imprisoned in the Luxembourg with me, was taken to the
tribunal and guillotined, and I, his principal, left. There were
two foreigners in the Convention, Anacharsis Clootz and myself. We were both put out of the Convention by the same
vote, arrested by the same order, and carried to prison together the same night. He was taken to the guillotine, and I
was again left. . . . Joseph Lebon, one of the vilest characters
that ever existed, and who made the streets of Arras run with
blood, was my *suppleant,* as member of the Convention for the
Pas de Calais. When I was put out of the Convention he came
and took my place. When I was liberated from prison and
voted again into the Convention, he was sent to the same
prison and took my place there, and he was sent to the guillotine instead of me. He supplied my place all the way through.

" One hundred and sixty-eight persons were taken out of the
Luxembourg in one night, and a hundred and sixty of them
guillotined next day, of which I knew I was to be one ; and
the manner I escaped that fate is curious, and has all the appearance of accident. The room in which I lodged was on the
ground floor, and one of a long range of rooms under a gallery,
and the door of it opened outward and flat against the wall ;
so that when it was open the inside of the door appeared outward, and the contrary when it was shut. I had three comrades, fellow prisoners with me, Joseph Vanhuile of Bruges,
since president of the municipality of that town, Michael and

Robbins Bastini of Louvain. When persons by scores and by hundreds were to be taken out of the prison for the guillotine it was always done in the night, and those who performed that office had a private mark or signal by which they knew what rooms to go to, and what number to take. We, as I have said, were four, and the door of our room was marked, unobserved by us, with that number in chalk ; but it happened, if happening is the proper word, that the mark was put on when the door was open and flat against the wall, and thereby came on the inside when we shut it at night ; and the destroying angel passed by it."

Paine did not hear of this chalk mark until afterwards. In his letter to Washington he says:

" I had been imprisoned seven months, and the silence of the executive part of the government of America (Mr. Washington) upon the case, and upon every thing respecting me, was explanation enough to Robespierre that he might proceed to extremities. A violent fever which had nearly terminated my existence was, I believe, the circumstance that preserved it. I was not in a condition to be removed, or to know of what was passing, or of what had passed, for more than a month. It makes a blank in my remembrance of life. The first thing I was informed of was the fall of Robespierre."

The probabilities are that the prison physician Marhaski, whom Paine mentions with gratitude, was with him when the chalk mark was made, and that there was some connivance in the matter. In the same letter he says:

" From about the middle of March (1794) to the fall of Robespierre, July 29, (9th of Thermidor,) the state of things in the prisons was a continued scene of horror. No man could count upon life for twenty-four hours. To such a pitch of rage and suspicion were Robespierre and his committee arrived, that it seemed as if they feared to leave a man to live. Scarcely a night passed in which ten, twenty, thirty, forty, fifty or more were not taken out of the prison, carried before a pretended tribunal in the morning, and guillotined before night. One hundred and sixty-nine were taken out of the Luxembourg one night in the month of July, and one hundred and sixty of them guillotined. A list of two hundred more, according to the report in the prison, was preparing a few days before Robespierre fell. In this last list I have good reason to believe I was included."

To this Paine adds the memorandum for his accusation found in Robespierre's note-book. Of course it was natural, especially with the memorandum, to accept the Robespierre mythology of the time without criticism. The massacres of July were not due to Robespierre, who during that time was battling with the Committee of Public Safety, at whose hands he fell on the 29th. At the close of June there was an alarm at preparations for an insurrection in Luxembourg prison, which caused a union of the Committee of Public Safety and the police, resulting in indiscriminate slaughter of prisoners. But Paine was discriminated. Barrère, long after, apologized to him for having signed "the warrant," by saying he felt himself in danger and was obliged to do it. Paine accepted the apology, and when Barrère had returned to France, after banishment, Paine introduced him to the English author, Lewis Goldsmith.[1] As Barrère did not sign the warrant for Paine's imprisonment, it must have been a warrant for his death, or for accusation at a moment when it was equivalent to a death sentence. Whatever danger Barrère had to fear, so great as to cause him to sacrifice Paine, it was

[1] "Mémoires de B. Barrère,"t. i., p. 80. Lewis Goldsmith was the author of "Crimes of the Cabinets."

not from Robespierre ; else it would not have continued to keep Paine in prison three months after
Robespierre's death.   As Robespierre's memorandum was for a " decree of accusation " against
Paine, separately, which might not have gone
against him, but possibly have dragged to light the
conspiracy against him, there would seem to be no
ground for connecting that " demand " with the
warrant signed by a Committee he did not attend.

Paine had good cause for writing as he did in
praise of " Forgetfulness."   During the period in
which he was unconscious with fever the horrors of
the prison reached their apogee.   On June 19th
the kindly gaoler, Benoit, was removed and tried ;
he was acquitted but not restored.   His place was
given to a cruel fellow named Gayard, who instituted a reign of terror in the prison.

There are many evidences that the good Benoit,
so warmly remembered by Paine, evaded the rigid
police regulations as to communications of prisoners with their friends outside, no doubt with precaution against those of a political character.   It is
pleasant to record an instance of this which was
the means of bringing beautiful rays of light into
Paine's cell.   Shortly before his arrest an English
lady had called on him, at his house in the Faubourg St. Denis, to ask his intervention in behalf
of an Englishman of rank who had been arrested.
Paine had now, however, fallen from power, and
could not render the requested service.   This lady
was the last visitor who preceded the officers who
arrested him.   But while he was in prison there
was brought to him a communication, in a lady's

handwriting, signed " A little corner of the World."
So far as can be gathered, this letter was of a poetical character, perhaps tinged with romance. It
was followed by others, all evidently meant to be-
guile the weary and fearful hours of a prisoner
whom she had little expectation of ever meeting
again. Paine, by the aid of Benoit, managed to
answer his " contemplative correspondent," as he
called her, signing, " The Castle in the Air."
These letters have never seen the light, but the
sweetness of this sympathy did, for many an hour,
bring into Paine's *oubliette* the oblivion of grief
described in the letter on " Forgetfulness," sent to
the lady after his liberation.

" Memory, like a beauty that is always present to hear herself flattered, is flattered by every one. But the absent and
silent goddess, Forgetfulness, has no votaries, and is never
thought of : yet we owe her much. She is the goddess of
ease, though not of pleasure. When the mind is like a room
hung with black, and every corner of it crowded with the most
horrid images imagination can create, this kind, speechless
maid, Forgetfulness, is following us night and day with her
opium wand, and gently touching first one and then another,
benumbs them into rest, and then glides away with the silence
of a departing shadow."

Paine was not forgotten by his old friends in
France. So soon as the excitement attending
Robespierre's execution had calmed a little, Lanthenas (August 7th) sent Merlin de Thionville a
copy of the " Age of Reason," which he had translated, and made his appeal.

" I think it would be in the well-considered interest of the
Republic, since the fall of the tyrants we have overthrown, to
re-examine the motives of Thomas Paine's imprisonment.

That re-examination is suggested by too many and sensible grounds to be related in detail. Every friend of liberty familiar with the history of our Revolution, and feeling the necessity of repelling the slanders with which despots are loading it in the eyes of nations, misleading them against us, will understand these grounds. Should the Committee of Public Safety, having before it no founded charge or suspicion against Thomas Paine, retain any scruples, and think that from my occasional conversation with that foreigner, whom the people's suffrage called to the national representation, and some acquaintance with his language, I might perhaps throw light upon their doubt, I would readily communicate to them all that I know about him. I request Merlin de Thionville to submit these considerations to the Committee."

Merlin was now a leading member of the Committee. On the following day Paine sent (in French) the following letters :

"CITIZENS, REPRESENTATIVES, AND MEMBERS OF THE COMMITTEE OF PUBLIC SAFETY : I address you a copy of a letter which I have to-day written to the Convention. The singular situation in which I find myself determines me to address myself to the whole Convention, of which you are a part.
                                        " THOMAS PAINE.
" Maison d'Arrèt du Luxembourg,
    Le 19 Thermidor, l'an 2 de la République, une et
    indivisible."

"CITIZEN REPRESENTATIVES : If I should not express myself with the energy I used formerly to do, you will attribute it to the very dangerous illness I have suffered in the prison of the Luxembourg. For several days I was insensible of my own existence ; and though I am much recovered, it is with exceeding great difficulty that I find power to write you this letter.

" But before I proceed further, I request the Convention to observe : that this is the first line that has come from me, either

to the Convention, or to any of the Committees, since my imprisonment,—which is approaching to Eight months.—Ah, my
friends, eight months' loss of Liberty seems almost a life-time
to a man who has been, as I have been, the unceasing defender
of Liberty for twenty years.

"I have now to inform the Convention of the reason of my
not having written before. It is a year ago that I had strong
reason to believe that Robespierre was my inveterate enemy,
as he was the enemy of every man of virtue and humanity.
The address that was sent to the Convention some time about
last August from Arras, the native town of Robespierre, I have
always been informed was the work of that hypocrite and the
partizans he had in the place. The intention of that address
was to prepare the way for destroying me, by making the People declare (though without assigning any reason) that I had
lost their confidence; the Address, however, failed of success,
as it was immediately opposed by a counter-address from St.
Omer which declared the direct contrary. But the strange
power that Robespierre, by the most consummate hypocrisy
and the most hardened cruelties, had obtained rendered any
attempt on my part to obtain justice not only useless but even
dangerous; for it is the nature of Tyranny always to strike a
deeper blow when any attempt has been made to repel a former
one. This being my situation I submitted with patience to the
hardness of my fate and waited the event of brighter days. I
hope they are now arrived to the nation and to me.

"Citizens, when I left the United States in the year 1787, I
promised to all my friends that I would return to them the
next year; but the hope of seeing a Revolution happily established in France, that might serve as a model to the rest of
Europe, and the earnest and disinterested desire of rendering
every service in my power to promote it, induced me to defer
my return to that country, and to the society of my friends,
for more than seven years. This long sacrifice of private

tranquillity, especially after having gone through the fatigues and dangers of the American Revolution which continued almost eight years, deserved a better fate than the long imprisonment I have silently suffered. But it is not the nation but a faction that has done me this injustice, and it is to the national representation that I appeal against that injustice. Parties and Factions, various and numerous as they have been, I have always avoided. My heart was devoted to all France, and the object to which I applied myself was the Constitution. The Plan which I proposed to the Committee, of which I was a member, is now in the hands of Barrère, and it will speak for itself.

"It is perhaps proper that I inform you of the cause assigned in the order for my imprisonment. It is that I am 'a Foreigner'; whereas, the *Foreigner* thus imprisoned was invited into France by a decree of the late national Assembly, and that in the hour of her greatest danger, when invaded by Austrians and Prussians. He was, moreover, a citizen of the United States of America, an ally of France, and not a subject of any country in Europe, and consequently not within the intentions of any of the decrees concerning Foreigners. But any excuse can be made to serve the purpose of malignity when it is in power.

"I will not intrude on your time by offering any apology for the broken and imperfect manner in which I have expressed myself. I request you to accept it with the sincerity with which it comes from my heart; and I conclude with wishing Fraternity and prosperity to France, and union and happiness to her representatives.

"Citizens, I have now stated to you my situation, and I can have no doubt but your justice will restore me to the Liberty of which I have been deprived.

"THOMAS PAINE.

"Luxembourg, Thermidor 19th, 2d year of the French Republic, one and indivisible."

No doubt this touching letter would have been effectual had it reached the Convention. But the Committee of Public Safety took care that no whisper even of its existence should be heard. Paine's participation in their fostered dogma, that *Robespierre le veut* explained all crimes, probably cost him three more months in prison. The lamb had confided its appeal to the wolf. Barrère, Billaud-Varennes, and Collot d'Herbois, by skilful use of the dead scapegoat, maintained their places on the Committee until September 1st, and after that influenced its counsels. At the same time Morris, as we have seen, was keeping Monroe out of his place. There might have been a serious reckoning for these men had Paine been set free, or his case inquired into by the Convention. And Thuriot was now on the Committee of Public Safety; he was eager to lay his own crimes on Robespierre, and to conceal those of the Committee. Paine's old friend, Achille Audibert, unsuspicious as himself of the real facts, sent an appeal (August 20th) to " Citizen Thuriot, member of the Committee of Public Safety."

" REPRESENTATIVE :—A friend of mankind is groaning in chains,—Thomas Paine, who was not so politic as to remain silent in regard to a man unlike himself, but dared to say that Robespierre was a monster to be erased from the list of men. From that moment he became a criminal ; the despot marked him as his victim, put him into prison, and doubtless prepared the way to the scaffold for him, as for others who knew him and were courageous enough to speak out.[1]

[1] It must be remembered that at this time it seemed the strongest recommendation of any one to public favor to describe him as a victim of Robespierre ; and Paine's friends could conceive no other cause for the detention of a man they knew to be innocent.

"Thomas Paine is an acknowledged citizen of the United States. He was the secretary of the Congress for the department of foreign affairs during the Revolution. He has made himself known in Europe by his writings, and especially by his 'Rights of Man.' The electoral assembly of the department of Pas-de-Calais elected him one of its representatives to the Convention, and commissioned me to go to London, inform him of his election, and bring him to France. I hardly escaped being a victim to the English Government with which he was at open war; I performed my mission; and ever since friendship has attached me to Paine. This is my apology for soliciting you for his liberation.

"I can assure you, Representative, that America was by no means satisfied with the imprisonment of a strong column of its Revolution. Please to take my prayer into consideration. But for Robespierre's villainy this friend of man would now be free. Do not permit liberty longer to see in prison a victim of the wretch who lives no more but by his crimes; and you will add to the esteem and veneration I feel for a man who did so much to save the country amidst the most tremendous crisis of our Revolution.

"Greeting, respect, and brotherhood,

"ACHILLE AUDIBERT, of Calais.

"No. 216 Rue de Bellechase, Fauborg St. Germaine."

Audibert's letter, of course, sank under the burden of its Robespierre myth to a century's sleep beside Paine's, in the Committee's closet.

Meanwhile, the regulation against any communication of prisoners with the outside world remaining in force, it was some time before Paine could know that his letter had been suppressed on its way to the Convention. He was thus late in discovering his actual enemies.

An interesting page in the annals of diplomacy remains to be written on the closing weeks of Morris in France. On August 14th he writes to Robert Morris: "I am preparing for my departure, but as yet can take no step, as there is a kind of interregnum in the government and Mr. Monroe is not yet received, at which he grows somewhat impatient." There was no such interregnum, and no such explanation was given to Monroe, who writes :

"I presented my credentials to the commissary of foreign affairs soon after my arrival [August 2d]; but more than a week had elapsed, and I had obtained no answer, when or whether I should be received. A delay beyond a few days surprised me, because I could discern no adequate or rational motive for it."[1]

It is plain that the statement of Paine, who was certainly in communication with the Committees a year later, is true, that Morris was in danger on account of the interception of compromising letters written by him. He needed time to dispose of his house and horses, and ship his wines, and felt it important to retain his protecting credentials. At any moment his friends might be expelled from the Committee, and their papers be examined. While the arrangements for Monroe's reception rested with Morris and this unaltered Committee, there was little prospect of Monroe's being installed at all. The new Minister was therefore compelled, as other Americans had been, to appeal directly to the Convention. That assembly responded at once, and he was received (August 28th) with highest honors. Morris had nothing to do with the arrangement. The historian Frédéric Masson,

---

[1] " View of the Conduct of the Executive in the Foreign Affairs of the United States," by James Monroe, p. 7.

alluding to the "unprecedented" irregularity of Morris in not delivering or receiving letters of recall, adds that Monroe found it important to state that he had acted without consultation with his predecessor.[1] This was necessary for a cordial reception by the Convention, but it invoked the cordial hatred of Morris, who marked him for his peculiar guillotine set up in Philadelphia.

So completely had America and Congress been left in the dark about Paine that Monroe was surprised to find him a prisoner. When at length the new Minister was in a position to consult the French Minister about Paine, he found the knots so tightly tied around this particular victim—almost the only one left in the Luxembourg of those imprisoned during the Terror—that it was difficult to untie them. The Minister of Foreign Affairs was now M. Bouchot, a weak creature who, as Morris said, would not wipe his nose without permission of the Committee of Public Safety. When Monroe opened Paine's case he was asked whether he had brought instructions. Of course he had none, for the administration had no suspicion that Morris had not, as he said, attended to the case.

When Paine recovered from his fever he heard that Monroe had superseded Morris.

"As soon as I was able to write a note legible enough to be read, I found a way to convey one to him [Monroe] by means of the man who lighted the lamps in the prison, and whose unabated friendship to me, from whom he never received any service, and with difficulty accepted any recompense, puts the character of Mr. Washington to shame. In a few days I re-

[1] " Le Départément des Affaires Étrangères," etc., p. 345.

ceived a message from Mr. Monroe, conveyed in a note from an intermediate person, with assurance of his friendship, and expressing a desire that I should rest the case in his hands. After a fortnight or more had passed, and hearing nothing farther, I wrote to a friend [Whiteside], a citizen of Philadelphia, requesting him to inform me what was the true situation of things with respect to me. I was sure that something was the matter; I began to have hard thoughts of Mr. Washington, but I was unwilling to encourage them. In about ten days I received an answer to my letter, in which the writer says: 'Mr. Monroe told me he had no order (meaning from the president, Mr. Washington) respecting you, but that he (Mr. Monroe) will do everything in his power to liberate you, but, from what I learn from the Americans lately arrived in Paris, you are not considered, either by the American government or by individuals, as an American citizen.'"

As the American government did regard Paine as an American citizen, and approved Monroe's demanding him as such, there is no difficulty in recognizing the source from which these statements were diffused among Paine's newly arriving countrymen. Morris was still in Paris.

On the receipt of Whiteside's note, Paine wrote a Memorial to Monroe, of which important parts—amounting to eight printed pages—are omitted from American and English editions of his works. In quoting this Memorial, I select mainly the omitted portions.[1] Paine says that before leaving London for the Convention, he consulted Minister Pinckney, who agreed with him that "it was for the interest of America that the system of European governments should be changed and placed

[1] The whole is published in French: "Mémoire de Thomas Payne, autographé et signé de sa main: addressé à M. Monroe, ministre des États-unis en France, pour réclamer sa mise en liberté comme Citoyen Américain, 10 Septembre, 1794. Villeneuve."

on the same principle with her own "; and adds :
" I have wished to see America the mother church
of government, and I have done my utmost to
exalt her character and her condition." He points
out that he had not accepted any title or office
under a foreign government, within the meaning
of the United States Constitution, because there
was no government in France, the Convention
being assembled to frame one ; that he was a
citizen of France only in the honorary sense in
which others in Europe and America were declared
such ; that no oath of allegiance was required or
given. The following paragraphs are from various
parts of the Memorial.

" They who propagate the report of my not being considered
as a citizen of America by government, do it to the prolonga-
tion of my imprisonment, and without authority ; for Congress,
as a government, has neither decided upon it, nor yet taken the
matter into consideration ; and I request you to caution such
persons against spreading such reports. . . .

" I know not what opinions have been circulated in America.
It may have been supposed there, that I had voluntarily and
intentionally abandoned America, and that my citizenship had
ceased by my own choice. I can easily conceive that there
are those in that Country who would take such a proceeding on
my part somewhat in disgust. The idea of forsaking old friendships for new acquaintances is not agreeable. I am a little
warranted in making this supposition by a letter I received
some time ago from the wife of one of the Georgia delegates,
in which she says, 'your friends on this side the water cannot
be reconciled to the idea of your abandoning America.' I
have never abandoned America in thought, word, or deed, and
I feel it incumbent upon me to give this assurance to the
friends I have in that country, and with whom I have always
intended, and am determined, if the possibility exists, to close
the scene of my life. It is there that I have made myself a
home. It is there that I have given the services of my best

days. America never saw me flinch from her cause in the most
gloomy and perilous of her situations : and I know there are
those in that Country who will not flinch from me. If I have
Enemies (and every man has some) I leave them to the enjoyment of their ingratitude. . . .

" It is somewhat extraordinary, that the Idea of my not being
a Citizen of America should have arisen only at the time that
I am imprisoned in France because, or on the pretence that, I
am a foreigner. The case involves a strange contradiction of
Ideas. None of the Americans who came to France whilst I
was in liberty, had conceived any such idea or circulated any
such opinion ; and why it should arise now is a matter yet to
be explained. However discordant the late American Minister,
Gouverneur Morris, and the late French Committee of Public
Safety were, it suited the purpose of both that I should be continued in arrestation. The former wished to prevent my return
to America, that I should not expose his misconduct ; and the
latter, lest I should publish to the world the history of its
wickedness. Whilst that Minister and that Committee continued, I had no expectation of liberty. I speak here of the
Committee of which Robespierre was a member. . . .

" I here close my Memorial and proceed to offer to you a
proposal, that appears to me suited to all the circumstances of
the case ; which is, that you reclaim me conditionally, until the
opinion of Congress can be obtained upon the subject of my
Citizenship of America, and that I remain in liberty under your
protection during that time. I found this proposal upon the
following grounds :

" First, you say you have no orders respecting me ; consequently you have no orders *not* to reclaim me ; and in this case
you are left discretionary judge whether to reclaim or not. My
proposal therefore unites a consideration of your situation with
my own.

" Secondly, I am put in arrestation because I am a foreigner. It is therefore necessary to determine to what Country
I belong. The right of determining this question cannot
appertain exclusively to the committee of public safety or
general surety ; because I appear to the Minister of the United
States, and shew that my citizenship of that Country is good
and valid, referring at the same time, through the agency of the

Minister, my claim of Right to the opinion of Congress,—it being a matter between two governments.

" Thirdly, France does not claim me for a citizen ; neither do I set up any claim of citizenship in France. The question is simply, whether I am or am not a citizen of America. I am imprisoned here on the decree for imprisoning Foreigners, because, say they, I was born in England. I say in answer, that, though born in England, I am not a subject of the English Government any more than any other American is who was born, as they all were, under the same government, or that the citizens of France are subjects of the French monarchy, under which they were born. I have twice taken the oath of abjuration to the British king and government, and of Allegiance to America. Once as a citizen of the State of Pennsylvania in 1776 ; and again before Congress, administered to me by the President, Mr. Hancock, when I was appointed Secretary in the office of foreign affairs in 1777. . . .

" Painful as the want of liberty may be, it is a consolation to me to believe that my imprisonment proves to the world that I had no share in the murderous system that then reigned. That I was an enemy to it, both morally and politically, is known to all who had any knowledge of me ; and could I have written French as well as I can English, I would publicly have exposed its wickedness, and shown the ruin with which it was pregnant. They who have esteemed me on former occasions, whether in America or England, will, I know, feel no cause to abate that esteem when they reflect, that imprisonment with preservation of character, is preferable to liberty with disgrace."

In a postscript Paine adds that " as Gouverneur Morris could not inform Congress of the cause of my arrestation, as he knew it not himself, it is to be supposed that Congress was not enough acquainted with the case to give any directions respecting me when you left." Which to the reader of the preceding pages will appear sufficiently naïve.

To this Monroe responded (September 18th) with a letter of warm sympathy, worthy of the

high-minded gentleman that he was. After ascribing the notion that Paine was not an American
to mental confusion, and affirming his determination to maintain his rights as a citizen of the
United States, Monroe says:

" It is unnecessary for me to tell you how much all your
countrymen, I speak of the great mass of the people, are interested in your welfare.   They have not forgotten the history of
their own revolution, and the difficult scenes through which
they passed ; nor do they review its several stages without
reviving in their bosoms a due sensibility of the merits of those
who served them in that great and arduous conflict.   The crime
of ingratitude has not yet stained, and I trust never will stain,
our national character.   You are considered by them, as not
only having rendered important services in our own revolution,
but as being on a more extensive scale, the friend of human
rights, and a distinguished and able advocate in favor of public
liberty.   To the welfare of Thomas Paine the Americans are
not and cannot be indifferent.   Of the sense which the President has always entertained of your merits, and of his friendly
disposition towards you, you are too well assured to require
any declaration of it from me.   That I forward his wishes in
seeking your safety is what I well know ; and this will form an
additional obligation on me to perform what I should otherwise
consider as a duty.

" You are, in my opinion, menaced by no kind of danger.
To liberate you, will be an object of my endeavors, and as soon
as possible.   But you must, until that event shall be accomplished, face your situation with patience and fortitude ; you
will likewise have the justice to recollect, that I am placed here
upon a difficult theatre, many important objects to attend to,
and with few to consult.   It becomes me in pursuit of those,
to regulate my conduct in respect to each, as to the manner
and the time, as will, in my judgment, be best calculated to
accomplish the whole.

" With great esteem and respect consider me personally your
friend,

"JAMES MONROE."

Monroe was indeed "placed upon a difficult theatre." Morris was showing a fresh letter from the President expressing unabated confidence in him, apologizing for his recall ; he still had friends in the Committee of Public Safety, to which Monroe had appealed in vain. The continued dread the conspirators had of Paine's liberation appears in the fact that Monroe's letter, written September 18th, did not reach Paine until October 18th, when Morris had reached the boundary line of Switzerland, which he entered on the 19th. He had left Paris (Sainport) October 14th, when Barrère, Billaud-Varennes, and Collot d'Herbois, no longer on the Committee, were under accusation, and their papers under investigation,—a search that resulted in their exile. Morris got across the line on an irregular passport.

While Monroe's reassuring letter to Paine was taking a month to penetrate his prison walls, he vainly grappled with the subtle obstacles. All manner of delays impeded the correspondence, the principal one being that he could present no instructions from the President concerning Paine. Of course he was fighting in the dark, having no suspicion that the imprisonment was due to his predecessor. At length, however, he received from Secretary Randolph a letter (dated July 30th), from which, though Paine was not among its specifications, he could select a sentence as basis of action : " We have heard with regret that several of our citizens have been thrown into prison in France, from a suspicion of criminal attempts˙ against the government. If they are guilty we are extremely sorry for it; if innocent we must protect them." What Paine had said in his Memorial of collusion between Morris and the Committee of Public Safety probably determined Monroe to apply no more in that quarter ; so he wrote (November 2d) to the Committee of General Surety. After stating the general principles and limitations of ministerial protection to an imprisoned countryman, he adds :

" The citizens of the United States cannot look back upon the time of their own revolution without recollecting among the names of their most distinguished patriots that of Thomas Paine ; the services he rendered to his country in its struggle for freedom have implanted in the hearts of his countrymen a sense of gratitude never to be effaced as long as they shall deserve the title of a just and generous people.

" The above-named citizen is at this moment languishing in prison, affected with a disease growing more intense from his confinement. I beg, therefore, to call your attention to his condition and to request you to hasten the moment when the law shall decide his fate, in case of any accusation against him, and if none, to restore him to liberty.

" Greeting and fraternity   " MONROE."

At this the first positive assertion of Paine's American citizenship the prison door flew open. He had been kept there solely " pour les interêts de l'Amérique," as embodied in Morris, and two days after Monroe undertook, without instructions, to affirm the real interests of America in Paine he was liberated.

" Brumaire, 13th. Third year of the French Republic.—The Committee of General Surety orders that the Citizen Thomas Paine be set at liberty, and the seals taken from his papers, on sight of these presents.

"Members of the Committee (signed) : Clauzel, Lesage, Senault, Bentabole, Reverchon, Goupilleau de Fontenai, Rewbell.

"Delivered to Clauzel, as Commissioner."

There are several interesting points about this little decree. It is signed by Bentabole, who had moved Paine's expulsion from the Convention. It orders that the seals be removed from Paine's papers, whereas none had been placed on them, the officers reporting them innocent. This same authority, which had ordered Paine's arrest, now, in ordering his liberation, shows that the imprisonment had never been a subject of French inquiry. It had ordered the seals but did not know whether they were on the papers or not. It was no concern of France, but only of the American Minister. It is thus further evident that when Monroe invited a trial of Paine there was not the least trace of any charge against him. And there was precisely the same absence of any accusation against Paine in the new Committee of Public Safety, to which Monroe's letter was communicated the same day.

Writing to Secretary Randolph (November 7th) Monroe says :

"He was actually a citizen of the United States, and of the United States only ; for the Revolution which parted us from Great Britain broke the allegiance which was before due to the Crown, of all who took our side. He was, of course, not a British subject ; nor was he strictly a citizen of France, for he came by invitation for the temporary purpose of assisting in the formation of their government only, and meant to withdraw to America when that should be completed. And what confirms this is the act of the Convention itself arresting him, by which he is declared a foreigner. Mr. Paine pressed my interference.

I told him I had hoped getting him enlarged without it ; but, if I did interfere, it could only be by requesting that he be tried, in case there was any charge against him, and liberated in case there was not. This was admitted. His correspondence with me is lengthy and interesting, and I may probably be able here-after to send you a copy of it. After some time had elapsed, without producing any change in his favor, I finally resolved to address the Committee of General Surety in his behalf, resting my application on the above principle. My letter was delivered by my Secretary in the Committee to the president, who as-sured him he would communicate its contents immediately to the Committee of Public Safety, and give me an answer as soon as possible. The conference took place accordingly between the two Committees, and, as I presume, on that night, or on the succeeding day ; for on the morning of the day after, which was yesterday, I was presented by the Secretary of the Com-mittee of General Surety with an order for his enlargement. I forwarded it immediately to the Luxembourg, and had it carried into effect ; and have the pleasure now to add that he is not only released to the enjoyment of liberty, but is in good spirits."

In reply, the Secretary of State (Randolph) in a letter to Monroe of March 8, 1795, says : " Your observations on our commercial relations to France, and your conduct as to Mr. Gardoqui's letter, prove your judgment and assiduity. Nor are your measures as to Mr. Paine, and the lady of our friend [Lafayette] less approved."

Thus, after an imprisonment of ten months and nine days, Thomas Paine was liberated from the prison into which he had been cast by a Minister of the United States.

CHAPTER IX.

A RESTORATION.

As in 1792 Paine had left England with the authorities at his heels, so in 1794 escaped Morris from France. The ex-Minister went off to play courtier to George III. and write for Louis XVIII. the despotic proclamation with which monarchy was to be restored in France"[1]; Paine sat in the house of a real American Minister, writing proclamations of republicanism to invade the empires. So passed each to his own place.

While the American Minister in Paris and his wife were nursing their predecessor's victim back into life, a thrill of joy was passing through European courts, on a rumor that the dreaded author had been guillotined. Paine had the satisfaction of reading, at Monroe's fireside, his own last words on the scaffold,[2] and along with it an invitation of

---

[1] Morris' royal proclamations are printed in full in his biography by Jared Sparks.

[2] "The last dying words of Thomas Paine. Executed at the Guillotine in France on the 1st of September, 1794." The dying speech begins: "Ye numerous spectators gathered around, pray give ear to my last words; I am determined to speak the Truth in these my last moments, altho' I have written and spoke nothing but lies all my life." There is nothing in the witless leaflet worth quoting. When Paine was burnt in effigy, in 1792, it appears to have been with accompaniments of the same kind. Before me is a small placard, which reads thus: "The Dying Speech and Confession of the Arch-Traitor Thomas Paine. Who was executed at Oakham on Thurs-

the Convention to return to its bosom. On December 7, 1794, Thibaudeau had spoken to that assembly in the following terms :

"It yet remains for the Convention to perform an act of justice. I reclaim one of the most zealous defenders of liberty —Thomas Paine. (*Loud applause.*) My reclamation is for a man who has honored his age by his energy in defence of the rights of humanity, and who is so gloriously distinguished by his part in the American revolution. A naturalized Frenchman[1] by a decree of the legislative assembly, he was nominated by the people. It was only by an intrigue that he was driven from the Convention, the pretext being a decree excluding foreigners from representing the French people. There were only two foreigners in the Convention ; one [Anacharsis. Clootz] is dead, and I speak not of him, but of Thomas Paine, who powerfully contributed to establish liberty in a country allied with the French Republic. I demand that he be recalled. to the bosom of the Convention." (*Applause.*)

The *Moniteur*, from which I translate, reports. the unanimous adoption of Thibaudeau's motion. But this was not enough. The Committee of Public Instruction, empowered to award pensions for literary services, reported (January 3, 1795) as the first name on their list, Thomas Paine. Chenier, in reading the report, claimed the honor of having originally suggested Paine's name as an honorary citizen of France, and denounced, amid applause, the decree against foreigners under which the great author had suffered.

day the 27th of December 1792. This morning the Officers usually attending on such occasions went in procession on Horseback to the County Gaol, and demanded the Body of the Arch-Traitor, and from thence proceeded with the Criminal drawn in a Cart by an Ass to the usual place of execution with his Pamphlet called the ' Rights of Man ' in his right hand."

[1] Here Thibaudeau was inexact. In the next sentence but one he rightly describes Paine as a foreigner. The allusion to " an intrigue " is significant.

" You have revoked that inhospitable decree, and we again see Thomas Paine, the man of genius without fortune, our colleague, dear to all friends of humanity,—a cosmopolitan, persecuted equally by Pitt and by Robespierre. Notable epoch in the life of this philosopher, who opposed the arms of Common Sense to the sword of Tyranny, the Rights of Man to the machiavelism of English politicians ; and who, by two immortal works, has deserved well of the human race, and consecrated liberty in the two worlds."

Poor as he was, Paine declined this literary pension. He accepted the honors paid him by the Convention, no doubt with a sorrow at the contrasted silence of those who ruled in America. Monroe, however, encouraged him to believe that he was still beloved there, and, as he got stronger, a great homesickness came upon him. The kindly host made an effort to satisfy him. On January 4th he (Monroe) wrote to the Committee of Public Safety :

" CITIZENS : The Decree just passed, bearing on the execution of Articles 23 and 24 of the Treaty of Friendship and Commerce between the two Republics, is of such great importance to my country, that I think it expedient to send it there officially, by some particularly confidential hand ; and no one seems to be better fitted for this errand than Thomas Paine. Having resided a long time in France, and having a perfect knowledge of the many vicissitudes which the Republic has passed, he will be able to explain and compare the happy lot she now enjoys. As he has passed the same himself, remaining faithful to his principles, his reports will be the more trustworthy, and consequently produce a better effect. But as Citizen Paine is a member of the Convention, I thought it better to submit this subject to your consideration. If this affair can be arranged, the Citizen will leave for America immediately, *via* Bordeaux, on an American vessel which will be prepared for him. As he has reason to fear the persecution of the English government, should he be taken prisoner, he desires that his departure may be kept a secret.

" JAS. MONROE."

The Convention alone could give a passport to one of its members, and as an application to it would make Paine's mission known, the Committee returned next day a negative answer.

"CITIZEN : We see with satisfaction and without surprise, that you attach some interest to sending officially to the United States the Decree which the National Convention has just made, in which are recalled and confirmed the reports of Friendship and Commerce existing between the two Republics.

"As to the design you express of confiding this errand to Citizen Thomas Paine, we must observe to you that the position he holds will not permit him to accept it.   Salutation and Friendship.

"CAMBACÉRÈS." [1]

Liberty's great defender gets least of it ! The large seal of the Committee—mottoed "Activity, Purity, Attention "—looks like a wheel of fortune ; but one year before it had borne from the Convention to prison the man it now cannot do without. France now especially needs the counsel of shrewd and friendly American heads.   There are indications that Jay in London is carrying the United States into Pitt's combination against the Republic, just as it is breaking up on the Continent.

Monroe's magnanimity towards Paine found its reward.   He brought to his house, and back into life, just the one man in France competent to give him the assistance he needed.   Comprehending the history of the Revolution, knowing the record of every actor in it, Paine was able to revise Monroe's impressions, and enable him to check calumnies circulated in America.   The despatches of

[1] State Archives of France.   États Unis, vol. xliii.   Monroe dates his letter, " 19th year of the American Republic."

Monroe are of high historic value, largely through knowledge derived from Paine.

Nor was this all. In Monroe's instructions emphasis was laid on the importance to the United States of the free navigation of the Mississippi and its ultimate control.[1] Paine's former enthusiasm in this matter had possibly been utilized by Gouverneur Morris to connect him, as we have seen, with Genêt's proceedings. The Kentuckians consulted Paine at a time when expulsion of the Spaniard was a patriotic American scheme. This is shown in a letter written by the Secretary of State (Randolph) to the President, February 27, 1794.

" Mr. Brown [Senator of Kentucky] has shown me a letter from the famous Dr. O'Fallon to Captain Herron, dated Oct. 18, 1793. It was intercepted, and he has permitted me to take the following extract :—' This plan (an attack on Louisiana) was digested between Gen. Clarke and me last Christmas. I framed the whole of the correspondence in the General's name, and corroborated it by a private letter of my own to Mr. Thomas Paine, of the National Assembly, with whom during the late war I was very intimate. His reply reached me but a few days since, enclosed in the General's despatches from the Ambassador." [2]

[1] " The conduct of Spain towards us is unaccountable and injurious. Mr. Pinckney is by this time gone over to Madrid as our envoy extraordinary to bring matters to a conclusion some way or other. But you will seize any favorable moment to execute what has been entrusted to you respecting the Mississippi."—*Randolph to Monroe*, February 15, 1795.

[2] Two important historical works have recently appeared relating to the famous Senator Brown. The first is a publication of the Filson Club : "The Political Beginnings of Kentucky," by John Mason Brown. The second is : " The Spanish Conspiracy," by Thomas Marshall Green (Cincinnati, Robert Clarke & Co., 1891). The intercepted letter quoted above has some bearing on the controversy between these authors. Apparently, Senator Brown, like many other good patriots, favored independent action in Kentucky when that seemed for the welfare of the United States, but, when the situation had changed, Brown is found co-operating with Washington and Randolph.

That such letters (freely written as they were at the beginning of 1793) were now intercepted indicates the seriousness of the situation time had brought on. The administration had soothed the Kentuckians by pledges of pressing the matter by negotiations. Hence Monroe's instructions, in carrying out which Paine was able to lend a hand.

In the State Archives at Paris (*États Unis*, vol. xliii.) there are two papers marked "Thomas Payne." The first urges the French Ministry to seize the occasion of a treaty with Spain to do a service to the United States : let the free navigation of the Mississippi be made by France a condition of peace. The second paper (endorsed " 3 Ventose, February 21, 1795 ") proposes that, in addition to the condition made to Spain, an effort should be made to include American interests in the negotiation with England, if not too late. The negotiation with England was then finished, but the terms unpublished. Paine recommended that the Convention should pass a resolution that freedom of the Mississippi should be a condition of peace with Spain, which would necessarily accept it ; and that, in case the arrangement with England should prove unsatisfactory, any renewed negotiations should support the just reclamations of their American ally for the surrender of the frontier posts and for depredations on their trade. Paine points out that such a declaration could not prolong the war a day, nor cost France an obole ; whereas it might have a decisive effect in the United States, especially if Jay's treaty with England should be reprehensible, and should be approved in America.

That generosity "would certainly raise the reputation of the French Republic to the most eminent
degree of splendour, and lower in proportion that
of her enemies." It would undo the bad effects of
the depredations of French privateers on American
vessels, which rejoiced the British party in the
United States and discouraged the friends of
liberty and humanity there. It would acquire for
France the merit which is her due, supply her
American friends with strength against the intrigues of England, and cement the alliance of the
Republics.

This able paper might have been acted on, but
for the anger in France at the Jay treaty.

While writing in Monroe's house, the invalid,
with an abscess in his side and a more painful sore
in his heart—for he could not forget that Washington had forgotten him,—receives tidings of new
events through cries in the street. In the month
of his release they had been resonant with yells as
the Jacobins were driven away and their rooms
turned to a Normal School. Then came shouts,
when, after trial, the murderous committeemen
were led to execution or exile. In the early weeks
of 1795 the dread sounds of retribution subside,
and there is a cry from the street that comes nearer
to Paine's heart—" Bread and the Constitution of
Ninety-three!" He knows that it is his Constitution for which they are really calling, for they cannot understand the Robespierrian adulteration of it
given out, as one said, as an opiate to keep the
country asleep. The people are sick of revolutionary rule. These are the people in whom Paine has

ever believed,—the honest hearts that summoned
him, as author of "The Rights of Man," to help form
their Constitution.   They, he knows, had to be deceived when cruel deeds were done, and heard of
such deeds with as much horror as distant peoples.
Over that Constitution for which they were clamor-
ing he and his lost friend Condorcet had spent
many a day of honest toil.   Of the original Committee of Nine appointed for the work, six had
perished by the revolution, one was banished, and
two remained—Sieyès and Paine.   That original
Committee had gradually left the task to Paine and
Condorcet,—Sieyès, because he had no real sympathy with republicanism, though he honored Paine.[1]
When afterwards asked how he had survived the
Terror, Sieyès answered, "I lived."   He lived by
bending, and now leads a Committee of Eleven on
the Constitution, while Paine, who did not bend, is
disabled.   Paine knows Sieyès well.   The people
will vainly try for the "Constitution of Ninety-
three."   They shall have no Constitution but of
Sieyès' making, and in it will be some element of
monarchy.   Sieyès presently seemed to retire from
the Committee, but old republicans did not doubt
that he was all the more swaying it.

[1] "Mr. Thomas Paine is one of those men who have contributed the
most to establish the liberty of America.   His ardent love of humanity, and
his hatred of every sort of tyranny, have induced him to take up in England
the defence of the French revolution, against the amphigorical declamation
of Mr. Burke.   His work has been translated into our language, and is universally known.   What French patriot is there who has not already, from
the bottom of his heart, thanked this foreigner for having strengthened our
cause by all the powers of his reason and reputation?   It is with pleasure
that I observe an opportunity of offering him the tribute of my gratitude
and my esteem for the truly philosophical application of talents so distinguished as his own."—Sieyès in the *Moniteur*, July 6, 1791.

So once more Paine seizes his pen ; his hand is
feeble, but his intellect has lost no fibre of force,
nor his heart its old faith.   His trust in man has
passed through the ordeal of seeing his friends—
friends of man—murdered by the people's Convention, himself saved by accident ; it has survived the
apparent relapse of Washington into the arms of
George the Third.   The ingratitude of his faith-
fully-served America is represented by an abscess in
his side, which may strike into his heart—in a sense
has done so—but will never reach his faith in
liberty, equality, and humanity.

Early in July the Convention is reading Paine's
"Dissertation on First Principles of Government."
His old arguments against hereditary right, or in-
vesting even an elective individual with extraordinary power, are repeated with illustrations from the
passing Revolution.

" Had a Constitution been established two years ago, as
ought to have been done, the violences that have since deso-
lated France and injured the character of the revolution,
would, in my opinion, have been prevented. The nation
would have had a bond of union, and every individual would
have known the line of conduct he was to follow. But, instead of this, a revolutionary government, a thing without either
principle or authority, was substituted in its place ; virtue or
crime depended upon accident ; and that which was patriotism
one day, became treason the next. All these things have followed from the want of a Constitution ; for it is the nature and
intention of a Constitution to prevent governing by party, by
establishing a common principle that shall limit and control the
power and impulse of party, and that says to all parties, *Thus
far shalt thou go, and no farther.* But in the absence of a Constitution men look entirely to party ; and instead of principle
governing party, party governs principle.

"An avidity to punish is always dangerous to liberty. It leads men to stretch, to misinterpret and to misapply even the best of laws. He that would make his own liberty secure, must guard even his enemy from oppression ; for if he violates this duty, he establishes a precedent that will reach himself."

Few of Paine's pamphlets better deserve study than this. In writing it, he tells us, he utilized the fragment of a work begun at some time not stated, which he meant to dedicate to the people of Holland, then contemplating a revolution. It is a condensed statement of the principles underlying the Constitution written by himself and Condorcet, now included among Condorcet's works. They who imagine that Paine's political system was that of the democratic demagogues may undeceive themselves by pondering this pamphlet. It has been pointed out, on a previous page of this work, that Paine held the representative to be not the voter's mouthpiece, but his delegated sovereignty. The representatives of a people are therefore its supreme power. The executive, the ministers, are merely as chiefs of the national police engaged in enforcing the laws. They are mere employés, without any authority at all, except of superintendence. "The executive department is official, and is subordinate to the legislative as the body is to the mind." The chief of these official departments is the judicial. In appointing officials the most important rule is, "never to invest any individual with extraordinary power ; for besides being tempted to misuse it, it will excite contention and commotion in the nation for the office."

All of this is in logical conformity with the same

author's " Rights of Man," which James Madison
declared to be an exposition of the principles on
which the United States government is based. It
would be entertaining to observe the countenance
of a President should our House of Representatives address him as a chief of national police.

Soon after the publication of Paine's " Dissertation " a new French Constitution was textually submitted for popular consideration. Although in many
respects it accorded fairly well with Paine's principles,
it contained one provision which he believed would
prove fatal to the Republic. This was the limitation of citizenship to payers of direct taxes, except
soldiers who had fought in one or more campaigns
for the Republic, this being a sufficient qualification.
This revolutionary disfranchisement of near half the
nation brought Paine to the Convention (July 7th)
for the first time since the fall of the Brissotins,
two years before. The scene at his return was impressive. A special motion was made by Lanthenas and unanimously adopted, "that permission
be granted Thomas Paine to deliver his sentiments
on the declaration of rights and the Constitution."
With feeble step he ascended the tribune, and stood
while a secretary read his speech. Of all present
this man had suffered most by the confusion of the
mob with the people, which caused the reaction on
which was floated the device he now challenged.
It is an instance of idealism rare in political history.
The speech opens with words that caused emotion.

" CITIZENS, The effects of a malignant fever, with which I
was afflicted during a rigorous confinement in the Luxembourg,
have thus long prevented me from attending at my post in the

bosom of the Convention; and the magnitude of the subject under discussion, and no other consideration on earth, could induce me now to repair to my station. A recurrence to the vicissitudes I have experienced, and the critical situations in which I have been placed in consequence of the French Revolution, will throw upon what I now propose to submit to the Convention the most unequivocal proofs of my integrity, and the rectitude of those principles which have uniformly influenced my conduct. In England I was proscribed for having vindicated the French Revolution, and I have suffered a rigorous imprisonment in France for having pursued a similar line of conduct. During the reign of terrorism I was a prisoner for eight long months, and remained so above three months after the era of the 10th Thermidor. I ought, however, to state, that I was not persecuted by the *people*, either of England or France. The proceedings in both countries were the effects of the despotism existing in their respective governments. But, even if my persecution had originated in the people at large, my principles and conduct would still have remained the same. Principles which are influenced and subject to the control of tyranny have not their foundation in the heart."

Though they slay him Paine will trust in the people. There seems a slight slip of memory; his imprisonment, by revolutionary calendar, lasted ten and a half months, or 315 days ; but there is no failure of conviction or of thought. He points out the inconsistency of the disfranchisement of indirect tax-payers with the Declaration of Rights, and the opportunity afforded partisan majorities to influence suffrage by legislation on the mode of collecting taxes. The soldier, enfranchised without other qualification, would find his children slaves.

" If you subvert the basis of the Revolution, if you dispense with principles and substitute expedients, you will extinguish that enthusiasm which has hitherto been the life and soul of the revolution ; and you will substitute in its place nothing but a cold indifference and self-interest, which will again degenerate into intrigue, cunning, and effeminacy."

There was an educational test of suffrage to which he did not object. " Where knowledge is a duty, ignorance is a crime." But in his appeal to pure principle simple-hearted Paine knew nothing of the real test of the Convention's votes. This white-haired man was the only eminent member of the Convention with nothing in his record to cause shame or fear. He almost alone among them had the honor of having risked his head rather than execute Louis, on whom he had looked as one man upon another. He alone had refused to enter the Convention when it abandoned the work for which it was elected and became a usurping tribunal. During two fearful years the true Republic had been in Paine's house and garden, where he conversed with his disciples ; or in Luxembourg prison, where he won all hearts, as did imprisoned George Fox, who reappeared in him, and where, beneath the knife whose fall seemed certain, he criticised consecrated dogmas. With this record Paine spoke that day to men who feared to face the honest sentiment of the harried peasantry. Some of the members had indeed been terrorized, but a majority shared the disgrace of the old Convention. They were jeered at on the streets. The heart of France was throbbing again, and what would become of these " Conventionnels," when their assembly should die in giving birth to a government ? They must from potentates become pariahs. Their aim now was to prolong their political existence. The constitutional narrowing of the suffrage was in anticipation of the decree presently appended, that two thirds of the new legislature should be chosen from the Convention.

Paine's speech was delivered against a foregone conclusion. This was his last appearance in the Convention. Out of it he naturally dropped when it ended (October 26, 1795), with the organization of the Directory. Being an American he would not accept candidature in a foreign government.

CHAPTER X.

MONROE, in a letter of September 15th to his relative, Judge Joseph Jones, of Fredericksburg, Virginia, after speaking of the Judge's son and his tutor at St. Germain, adds :

" As well on his account as that of our child, who is likewise at St. Germain, we had taken rooms there, with the intention of occupying for a month or two in the course of the autumn, but fear it will not be in our power to do so, on account of the ill-health of Mr. Paine, who has lived in my house for about ten months past. He was upon my arrival confined in the Luxembourg, and released on my application ; after which, being ill, he has remained with me. For some time the prospect of his recovery was good ; his malady being an abscess in his side, the consequence of a severe fever in the Luxembourg. Latterly his symptoms have become worse, and the prospect now is that he will not be able to hold out more than a month or two at the furthest. I shall certainly pay the utmost attention to this gentleman, as he is one of those whose merits in our Revolution were most distinguished." [1]

Paine's speech in the Convention told sadly on his health. Again he had to face death. As when, in 1793, the guillotine rising over him, he had set about writing his last bequest, the "Age of Reason," he now devoted himself to its completion. The

---

[1] I am indebted to Mrs. Gouverneur, of Washington, for this letter, which is among the invaluable papers of her ancestor, President Monroe, which surely should be secured for our national archives.

manuscript of the second part, begun in prison, had been in the printer's hands some time before Monroe wrote of his approaching end. When the book appeared, he was so low that his death was again reported.

So far as France was concerned, there was light about his eventide. "Almost as suddenly," so he wrote, " as the morning light dissipates darkness, did the establishment of the Constitution change the face of affairs in France. Security succeeded to terror, prosperity to distress, plenty to famine, and confidence increased as the days multiplied." This may now seem morbid optimism, but it was shared by the merry youth, and the pretty dames, whose craped arms did not prevent their sandalled feet and Greek-draped forms from dancing in their transient Golden Age. Of all this, we may be sure, the invalid hears many a beguiling story from Madame Monroe.

But there is a grief in his heart more cruel than death. The months have come and gone,—more than eighteen,—since Paine was cast into prison, but as yet no word of kindness or inquiry had come from Washington. Early in the year, on the President's sixty-third birthday, Paine had written him a letter of sorrowful and bitter reproach, which Monroe persuaded him not to send, probably because of its censures on the ministerial failures of Morris, and " the pusillanimous conduct of Jay in England." It now seems a pity that Monroe did not encourage Paine to send Washington, in substance, the personal part of his letter, which was in the following terms :

" As it is always painful to reproach those one would wish to respect, it is not without some difficulty that I have taken the resolution to write to you. The danger to which I have been exposed cannot have been unknown to you, and the guarded silence you have observed upon that circumstance, is what I ought not to have expected from you, either as a friend or as a President of the United States.

" You knew enough of my character to be assured that I could not have deserved imprisonment in France, and, without knowing anything more than this, you had sufficient ground to have taken some interest for my safety. Every motive arising from recollection ought to have suggested to you the consistency of such a measure. But I cannot find that you have so much as directed any enquiry to be made whether I was in prison or at liberty, dead or alive ; what the cause of that imprisonment was, or whether there was any service or assistance you could render. Is this what I ought to have expected from America after the part I had acted towards her ? Or, will it redound to her honor or to your's that I tell the story ?

" I do not hesitate to say that you have not served America with more fidelity, or greater zeal, or greater disinterestedness, than myself, and perhaps with not better effect. After the revolution of America had been established, you rested at home to partake its advantages, and I ventured into new scenes of difficulty to extend the principles which that revolution had produced. In the progress of events you beheld yourself a president in America and me a prisoner in France : you folded your arms, forgot your friend, and became silent.

" As everything I have been doing in Europe was connected with my wishes for the prosperity of America, I ought to be the more surprised at this conduct on the part of her government. It leaves me but one mode of explanation, which is, that everything is not as it ought to be amongst you, and that the presence of a man who might disapprove, and who had credit enough with the country to be heard and believed, was not wished for. This was the operating motive of the despotic faction that imprisoned me in France (though the pretence was, that I was a foreigner) ; and those that have been silent towards me in America, appear to me to have acted from the same motive. It is impossible for me to discover any other."

Unwilling as all are to admit anything disparaging to Washington, justice requires the fair consideration of Paine's complaint.   There were in his hands many letters proving Washington's friendship, and his great appreciation of Paine's services.   Paine had certainly done nothing to forfeit his esteem.   The " Age of Reason " had not appeared in America early enough to affect the matter, even should we suppose it offensive to a deist like Washington.   The dry approval, forwarded by the Secretary of State, of Monroe's reclamation of Paine, enhanced the grievance.   It admitted Paine's American citizenship.   It was not then an old friend unhappily beyond his help, but a fellow-citizen whom he could legally protect, whom the President had left to languish in prison, and in hourly danger of death.   During six months he saw no visitor, he heard no word, from the country for which he had fought.   To Paine it could appear only as a sort of murder.   And, although he kept back the letter, at his friend's desire, he felt that it might yet turn out to be murder.   Even so it seemed, six months later, when the effects of his imprisonment, combined with his grief at Washington's continued silence (surely Monroe must have written on the subject), brought him to death's door.   One must bear in mind also the disgrace, the humiliation of it, for a man who had been reverenced as a founder of the American Republic, and its apostle in France.   This, indeed, had made his last three months in prison, after there had been ample time to hear from Washington, heavier than all the others.   After the fall of

Robespierre the prisons were rapidly emptied—
from twenty to forty liberations daily,—the one
man apparently forgotten being he who wrote, " in
the times that tried men's souls," the words that
Washington ordered to be read to his dispirited
soldiers.

And now death approaches.   If there can be any
explanation of this long neglect and silence, knowledge of it would soothe the author's dying pillow ;
and though there be little probability that he can
hold out so long, a letter (September 20th) is sent
to Washington, under cover to Franklin Bache.

"SIR,—I had written you a letter by Mr. Letombe, French
consul, but, at the request of Mr. Monroe, I withdrew it, and
the letter is still by me.   I was the more easily prevailed upon
to do this, as it was then my intention to have returned to
America the latter end of the present year (1795 ;) but the
illness I now suffer prevents me.   In case I had come, I should
have applied to you for such parts of your official letters (and
your private ones, if you had chosen to give them) as contained
any instructions or directions either to Mr. Monroe, to Mr.
Morris, or to any other person, respecting me ; for after you
were informed of my imprisonment in France it was incumbent
on you to make some enquiry into the cause, as you might very
well conclude that I had not the opportunity of informing you
of it.   I cannot understand your silence upon this subject upon
any other ground, than as connivance at my imprisonment ;
and this is the manner in which it is understood here, and will
be understood in America, unless you will give me authority
for contradicting it.   I therefore write you this letter, to
propose to you to send me copies of any letters you have
written, that I may remove this suspicion.   In the Second Part
of the "Age of Reason," I have given a memorandum from the
handwriting of Robespierre, in which he proposed a decree of
accusation against me 'for the interest of America as well as
of France.'   He could have no cause for putting America in

the case, but by interpreting the silence of the American government into connivance and consent.   I was imprisoned on the
ground of being born in England ; and your silence in not
inquiring the cause of that imprisonment, and reclaiming me
against it, was tacitly giving me up.   I ought not to have
suspected you of treachery ; but whether I recover from the
illness I now suffer, or not, I shall continue to think you
treacherous, till you give me cause to think otherwise.   I am
sure you would have found yourself more at your ease had you
acted by me as you ought ; for whether your desertion of me
was intended to gratify the English government, or to let me
fall into destruction in France that you might exclaim the
louder against the French Revolution ; or whether you hoped
by my extinction to meet with less opposition in mounting up
the American government ; either of these will involve you in
reproach you will not easily shake off.

" THOMAS PAINE."

This is a bitter letter, but it is still more a sorrowful one.   In view of what Washington had written
of Paine's services, and for the sake of twelve years
of *camaraderie,* Washington should have over-
looked the sharpness of a deeply wronged and
dying friend, and written to him what his Minister
in France had reported.   My reader already knows,
what the sufferer knew not, that a part of Paine's
grievance against Washington was unfounded.
Washington could not know that the only charge
against Paine was one trumped up by his own
Minister in France.   But, if he ever saw the letter
just quoted, he must have perceived that Paine
was laboring under an error in supposing that no
inquiry had been made into his case.   There are
facts antecedent to the letter showing that his complaint had a real basis.   For instance, in a letter to
Monroe (July 30th), the President's interest was

expressed in two other American prisoners in France—Archibald Hunter and Shubael Allen,— but no word was said of Paine. There was certainly a change in Washington towards Paine, and the following may have been its causes.

1. Paine had introduced Genêt to Morris, and probably to public men in America. Genêt had put an affront on Morris, and taken over a demand for his recall, with which Morris connected Paine. In a letter to Washington (private) Morris falsely insinuated that Paine had incited the actions of Genêt which had vexed the President.

2. Morris, perhaps in fear that Jefferson, influenced by Americans in Paris, might appoint Paine to his place, had written to Robert Morris in Philadelphia slanders of Paine, describing him as a sot and an object of contempt. This he knew would reach Washington without passing under the eye of Paine's friend, Jefferson.

3. In a private letter Morris related that Paine had visited him with Colonel Oswald, and treated him insolently. Washington particularly disliked Oswald, an American journalist actively opposing his administration.

4. Morris had described Paine as intriguing against him, both in Europe and America, thus impeding his mission, to which the President attached great importance.

5. The President had set his heart on bribing England with a favorable treaty of commerce to give up its six military posts in America. The most obnoxious man in the world to England was Paine. Any interference in Paine's behalf would

not only have offended England, but appeared as a sort of repudiation of Morris' intimacy with the English court. The (alleged) reclamation of Paine by Morris had been kept secret by Washington even from friends so intimate (at the time) as Madison, who writes of it as having never been done. So carefully was avoided the publication of anything that might vex England.

6. Morris had admonished the Secretary of State that if Paine's imprisonment were much noticed it might endanger his life. So conscience was free to jump with policy.

What else Morris may have conveyed to Washington against Paine can be only matter for conjecture; but what he was capable of saying about those he wished to injure may be gathered from various letters of his. In one (December 19, 1795) he tells Washington that he had heard from a trusted informant that his Minister, Monroe, had told various Frenchmen that "he had no doubt but that, if they would do what was proper here, he and his friends would turn out Washington."

Liability to imposition is the weakness of strong natures. Many an Iago of canine cleverness has made that discovery. But, however Washington's mind may have been poisoned towards Paine, it seems unaccountable that, after receiving the letter of September 20th, he did not mention to Monroe, or to somebody, his understanding that the prisoner had been promptly reclaimed. His silence looks as if he had not received the letter. After Edmund Randolph's resignation his successor, Pickering, suppressed a document that would have exculpated

him in Washington's eyes, and it is now among the
Pickering papers.   Paine had an enemy in Pickering.   The letter of Paine was sent under cover to
Benjamin Franklin Bache, of the *General Advertiser*, with whom as with other republicans Washington had no intercourse.   Pickering may therefore have had official opportunity to intercept it.
The President was no longer visited by his old
friends, Madison and others, and they could not
discuss with him the intelligence they were receiving about Paine.   Madison, in a letter to Jefferson
(dated at Philadelphia, January 10, 1796), says :

> " I have a letter from Thomas Paine which breathes the same
> sentiments, and contains some keen observations on the ad-
> ministration of the government here.   It appears that the neg-
> lect to claim him as an American citizen when confined by
> Robespierre, or even to interfere in any way whatever in his
> favor, has filled him with an indelible rancor against the
> President, to whom it appears he has written on the subject
> [September 20, 1795].   His letter to me is in the style of a dy-
> ing one, and we hear that he is since dead of the abscess in
> his side, brought on by his imprisonment.   His letter desires
> that he may be remembered to you."

Whatever the explanation may be, no answer
came from Washington.   After waiting a year
Paine employed his returning strength in embody-
ing the letters of February 22d and September 20th,
with large additions, in a printed *Letter to George
Washington*.   The story of his imprisonment and
death sentence here for the first time really reached
the American people.   His personal case is made
preliminary to an attack on Washington's whole
career.   The most formidable part of the pamphlet
was the publication of Washington's letter to the

Committee of Public Safety, which, departing from its rule of secrecy (in anger at the British Treaty), thus delivered a blow not easily answerable. The President's letter was effusive about the " alliance," " closer bonds of friendship," and so forth,—phrases which, just after the virtual transfer of our alliance to the enemy of France, smacked of perfidy. Paine attacks the treaty, which is declared to have put American commerce under foreign dominion. " The sea is not free to her. Her right to navigate is reduced to the right of escaping ; that is, until some ship of England or France stops her vessels and carries them into port." The ministerial misconduct of Gouverneur Morris, and his neglect of American interests, are exposed in a sharp paragraph. Washington's military mistakes are relentlessly raked up, with some that he did not commit, and the credit given him for victories won by others heavily discounted.

That Washington smarted under this pamphlet appears by a reference to it in a letter to David Stuart, January 8, 1797. Speaking of himself in the third person, he says : " Although he is soon to become a private citizen, his opinions are to be knocked down, and his character reduced as low as they are capable of sinking it, even by resorting to absolute falsehoods. As an evidence whereof, and of the plan they are pursuing, I send you a letter of Mr. Paine to me, printed in this city [Philadelphia], and disseminated with great industry." In the same letter he says : " Enclosed you will receive also a production of Peter Porcupine, alias William Cobbett. Making allowances for the asperity of an Englishman, for some of his strong and coarse expressions, and a want of official information as to many facts, it is not a bad thing."[1]   Cobbett's answer to Paine's personal grievance was really an arraignment of the President.   He undertakes to prove that the French Convention was a real government, and that by membership in it Paine had forfeited his American citizenship.   But Monroe had formally claimed Paine as an American citizen, and the President had officially endorsed that claim.   That this approval was unknown to Cobbett is a remarkable fact, showing that even such small and tardy action in Paine's favor was kept secret from the President's new British and Federalist allies.

For the rest it is a pity that Washington did not specify the "absolute falsehoods" in Paine's pamphlet, if he meant the phrase to apply to that.   It might assist us in discovering just how the case stood in his mind.   He may have been indignant at the suggestion of his connivance with Paine's imprisonment; but, as a matter of fact, the President had been brought by his Minister into the conspiracy which so nearly cost Paine his life.

On a review of the facts, my own belief is that the heaviest part of Paine's wrong came indirectly from Great Britain.   It was probably one more instance of Washington's inability to weigh any injustice against an interest of this country.   He ignored compacts of capitulation in the cases of Burgoyne and Asgill, in the Revolution ; and when

---

[1] " Porcupine's Political Censor, for December, 1796.   A Letter to the Infamous Tom. Paine, in answer to his letter to General Washington."

convinced that this nation must engage either in war or commercial alliance with England he virtually broke faith with France.[1] To the new alliance he sacrificed his most faithful friends Edmund Randolph and James Monroe; and to it, mainly, was probably due his failure to express any interest in England's outlaw, Paine. For this might gain publicity and offend the government with which Jay was negotiating. Such was George Washington. Let justice add that he included himself in the list of patriotic martyrdoms. By sacrificing France and embracing George III. he lost his old friends, lost the confidence of his own State, incurred denunciations that, in his own words, "could scarcely be applied to a Nero, a notorious defaulter, or even to a common pickpocket." So he wrote before Paine's pamphlet appeared, which, save in the personal matter, added nothing to the general accusations. It is now forgotten that with one exception—Johnson—no President ever went out of office so loaded with odium as Washington. It was the penalty of Paine's power that, of the thousand reproaches, his alone survived to recoil on his memory when the issues and the circumstances that explain if they cannot justify his pam-

---

[1] In a marginal note on Monroe's "View, etc.," found among his papers, Washington writes: "Did then the situation of our affairs admit of any other alternative than negotiation or war?" (Sparks' "Washington," xi., p. 505). Since writing my "Life of Randolph," in which the history of the British treaty is followed, I found in the French Archives (États-Unis, vol. ii., doc. 12) Minister Fauchet's report of a conversation with Secretary Randolph in which he (Randolph) said: "What would you have us do? We could not end our difficulties with the English but by a war or a friendly treaty. We were not prepared for war; it was necessary to negotiate." It is now tolerably certain that there was "bluff" on the part of the British players, in London and Philadelphia, but it won.

phlet, are forgotten. It is easy for the Washington worshipper of to-day to condemn Paine's pamphlet, especially as he is under no necessity of answering it. But could he imagine himself abandoned to long imprisonment and imminent death by an old friend and comrade, whose letters of friendship he cherished, that friend avowedly able to protect him, with no apparent explanation of the neglect but deference to an enemy against whom they fought as comrades, an unprejudiced reader would hardly consider Paine's letter unpardonable even where unjust. Its tremendous indignation is its apology so far as it needs apology. A man who is stabbed cannot be blamed for crying out. It is only in poetry that dying Desdemonas exonerate even their deluded slayers. Paine, who when he wrote these personal charges felt himself dying of an abscess traceable to Washington's neglect, saw not Iago behind the President. His private demand for explanation, sent through Bache, was answered only with cold silence. "I have long since resolved," wrote Washington to Governor Stone (December 6, 1795), "for the present time at least, to let my calumniators proceed without any notice being taken of their invectives by myself, or by any others with my participation or knowledge." But now, nearly a year later, comes Paine's pamphlet, which is not made up of invectives, but of statements of fact. If, in this case, Washington sent, to one friend at least, Cobbett's answer to Paine, despite its errors which he vaguely mentions, there appears no good reason why he should not have specified those errors, and Paine's also. By his silence, even in the confidence of friendship, the truth which might have come to light was suppressed beyond his grave. For such silence the best excuse to me imaginable is that, in ignorance of the part Morris had acted, the President's mind may have been in bewilderment about the exact facts.

As for Paine's public letter, it was an answer to Washington's unjustifiable refusal to answer his private one. It was the natural outcry of an ill and betrayed man to one whom we now know to have been also betrayed. Its bitterness and wrath measure the greatness of the love that was wounded. The mutual personal services of Washington and Paine had continued from the beginning of the American revolution to the time of Paine's departure for Europe in 1787. Although he recognized, as Washington himself did, the commander's mistakes Paine had magnified his successes ; his all-powerful pen defended him against loud charges on account of the retreat to the Delaware, and the failures near Philadelphia. In those days what "Common Sense" wrote was accepted as the People's verdict. It is even doubtful whether the proposal to supersede Washington might not have succeeded but for Paine's fifth *Crisis*.[1] The

---

[1] "When a party was forming, in the latter end of seventy-seven and beginning of seventy-eight, of which John Adams was one, to remove Mr. Washington from the command of the army, on the complaint that *he did nothing*, I wrote the fifth number of the *Crisis*, and published it at Lancaster (Congress then being at Yorktown, in Pennsylvania), to ward off that meditated blow ; for though I well knew that the black times of seventy-six were the natural consequence of his want of military judgment in the choice of positions into which the army was put about New York and New Jersey, I could see no possible advantage, and nothing but mischief, that could arise by distracting the army into parties, which would have been the case had the intended motion gone on."—Paine's Letter iii to the People of the United States (1802).

personal relations between the two had been even affectionate. We find Paine consulting him about his projected publications at little oyster suppers in his own room ; and Washington giving him one of his two overcoats, when Paine's had been stolen. Such incidents imply many others never made known ; but they are represented in a terrible epigram found among Paine's papers,— " Advice to the statuary who is to execute the statue of Washington.

> "Take from the mine the coldest, hardest stone,
> It needs no fashion : it is Washington.
> But if you chisel, let the stroke be rude,
> And on his heart engrave—Ingratitude."

Paine never published the lines. Washington being dead, old memories may have risen to restrain him ; and he had learned more of the treacherous influences around the great man which had poisoned his mind towards other friends besides himself. For his pamphlet he had no apology to make. It was a thing inevitable, volcanic, and belongs to the history of a period prolific in intrigues, of which both Washington and Paine were victims.

CHAPTER XI.

"THE AGE OF REASON."

THE reception which the "Age of Reason" met is its sufficient justification. The chief priests and preachers answered it with personal abuse and slander, revealing by such fruits the nature of their tree, and confessing the feebleness of its root, either in reason or human affection.

Lucian, in his "Ζεὺς τραγῳδός," represents the gods as invisibly present at a debate, in Athens, on their existence. Damis, who argues from the evils of the world that there are no gods, is answered by Timocles, a theological professor with large salary. The gods feel doleful, as the argument goes against them, until their champion breaks out against Damis,—"You blasphemous villain, you! Wretch! Accursed monster!" The chief of the gods takes courage, and exclaims: "Well done, Timocles! give him hard words. That is your strong point. Begin to reason and you will be dumb as a fish."

So was it in the age when the Twilight of the Gods was brought on by faith in the Son of Man. Not very different was it when this Son of Man, dehumanized by despotism, made to wield the thunderbolts of Jove, reached in turn his inevitable

Twilight. The man who pointed out the now admitted survivals of Paganism in the despotic system then called Christianity, who said, "the church has set up a religion of pomp and revenue in the pretended imitation of a person whose life was humility and poverty," was denounced as a sot and an adulterer. These accusations, proved in this work unquestionably false, have accumulated for generations, so that a mountain of prejudice must be tunnelled before any reader can approach the "Age of Reason" as the work of an honest and devout mind.

It is only to irrelevant personalities that allusion is here made. Paine was vehement in his arraignment of Church and Priesthood, and it was fair enough for them to strike back with animadversions on Deism and Infidelity. But it was no answer to an argument against the antiquity of Genesis to call Paine a drunkard, had it been true. This kind of reply was heard chiefly in America. In England it was easy for Paine's chief antagonist, the Bishop of Llandaff, to rebuke Paine's strong language, when his lordship could sit serenely in the House of Peers with knowledge that his opponent was answered with handcuffs for every Englishman who sold his book. But in America, slander had to take the place of handcuffs.

Paine is at times too harsh and militant. But in no case does he attack any person's character. Nor is there anything in his language, wherever objectionable, which I have heard censured when uttered on the side of orthodoxy. It is easily forgotten that Luther desired the execution of a

rationalist, and that Calvin did burn a Socinian.
The furious language of Protestants against Rome,
and of Presbyterians against the English Church,
is considered even heroic, like the invective
ascribed to Christ, " Generation of vipers, how can
you escape the damnation of hell !"   Although
vehement language grates on the ear of an age
that understands the real forces of evolution, the
historic sense remembers that moral revolutions
have been made with words hard as cannon-balls.
It was only when soft phrases about the evil of
slavery, which " would pass away in God's good
time," made way for the abolitionist denunciation
of the Constitution as " an agreement with hell,"
that the fortress began to fall.   In other words,
reforms are wrought by those who are in earnest.[1]
It is difficult in our time to place one's self in the
situation of a heretic of Paine's time.   Darwin,
who is buried in Westminster, remembered the
imprisonment of some educated men for opinions
far less heretical than his own.   George III.
egoistic insanity appears (1892) to have been inherited by an imperial descendant, and should
Germans be presently punished for their religion,
as Paine's early followers were in England, we
shall again hear those words that are the " half-
battles " preceding victories.

There is even greater difficulty in the appreciation by one generation of the inner sense of the

---

[1] " In writing upon this, as upon every other subject, I speak a language
plain and intelligible.   I deal not in hints and intimations.   I have several
reasons for this : first, that I may be clearly understood ; secondly, that it
may be seen I am in earnest ; and thirdly, because it is an affront to truth
to treat falsehood with complaisance."—Paine's reply to Bishop Watson.

language of a past one.   The common notion that
Paine's "Age of Reason" abounds in "vulgarity" is
due to the lack of literary culture in those—probably
few—who have derived that impression from its
perusal.   It is the fate of all genius potent enough
to survive a century that its language will here and
there seem coarse.   The thoughts of Boccaccio,
Rabelais, Shakespeare,—whose works are com-
monly expurgated,—are so modern that they are
not generally granted the allowances conceded to
writers whose ideas are as antiquated as their
words.   Only the instructed minds can set their
classic nudities in the historic perspective that
reveals their innocency and value.   Paine's book
has done as much to modify human belief as any
ever written.   It is one of the very few religious
works of the last century which survives in unsec-
tarian circulation.   It requires a scholarly perception to recognize in its occasional expressions, by
some called "coarse," the simple Saxon of Norfolkshire.   Similar expressions abound in pious
books of the time ; they are not censured, because
they are not read.   His refined contemporary
antagonists—Dr. Watson and Dr. Priestley—
found no fault with Paine's words, though the former twice accuses his assertions as "indecent."   In
both cases, however, Paine is pointing out some biblical triviality or indecency—or what he conceived
such.   I have before me original editions of both
Parts of the "Age of Reason" printed from Paine's
manuscripts.   Part First may be read by the most
prudish parent to a daughter, without an omission.
In Part Second six or seven sentences might be

omitted by the parent, where the writer deals,
without the least prurience, with biblical narratives
that can hardly be daintily touched.   Paine would
have been astounded at the suggestion of any impropriety in his expressions.   He passes over four-
fifths of the passages in the Bible whose grossness
he might have cited in support of his objection to
its immorality.   "Obscenity," he says, "in matters
of faith, however wrapped up, is always a token
of fable and imposture ; for it is necessary to our
serious belief in God that we do not connect it with
stories that run, as this does, into ludicrous inter-
pretations.   The story [of the miraculous concep-
tion] is, upon the face of it, the same kind of story
as that of Jupiter and Leda."

Another fostered prejudice supposes "The Age of
Reason" largely made up of scoffs.   The Bishop of
Llandaff, in his reply to Paine, was impressed by
the elevated Theism of the work, to portions of
which he ascribed "a philosophical sublimity."[1]
Watson apparently tried to constrain his ecclesi-
astical position into English fair play, so that
his actual failures to do so were especially misleading, as many knew Paine only as represented by
this eminent antagonist.   For instance, the Bishop
says, "Moses you term a coxcomb, etc."   But
Paine, commenting on Numbers xii., 3, "Moses
was very meek, above all men," had argued that
Moses could not have written the book, for "If
Moses said this of himself he was a coxcomb."
Again the Bishop says Paine terms Paul "a fool."
But Paine had quoted from Paul, "'Thou fool, that

---

[1] "An Apology for the Bible. By R. Llandaff" [Dr. Richard Watson].

which thou sowest is not quickened except it die.'
To which [he says] one might reply in his own
language, and say, 'Thou fool, Paul, that which
thou sowest is not quickened except it die not.'"

No intellect that knows the law of literature,
that deep answers only unto deep, can suppose that
the effect of Paine's "Age of Reason," on which
book the thirty years' war for religious freedom
in England was won, after many martyrdoms, came
from a scoffing or scurrilous work.   It is never
Paine's object to raise a laugh ; if he does so it is
because of the miserable baldness of the dogmas,
and the ignorant literalism, consecrated in the
popular mind of his time.   Through page after page
he peruses the Heavens, to him silently declaring
the glory of God, and it is not laughter but awe
when he asks, " From whence then could arise the
solitary and strange conceit, that the Almighty,
who had millions of worlds equally dependent on
his protection, should quit the care of all the rest,
and come to die in our world, because, they say,
one man and one woman had eaten an apple !"

In another work Paine finds allegorical truth in
the legend of Eden.   The comparative mythologists of to-day, with many sacred books of the
East, can find mystical meaning and beauty in
many legends of the Bible wherein Paine could see
none, but it is because of their liberation by the
rebels of last century from bondage to the petti-
ness of literalism.   Paine sometimes exposes an
absurdity with a taste easily questionable by a
generation not required like his own to take such
things under foot of the letter.   But his spirit is

never flippant, and the sentences that might so
seem to a casual reader are such as Browning
defended in his " Christmas Eve."

> " If any blames me,
> Thinking that merely to touch in brevity
> The topics I dwell on, were unlawful—
> Or, worse, that I trench, with undue levity,
> On the bounds of the Holy and the awful,
> I praise the heart, and pity the head of him,
> And refer myself to THEE, instead of him ;
> Who head and heart alike discernest,
> Looking below light speech we utter,
> When the frothy spume and frequent sputter
> Prove that the soul's depths boil in earnest ! "

Even Dr. James Martineau, whose reverential
spirit no one can question, once raised a smile in
his audience, of which the present writer was one,
by saying that the account of the temptation of
Jesus, if true, must have been reported by
himself, or "by the only other party present."
Any allusion to the devil in our day excites a smile.
But it was not so in Paine's day, when many
crossed themselves while speaking of this dark
prince.   Paine has " too much respect for the moral
character of Christ " to suppose that he told the
story of the devil showing him all the kingdoms
of the world.   " How happened it that he did not
discover America ; or is it only with *kingdoms* that
his sooty highness has any interest ? "   This is not
flippancy ; it was by following the inkstand Luther
threw at the devil with equally vigorous humor
that the grotesque figure was eliminated, leaving
the reader of to-day free to appreciate the profound significance of the Temptation.

How free Paine is from any disposition to play
to pit or gallery, any more than to dress circle, is
shown in his treatment of the Book of Jonah. It
is not easy to tell the story without exciting laughter; indeed the proverbial phrases for exaggeration,
—"a whale," a "fish story,"—probably came from
Jonah. Paine's smile is slight. He says, "it
would have approached nearer to the idea of a
miracle if Jonah had swallowed the whale"; but
this is merely in passing to an argument that miracles, in the early world, would hardly have represented Divinity. Had the fish cast up Jonah in the
streets of Nineveh the people would probably have
been affrighted, and fancied them both devils.
But in the second Part of the work there is a very
impressive treatment of the Book of Jonah. This
too is introduced with a passing smile—"if credulity could swallow Jonah and the whale it could
swallow anything." But it is precisely to this supposed "scoffer" that we owe the first interpretation
of the profound and pathetic significance of the
book, lost sight of in controversies about its
miracle. Paine anticipates Baur in pronouncing it
a poetical work of Gentile origin. He finds in it
the same lesson against intolerance contained in
the story of the reproof of Abraham for piously
driving the suffering fire-worshipper from his tent.
(This story is told by the Persian Saadi, who also
refers to Jonah: "And now the whale swallowed
Jonah : the sun set.") In the prophet mourning for
his withered gourd, while desiring the destruction
of a city, Paine finds a satire ; in the divine rebuke
he hears the voice of a true God, and one very

different from the deity to whom the Jews ascribed massacres. The same critical acumen is shown in his treatment of the Book of Job, which he believes to be also of Gentile origin, and much admires.

The large Paine Mythology cleared aside, he who would learn the truth about this religious teacher will find in his way a misleading literature of uncritical eulogies. Indeed the pious prejudices against Paine have largely disappeared, as one may see by comparing the earlier with the later notices of him in religious encyclopædias. But though he is no longer placed in an infernal triad as in the old hymn—" The world, the devil, and Tom Paine"—and his political services are now candidly recognized, he is still regarded as the propagandist of a bald illiterate deism. This, which is absurdly unhistorical, Paine having been dealt with by eminent critics of his time as an influence among the educated, is a sequel to his long persecution. For he was relegated to the guardianship of an unlearned and undiscriminating radicalism, little able to appreciate the niceties of his definitions, and was gilded by its defensive commonplaces into a figurehead. Paine therefore has now to be saved from his friends more perhaps than from his enemies. It has been shown on a former page that his governmental theories were of a type peculiar in his time. Though such writers as Spencer, Frederic Harrison, Bagehot, and Dicey have familiarized us with his ideas, few of them have the historic perception which enables Sir George Trevelyan to recognize Paine's connection with them. It must now be added that Paine's religion was of a still more

peculiar type. He cannot be classed with deists of
the past or theists of the present. Instead of being
the mere iconoclast, the militant assailant of Christian beliefs, the "infidel" of pious slang, which even
men who should know better suppose, he was an
exact thinker, a slow and careful writer, and his
religious ideas, developed through long years, require and repay study.

The dedication of "The Age of Reason" places
the work under the "protection" of its author's
fellow-citizens of the United States. To-day the
trust comes to many who really are such as Paine
supposed all of his countrymen to be,—just and
independent lovers of truth and right. We shall
see that his trust was not left altogether unfulfilled
by a multitude of his contemporaries, though they
did not venture to do justice to the man. Paine
had idealized his countrymen, looking from his
prison across three thousand miles. But, to that
vista of space, a century of time had to be added
before the book which fanatical Couthon suppressed, and the man whom murderous Barrère
sentenced to death, could both be fairly judged by
educated America.

"The Age of Reason" is in two Parts, published
in successive years. These divisions are interesting as memorials of the circumstances under which
they were written and published,—in both cases
with death evidently at hand. But taking the two
Parts as one work, there appears to my own mind a
more real division : a part written by Paine's century, and another originating from himself. Each
of these has an important and traceable evolution.

I. The first of these divisions may be considered, fundamentally, as a continuation of the old revolution against arbitrary authority. Carlyle's humor covers a profound insight when he remarks that Paine, having freed America with his " Common Sense," was resolved to free this whole world, and perhaps the other ! All the authorities were and are interdependent. "If thou release this man thou art not Cæsar's friend," cried the Priest to Pilate. The proconsul must face the fact that in Judea Cæsarism rests on the same foundation with Jahvism. Authority leans on authority; none can stand alone. It is still a question whether political revolutions cause or are caused by religious revolutions. Buckle maintained that the French Revolution was chiefly due to the previous overthrow of spiritual authority; Rocquain, that the political *régime* was shaken before the philosophers arose.[1] In England religious changes seem to have usually followed those of a political character, not only in order of time, but in character. In beginning the "Age of Reason," Paine says :

" Soon after I had published the pamphlet 'Common Sense' in America I saw the exceeding probability that a revolution in the system of government would be followed by a revolution in the system of religion. The adulterous connection of church and state, wherever it had taken place, whether Jewish, Christian, or Turkish, had so effectually prohibited by pains and penalties every discussion upon established creeds, and upon first principles of religion, that until the system of government should be changed those subjects could not be

[1] Felix Rocquain's fine work, " L'Esprit révolutionnaire avant la Révolution," has lately been well condensed and translated by Miss Hunting, of London, with an excellent introduction by Professor Huxley.

brought fairly and openly before the world ; but that whenever
this should be done a revolution in the system of religion
would follow. Human inventions and priestcraft would be
detected ; and man would return to the pure, unmixed, and
unadulterated belief of one God and no more."

The historical continuity of the critical negations
of Paine with the past is represented in his title.
The Revolution of 1688,—the secular arm transferring the throne from one family to another,—
brought the monarchical superstition into doubt ;
straightway the Christian authority was shaken.
One hundred years before Paine's book, appeared
Charles Blount's " Oracles of Reason." Macaulay
describes Blount as the head of a small school of
" infidels," troubled with a desire to make converts ;
his delight was to worry the priests by asking them
how light existed before the sun was made, and
where Eve found thread to stitch her fig-leaves. But
to this same Blount, Macaulay is constrained to
attribute emanicipation of the press in England.

Blount's title was taken up in America by Ethan
Allen, leader of the " Green Mountain Boys."
Allen's "Oracles of Reason " is forgotten ; he is
remembered by his demand (1775) for the surrender of Fort Ticonderoga, " in the name of Jehovah
and the Continental Congress." The last five
words of this famous demand would have been a
better title for the book. It introduces the nation
to a Jehovah qualified by the Continental Congress.
Ethan Allen's deity is no longer a King of kings :
arbitrariness has disappeared ; men are summoned
to belief in a governor administering laws inherent
in the constitution of a universe co-eternal with

himself, and with which he is interdependent. His
administration is not for any divine glory, but, in
anticipation of our constitutional preamble, to
"promote the general welfare." The old Puritan
alteration in the Lord's Prayer, "Thy Commonwealth come !" would in Allen's church have been
"Thy Republic come !" That is, had he admitted
prayer, which to an Executive is of course out of
place. It must not, however, be supposed that
Ethan Allen is conscious that his system is inspired
by the Revolution. His book is a calm, philosophical analysis of New England theology and metaphysics ; an attempt to clear away the ancient biblical science and set Newtonian science in its place ;
to found what he conceives " Natural Religion."

In editing his " Account of Arnold's Campaign
in Quebec," John Joseph Henry says in a footnote
that Paine borrowed from Allen. But the aged
man was, in his horror of Paine's religion, betrayed
by his memory. The only connection between the
books runs above the consciousness of either writer.
There was necessarily some resemblance between
negations dealing with the same narratives, but a
careful comparison of the books leaves me doubtful whether Paine ever read Allen. His title may
have been suggested by Blount, whose " Oracles of
Reason " was in the library of his assistant at Bordentown, John Hall. The works are distinct in
aim, products of different religious climes. Allen
is occupied mainly with the metaphysical, Paine
with quite other, aspects of their common subject.
There is indeed a conscientious originality in the
freethinkers who successively availed themselves

of the era of liberty secured by Blount. Collins, Bol-
ingbroke, Hume, Toland, Chubb, Woolston, Tindal,
Middleton, Annet, Gibbon,—each made an examination for himself, and represents a distinct chapter in the religious history of England. Annet's
" Free Inquirer," aimed at enlightenment of the lower classes, proved that free thought was tolerated
only as an aristocratic privilege; the author was
pilloried, just thirty years before the cheapening of
the " Rights of Man " led to Paine's prosecution.
Probably Morgan did more than any of the deists
to prepare English ground for Paine's sowing, by
severely criticising the Bible by a standard of civilized ethics, so far as ethics were civilized in the
early eighteenth century. But none of these writers touched the deep chord of religious feeling in
the people. The English-speaking people were
timid about venturing too much on questions which
divided the learned, and were content to express
their protest against the worldliness of the Church,
and faithlessness to the lowly Saviour, by following
pietists and enthusiasts. The learned clergy, generally of the wealthy classes, were largely deistical,
but conservative. They gradually perceived that
the political and the theological authority rested on
the same foundation. So between the deists and
the Christians there was, as Leslie Stephen says,
a " comfortable compromise, which held together
till Wesley from one side, and Thomas Paine from
another, forced more serious thoughts on the age." [1]

While " The Age of Reason " is thus, in one
aspect, the product of its time, the renewal of an

[1] " History of English Thought in the Eighteenth Century."

old siege—begun far back indeed as Celsus,—its intellectual originality is none the less remarkable. Paine is more complete master of the comparative method than Tindal in his "Christianity as old as the Creation." In his studies of "Christian Mythology" (his phrase), one is surprised by anticipations of Baur and Strauss. These are all the more striking by reason of his homely illustrations. Thus, in discussing the liabilities of ancient manuscripts to manipulation, he mentions in his second Part that in the first, printed less than two years before, there was already a sentence he never wrote; and contrasts this with the book of nature wherein no blade of grass can be imitated or altered.[1] He distinguishes the historical Jesus from the mythical Christ with nicety, though none had previously done this. He is more discriminating than the early deists in his explanations of the scriptural marvels which he discredits. There was not the invariable alternative of imposture with which the orthodoxy of his time had been accustomed to deal. He does indeed suspect Moses with his rod of conjuring, and thinks no better of those who pretended knowledge of future events; but the incredible narratives are traditions, fables, and occasionally "downright lies."

[1] The sentence imported into Paine's Part First is: "The book of Luke was carried by one voice only." I find the words added as a footnote in the Philadelphia edition, 1794, p. 33. While Paine in Paris was utilizing the ascent of the footnote to his text, Dr. Priestley in Pennsylvania was using it to show Paine's untrustworthiness. ("Letters to a Philosophical Unbeliever," p. 73.) But it would appear, though neither discovered it, that Paine's critic was the real offender. In quoting the page, before answering it, Priestley incorporated in the text the footnote of an American editor. Priestley could not of course imagine such editorial folly, but all the same the reader may here see the myth-insect already building the Paine Mythology.

" It is not difficult to discover the progress by which even simple supposition, with the aid of credulity, will in time grow into a lie, and at last be told as a fact; and wherever we can find a charitable reason for a thing of this kind we ought not to indulge a severe one." Paine's use of the word "lies" in this connection is an archaism. Carlyle told me that his father always spoke of such tales as " The Arabian Nights " as " downright lies " ; by which he no doubt meant fables without any indication of being such, and without any moral. Elsewhere Paine uses "lie " as synonymous with "fabulous "; when he means by the word what it would now imply, "wilful " is prefixed. In the Gospels he finds "inventions " of Christian Mythologists—tales founded on vague rumors, relics of primitive works of imagination mistaken for history,—fathered upon disciples who did not write them.

His treatment of the narrative of Christ's resurrection may be selected as an example of his method. He rejects Paul's testimony, and his five hundred witnesses to Christ's reappearance, because the evidence did not convince Paul himself, until he was struck by lightning, or otherwise converted. He finds disagreements in the narratives of the gospels, concerning the resurrection, which, while proving there was no concerted imposture, show that the accounts were not written by witnesses of the events ; for in this case they would agree more nearly. He finds in the narratives of Christ's reappearances,—" suddenly coming in and going out when doors are shut, vanishing out of sight and appearing again,"—and the lack of details, as to his dress, etc., the familiar signs of a ghost-story, which is apt to be told in different ways. " Stories of this kind had been told of the assassination of Julius Cæsar, not many years before, and they generally have their origin in violent deaths, or in the execution of innocent persons. In cases of this kind compassion lends its aid, and benevolently stretches the story. It goes on a little and a little further, till it becomes a most certain truth. Once start a ghost, and credulity fills up its life and assigns the cause of its appearance." The moral and religious importance of the resurrection would thus be an afterthought. The secrecy and privacy of the alleged appearances of Christ after death are, he remarks, repugnant to the supposed end of convincing the world.[1]

Paine admits the power of the deity to make a revelation. He therefore deals with each of the more notable miracles on its own evidence, adhering to his plan of bringing the Bible to judge the Bible. Such an investigation, written with lucid style and quaint illustration, without one timid or uncandid sentence, coming from a man whose services and sacrifices for humanity were great, could not have failed to give the " Age of Reason " long life, even had these been its only qualities. Four years

[1] In 1778 Lessing set forth his " New Hypothesis of the Evangelists," that they had independently built on a basis derived from some earlier Gospel of the Hebrews,—a theory now confirmed by the recovered fragments of that lost Memoir, collected by Dr. Nicholson of the Bodleian Library. It is tolerably certain that Paine was unacquainted with Lessing's work, when he became convinced, by variations in the accounts of the resurrection, that some earlier narrative "became afterwards the foundation of the four books ascribed to Matthew, Mark, Luke, and John,"—these being, traditionally, eye-witnesses.

before the book appeared, Burke said in Parliament: "Who, born within the last forty years, has read one word of Collins, and Toland, and Tindal, and Chubb, and Morgan, and the whole race who call themselves freethinkers?" Paine was, in one sense, of this intellectual pedigree; and had his book been only a digest and expansion of previous negative criticisms, and a more thorough restatement of theism, these could have given it but a somewhat longer life; the "Age of Reason" must have swelled Burke's list of forgotten freethinking books. But there was an immortal soul in Paine's book. It is to the consideration of this its unique life, which has defied the darts of criticism for a century, and survived its own faults and limitations, that we now turn.

II. Paine's book is the uprising of the human HEART against the Religion of Inhumanity.

This assertion may be met with a chorus of denials that there was, or is, in Christendom any Religion of Inhumanity. And, if Thomas Paine is enjoying the existence for which he hoped, no heavenly anthem would be such music in his ears as a chorus of stormiest denials from earth reporting that the Religion of Inhumanity is so extinct as to be incredible. Nevertheless, the Religion of Inhumanity did exist, and it defended against Paine a god of battles, of pomp, of wrath; an instigator of race hatreds and exterminations; an establisher of slavery; a commander of massacres in punishment of theological beliefs; a sender of lying spirits to deceive men, and of destroying angels to afflict them with plagues;

a creator of millions of human beings under a certainty of their eternal torture by devils and fires of his own creation. This apotheosis of Inhumanity is here called a religion, because it managed to survive from the ages of savagery by violence of superstition, to gain a throne in the Bible by killing off all who did not accept its authority to the letter, and because it was represented by actual inhumanities. The great obstruction of Science and Civilization was that the Bible was quoted in sanction of war, crusades against alien religions, murders for witchcraft, divine right of despots, degradation of reason, exaltation of credulity, punishment of opinion and unbiblical discovery, contempt of human virtues and human nature, and costly ceremonies before an invisible majesty, which, exacted from the means of the people, were virtually the offering of human sacrifices.

There had been murmurs against this consecrated Inhumanity through the ages, dissentients here and there ; but the Revolution began with Paine. Nor was this accidental. He was just the one man in the world who had undergone the training necessary for this particular work.

The higher clergy, occupied with the old textual controversy, proudly instructing Paine in Hebrew or Greek idioms, little realized their ignorance in the matter now at issue. Their ignorance had been too carefully educated to even imagine the University in which words are things, and things the word, and the many graduations passed between Thetford Quaker meeting and the French

Convention.   What to scholastics, for whom
humanities meant ancient classics, were the
murders and massacres of primitive tribes, declared
to be the word and work of God ?   Words, mere
words.   They never saw these things.   But Paine
had seen that war-god at his work.   In childhood
he had seen the hosts of the Defender of the Faith
as, dripping with the blood of Culloden and In-
verness, they marched through Thetford ; in manhood he had seen the desolations wrought " by the
grace of " that deity to the royal invader of
America ; he had seen the massacres ascribed to
Jahve repeated in France, while Robespierre and
Couthon were establishing worship of an infra-
human deity.   By sorrow, poverty, wrong, through
long years, amid revolutions and death-agonies,
the stay-maker's needle had been forged into a pen
of lightning.   No Oxonian conductor could avert
that stroke, which was not at mere irrationalities,
but at a huge idol worshipped with human sacrifices.

The creation of the heart of Paine, historically
traceable, is so wonderful, its outcome seems so
supernatural, that in earlier ages he might have
been invested with fable, like some Avatar.   Of
some such man, no doubt, the Hindu poets
dreamed in their picture of young Arguna (in the
Bhagavatgîtâ).   The warrior, borne to the battlefield in his chariot, finds arrayed against him his
kinsmen, friends, preceptors.   He bids his
charioteer pause ; he cannot fight those he loves.
His charioteer turns : 't is the radiant face of divine
Chrishna, his Saviour !   Even He has led him to
this grievous contention with kinsmen, and those

to whose welfare he was devoted. Chrishna instructs his disciple that the war is an illusion; it is the conflict by which, from age to age, the divine life in the world is preserved. " This imperishable devotion I declared to the sun, the sun delivered it to Manu, Manu to Ikshâku; handed down from one to another it was studied by the royal sages. In the lapse of time that devotion was lost. It is even the same discipline which I this day communicate to thee, for thou art my servant and my friend. Both thou and I have passed through many births. Mine are known to me; thou knowest not of thine. I am made evident by my own power : as often as there is a decline of virtue, and an insurrection of wrong and injustice in the world, I appear."

Paine could not indeed know his former births; and, indeed, each former self of his—Wycliffe, Fox, Roger Williams—was sectarianized beyond recognition. He could hardly see kinsmen in the Unitarians, who were especially eager to disown the heretic affiliated on them by opponents; nor in the Wesleyans, though in him was the blood of their apostle, who declared salvation a present life, free to all. In a profounder sense, Paine was George Fox. Here was George Fox disowned, freed from his accidents, naturalized in the earth and humanized in the world of men. Paine is explicable only by the intensity of his Quakerism, consuming its own traditions as once the church's ceremonies and sacraments. On him, in Thetford meeting-house, rolled the burden of that Light that enlighteneth every man, effacing distinctions of rank, race, sex, making all equal, clearing away privilege, whether of priest or mediator, subjecting all scriptures to its immediate illumination.

This faith was a fearful heritage to carry, even in childhood, away from the Quaker environment which, by mixture with modifying "survivals," in habit and doctrine, cooled the fiery gospel for the average tongue. The intermarriage of Paine's father with a family in the English Church brought the precocious boy's Light into early conflict with his kindred, his little lamp being still fed in the meeting-house. A child brought up without respect for the conventional symbols of religion, or even with pious antipathy to them, is as if born with only one spiritual skin ; he will bleed at a touch.

"I well remember, when about seven or eight years of age, hearing a sermon read by a relation of mine, who was a great devotee of the Church, upon the subject of what is called *redemption by the death of the Son of God*. After the sermon was ended I went into the garden, and as I was going down the garden steps, (for I perfectly remember the spot), I revolted at the recollection of what I had heard, and thought to myself that it was making God Almighty act like a passionate man, that killed his son when he could not revenge himself in any other way ; and, as I was sure a man would be hanged that did such a thing, I could not see for what purpose they preached such sermons. This was not one of that kind of thoughts that had anything in it of childish levity ; it was to me a serious reflection, arising from the idea I had, that God was too good to do such an action, and also too almighty to be under any necessity of doing it. I believe in the same manner at this moment ; and I moreover believe that any system of religion that has anything in it which shocks the mind of a child, cannot be a true system."

The child took his misgivings out into the garden ; he would not by a denial shock his aunt Cocke's faith as his own had been shocked. For many years he remained silent in his inner garden, nor ever was drawn out of it until he found the abstract dogma of the death of God's Son an altar for sacrificing men, whom he reverenced as all God's sons. What he used to preach at Dover and Sandwich cannot now be known. His ignorance of Greek and Latin, the scholastic "humanities," had prevented his becoming a clergyman, and introduced him to humanities of another kind. His mission was then among the poor and ignorant.[1] Sixteen years later he is in Philadelphia, attending the English Church, in which he had been confirmed. There were many deists in that Church, whose laws then as now were sufficiently liberal to include them. In his "Common Sense" (published January 10, 1776) Paine used the reproof of Israel (I. Samuel) for desiring a King. John Adams, a Unitarian and monarchist, asked him if he really believed in the inspiration of the Old Testament. Paine said he did not, and intended at a later period to publish his opinions on the subject. There was nothing inconsistent in Paine's believing that a passage confirmed by his own Light was a divine direction, though contained in a book whose alleged inspiration throughout he did not accept. Such was the Quaker principle. Before that, soon after his arrival in the country, when he found African Slavery supported by the Old Testament, Paine had repudiated the authority of that book; he declares it abolished by "Gospel light,"

---

[1] "Old John Berry, the late Col. Hay's servant, told me he knew Paine very well when he was at Dover—had heard him preach there—thought him a staymaker by trade."—W. Weedon, of Glynde, quoted in *Notes and Queries* (London), December 29, 1866.

which includes man-stealing among the greatest
crimes. When, a year later, on the eve of the
Revolution, he writes "Common Sense," he has
another word to say about religion, and it is
strictly what the human need of the hour demands.
Whatever his disbeliefs, he could never sacrifice
human welfare to them, any more than he would
suffer dogmas to sacrifice the same. It would have
been a grievous sacrifice of the great cause of
republican independence, consequently of religious
liberty, had he introduced a theological controversy
at the moment when it was of vital importance that
the sects should rise above their partition-walls and
unite for a great common end. The Quakers,
deistical as they were, preserved religiously the
"separatism" once compulsory; and Paine proved
himself the truest Friend among them when he was
"moved" by the Spirit of Humanity, for him at
length the Holy Spirit, to utter (1776) his brave
cheer for Catholicity.

"As to religion, I hold it to be the indispensable duty of all
governments to protect all conscientious professors thereof, and
I know of no other business which government hath to do
therewith. Let a man throw aside that narrowness of soul, that
selfishness of principle, which the niggards of all professions are
so unwilling to part with, and he will be at once delivered of his
fears on that head. Suspicion is the companion of mean souls,
and the bane of all good society. For myself, I fully and con-
scientiously believe, that it is the will of the Almighty that
there should be a diversity of religious opinions amongst us: it
affords a larger field for our Christian kindness. Were we all
of one way of thinking, our religious dispositions would want
matter for probation; and, on this liberal principle, I look on
the various denominations among us to be like children of the
same family, differing only in what is called their Christian
names."

There was no pedantry whatever about Paine, this obedient son of Humanity. He would defend Man against men, against sects and parties; he would never quarrel about the botanical label of a tree bearing such fruits as the Declaration of Independence. But no man better knew the power of words, and that a botanical error may sometimes result in destructive treatment of the tree. For this reason he censured the Quakers for opposing the Revolution on the ground that, in the words of their testimony (1776), "the setting up and putting down kings and governments is God's peculiar prerogative." Kings, he answers, are not removed by miracles, but by just such means as the Americans were using. "Oliver Cromwell thanks you. Charles, then, died not by the hands of man; and should the present proud imitator of him come to the same untimely end, the writers and publishers of the Testimony are bound, by the doctrine it contains, to applaud the fact."

Paine was a Christian. In his "Epistle to Quakers" he speaks of the dispersion of the Jews as "foretold by our Saviour." In his famous first *Crisis* he exhorts the Americans not to throw "the burden of the day upon Providence, but 'show your faith by your works,' that God may bless you." For in those days there was visible to such eyes as his, as to anti-slavery eyes in our civil war,

"A fiery Gospel writ in burnished rows of steel."

The Republic, not American but Human, became Paine's religion. "Divine Providence intends this country to be the asylum of persecuted virtue from every quarter of the globe." So he had written before the Declaration of Independence. In 1778 he finds that there still survives some obstructive superstition among English churchmen in America about the connection of Protestant Christianity with the King. In his seventh *Crisis* (November 21, 1778) he wrote sentences inspired by his new conception of religion.

" In a Christian and philosophical sense, mankind seem to have stood still at individual civilization, and to retain as nations all the original rudeness of nature. . . . As individuals we profess ourselves Christians, but as nations we are heathens, Romans, and what not. I remember the late Admiral Saunders declaring in the House of Commons, and that in the time of peace, ' That the city of Madrid laid in ashes was not a sufficient atonement for the Spaniards taking off the rudder of an English sloop of war.'. . . The arm of Britain has been spoken of as the arm of the Almighty, and she has lived of late as if she thought the whole world created for her diversion. Her politics, instead of civilizing, has tended to brutalize mankind, and under the vain unmeaning title of ' Defender of the Faith,' she has made war like an Indian on the Religion of Humanity."[1]

Thus, forty years before Auguste Comte sat, a youth of twenty, at the feet of Saint Simon, learning the principles now known as " The Religion of Humanity," Thomas Paine had not only minted the name, but with it the idea of international civilization, in which nations are to treat each other as gentlemen in private life. National honor was, he said, confused with " bullying "; but " that which is the best character for an indi-

[1] Mr. Thaddeus B. Wakeman, an eminent representative of the " Religion of Humanity," writes me that he has not found this phrase in any work earlier than Paine's *Crisis*, vii.

vidual is the best character for a nation." The
great and pregnant idea was, as in the previous
instances, occasional. It was a sentence passed
upon the " Defender-of-the-Faith " superstition,
which detached faith from humanity, and had
pressed the Indian's tomahawk into the hands of
Jesus.

At the close of the American Revolution there
appeared little need for a religious reformation.
The people were happy, prosperous, and, there
being no favoritism toward any sect under the new
state constitutions, but perfect equality and freedom, the Religion of Humanity meant sheathing of
controversial swords also. It summoned every man
to lend a hand in repairing the damages of war,
and building the new nationality. Paine therefore
set about constructing his iron bridge of thirteen
symbolic ribs, to overleap the ice-floods and quick-
sands of rivers. His assistant in this work, at
Bordentown, New Jersey, John Hall, gives us in
his journal, glimpses of the religious ignorance and
fanaticism of that region. But Paine showed no
aggressive spirit towards them. " My employer,"
writes Hall (1786), has *Common Sense* enough to
disbelieve most of the common systematic theories
of Divinity, but does not seem to establish any for
himself." In all of his intercourse with Hall (a
Unitarian just from England), and his neighbors,
there is no trace of any disposition to deprive any
one of a belief, or to excite any controversy. Humanity did not demand it, and by that direction he
left the people to their weekly toils and Sunday
sermons.

But when (1787) he was in England, Humanity gave another command. It was obeyed in the eloquent pages on religious liberty and equality in " The Rights of Man." Burke had alarmed the nation by pointing out that the Revolution in France had laid its hand on religion. The cry was raised that religion was in danger. Paine then uttered his impressive paradox :

" Toleration is not the opposite of intoleration, but the counterfeit of it. Both are despotisms. The one assumes the right of withholding liberty of conscience, and the other of granting it. The one is the pope armed with fire and faggot, the other is the pope selling or granting indulgences. . . . Toleration by the same assumed authority by which it tolerates a man to pay his worship, presumptuously and blasphemously sets itself up to tolerate the Almighty to receive it. . . . Who then art thou, vain dust and ashes, by whatever name thou art called, whether a king, a bishop, a church or a state, a parliament or anything else, that obtrudest thine insignificance between the soul of man and his maker ? Mind thine own concerns. If he believes not as thou believest, it is a proof that thou believest not as he believeth, and there is no earthly power can determine between you. . . . Religion, without regard to names, as directing itself from the universal family of mankind to the divine object of all adoration, is man bringing to his maker the fruits of his heart ; and though these fruits may differ like the fruits of the earth, the grateful tribute of every one is accepted.

This, which I condense with reluctance, was the affirmation which the Religion of Humanity needed in England. But when he came to sit in the French Convention a new burden rolled upon him. There was Marat with the Bible always before him, picking out texts that justified his murders ; there were Robespierre and Couthon invoking the God of Nature to sanction just such massacres as Marat found in his Bible ; and there were crude "atheists" consecrating the ferocities of nature more dangerously than if they had named them Siva, Typhon, or Satan.   Paine had published the rights of man for men ; but here human hearts and minds had been buried under the superstitions of ages.   The great mischief had ensued, to use his own words, "by the possession of power before they understood principles : they earned liberty in words but not in fact." Exhumed suddenly, as if from some Nineveh, resuscitated into semi-conscious strength, they remembered only the methods of the allied inquisitors and tyrants they were overthrowing ; they knew no justice but vengeance ; and when on crumbled idols they raised forms called " Nature " and " Reason," old idols gained life in the new forms.   These were the gods which had but too literally created, by the slow evolutionary force of human sacrifices, the new revolutionary priesthood.   Their massacres could not be questioned by those who acknowledged the divine hand in the slaughter of Canaanites.[1]

[1] On August 10, 1793, there was a sort of communion of the Convention around the statue of Nature, whose breasts were fountains of water. Hérault de Séchelles, at that time president, addressed the statue : " Sovereign of the savage and of the enlightened nations, O Nature, this great people, gathered at the first beam of day before thee, is free ! It is in thy bosom, it is in thy sacred sources, that it has recovered its rights, that it has regenerated itself after traversing so many ages of error and servitude : it must return to the simplicity of thy ways to rediscover liberty and equality. O Nature ! receive the expression of the eternal attachment of the French people for thy laws ; and may the teeming waters gushing from thy breasts, may this pure beverage which refreshed the first human beings, consecrate in this Cup of Fraternity and Equality the vows that France makes thee this day,—the most beautiful that the sun has illumined since it was suspended in the immensity of space." The cup passed around from lip to lip, amid fervent ejaculations. Next year Nature's breasts issued Hérault's blood.

The Religion of Humanity again issued its command to its minister. The "Age of Reason" was written, in its first form, and printed in French. "Couthon," says Lanthenas, "to whom I sent it, seemed offended with me for having translated it."[1] Couthon raged against the priesthood, but could not tolerate a work which showed vengeance to be atheism, and compassion—not merely for men, but for animals—true worship of God. On the other hand, Paine's opposition to atheism would appear to have brought him into danger from another quarter, in which religion could not be distinguished from priestcraft. In a letter to Samuel Adams Paine says that he endangered his life by opposing the king's execution, and "a second time by opposing atheism." Those who denounce the "Age of Reason" may thus learn that red-handed Couthon, who hewed men to pieces before his Lord, and those who acknowledged no Lord, agreed with them. Under these menaces the original work was as I have inferred, suppressed. But the demand of Humanity was peremptory, and Paine re-wrote it all, and more. When it appeared he was a prisoner; his life was in Couthon's hands. He had personally nothing to gain by its publication—neither wife, child, nor relative to reap benefit by its sale. It was published as purely for the good of mankind as any work ever written. Nothing could be more simply true than his declaration, near the close of life:

---

[1] The letter of Lanthenas to Merlin de Thionville, of which the original French is before me, is quoted in an article in *Scribner*, September, 1880, by Hon. E. B. Washburne (former Minister to France); it is reprinted in Remsburg's compilation of testimonies: "Thomas Paine, the Apostle of Religious and Political Liberty" (1880). See also p. 135 of this volume.

"As in my political works my motive and object have been to give man an elevated sense of his own character, and free him from the slavish and superstitious absurdity of monarchy and hereditary government, so, in my publications on religious subjects, my endeavors have been directed to bring man to a right use of the reason that God has given him ; to inpress on him the great principles of divine morality, justice, and mercy, and a benevolent disposition to all men, and to all creatures ; and to inspire in him a spirit of trust, confidence and consolation, in his Creator, unshackled by the fables of books pretending to be the word of God."

It is misleading at the present day to speak of Paine as an opponent of Christianity. This would be true were Christianity judged by the authorized formulas of any church ; but nothing now acknowledged as Christianity by enlightened Christians of any denomination was known to him. In our time, when the humanizing wave, passing through all churches, drowns old controversies, floats the dogmas, till it seems ungenerous to quote creeds and confessions in the presence of our "orthodox" lovers of man—even "totally depraved" and divinely doomed man—the theological eighteenth century is inconceivable. Could one wander from any of our churches, unless of the Christian Pagans or remote villagers *(pagani)*, into those of the last century, he would find himself moving in a wilderness of cinders, with only the plaintive song of John and Charles Wesley to break the solitude. If he would hear recognition of the human Jesus, on whose credit the crowned Christ is now maintained, he would be sharply told that it were a sin to "know Christ after the flesh," and must seek such recognition among those stoned as infidels. Three

noble and pathetic tributes to the Man of Nazareth
are audible from the last century—those of Rousseau, Voltaire, and Paine.   From its theologians
and its pulpits not one!   Should the tribute of
Paine be to-day submitted, without his name, to
our most eminent divines, even to leading American and English Bishops, beside any theological
estimate of Christ from the same century, the Jesus
of Paine would be surely preferred.

Should our cultured Christian of to-day press beyond those sectarian, miserable controversies of the
eighteenth century, known to him now as cold
ashes, into the seventeenth century, he would find
himself in a comparatively embowered land ; that
is, in England, and in a few oases in America—like
that of Roger Williams in Rhode Island.   In England he would find brain and heart still in harmony,
as in Tillotson and South ; still more in Bishop
Jeremy Taylor, "Shakespeare of divines."   He
would hear this Jeremy reject the notions of original sin and transmitted guilt, maintain the "liberty
of prophesying," and that none should suffer for
conclusions concerning a book so difficult of interpretation as the Bible.   In those unsophisticated
years Jesus and the disciples and the Marys still
wore about them the reality gained in miracle-plays.
What Paine need arise where poets wrote the creed,
and men knew the Jesus of whom Thomas Dekker
wrote :

> " The best of men
> That e'er wore earth about him was a sufferer ;
> A soft, meek, patient, humble, tranquil spirit,
> The first true gentleman that ever breathed."

Dean Swift, whose youth was nourished in that living age, passed into the era of dismal disputes, where he found the churches "dormitories of the living as well as of the dead." Some ten years before Paine's birth the Dean wrote : " Since the union of Divinity and Humanity is the great Article of our Religion, 't is odd to see some clergymen, in their writings of Divinity, wholly devoid of Humanity." Men have, he said, enough religion to hate, but not to love. Had the Dean lived to the middle of the eighteenth century he might have discovered exceptions to this holy heartlessness, chiefly among those he had traditionally feared—the Socinians. These, like the Magdalene, were seeking the lost humanity of Jesus. He would have sympathized with Wesley, who escaped from " dormitories of the living " far enough to publish the Life of a Socinian (Firmin), with the brave apology, ."I am sick of opinions, give me the life." But Socianism, in eagerness to disown its bolder children, presently lost the heart of Jesus, and when Paine was recovering it the best of them could not comprehend his separation of the man from the myth. So came on the desiccated Christianity of which Emerson said, even among the Unitarians of fifty years ago, " The prayers and even the dogmas of our church are like the zodiac of Denderah, wholly insulated from anything now extant in the life and business of the people." Emerson may have been reading Paine's idea that Christ and the Twelve were mythically connected with Sun and Zodiac, this speculation being an indication of their distance

from the Jesus he tenderly revered. If Paine rent
the temple-veils of his time, and revealed the stony
images behind them, albeit with rudeness, let it
not be supposed that those forms were akin to
the Jesus and the Marys whom skeptical criticism
is re-incarnating, so that they dwell with us.   Outside Paine's heart the Christ of his time was not
more like the Jesus of our time than Jupiter was
like the Prometheus he bound on a rock.   The
English Christ was then not a Son of Man, but a
Prince of Dogma, bearing handcuffs for all who
reasoned about him ; a potent phantasm that tore
honest thinkers from their families and cast them
into outer darkness, because they circulated the
works of Paine, which reminded the clergy that
the Jesus even of their own Bible sentenced those
only who ministered not to the hungry and naked.
the sick and in prison.   Paine's religious culture
was English.   There the brain had retreated to
deistic caves, the heart had gone off to " Sal-
vationism " of the time ; the churches were given
over to the formalist and the politician, who carried
divine sanction to the repetition of biblical oppressions and massacres by Burke and Pitt.   And in
all the world there had not been one to cry
Sursum Corda against the consecrated tyranny
until that throb of Paine's heart which brought on
it the vulture.   But to-day, were we not swayed by
names and prejudices, it would bring on that
prophet of the divine humanity, even the Christian
dove.

Soon after the appearance of Part First of the
" Age of Reason " it was expurgated of its negative

criticisms, probably by some English Unitarians, and published as a sermon, with text from Job xi., 7: "Canst thou by searching find out God? Canst thou find out the Almighty to perfection?" It was printed anonymously; and were its sixteen pages read in any orthodox church to-day it would be regarded as admirable. It might be criticised by left wings as somewhat old-fashioned in the warmth of its theism. It is fortunate that Paine's name was not appended to this doubtful use of his work, for it would have been a serious misrepresentation.[1] That his Religion of Humanity took the deistical form was an evolutionary necessity. English deism was not a religion, but at first a philosophy, and afterwards a scientific generalization. Its founder, as a philosophy, Herbert of Cherbury, had created the matrix in which was formed the Quaker religion of the "inner light," by which Paine's childhood was nurtured; its founder as a scientific theory of creation, Sir Isaac Newton, had determined the matrix in which all unorthodox systems should originate. The real issue was between a sanctified ancient science and a modern science. The utilitarian English race, always the stronghold of science, had established the freedom of the new deism, which thus became the mould into which all unorthodoxies ran. From the time of Newton, English and American thought

---

[1] "A Lecture on the Existence and Attributes of the Deity, as Deduced from a Contemplation of His Works. M,DCC,XCV." The copy in my possession is inscribed with pen: "This was J. Joyce's copy, and noticed by him as Paine's work." Mr. Joyce was a Unitarian minister. It is probable that the suppression of Paine's name was in deference to his outlawry, and to the dread, by a sect whose legal position was precarious, of any suspicion of connection with "Painite" principles.

and belief have steadily become Unitarian. The dualism of Jesus, the thousand years of faith which gave every soul its post in a great war between God and Satan, without which there would have been no church, has steadily receded before a monotheism which, under whatever verbal disguises, makes the deity author of all evil. English Deism prevailed only to be reconquered into alliance with a tribal god of antiquity, developed into the tutelar deity of Christendom. And this evolution involved the transformation of Jesus into Jehovah, deity of a "chosen" or "elect" people. It was impossible for an apostle of the international republic, of the human brotherhood, whose Father was degraded by any notion of favoritism to a race, or to a "first-born son," to accept a name in which foreign religions had been harried, and Christendom established on a throne of thinkers' skulls. The philosophical and scientific deism of Herbert and Newton had grown cold in Paine's time, but it was detached from all the internecine figure-heads called gods; it appealed to the reason of all mankind; and in that manger, amid the beasts, royal and revolutionary, was cradled anew the divine humanity.

Paine wrote "Deism" on his banner in a militant rather than an affirmative way. He was aiming to rescue the divine Idea from traditional degradations in order that he might with it confront a revolutionary Atheism defying the celestial monarchy. In a later work, speaking of a theological book, "An Antidote to Deism," he remarks: "An antidote to Deism must be Atheism." So far

as it is theological, the "Age of Reason" was
meant to combat Infidelity.   It raised before the
French the pure deity of Herbert, of Newton, and
other English deists whose works were unknown in
France.   But when we scrutinize Paine's positive
Theism we find a distinctive nucleus forming within
the nebulous mass of deistical speculations.   Paine
recognizes a deity only in the astronomic laws and
intelligible order of the universe, and in the corresponding reason and moral nature of man.   Like
Kant, he was filled with awe by the starry heavens
and man's sense of right.[1]   The first part of the
"Age of Reason" is chiefly astronomical; with
those celestial wonders he contrasts such stories as
that of Samson and the foxes.   "When we contemplate the immensity of that Being who directs
and governs the incomprehensible Whole, of which
the utmost ken of human sight can discover but a
part, we ought to feel shame at calling such paltry
stories the word of God."   Then turning to the
Atheist he says : "We did not make ourselves; we
did not make the principles of science, which we
discover and apply but cannot alter."   The only
revelation of God in which he believes is "the universal display of himself in the works of creation,
and that repugnance we feel in ourselves to bad
actions, and disposition to do good ones."   "The
only idea we can have of serving God, is that of

[1] Astronomy, as we know, he had studied profoundly. In early life he had
studied astronomic globes, purchased at the cost of many a dinner, and the
orrery, and attended lectures at the Royal Society.   In the "Age of
Reason" he writes, twenty-one years before Herschel's famous paper on the
Nebulæ : "The probability is that each of those fixed stars is also a sun,
round which another system of worlds or planets, though too remote for us.
to discover, performs its revolutions."

contributing to the happiness of the living creation
that God has made."

It thus appears that in Paine's Theism the deity
is made manifest, not by omnipotence, a word I do
not remember in his theories, but in this correspondence of universal order and bounty with reason
and conscience, and the humane heart. In later
works this speculative side of his Theism presented
a remarkable Zoroastrian variation. When pressed
with Bishop Butler's terrible argument against previous Deism,—that the God of the Bible is no more
cruel than the God of Nature,—Paine declared his
preference for the Persian religion, which exon-
erated the deity from responsibility for natural
evils, above the Hebrew which attributed such
things to God. He was willing to sacrifice God's
omnipotence to his humanity. He repudiates every
notion of a devil, but was evidently unwilling to
ascribe the unconquered realms of chaos to the
divine Being in whom he believed.

Thus, while theology was lowering Jesus to a
mere King, glorying in baubles of crown and throne,
pleased with adulation, and developing him into an
authorizor of all the ills and agonies of the world,
so depriving him of his humanity, Paine was
recovering from the universe something like the
religion of Jesus himself. "Why even of yourselves judge ye not what is right." In affirming
the Religion of Humanity, Paine did not mean
what Comte meant, a personification of the con-
tinuous life of our race[1]; nor did he merely mean

---

[1] Paine's friend and fellow-prisoner, Anacharsis Clootz, was the first to
describe Humanity as " L'Être Suprême."

benevolence towards all living creatures. He
affirmed a Religion based on the authentic divinity
of that which is supreme in human nature and distinctive of it. The sense of right, justice, love,
mercy, is God himself in man ; this spirit judges all
things,—all alleged revelations, all gods. In
affirming a deity too good, loving, just, to do what
is ascribed to Jahve, Paine was animated by the
same spirit that led the early believer to turn from
heartless elemental gods to one born of woman,
bearing in his breast a human heart. Pauline
theology took away this human divinity, and
effected a restoration, by making the Son of Man
Jehovah, and commanding the heart back from its
seat of judgment, where Jesus had set it. " Shall
the clay say to the potter, why hast thou formed me
thus ? " " Yes," answered Paine, " if the thing felt
itself hurt, and could speak." He knew as did
Emerson, whom he often anticipates, that " no god
dare wrong a worm."

The force of the " Age of Reason " is not in its
theology, though this ethical variation of Deism in
the direction of humanity is of exceeding interest
to students who would trace the evolution of avatars
and incarnations. Paine's theology was but gradually developed, and in this work is visible only as a
tide beginning to rise under the fiery orb of his
religious passion. For abstract theology he cares
little. " If the belief of errors not morally bad did
no mischief, it would make no part of the moral
duty of man to oppose and remove them." He
evinces regret that the New Testament, containing
so many elevated moral precepts, should, by lean-

ing on supposed prophecies in the Old Testament, have been burdened with its barbarities. "It must follow the fate of its foundation." This fatal connection, he knows, is not the work of Jesus; he ascribes it to the church which evoked from the Old Testament a crushing system of priestly and imperial power reversing the benign principles of Jesus. It is this oppression, the throne of all oppressions, that he assails. His affirmations of the human deity are thus mainly expressed in his vehement denials.

This long chapter must now draw to a close. It would need a volume to follow thoroughly the argument of this epoch-making book, to which I have here written only an introduction, calling attention to its evolutionary factors, historical and spiritual. Such then was the new Pilgrim's Progress. As in that earlier prison, at Bedford, there shone in Paine's cell in the Luxembourg a great and imperishable vision, which multitudes are still following. The book is accessible in many editions. The Christian teacher of to-day may well ponder this fact. The atheists and secularists of our time are printing, reading, revering a work that opposes their opinions. For above its arguments and criticisms they see the faithful heart contending with a mighty Apollyon, girt with all the forces of revolutionary and royal Terrorism. Just this one Englishman, born again in America, confronting George III. and Robespierre on earth and tearing the like of them from the throne of the universe! Were it only for the grandeur of this spectacle in the past Paine would maintain his hold on thoughtful minds.

But in America the hold is deeper than that. In this self-forgetting insurrection of the human heart against deified Inhumanity there is an expression of the inarticulate wrath of humanity against continuance of the same wrong. In the circulation throughout the earth of the Bible as the Word of God, even after its thousand serious errors of translation are turned, by exposure, into falsehoods ; in the deliverance to savages of a scriptural sanction of their tomahawks and poisoned arrows ; in the diffusion among cruel tribes of a religion based on human sacrifice, after intelligence has abandoned it; in the preservation of costly services to a deity who "needs nothing at men's hands," beside hovels of the poor who need much ; in an exemption of sectarian property from taxation which taxes every man to support the sects, and continues the alliance of church and state ; in these things, and others— the list is long—there is still visible, however refined, the sting and claw of the Apollyon against whom Paine hurled his far-reaching dart. The "Age of Reason" was at first published in America by a religious house, and as a religious book. It was circulated in Virginia by Washington's old friend, Parson Weems. It is still circulated, though by supposed unbelievers, as a religious book, and such it is.

Its religion is expressed largely in those same denunciations which theologians resent. I have explained them ; polite agnostics apologize for them, or cast Paine over as a Jonah of the rationalistic ship. But to make one expression more gentle would mar the work. As it stands, with all its vio-

lences and faults, it represents, as no elaborate or
polite treatise could, the agony and bloody sweat
of a heart breaking in the presence of crucified
Humanity.   What dear heads, what noble hearts
had that man seen laid low ; what shrieks had he
heard in the desolate homes of the Condorcets, the
Brissots ; what Canaanite and Midianite massacres
had he seen before the altar of Brotherhood,
erected by himself !   And all because every human
being had been taught from his cradle that there is
something more sacred than humanity, and to
which man should be sacrificed.   Of all those massacred thinkers not one voice remains : they have
gone silent : over their reeking guillotine sits the
gloating Apollyon of Inhumanity.   But here is one
man, a prisoner, preparing for his long silence. He
alone can speak for those slain between the throne
and the altar.   In these outbursts of laughter and
tears, these outcries that think not of literary style,
these appeals from surrounding chaos to the starry
realm of order, from the tribune of vengeance to
the sun shining for all, this passionate horror of
cruelty in the powerful which will brave a heartless
heaven or hell with its immortal indignation,—in
all these the unfettered mind may hear the wail of
enthralled Europe, sinking back choked with its
blood, under the chain it tried to break.   So long
as a link remains of the same chain, binding reason
or heart, Paine's " Age of Reason " will live.   It is
not a mere book—it is a man's heart.

CHAPTER XII.

FRIENDSHIPS.

BARON PICHON, who had been a sinuous Secretary of Legation in America under Genêt and Fauchet, and attached to the Foreign Office in France under the Directory, told George Ticknor, in 1837, that "Tom Paine, who lived in Monroe's house at Paris, had a great deal too much influence over Monroe."[1] The Baron, apart from his prejudice against republicanism (Talleyrand was his master), knew more about American than French politics at the time of Monroe's mission in France. The agitation caused in France by Jay's negotiations in England, and rumors set afloat by their secrecy,—such secrecy being itself felt as a violation of good faith—rendered Monroe's position unhappy and difficult. After Paine's release from prison, his generous devotion to France, undiminished by his wrongs, added to the painful illness that reproached the Convention's negligence, excited a chivalrous enthusiasm for him. The tender care of Mr. and Mrs. Monroe for him, the fact that this faithful friend of France was in their house, were circumstances of international importance. Of Paine's fidelity to republican principles,

[1] " Life of George Ticknor," ii., p. 113.

and his indignation at their probable betrayal in England, there could be no doubt in any mind. He was consulted by the French Executive, and was virtually the most important *attaché* of the United States Legation. The "intrigue" of which Thibaudeau had spoken, in Convention, as having driven Paine from that body, was not given to the public, but it was well understood to involve the American President. If Paine's suffering represented in London Washington's deference to England, all the more did he stand to France as a representative of those who in America were battling for the Alliance. He was therefore a tower of strength to Monroe. It will be seen by the subjoined letter that while he was Monroe's guest it was to him rather than the Minister that the Foreign Office applied for an introduction of a new Consul to Samuel Adams, Governor of Massachusetts—a Consul with whom Paine was not personally acquainted. The general feeling and situation in France at the date of this letter (March 6th), and the anger at Jay's secret negotiations in England, are reflected in it:

"MY DEAR FRIEND,—Mr. Mozard, who is appointed Consul, will present you this letter. He is spoken of here as a good sort of man, and I can have no doubt that you will find him the same at Boston. When I came from America it was my intention to return the next year, and I have intended the same every year since. The case I believe is, that as I am embarked in the revolution, I do not like to leave it till it is finished, notwithstanding the dangers I have run. I am now almost the only survivor of those who began this revolution, and I know not how it is that I have escaped. I know however that I owe nothing to the government of America. The

executive department has never directed either the former or
the present Minister to enquire whether I was dead or alive,
in prison or in liberty, what the cause of the imprisonment
was, and whether there was any service or assistance it could
render.   Mr. Monroe acted voluntarily in the case, and reclaimed me as an American citizen ; for the pretence for my
imprisonment was that I was a foreigner, born in England.

"The internal scene here from the 31 of May 1793 to the
fall of Robespierre has been terrible.   I was shut up in the
prison of the Luxembourg eleven months, and I find by the
papers of Robespierre that have been published by the Convention since his death, that I was designed for a worse fate.
The following memorandum is in his own handwriting :
'Démander que Thomas Paine soit décrété d'accusation pour
les interêts de l'Amérique autant que de la France.'

"You will see by the public papers that the successes of the
French arms have been and continue to be astonishing, more
especially since the fall of Robespierre, and the suppression
of the system of Terror.   They have fairly beaten all the
armies of Austria, Prussia, England, Spain, Sardignia, and
Holland.   Holland is entirely conquered, and there is now a
revolution in that country.

"I know not how matters are going on your side the water,
but I think everything is not as it ought to be.   The appointment of G. Morris to be Minister here was the most unfortunate
and the most injudicious appointment that could be made.   I
wrote this opinion to Mr. Jefferson at the time, and I said the
same to Morris.   Had he not been removed at the time he
was I think the two countries would have been involved in
a quarrel, for it is a fact, that he would either have been
ordered away or put in arrestation ; for he gave every reason
to suspect that he was secretly a British Emissary.

"What Mr. Jay is about in England I know not ; but is it
possible that any man who has contributed to the Independence of America, and to free her from the tyranny of the
British Government, can read without shame and indignation
the note of Jay to Grenville ?   That the *United States has no
other resource than in the justice and magnanimity of his Majesty*,
is a satire upon the Declaration of Independence, and exhibits
[such] a spirit of meanness on the part of America, that, were

it true, I should be ashamed of her. Such a declaration may suit the spaniel character of Aristocracy, but it cannot agree with manly character of a Republican.

"Mr. Mozard is this moment come for this letter, and he sets off directly.—God bless you, remember me among the circle of our friends, and tell them how much I wish to be once more among them.

"THOMAS PAINE." [1]

There are indications of physical feebleness as well as haste in this letter. The spring and summer brought some vigor, but, as we have seen by Monroe's letter to Judge Jones, he sank again, and in the autumn seemed nearing his end. Once more the announcement of his death appeared in England, this time bringing joy to the orthodox. From the same quarter, probably, whence issued, in 1793, "Intercepted Correspondence from Satan to Citizen Paine," came now (1795) a folio sheet: "Glorious News for Old England. The British Lyon rous'd; or John Bull for ever.

"The Fox has lost his Tail
The Ass has done his Braying,
The Devil has got Tom Paine."

Good-hearted as Paine was, it must be admitted that he was cruelly persistent in disappointing these British obituaries. Despite anguish, fever, and abscess—this for more than a year eating into his side,—he did not gratify those prayerful expectations by becoming a monument of divine retribution. Nay, amid all these sufferings he had managed to finish Part Second of the "Age of Reason," write the "Dissertation on Government," and give

[1] Mr. Spofford, Librarian of Congress, has kindly copied this letter for me. from the original, among the papers of George Bancroft.

the Address before the Convention.   Nevertheless
when, in November, he was near death's door,
there came from England tidings grievous enough
to crush a less powerful constitution.   It was
reported that many of his staunchest old friends
had turned against him on account of his heretical
book.   This report seemed to find confirmation in
the successive volumes of Gilbert Wakefield in
reply to the two Parts of Paine's book.   Wakefield
held Unitarian opinions, and did not defend the
real fortress besieged by Paine.   He was enraged
that Paine should deal with the authority of the
Bible, and the orthodox dogmas, as if they were
Christianity, ignoring unorthodox versions altogether.   This, however, hardly explains the extreme and coarse vituperation of these replies,
which shocked Wakefield's friends.[1]   Although in
his thirty-eighth year at this time, Wakefield was
not old enough to escape the *sequelæ* of his former
clericalism.   He had been a Fellow of Jesus College, Cambridge, afterwards had a congregation,
and had continued his connection with the English
Church after he was led, by textual criticism, to
adopt Unitarian opinions.   He had great reputation as a linguist, and wrote Scriptural expositions
and retranslations.   But few read his books, and he
became a tutor in a dissenting college at Hackney,
mainly under influence of the Unitarian leaders,

---

[1] "The office of ' castigation ' was unworthy of our friend's talents, and
detrimental to his purpose of persuading others.   Such a contemptuous
treatment, even of an unfair disputant, was also too well calculated to
depreciate in the public estimation that benevolence of character by which
Mr. Wakefield was so justly distinguished."—" Life of Gilbert Wakefield,"
1804, ii., p. 33.

Price and Priestley. Wakefield would not condescend to any connection with a dissenting society,
and his career at Hackney was marked by arrogant
airs towards Unitarians, on account of a university
training, then not open to dissenters. He attacked
Price and Priestley, his superiors in every respect,
apart from their venerable position and services,
in a contemptuous way; and, in fact, might be
brevetted a prig, with a fondness for coarse
phrases, sometimes printed with blanks. He flew
at Paine as if he had been waiting for him; his
replies, not affecting any vital issue, were displays
of linguistic and textual learning, set forth on the
background of Paine's page, which he black-
ened. He exhausts his large vocabulary of vilifi-
cation on a book whose substantial affirmations he
concedes; and it is done in the mean way of appro-
priating the credit of Paine's arguments.

Gilbert Wakefield was indebted to the excitement raised by Paine for the first notice taken by
the general public of anything he ever wrote. Paine,
however, seems to have been acquainted with a
sort of autobiography which he had published in
1792. In this book Wakefield admitted with shame
that he had subscribed the Church formulas when
he did not believe them, while indulging in flings
at Price, Priestley, and others, who had suffered for
their principles. At the same time there were
some things in Wakefield's autobiography which
could not fail to attract Paine : it severely attacked
slavery, and also the whole course of Pitt towards
France. This was done with talent and courage.
It was consequently a shock when Gilbert Wake-

field's outrageous abuse of himself came to the
invalid in his sick-room.   It appeared to be an
indication of the extent to which he was abandoned
by the Englishmen who had sympathized with his
political principles, and to a large extent with his
religious views.   This acrimonious repudiation
added groans to Paine's sick and sinking heart,
some of which were returned upon his Socinian
assailant, and in kind.   This private letter my
reader must see, though it was meant for no eye
but that of Gilbert Wakefield.   It is dated at
Paris, November 19, 1795.

"DEAR SIR,—When you prudently chose, like a starved
apothecary, to offer your eighteenpenny antidote to those who
had taken my two-and-sixpenny Bible-purge,[1] you forgot that
although my dose was rather of the roughest, it might not be
the less wholesome for possessing that drastick quality ; and if
I am to judge of its salutary effects on your infuriate polemic
stomach, by the nasty things it has made you bring away, I
think you should be the last man alive to take your own
panacea.   As to the collection of words of which you boast
the possession, nobody, I believe, will dispute their amount, but
every one who reads your answer to my 'Age of Reason'
will wish there were not so many scurrilous ones among them ;
for though they may be very usefull in emptying your gall-
bladder they are too apt to move the bile of other people.
   "Those of Greek and Latin are rather foolishly thrown
away, I think, on a man like me, who, you are pleased to say, is
'the greatest ignoramus in nature': yet I must take the
liberty to tell you, that wisdom does not consist in the mere
knowledge of language, but of things.
   "You recommend me to *know myself,*—a thing very easy to advise, but very difficult to practice, as I learn from your own book ;
for you take yourself to be a meek disciple of Christ, and yet
give way to passion and pride in every page of its composition.

[1] These were the actual prices of the books.

" You have raised an ant-hill about the roots of my sturdy
oak, and it may amuse idlers to see your work ; but neither its
body nor its branches are injured by you ; and I hope the shade
of my Civic Crown may be able to preserve your little contriv-
ance, at least for the season.

" When you have done as much service to the world by your
writings, and suffered as much for them, as I have done, you
will be better entitled to dictate : but although I know you to
be a keener politician than Paul, I can assure you, from my
experience of mankind, that you do not much commend the
Christian doctrines to them by announcing that it requires the
labour of a learned life to make them understood.

" May I be permitted, after all, to suggest that your truly
vigorous talents would be best employed in teaching men to
preserve their liberties exclusively,—leaving to that God who
made their immortal souls the care of their eternal welfare.

              " I am, dear Sir,
                      " Your true well-wisher,
                                  " THO. PAINE.
" To GILBERT WAKEFIELD, A. B."

After a first perusal of this letter has made its
unpleasant impression, the reader will do well to
read it again.   Paine has repaired to his earliest
Norfolkshire for language appropriate to the coarser
tongue of his Nottinghamshire assailant; but it
should be said that the offensive paragraph, the
first, is a travesty of one written by Wakefield. In
his autobiography, after groaning over his books
that found no buyers, a veritable " starved apothecary," Wakefield describes the uneasiness caused
by his pamphlet on " Religious Worship " as proof
that the disease was yielding to his " potion."   He
says that " as a physician of spiritual maladies "
he had seconded " the favourable operation of
the first prescription,"—and so forth. Paine, in
using the simile, certainly allows the drugs and

phials of his sick-room to enter it to a disagreeable extent, but we must bear in mind that we are looking over his shoulder. We must also, by the same consideration of its privacy, mitigate the letter's egotism. Wakefield's ant-hill protected by the foliage, the "civic crown," of Paine's oak which it has attacked,—gaining notice by the importance of the work it belittles,—were admirable if written by another ; and the egotism is not without some warrant. It is the rebuke of a scarred veteran of the liberal army to the insults of a subaltern near twenty years his junior. It was no doubt taken to heart. For when the agitation which Gilbert Wakefield had contributed to swell, and to lower, presently culminated in handcuffs for the circulators of Paine's works, he was filled with anguish. He vainly tried to resist the oppression, and to call back the Unitarians, who for twenty-five years continued to draw attention from their own heresies by hounding on the prosecution of Paine's adherents.[1] The prig perished ; in his place stood

[1] " But I would not forcibly suppress this book ["Age of Reason"] ; much less would I punish (O my God, be such wickedness far from me, or leave me destitute of thy favour in the midst of this perjured and sanguinary generation !) much less would I punish, by fine or imprisonment, from any possible consideration, the publisher or author of these pages."—Letter of Gilbert Wakefield to Sir John Scott, Attorney General, 1798. For evidence of Unitarian intolerance see the discourse of W. J. Fox on " The Duties of Christians towards Deists " (Collected Works, vol. i.). In this discourse, October 24, 1819, on the prosecution of Carlile for publishing the "Age of Reason," Mr. Fox expresses his regret that the first prosecution should have been conducted by a Unitarian. " Goaded," he says, " by the calumny which would identify them with those who yet reject the Saviour, they have, in repelling so unjust an accusation, caught too much of the tone of their opponents, and given the most undesirable proof of their affinity to other Christians by that unfairness towards the disbeliever which does not become any Christian." Ultimately Mr. Fox became the champion of all the principles of " The Age of Reason " and " The Rights of Man."

a martyr of the freedom bound up with the work
he had assailed. Paine's other assailant, the
Bishop of Llandaff, having bent before Pitt, and
episcopally censured the humane side he once
espoused, Gilbert Wakefield answered him with
a boldness that brought on him two years'
imprisonment. When he came out of prison
(1801) he was received with enthusiasm by all of
Paine's friends, who had forgotten the wrong
so bravely atoned for. Had he not died in
the same year, at the age of forty-five, Gilbert
Wakefield might have become a standard-bearer
of the freethinkers.

Paine's recovery after such prolonged and perilous suffering was a sort of resurrection. In April
(1796) he leaves Monroe's house for the country,
and with the returning life of nature his strength is
steadily recovered. What to the man whose years
of anguish, imprisonment, disease, at last pass
away, must have been the paths and hedgerows of
Versailles, where he now meets the springtide, and
the more healing sunshine of affection ! Risen
from his thorny bed of pain—

> " The meanest floweret of the vale,
> The simplest note that swells the gale,
> The common sun, the air, the skies,
> To him are opening paradise."

So had it been even if nature alone had surrounded him. But Paine had been restored by
the tenderness and devotion of friends. Had it
not been for friendship he could hardly have been
saved. We are little able, in the present day, to

appreciate the reverence and affection with which Thomas Paine was regarded by those who saw in him the greatest apostle of liberty in the world. Elihu Palmer spoke a very general belief when he declared Paine "probably the most useful man that ever existed upon the face of the earth." This may sound wild enough on the ears of those to whom Liberty has become a familiar drudge. There was a time when she was an ideal Rachel, to win whom many years of terrible service were not too much ; but now in the garish day she is our prosaic Leah,—a serviceable creature in her way, but quite unromantic. In Paris there were ladies and gentlemen who had known something of the cost of Liberty,—Colonel and Mrs. Monroe, Sir Robert and Lady Smith, Madame Lafayette, Mr. and Mrs. Barlow, M. and Madame De Bonneville. They had known what it was to watch through anxious nights with terrors surrounding them. He who had suffered most was to them a sacred person. He had come out of the succession of ordeals, so weak in body, so wounded by American ingratitude, so sore at heart, that no delicate child needed more tender care. Set those ladies and their charge a thousand years back in the poetic past, and they become Morgan le Fay, and the Lady Nimue, who bear the wounded warrior away to their Avalon, there to be healed of his grievous hurts. Men say their Arthur is dead, but their love is stronger than death. And though the service of these friends might at first have been reverential, it had ended with attachment, so great was Paine's power, so wonderful and pathetic his memories, so charming the play of his wit, so full his response to kindness.

One especially great happiness awaited him when he became convalescent. Sir Robert Smith, a wealthy banker in Paris, made his acquaintance, and he discovered that Lady Smith was no other than "The Little Corner of the World," whose letters had carried sunbeams into his prison.[1] An intimate friendship was at once established with Sir Robert and his lady, in whose house, probably at Versailles, Paine was a guest after leaving the Monroes. To Lady Smith, on discovering her, Paine addressed a poem,—"The Castle in the Air to the Little Corner of the World":

"In the region of clouds, where the whirlwinds arise,
   My Castle of Fancy was built;
The turrets reflected the blue from the skies,
   And the windows with sunbeams were gilt.

"The rainbow sometimes, in its beautiful state,
   Enamelled the mansion around;
And the figures that fancy in clouds can create
   Supplied me with gardens and ground.

"I had grottos, and fountains, and orange-tree groves,
   I had all that enchantment has told;
I had sweet shady walks for the gods and their loves,
   I had mountains of coral and gold.

"But a storm that I felt not had risen and rolled,
   While wrapped in a slumber I lay;
And when I looked out in the morning, behold,
   My Castle was carried away.

---

[1] Sir Robert Smith (Smythe in the Peerage List) was born in 1744, and married, first, Miss Blake of London (1776). The name of the second Lady Smith, Paine's friend, before her marriage I have not ascertained.

" It passed over rivers and valleys and groves,
    The world it was all in my view ;
I thought of my friends, of their fates, of their loves,
    And often, full often, of YOU.

" At length it came over a beautiful scene,
    That nature in silence had made ;
The place was but small, but 't was sweetly serene,
    And chequered with sunshine and shade.

" I gazed and I envied with painful good will,
    And grew tired of my seat in the air ;
When all of a sudden my Castle stood still,
    As if some attraction were there.

" Like a lark from the sky it came fluttering down,
    And placed me exactly in view,
When whom should I meet in this charming retreat,
    This corner of calmness, but—YOU.

" Delighted to find you in honour and ease,
    I felt no more sorrow nor pain ;
But the wind coming fair, I ascended the breeze,
    And went back with my Castle again."

Paine was now a happy man. The kindness
that rescued him from death was followed by the
friendship that beguiled him from horrors of the
past. From gentle ladies he learned that beyond
the Age of Reason lay the forces that defeat Giant
Despair.

" To reason [so he writes to Lady Smith] against feelings is
as vain as to reason against fire : it serves only to torture the
torture, by adding reproach to horror. All reasoning with
ourselves in such cases acts upon us like the reasoning of
another person, which, however kindly done, serves but to
insult the misery we suffer. If Reason could remove the
pain, Reason would have prevented it. If she could not do

the one, how is she to perform the other? In all such cases we must look upon Reason as dispossessed of her empire, by a revolt of the mind. She retires to a distance to weep, and the ebony sceptre of Despair rules alone. All that Reason can do is to suggest, to hint a thought, to signify a wish, to cast now and then a kind of bewailing look, to hold up, when she can catch the eye, the miniature shaded portrait of Hope; and though dethroned, and can dictate no more, to wait upon us in the humble station of a handmaid."

The mouth of the rescued and restored captive was filled with song. Several little poems were circulated among his friends, but not printed; among them the following:

"CONTENTMENT; OR, IF YOU PLEASE, CONFESSION. *To Mrs. Barlow, on her pleasantly telling the author that, after writing against the superstition of the Scripture religion, he was setting up a religion capable of more bigotry and enthusiasm, and more dangerous to its votaries—that of making a religion of Love.*

"O could we always live and love,
    And always be sincere,
I would not wish for heaven above,
    My heaven would be here.

"Though many countries I have seen,
    And more may chance to see,
My *Little Corner of the World*
    Is half the world to me.

"The other half, as you may guess,
    America contains;
And thus, between them, I possess
    The whole world for my pains.

"I 'm then contented with my lot,
    I can no happier be;
For neither world I 'm sure has got
    So rich a man as me.

" Then send no fiery chariot down
    To take me off from hence,
But leave me on my heavenly ground—
    This prayer is *common sense.*

" Let others choose another plan,
    I mean no fault to find ;
The true theology of man
    Is happiness of mind."

Paine gained great favor with the French government and fame throughout Europe by his
pamphlet, "The Decline and Fall of the English
System of Finance," in which he predicted the suspension of the Bank of England, which followed
the next year.   He dated the pamphlet April 8th,
and the Minister of Foreign Affairs is shown, in
the Archives of that office, to have ordered, on
April 27th, a thousand copies.   It was translated
in all the languages of Europe, and was a terrible
retribution for the forged assignats whose distribution in France the English government had considered a fair mode of warfare.   This translation
" into all the languages of the continent " is mentioned by Ralph Broome, to whom the British
government entrusted the task of answering the
pamphlet.[1] As Broome's answer is dated June 4th,
this circulation in six or seven weeks is remarkable.
The proceeds were devoted by Paine to the relief
of prisoners for debt in Newgate, London.[2]

---

[1] " Observations on Mr. Paine's Pamphlet," etc. Broome escapes the
charge of prejudice by speaking of " Mr. Paine, whose abilities I admire
and deprecate in a breath." Paine's pamphlet was also replied to by
George Chalmers (" Oldys ") who had written the slanderous biography.

[2] Richard Carlile's sketch of Paine, p. 20. This large generosity to English sufferers appears the more characteristic beside the closing paragraph of

The concentration of this pamphlet on its immediate subject, which made it so effective, renders it of too little intrinsic interest in the present day to delay us long, especially as it is included in all editions of Paine's works. It possesses, however, much biographical interest as proving the intellectual power of Paine while still but a convalescent. He never wrote any work involving more study and mastery of difficult details. It was this pamphlet, written in Paris, while " Peter Porcupine," in America, was rewriting the slanders of "Oldys," which revolutionized Cobbett's opinion of Paine, and led him to try and undo the injustice he had wrought.

It now so turned out that Paine was able to repay all the kindnesses he had received. The relations between the French government and Monroe, already strained, as we have seen, became in the spring of 1796 almost intolerable. The Jay treaty seemed to the French so incredible that, even after it was ratified, they believed that the Representatives would refuse the appropriation needed for its execution. But when tidings came that this effort of the House of Representatives had been crushed by a menaced *coup d'état*, the ideal America fell in France, and was broken in

---

Paine's pamphlet, "As an individual citizen of America, and as far as an individual can go, I have revenged (if I may use the expression without any immoral meaning) the piratical depredations committed on American commerce by the English government. I have retaliated for France on the subject of finance : and I conclude with retorting on Mr. Pitt the expression he used against France, and say, that the English system of finance ' is on the verge, nay even in the gulf of bankruptcy.' "

Concerning the false French assignats forged in England, see Louis Blanc's " History of the Revolution," vol. xii., p. 101.

fragments. Monroe could now hardly have remained save on the credit of Paine with the
French. There was, of course, a fresh accession
of wrath towards England for this appropriation
of the French alliance. Paine had been only the
first sacrifice on the altar of the new alliance ; now
all English families and all Americans in Paris
except himself were likely to become its victims.
The English-speaking residents there made one
little colony, and Paine was sponsor for them all.
His fatal blow at English credit proved the formidable power of the man whom Washington had
delivered up to Robespierre in the interest of Pitt.
So Paine's popularity reached its climax ; the
American Legation found through him a *modus*
vivendi with the French government ; the families
which had received and nursed him in his weakness found in his intimacy their best credential.
Mrs. Joel Barlow especially, while her husband was
in Algeria, on the service of the American government, might have found her stay in Paris unpleasant but for Paine's friendship. The importance of
his guarantee to the banker, Sir Robert Smith,
appears by the following note, written at Versailles,
August 13th :

"CITIZEN MINISTER : The citizen Robert Smith, a very
particular friend of mine, wishes to obtain a passport to go to
Hamburg, and I will be obliged to you to do him that favor.
Himself and family have lived several years in France, for he
likes neither the government nor the climate of England. He
has large property in England, but his Banker in that country
has refused sending him remittances. This makes it necessary
for him to go to Hamburg, because from there he can draw

his money out of his Banker's hands, which he cannot do
whilst in France. His family remains in France.—*Salut et
fraternité.*

"THOMAS PAINE." [1]

Amid his circle of cultured and kindly friends
Paine had dreamed of a lifting of the last cloud
from his life, so long overcast. His eyes were
strained to greet that shining sail that should bring
him a response to his letter of September to Washington, in his heart being a great hope that his
apparent wrong would be explained as a miserable
mistake, and that old friendship restored. As
the reader knows, the hope was grievously disappointed. The famous public letter to Washington
(August 3d), which was not published in France,
has already been considered, in advance of its
chronological place. It will be found, however, of
more significance if read in connection with the
unhappy situation, in which all of Paine's friends,
and all Americans in Paris, had been brought by
the Jay treaty. From their point of view the deliverance of Paine to prison and the guillotine was
only one incident in a long-planned and systematic
treason, aimed at the life of the French republic.
Jefferson in America, and Paine in France, represented the faith and hope of republicans that the
treason would be overtaken by retribution and
reversal.

[1] Soon after Jefferson became President Paine wrote to him, suggesting
that Sir Robert's firm might be safely depended on as the medium of American financial transactions in Europe.

CHAPTER XIII.

THEOPHILANTHROPY.

In the ever-recurring controversies concerning Paine and his "Age of Reason" we have heard many triumphal claims. Christianity and the Church, it is said, have advanced and expanded, unharmed by such criticisms. This is true. But there are several fallacies implied in this mode of dealing with the religious movement caused by Paine's work. It assumes that Paine was an enemy of all that now passes under the name of Christianity—a title claimed by nearly a hundred and fifty different organizations, with some of which (as the Unitarians, Universalists, Broad Church, and Hicksite Friends) he would largely sympathize. It further assumes that he was hostile to all churches, and desired or anticipated their destruction. Such is not the fact. Paine desired and anticipated their reformation, which has steadily progressed. At the close of the "Age of Reason" he exhorts the clergy to "preach something that is edifying, and from texts that are known to be true."

"The Bible of the creation is inexhaustible in texts. Every part of science, whether connected with the geometry of the universe, with the systems of animal and vegetable life, or with the properties of inanimate matter, is a text for devotion as well as for philosophy—for gratitude as for human improve-

ment.   It will perhaps be said, that, if such a revolution in the
system of religion takes place, every preacher ought to be a
philosopher.   *Most certainly.*   And every house of devotion a
school of science.   It has been by wandering from the immut-
able laws of science, and the right use of reason, and setting
up an invented thing called revealed religion, that so many
wild and blasphemous conceits nave been formed of the Almighty.   The Jews have made him the assassin of the human
species, to make room for the religion of the Jews.   The
Christians have made him the murderer of himself, and the
founder of a new religion, to supersede and expel the Jewish
religion.   And to find pretence and admission for these things
they must have supposed his power and his wisdom imperfect,
or his will changeable ; and the changeableness of the will is
the imperfection of the judgment.   The philosopher knows
that the laws of the Creator have never changed with respect
either to the principles of science, or the properties of matter.
Why then is it to be supposed they have changed with respect
to man ? "

To the statement that Christianity has not been
impeded by the " Age of Reason," it should be
added that its advance has been largely due to
modifications rendered necessary by that work.
The unmodified dogmas are represented in small
and eccentric communities.   The advance has been
under the Christian name, with which Paine had no
concern ; but to confuse the word " Christianity "
with the substance it labels is inadmissible.   England wears the device of St. George and the Dragon ;
but English culture has reduced the saint and
dragon to a fable.

The special wrath with which Paine is still visited,
above all other deists put together, or even atheists,
is a tradition from a so-called Christianity which his
work compelled to capitulate.   That system is now

nearly extinct, and the *vendetta* it bequeathed should now end. The capitulation began immediately with the publication of the Bishop of Llandaff's " Apology for the Bible," a title that did not fail to attract notice when it appeared (1796). There were more than thirty replies to Paine, but they are mainly taken out of the Bishop's "Apology," to which they add nothing. It is said in religious encyclopedias that Paine was "answered" by one and another writer, but in a strict sense Paine was never answered, unless by the successive surrenders referred to. As Bishop Watson's "Apology" is adopted by most authorities as the sufficient "answer," it may be here accepted as a representative of the rest. Whether Paine's points dealt with by the Bishop are answerable or not, the following facts will prove how uncritical is the prevalent opinion that they were really answered.

Dr. Watson concedes generally to Paine the discovery of some "real difficulties" in the Old Testament, and the exposure, in the Christian grove, of "a few unsightly shrubs, which good men had wisely concealed from public view" (p. 44).[1] It is not Paine that here calls some "sacred" things unsightly, and charges the clergy with concealing them—it is the Bishop. Among the particular and direct concessions made by the Bishop are the following :

1. That Moses may not have written every part of the Pentateuch. Some passages were probably written by later hands, transcribers or editors (pp.

---

[1] Carey's edition, Philadelphia, 1796.

9–11, 15). [If human reason and scholarship are admitted to detach any portions, by what authority can they be denied the right to bring all parts of the Pentateuch, or even the whole Bible, under their human judgment?]

2. The law in Deuteronomy giving parents the right, under certain circumstances, to have their children stoned to death, is excused only as a " humane restriction of a power improper to be lodged with any parent " (p. 13). [Granting the Bishop's untrue assertion, that the same " improper " power was arbitrary among the Romans, Gauls, and Persians, why should it not have been abolished in Israel? And if Dr. Watson possessed the right to call any law established in the Bible "improper," how can Paine be denounced for subjecting other things in the book to moral condemnation? The moral sentiment is not an episcopal prerogative.]

3. The Bishop agrees that it is " the opinion of many learned men and good Christians " that the Bible, though authoritative in religion, is fallible in other respects, "relating the ordinary history of the times " (p. 23). [What but human reason, in the absence of papal authority, is to draw the line between the historical and religious elements in the Bible?]

4. It is conceded that "Samuel did not write any part of the second book bearing his name, and only a part of the first " (p. 24). [One of many blows dealt by this prelate at confidence in the Bible.]

5. It is admitted that Ezra contains a contradiction in the estimate of the numbers who returned from Babylon ; it is attributed to a transcriber's

mistake of one Hebrew figure for another (p. 30).
[Paine's question here had been: "What certainty
then can there be in the Bible for anything"? It
is no answer to tell him how an error involving a
difference of 12,542 people may perhaps have occurred.]

5. It is admitted that David did not write some
of the Psalms ascribed to him (p. 131).

7. "It is acknowledged that the order of time is
not everywhere observed" [in Jeremiah]; also that
this prophet, fearing for his life, suppressed the
truth [as directed by King Zedekiah]. "He was
under no obligation to tell the whole [truth] to
men who were certainly his enemies and no good
subjects of the king" (pp. 36, 37). [But how can
it be determined how much in Jeremiah is the
"word of God," and how much uttered for the
casual advantage of himself or his king?]

8. It is admitted that there was no actual fulfilment of Ezekiel's prophecy, "No foot of man shall
pass through it [Egypt], nor foot of beast shall
pass through it, for forty years" (p. 42).

9. The discrepancies between the genealogies of
Christ, in Matthew and Luke, are admitted : they
are explained by saying that Matthew gives the
genealogy of Joseph, and Luke that of Mary ; and
that Matthew commits "an error" in omitting three
generations between Joram and Ozias (p. 48.)
[Paine had asked, why might not writers mistaken
in the natural genealogy of Christ be mistaken also
in his celestial genealogy? To this no answer was
attempted.]

Such are some of the Bishop's direct admissions.

There are other admissions in his silences and evasions. For instance, having elaborated a theory as
to how the error in Ezra might occur, by the close
resemblance of Hebrew letters representing widely
different numbers, he does not notice Nehemiah's
error in the same matter, pointed out by Paine,—
a self-contradiction, and also a discrepancy with
Ezra, which could not be explained by his theory.
He says nothing about several other contradictions
alluded to by Paine. The Bishop's evasions are
sometimes painful, as when he tries to escape the
force of Paine's argument, that Paul himself was
not convinced by the evidences of the resurrection
which he adduces for others. The Bishop says:
" That Paul had so far resisted the evidence which
the apostles had given of the resurrection and
ascension of Jesus, as to be a persecutor of the disciples of Christ, is certain ; but I do not remember
the place where he declares that he had not believed
them." But when Paul says, " I verily thought
with myself that I ought to do many things contrary to the name of Jesus of Nazareth," surely
this is inconsistent with his belief in the resurrection and ascension. Paul declares that when it
was the good pleasure of God "to reveal his Son
in me," immediately he entered on his mission.
He " was not disobedient to the heavenly vision."
Clearly then Paul had not been convinced of the
resurrection and ascension until he saw Christ in a
vision.

In dealing with Paine's moral charges against
the Bible the Bishop has left a confirmation of all
that I have said concerning the Christianity of his

time. An "infidel" of to-day could need no better moral arguments against the Bible than those framed by the Bishop in its defence. He justifies the massacre of the Canaanites on the ground that they were sacrificers of their own children to idols, cannibals, addicted to unnatural lust. Were this true it would be no justification; but as no particle of evidence is adduced in support of these utterly unwarranted and entirely fictitious accusations, the argument now leaves the massacre without any excuse at all. The extermination is not in the Bible based on any such considerations, but simply on a divine command to seize the land and slay its inhabitants. No legal right to the land is suggested in the record; and, as for morality, the only persons spared in Joshua's expedition were a harlot and her household, she having betrayed her country to the invaders, to be afterwards exalted into an ancestress of Christ. Of the cities destroyed by Joshua it is said: "It was of Jehovah to harden their hearts, to come against Israel in battle, that he might utterly destroy them, that they might have no favor, but that he might destroy them, as Jehovah commanded Moses" (Joshua xi., 20). As their hearts were thus in Jehovah's power for hardening, it may be inferred that they were equally in his power for reformation, had they been guilty of the things alleged by the Bishop. With these things before him, and the selection of Rahab for mercy above all the women in Jericho— every woman slain save the harlot who delivered them up to slaughter—the Bishop says: "The destruction of the Canaanites exhibits to all nations,

in all ages, a signal proof of God's displeasure
against sin."

The Bishop rages against Paine for supposing
that the commanded preservation of the Midianite
maidens, when all males and married women were
slain, was for their " debauchery."

"Prove this, and I will allow that Moses was the horrid
monster you make him—prove this, and I will allow that the
Bible is what you call it—'a book of lies, wickedness, and
blasphemy'—prove this, or excuse my warmth if I say to you,
as Paul said to Elymas the sorcerer, who sought to turn away
Sergius Paulus from the faith, ' O full of all subtilty, and of all
mischief, thou child of the devil, thou enemy of all righteous-
ness, wilt thou not cease to pervert the right ways of the
Lord ?'—I did not, when I began these letters, think that I
should have been moved to this severity of rebuke, by anything you could have written ; but when so gross a misrepresentation is made of God's proceedings, coolness would be a
crime."

And what does my reader suppose is the alternative claimed by the prelate's foaming mouth ? The
maidens, he declares, were not reserved for debauchery, but for slavery !

Little did the Bishop foresee a time when, of
the two suppositions, Paine's might be deemed the
more lenient. The subject of slavery was then
under discussion in England, and the Bishop is
constrained to add, concerning this enslavement of
thirty-two thousand maidens, from the massacred
families, that slavery is "a custom abhorrent from
our manners, but everywhere practised in former times, and still practised in countries where
the benignity of the Christian religion has not
softened the ferocity of human nature." Thus,
Jehovah is represented as not only ordering the

wholesale murder of the worshippers of another
deity, but an adoption of their "abhorrent" and
inhuman customs.

This connection of the deity of the Bible with
"the ferocity of human nature" in one place, and
its softening in another, justified Paine's solemn
rebuke to the clergy of his time.

"Had the cruel and murderous orders with which the Bible
is filled, and the numberless torturing executions of men,
women, and children, in consequence of those orders, been
ascribed to some friend whose memory you revered, you
would have glowed with satisfaction at detecting the falsehood of the charge, and gloried in defending his injured fame.
It is because ye are sunk in the cruelty of superstition, or feel
no interest in the honor of your Creator, that ye listen to the
horrid tales of the Bible, or hear them with callous indifference."

This is fundamentally what the Bishop has to
answer, and of course he must resort to the terrible
Tu quoque of Bishop Butler. Dr. Watson says he
is astonished that "so acute a reasoner" should
reproduce the argument.

"You profess yourself to be a deist, and to believe that
there is a God, who created the universe, and established the
laws of nature, by which it is sustained in existence. You
profess that from a contemplation of the works of God you
derive a knowledge of his attributes; and you reject the
Bible because it ascribes to God things inconsistent (as you
suppose) with the attributes which you have discovered to
belong to him; in particular, you think it repugnant to his
moral justice that he should doom to destruction the crying
and smiling infants of the Canaanites. Why do you not maintain it to be repugnant to his moral justice that he should
suffer crying or smiling infants to be swallowed up by an
earthquake, drowned by an inundation, consumed by fire,
starved by a famine, or destroyed by a pestilence?"

Dr. Watson did not, of course, know that he was following Bishop Butler in laying the foundations of atheism, though such was the case. As was said in my chapter on the "Age of Reason," this dilemma did not really apply to Paine. His deity was inferred, despite all the disorders in nature, exclusively from its apprehensible order without, and from the reason and moral nature of man. He had not dealt with the problem of evil, except implicitly, in his defence of the divine goodness, which is inconsistent with the responsibility of his deity for natural evils, or for anything that would be condemned by reason and conscience if done by man. It was thus the Christian prelate who had abandoned the primitive faith in the divine humanity for a natural deism, while the man he calls a "child of the devil" was defending the divine humanity.

This then was the way in which Paine was "answered," for I am not aware of any important addition to the Bishop's "Apology" by other opponents. I cannot see how any Christian of the present time can regard it otherwise than as a capitulation of the system it was supposed to defend, however secure he may regard the Christianity of to-day. It subjects the Bible to the judgment of human reason for the determination of its authorship, the integrity of its text, and the correction of admitted errors in authorship, chronology, and genealogy ; it admits the fallibility of the writers in matters of fact ; it admits that some of the moral laws of the Old Testament are "improper" and others, like slavery, belonging to "the ferocity of human nature " ; it admits the non-fulfilment of one prophet's prediction, and the self-interested suppression of truth by another; and it admits that "good men" were engaged in concealing these "unsightly" things.　Here are gates thrown open for the whole "Age of Reason."

The unorthodoxy of the Bishop's "Apology" does not rest on the judgment of the present writer alone.　If Gilbert Wakefield presently had to reflect on his denunciations of Paine from the inside of a prison, the Bishop of Llandaff had occasion to appreciate Paine's ideas on "mental lying" as the Christian infidelity.　The Bishop, born in the same year (1737) with the two heretics he attacked— Gibbon and Paine—began his career as a professor of chemistry at Cambridge (1764), but seven years later became Regius professor of divinity there. His posthumous papers present a remarkable picture of the church in his time.　In replying to Gibbon he studied first principles, and assumed a brave stand against all intellectual and religious coercion. On the episcopal bench he advocated a liberal policy toward France.　In undertaking to answer Paine he became himself unsettled ; and at the very moment when unsophisticated orthodoxy was hailing him as its champion, the sagacious magnates of Church and State proscribed him.　He learned that the king had described him as "impracticable" ; with bitterness of soul he saw prelates of inferior rank and ability promoted over his head.　He tried the effect of a political recantation, in one of his charges ; and when Williams was imprisoned for publishing the "Age of Reason," and Gilbert Wakefield for rebuking his "Charge," this former

champion of free speech dared not utter a protest.
But by this servility he gained nothing. He seems
to have at length made up his mind that if he was
to be punished for his liberalism he would enjoy it.
While preaching on " Revealed Religion " he saw
the Bishop of London shaking his head. In 1811,
five years before his death, he writes this significant
note : " I have treated my divinity as I, twenty-
five years ago, treated my chemical papers : I have
lighted my fire with the labour of a great portion
of my life." [1]

Next to the " Age of Reason," the book that
did most to advance Paine's principles in England was, as I believe, Dr. Watson's " Apology for
the Bible."   Dean Swift had warned the clergy that
if they began to reason with objectors to the creeds
they would awaken skepticism. Dr. Watson fulfilled this prediction. He pointed out, as Gilbert
Wakefield did, some exegetical and verbal errors
in Paine's book, but they no more affected its main
purpose and argument than the grammatical mistakes in " Common Sense " diminished its force in the
American Revolution. David Dale, the great manu-

[1] Patrick Henry's Answer to the " Age of Reason " shared the like fate.
" When, during the first two years of his retirement, Thomas Paine's
'Age of Reason' made its appearance, the old statesman was moved
to write out a somewhat elaborate treatise in defence of the truth of
Christianity. This treatise it was his purpose to have published. ' He read
the manuscript to his family as he progressed with it, and completed it a
short time before his death' [1799]. When it was finished, however, ' being diffident about his own work,' and impressed also by the great ability of
the replies to Paine which were then appearing in England, ' he directed his
wife to destroy' what he had written. She ' complied literally with his
directions,' and thus put beyond the chance of publication a work which
seemed, to some who heard it, ' the most eloquent and unanswerable argument in defence of the Bible which was ever written.' "—Fontaine MS.
quoted in Tyler's " Patrick Henry."

facturer at Paisley, distributed three thousand copies of the "Apology" among his workmen. The books carried among them extracts from Paine, and the Bishop's admissions. Robert Owen married Dale's daughter, and presently found the Paisley workmen a ripe harvest for his rationalism and radicalism.

Thus, in the person of its first clerical assailant, began the march of the "Age of Reason" in England. In the Bishop's humiliations for his concessions to truth, were illustrated what Paine had said of his system's falsity and fraudulence. After the Bishop had observed the Bishop of London manifesting disapproval of his sermon on "Revealed Religion" he went home and wrote: "What is this thing called Orthodoxy, which mars the fortunes of honest men? It is a sacred thing to which every denomination of Christians lays exclusive claim, but to which no man, no assembly of men, since the apostolic age, can prove a title." There is now a Bishop of London who might not acknowledge the claim even for the apostolic age. The principles, apart from the particular criticisms, of Paine's book have established themselves in the English Church. They were affirmed by Bishop Wilson in clear language: "Christian duties are founded on reason, not on the sovereignty of God commanding what he pleases: God cannot command us what is not fit to be believed or done, all his commands being founded in the necessities of our nature." It was on this principle that Paine declared that things in the Bible, "not fit to be believed or done," could not be divine commands.

His book, like its author, was outlawed, but men
more heretical are now buried in Westminster Ab-
bey, and the lost bones of Thomas Paine are really
reposing in those tombs. It was he who compelled
the hard and heartless Bibliolatry of his time to
repair to illiterate conventicles, and the lovers of
humanity, true followers of the man of Nazareth,
to abandon the crumbling castle of dogma, preserving its creeds as archaic bric-a-brac. As his " Rights
of Man " is now the political constitution of England, his " Age of Reason" is in the growing constitution of its Church,—the most powerful organization in Christendom because the freest and most
inclusive.

The excitement caused in England by the "Age
of Reason," and the large number of attempted
replies to it, were duly remarked by the *Moniteur*
and other French journals. The book awakened
much attention in France, and its principles were
reproduced in a little French book entitled " A
Manual of the Theoantropophiles." This appeared
in September, 1796. In January, 1797, Paine, with
five families, founded in Paris the church of Theophilanthropy,—a word, as he stated in a letter to
Erskine " compounded of three Greek words, signi-
fying God, Love, and Man. The explanation given
to this word is *Lovers of God and Man,* or *Adorers
of God and Friends of Man."* The society opened
" in the street Denis, No. 34, corner of Lombard
Street." " The Theophilanthropists believe in the
existence of God, and the immortality of the soul."
The inaugural discourse was given by Paine. It
opens with these words : " Religion has two prin-

cipal enemies, Fanaticism and Infidelity, or that which is called atheism. The first requires to be combated by reason and morality, the other by natural philosophy." The discourse is chiefly an argument for a divine existence based on motion, which, he maintains, is not a property of matter. It proves a Being "at the summit of all things." At the close he says :

"The society is at present in its infancy, and its means are small ; but I wish to hold in view the subject I allude to, and instead of teaching the philosophical branches of learning as ornamental branches only, as they have hitherto been taught, to teach them in a manner that shall combine theological knowledge with scientific instruction. To do this to the best advantage, some instruments will be necessary for the purpose of explanation, of which the society is not yet possessed. But as the views of the Society extend to public good, as well as to that of the individual, and as its principles can have no enemies, means may be devised to procure them. If we unite to the present instruction a series of lectures on the ground I have mentioned, we shall, in the first place, render theology the most entertaining of all studies. In the next place, we shall give scientific instruction to those who could not otherwise obtain it. The mechanic of every profession will there be taught the mathematical principles necessary to render him proficient in his art. The cultivator will there see developed the principles of vegetation ; while, at the same time, they will be led to see the hand of God in all these things."

A volume of 214 pages put forth at the close of the year shows that the Theophilanthropists sang theistic and humanitarian hymns, and read Odes ; also that ethical readings were introduced from the Bible, and from the Chinese, Hindu, and Greek authors. A library was established ("rue Neuve-Etienne-l'Estrapade, No. 25) at which was issued (1797), "Instruction Élémentaire sur la

Morale religieuse,"—this being declared to be morality based on religion.

Thus Paine, pioneer in many things, helped to found the first theistic and ethical society.

It may now be recognized as a foundation of the Religion of Humanity. It was a great point with Paine that belief in the divine existence was the one doctrine common to all religions. On this rock the Church of Man was to be built. Having vainly endeavored to found the international Republic he must repair to an ideal moral and human world. Robespierre and Pitt being unfraternal he will bring into harmony the sages of all races. It is a notable instance of Paine's unwillingness to bring a personal grievance into the sacred presence of Humanity that one of the four festivals of Theophilanthropy was in honor of Washington, while its catholicity was represented in a like honor to St. Vincent de Paul. The others so honored were Socrates and Rousseau. These selections were no doubt mainly due to the French members, but they could hardly have been made without Paine's agreement. It is creditable to them all that, at a time when France believed itself wronged by Washington, his services to liberty should alone have been remembered. The flowers of all races, as represented in literature or in history, found emblematic association with the divine life in nature through the flowers that were heaped on a simple altar, as they now are in many churches and chapels. The walls were decorated with ethical mottoes, enjoining domestic kindness and public benevolence.

Paine's pamphlet of this year (1797) on "Agrarian Justice" should be considered part of the theophilanthropic movement. It was written as a proposal to the French government, at a time when readjustment of landed property had been rendered necessary by the Revolution.[1] It was suggested by a sermon printed by the Bishop of Llandaff, on "The wisdom and goodness of God in having made both rich and poor." Paine denies that God made rich and poor : "he made only male and female, and gave them the earth for their inheritance." The earth, though naturally the equal possession of all, has been necessarily appropriated by individuals, because their improvements, which alone render its productiveness adequate to human needs, cannot be detached from the soil. Paine maintains that these private owners do nevertheless owe mankind ground-rent. He therefore proposes a tithe,—not for God, but for man. He advises that at the time when the owner will feel it least,—when property is passing by inheritance from one to another,—the tithe shall be taken from it. Personal property also owes a debt to society, without which wealth could not exist,—as in the case of one alone on an island. By a careful estimate he estimates that a tithe on inheritances would give every person, on reaching majority, fifteen pounds, and after the age of fifty an annuity of ten pounds, leaving a substantial surplus for charity. The practical scheme submitted is enforced by practical rather than theoretical con-

[1] " Thomas Payne à la Législature et au Directoire : ou la Justice Agraire Opposée à la Loi et aux Privilèges Agraires."

siderations. Property is always imperilled by poverty, especially where wealth and splendor have lost their old fascinations, and awaken emotions of disgust.

" To remove the danger it is necessary to remove the antipathies, and this can only be done by making property productive of a national blessing, extending to every individual. When the riches of one man above another shall increase the national fund in the same proportion ; when it shall be seen that the prosperity of that fund depends on the prosperity of individuals ; when the more riches a man acquires, the better it shall be for the general mass ; it is then that antipathies will cease, and property be placed on the permanent basis of national interest and protection.

" I have no property in France to become subject to the plan I propose. What I have, which is not much, is in the United States of America. But I will pay one hundred pounds sterling towards this fund in France, the instant it shall be established ; and I will pay the same sum in England, whenever a similar establishment shall take place in that country."

The tithe was to be given to rich and poor alike, including owners of the property tithed, in order that there should be no association of alms with this "agrarian justice."

About this time the priesthood began to raise their heads again. A report favorable to a restoration to them of the churches, the raising of bells, and some national recognition of public worship, was made by Camille Jordan for a committee on the subject. The jesuitical report was especially poetical about church bells, which Paine knew would ring the knell of the Republic. He wrote a theophilanthropic letter to Camille Jordan, from which I quote some paragraphs.

" You claim a privilege incompatible with the Constitution, and with Rights. The Constitution protects equally, as it ought to do, every profession of religion ; it gives no exclusive privilege to any. The churches are the common property of all the people ; they are national goods, and cannot be given exclusively to any one profession, because the right does not exist of giving to any one that which appertains to all. It would be consistent with right that the churches should be sold, and the money arising therefrom be invested as a fund for the education of children of poor parents of every profession, and, if more than sufficient for this purpose, that the surplus be appropriated to the support of the aged poor. After this every profession can erect its own place of worship, if it choose—support its own priests, if it choose to have any— or perform its worship without priests, as the Quakers do."

" It is a want of feeling to talk of priests and bells whilst so many infants are perishing in the hospitals, and aged and infirm poor in the streets. The abundance that France possesses is sufficient for every want, if rightly applied ; but priests and bells, like articles of luxury, ought to be the least articles of consideration."

" No man ought to make a living by religion. It is dishonest to do so. Religion is not an act that can be performed by proxy. One person cannot act religion for another. Every person must perform it for himself ; and all that a priest can do is to take from him ; he wants nothing but his money, and then to riot in the spoil and laugh at his credulity. The only people who, as a professional sect of Christians, provide for the poor of their society, are people known by the name of Quakers. These men have no priests. They assemble quietly in their places of worship, and do not disturb their neighbors with shows and noise of bells. Religion does not unite itself to show and noise. True religion is without either.'

" One good schoolmaster is of more use than a hundred priests. If we look back at what was the condition of France under the *ancien régime*, we cannot acquit the priests of corrupting the morals of the nation."

"Why has the Revolution of France been stained with crimes, while the Revolution of the United States of America was not? Men are physically the same in all countries; it is education that makes them different. Accustom a people to believe that priests, or any other class of men, can forgive sins, and you will have sins in abundance."

While Thomas Paine was thus founding in Paris a religion of love to God expressed in love to man, his enemies in England were illustrating by characteristic fruits the dogmas based on a human sacrifice. The ascendency of the priesthood of one church over others, which he was resisting in France, was exemplified across the channel in the prosecution of his publisher, and the confiscation of a thousand pounds which had somehow fallen due to Paine.[1] The "Age of Reason," amply advertised by its opponents, had reached a vast circulation, and a prosecution of its publisher, Thomas Williams, for blasphemy, was instituted in the King's Bench. Williams being a poor man, the defence was sustained by a subscription.[2] The trial occurred June 24th. The extent to which the English reign of terror had gone was shown in the fact that Erskine was now the prosecutor; he who five years before had defended the " Rights of Man," who had left the court in a carriage drawn by the people, now stood in the same room to assail the most sacred of rights. He began with a menace to the

[1] This loss, mentioned by Paine in a private note, occurred about the time when he had devoted the proceeds of his pamphlet on English Finance, a very large sum, to prisoners held for debt in Newgate. I suppose the thousand pounds were the proceeds of the " Age of Reason."

[2] " Subscriptions (says his circular) will be received by J. Ashley, Shoemaker, No. 6 High Holborn; C. Cooper, Grocer, New Compton-st., Soho; G. Wilkinson, Printer, No. 115 Shoreditch; J. Rhynd, Printer, Ray-st., Clerkenwell; R. Hodgson, Hatter, No. 29 Brook-st., Holborn." It will be observed that the defence of free printing had fallen to humble people.

defendant's counsel (S. Kyd) on account of a notice
served on the prosecution, foreshadowing a search
into the Scriptures.[1] "No man," he cried, "deserves to be upon the Rolls of the Court who dares,
as an Attorney, to put his name to such a notice.
It is an insult to the authority and dignity of the
Court of which he is an officer; since it seems to
call in question the very foundations of its jurisdiction." So soon did Erskine point the satire of
the fable he quoted from Lucian, in Paine's defence,
of Jupiter answering arguments with thunderbolts.
Erskine's argument was that the King had taken
a solemn oath "to maintain the Christian Religion as it is promulgated by God in the Holy
Scriptures." "Every man has a right to investi-
gate, with modesty and decency, controversial
points of the Christian religion; but no man, consistently with a law which only exists under its
sanction, has a right not only broadly to deny its
very existence, but to pour forth a shocking and
insulting invective, etc." The law, he said, permits,
by a like principle, the intercourse between the
sexes to be set forth in plays and novels, but punishes such as "address the imagination in a manner
to lead the passions into dangerous excesses."
Erskine read several passages from the "Age of
Reason," which, their main point being omitted,
seemed mere aimless abuse. In his speech, he
quoted as Paine's words of his own collocation,

[1] "The King *v*. Thomas Williams for Blasphemy.—Take notice that the
Prosecutors of the Indictment against the above named Defendant will upon
the Trial of this cause be required to produce a certain Book described in
the said Indictment to be the Holy Bible.—John Martin, Solicitor for the
Defendant. Dated the 17th day of June 1797."

representing the author as saying, "The Bible teaches nothing but 'lies, obscenity, cruelty, and injustice.'" This is his entire and inaccurate rendering of what Paine,—who always distinguishes the "Bible" from the "New Testament,"—says at the close of his comment on the massacre of the Midianites and appropriation of their maidens :

"People in general know not what wickedness there is in this pretended word of God. Brought up in habits of superstition, they take it for granted that the Bible [Old Testament] is true, and that it is good ; they permit themselves not to doubt it ; and they carry the ideas they form of the benevolence of the Almighty to the book they have been taught to believe was written by his authority. Good heavens ! it is quite another thing ! it is a book of lies, wickedness, and blasphemy ; for what can be greater blasphemy than to ascribe the wickedness of man to the orders of the Almighty ?"

Erskine argued that the sanction of Law was the oath by which judges, juries, witnesses administered law and justice under a belief in "the revelation of the unutterable blessings which shall attend their observances, and the awful punishments which shall await upon their transgressions." The rest of his opening argument was, mainly, that great men had believed in Christianity.

Mr. Kyd, in replying, quoted from the Bishop of Llandaff's "Answer to Gibbon" : "I look upon the right of private judgment, in every respect concerning God and ourselves, as superior to the control of human authority" ; and his claim that the Church of England is distinguished from Mahometanism and Romanism by its permission of every man to utter his opinion freely. He also cites Dr. Lardner, and

Dr. Waddington, the Bishop of Chichester, who
declared that Woolston "ought not to be punished
for being an infidel, nor for writing against the
Christian religion." He quoted Paine's profession
of faith on the first page of the incriminated book :
"I believe in one God and no more; I hope for
happiness, beyond this life ; I believe in the equality
of men, and I believe that religious duties consist
in doing justice, loving mercy, and endeavouring to
make our fellow creatures happy." He also quoted
Paine's homage to the character of Jesus. He
defied the prosecution to find in the "Age of Reason" a single passage "inconsistent with the most
chaste, the most correct system of morals," and
declared the very passages selected for indictment
pleas against obscenity and cruelty. Mr. Kyd
pointed out fourteen narratives in the Bible (such
as Sarah giving Hagar to Abraham, Lot and his
daughters, etc.) which, if found in any other book,
would be pronounced obscene. He was about to
enumerate instances of cruelty when the judge,
Lord Kenyon, indignantly interrupted him, and
with consent of the jury said he could only allow
him to cite such passages without reading them.
(Mr. Kyd gratefully acknowledged this release
from the "painful task" of reading such horrors
from the "Word of God"!) One of the interesting things about this trial was the disclosure of the
general reliance on Butler's "Analogy," used by
Bishop Watson in his reply to Paine,—namely,
that the cruelties objected to in the God of the
Bible are equally found in nature, through
which deists look up to their God. When Kyd,

after quoting from Bishop Watson, said, "Gentlemen, observe the weakness of this answer," Lord
Kenyon exclaimed : "I cannot sit in this place and
hear this kind of discussion." Kyd said : "My
Lord, I stand here on the privilege of an advocate
in an English Court of Justice : this man has applied
to me to defend him ; I have undertaken his defence ; and I have often heard your Lordship
declare, that every man had a right to be defended.
I know no other mode by which I can seriously
defend him against this charge, than that which I
am now pursuing; if your Lordship wish to prevent me from pursuing it, you may as well tell me
to abandon my duty to my client at once." Lord
Kenyon said : "Go on, Sir." Returning to the
analogy of the divinely ordered massacres in the
Bible with the like in nature, Kyd said :

"Gentlemen, this is reasoning by comparison ; and reasoning
by comparison is often fallacious. On the present occasion the
fallacy is this : that, in the first case, the persons perish by the
operation of the general laws of nature, not suffering punishment for a crime ; whereas, in the latter, the general laws of
nature are suspended or transgressed, and God commands the
slaughter to avenge his offended will. Is this then a satisfactory
answer to the objection ?   I think it is not ; another may think
so too ; which it may be fairly supposed the Author did ; and
then the objection, as to him, remains in full force, and he
cannot, from insisting upon it, be fairly accused of malevolent
intention."

In his answer Erskine said : "The history of
man is the history of man's vices and passions,
which could not be censured without adverting to
their existence; many of the instances that have
been referred to were recorded as memorable

warnings and examples for the instruction of mankind." But for this argument Erskine was indebted
to his old client, Paine, who did not argue against
the things being recorded, but against the belief
"that the inhuman and horrid butcheries of men,
women, and children, told of in those books, were
done, as those books say they were done, at the
command of God." Paine says: "Those accounts
are nothing to us, nor to any other persons, unless
it be to the Jews, as a part of the history of their
nation; and there is just as much of the word of
God in those books as there is in any of the histories of France, or Rapin's 'History of England,' or
the history of any other country."

As in Paine's own trial in 1792, the infallible
scheme of a special jury was used against Williams.
Lord Kenyon closed his charge with the words:
"Unless it was for the most malignant purposes, I
cannot conceive how it was published. It is, however, for you to judge of it, and to do justice
between the Public and the Defendant."

"The jury instantly found the Defendant—
Guilty."

Paine at once wrote a letter to Erskine, which
was first printed in Paris. He calls attention to the
injustice of the special jury system, in which all the
jurymen are nominated by the crown. In London
a special jury generally consists of merchants.
"Talk to some London merchants about scripture,
and they will understand you mean scrip, and tell
you how much it is worth at the Stock Exchange.
Ask them about Theology, and they will say they
know no such gentleman upon 'Change." He also

declares that Lord Kenyon's course in preventing Mr. Kyd from reading passages from the Bible was irregular, and contrary to words, which he cites, used by the same judge in another case.

This Letter to Erskine contains some effective passages. In one of these he points out the sophistical character of the indictment in declaring the " Age of Reason " a blasphemous work, tending to bring in contempt the holy scriptures. The charge should have stated that the work was intended to prove certain books not the holy scriptures. " It is one thing if I ridicule a work as being written by a certain person ; but it is quite a different thing if I write to prove that such a work was not written by such person. In the first case I attack the person through the work ; in the other case I defend the honour of the person against the work." After alluding to the two accounts in Genesis of the creation of man, according to one of which there was no Garden of Eden and no forbidden tree, Paine says :

" Perhaps I shall be told in the cant language of the day, as I have often been told by the Bishop of Llandaff and others, of the great and laudable pains that many pious and learned men have taken to explain the obscure, and reconcile the contradictory, or, as they say, the seemingly contradictory passages of the Bible. It is because the Bible needs such an undertaking, that is one of the first causes to suspect it is *not* the word of God : this single reflection, when carried home to the mind, is in itself a volume. What ! does not the Creator of the Universe, the Fountain of all Wisdom, the Origin of all Science, the Author of all Knowledge, the God of Order and of Harmony, know how to write ? When we contemplate the vast economy of the creation, when we behold the unerring regularity of the visible solar system, the perfection with which all its several parts revolve, and by corresponding assemblage form a whole ;—when we launch our eye into the boundless ocean of space, and see ourselves surrounded by innumerable worlds, not one of which varies from its appointed place—when we trace the power of a Creator, from a mite to an elephant, from an atom to an universe, can we suppose that the mind [which] could conceive such a design, and the power that executed it with incomparable perfection, cannot write without inconsistence ; or that a book so written can be the work of such a power? The writings of Thomas Paine, even of Thomas Paine, need no commentator to explain, compound, arrange, and re-arrange their several parts, to render them intelligible— he can relate a fact, or write an essay, without forgetting in one page what he has written in another ; certainly then, did the God of all perfection condescend to write or dictate a book, that book would be as perfect as himself is perfect : The Bible is not so, and it is confessedly not so, by the attempts to mend it."

Paine admonishes Erskine that a prosecution to preserve God's word, were it really God's word, would be like a prosecution to prevent the sun from falling out of heaven ; also that he should be able to comprehend that the motives of those who declare the Bible not God's word are religious. He then gives him an account of the new church of Theophilanthropists in Paris, and appends his discourse before that society.

In the following year, Paine's discourse to the Theophilanthropists was separately printed by Clio Rickman, with a sentence from Shakespeare in the title-page : " I had as lief have the foppery of freedom as the morality of imprisonment." There was also the following dedication :

" The following little Discourse is dedicated to the enemies of Thomas Paine, by one who has known him long and inti-

mately, and who is convinced that he is the enemy of no man.
It is printed to do good, by a well wisher to the world. By
one who thinks that discussion should be unlimited, that all
coercion is error ; and that human beings should adopt no
other conduct towards each other but an appeal to truth and
reason."

Paine wrote privately, in the same sense as to
Erskine, to his remonstrating friends. In one such
letter (May 12th) he goes again partly over the
ground. "You," he says, "believe in the Bible
from the accident of birth, and the Turks believe
in the Koran from the same accident, and each
calls the other *infidel*. This answer to your letter
is not written for the purpose of changing your
opinion. It is written to satisfy you, and some
other friends whom I esteem, that my disbelief of
the Bible is founded on a pure and religious belief
in God." "All are infidels who believe falsely of
God." "Belief in a cruel God makes a cruel
man."

Paine had for some time been attaining unique
fame in England. Some publisher had found it
worth while to issue a book, entitled "Tom Paine's
Jests : Being an entirely new and select Collection
of Patriotic Bon Mots, Repartees, Anecdotes, Epi-
grams, &c., on Political Subjects. By Thomas
Paine." There are hardly a half dozen items by
Paine in the book (72 pages), which shows that
his name was considered marketable. The government had made the author a cause. Erskine,
who had lost his office as Attorney-General for
the Prince of Wales by becoming Paine's counsel
in 1792, was at once taken back into favor after

prosecuting the " Age of Reason," and put on his way to become Lord Erskine. The imprisonment of Williams caused a reaction in the minds of those who had turned against Paine. Christianity suffered under royal patronage. The terror manifested at the name of Paine—some were arrested even for showing his portrait—was felt to be political. None of the aristocratic deists, who wrote for the upper classes, were dealt with in the same way. Paine had proclaimed from the housetops what, as Dr. Watson confessed, scholars were whispering in the ear. There were lampoons of Paine, such as those of Peter Pindar (Rev. John Wolcott), but they only served to whet popular curiosity concerning him.[1] The " Age of Reason " had passed through several editions before it was outlawed, and every copy of it passed through many hands. From the prosecution and imprisonment of Williams may be dated the consolidation of the movement for the " Rights of Man," with antagonism to the kind of Christianity which that injustice illustrated. Political liberalism and heresy thenceforth progressed in England, hand in hand.

[1] " I have preserved," says Royall Tyler, " an epigram of Peter Pindar's, written originally in a blank leaf of a copy of Paine's ' Age of Reason,' and not inserted in any of his works.

> " ' Tommy Paine wrote this book to prove that the bible
> Was an old woman's dream of fancies most idle ;
> That Solomon's proverbs were made by low livers,
> That prophets were fellows who sang semiquavers ;
> That religion and miracles all were a jest,
> And the devil in torment a tale of the priest.
> Though Beelzebub's absence from hell I 'll maintain,
> Yet we all must allow that the Devil's in Paine.' "

CHAPTER XIV.

THE REPUBLICAN ABDIEL.

THE sight of James Monroe and Thomas Paine in France, representing Republican America, was more than Gouverneur Morris could stand. He sent to Washington the abominable slander of Monroe already quoted (ii., p. 173), and the Minister's recall came at the close of 1796.[1] Monroe could not sail in midwinter with his family, so they remained until the following spring. Paine made preparations to return to America with them, and accompanied them to Havre ; but he found so many "british frigates cruising in sight" (so he writes Jefferson) that he did not " trust [himself] to their discretion, and the more so as [he] had no confidence in the Captain of the Dublin Packet." Sure enough this Captain Clay was friendly enough

[1] This sudden recall involved Monroe in heavy expenses, which Congress afterwards repaid. I am indebted to Mr. Frederick McGuire, of Washington, for the manuscript of Monroe's statement of his expenses and annoyances caused by his recall, which he declares due to "the representations which were made to him [Washington] by those in whom he confided." He states that Paine remained in his house a year and a half, and that he advanced him 250 louis d'or. For these services to Paine, he adds, "no claims were ever presented on my part, nor is any indemnity now desired." This money was repaid ($1,188) to Monroe by an Act of Congress, April 7, 1831. The advances are stated in the Act to have been made "from time to time," and were no doubt regarded by both Paine and Monroe as compensated by the many services rendered by the author to the Legation.

with the British cruiser which lay in wait to catch Paine, but only succeeded in finding his letter to Jefferson. Before returning from Havre to Paris he wrote another letter to Vice-President Jefferson.

"HAVRE, May 14th, 1797.

"DEAR SIR,—I wrote to you by the Ship Dublin Packet, Captain Clay, mentioning my intention to have returned to America by that Vessel, and to have suggested to some Member of the House of Representatives the propriety of calling Mr. Monroe before them to have enquired into the state of their affairs in France. This might have laid the foundation for some resolves on their part that might have led to an accomodation with France, for that House is the only part of the American Government that have any reputation here. I apprised Mr. Monroe of my design, and he wishes to be called up.

"You will have heard before this reaches you that the Emperor has been obliged to sue for peace, and to consent to the establishment of the new republic in Lombardy. How France will proceed with respect to England, I am not, at this distance from Paris, in the way of knowing, but am inclined to think she meditates a descent upon that Country, and a revolution in its Government. If this should be the plan, it will keep me in Europe at least another year.

" As the british party has thrown the American commerce into wretched confusion, it is necessary to pay more attention to the appointment of Consuls in the ports of france, than there was occasion to do in time of peace ; especially as there is now no Minister, and Mr. Skipwith, who stood well with the Government here, has resigned. Mr. Cutting, the Consul for Havre, does not reside at it, and the business is altogether in the hands of De la Motte, the Vice Consul, who is a frenchman, [and] cannot have the full authority proper for the office in the difficult state matters are now in. I do not mention this to the disadvantage of Mr. Cutting, for no man is more proper than himself if he thought it an object to attend to.

" I know not if you are acquainted with Captain Johnson of Massachusetts—he is a staunch man and one of the oldest

American Captains in the American employ. He is now
settled at Havre and is a more proper man for a Vice Consul
than La Motte. You can learn his character from Mr. Monroe.
He has written to some of his friends to have the appointment
and if you can see an opportunity of throwing in a little service for him, you will do a good thing. We have had several
reports of Mr. Madison's coming. He would be well received
as an individual, but as an Envoy of John Adams he could do
nothing.

"THOMAS PAINE."

The following, in Paine's handwriting, is copied
from the original in the Morrison papers, at the
British Museum. It was written in the summer of
1797, when Lord Malmsbury was at Lille in negotiation for peace. The negotiations were broken
off because the English commissioners were un-
authorized to make the demanded restorations to
Holland and Spain. Paine's essay was no doubt
sent to the Directory in the interests of peace, suggesting as it does a compromise, as regards the
Cape of Good Hope.

"CAPE OF GOOD HOPE.—It is very well known that Dundas, the English Minister for Indian affairs, is tenacious of
holding the Cape of Good Hope, because it will give to the
English East India Company a monopoly of the commerce of
India; and this, on the other hand, is the very reason that
such a claim is inadmissible by France, and by all the nations
trading in India and to Canton, and would also be injurious to
Canton itself.—We pretend not to know anything of the nego-
ciations at Lille, but it is very easy to see, from the nature of
the case, what ought to be the condition of the Cape. It ought
to be a free port open to the vessels of all nations trading to
any part of the East Indias. It ought also to be a neutral port
at all times, under the guarantee of all nations; the expense of
keeping the port in constant repair to be defrayed by a tonnage

tax to be paid by every vessel, whether of commerce or of war, and in proportion to the time of their stay.—Nothing then remains but with respect to the nation who shall be the port-master ; and this ought to be the Dutch, because they under-stand the business best. As the Cape is a half-way stage between Europe and India, it ought to be considered as a tavern, where travellers on a long journey put up for rest and refreshment.—T. P."

The suspension of peace negotiations,[1] and the bloodless defeat of Pichigru's conspiracy of 18 Fructidor (September 4th) were followed by a pamphlet addressed to " The People of France and the French Armies." This little work is of historical value, in connection with 18 Fructidor, but it was evidently written to carry two practical points. The first was, that if the war with England must con-tinue it should be directed to the end of breaking the Anglo-Germanic compact. England has the right to her internal arrangements, but this is an external matter. While "with respect to England it has been the cause of her immense national debt, the ruin of her finances, and the insolvency of her bank," English intrigues on the continent " are generated by, and act through, the medium of this Anglo-Germanic compound. It will be necessary to dissolve it. Let the elector retire to his elector-ate, and the world will have peace." Paine's other

---

[1] In a letter to Duane, many years later, Paine relates the following story concerning the British Union : " When Lord Malmsbury arrived in Paris, in the time of the Directory Government, to open a negociation for a peace, his credentials ran in the old style of ' George, by the grace of God, of Great Britain, *France*, and Ireland, king.' Malmsbury was informed that although the assumed title of king of France, in his credentials, would not prevent France opening a negociation, yet that no treaty of peace could be con-cluded until that assumed title was removed. Pitt then hit on the Union Bill, under which the assumed title of king of France was discontinued."

main point is, that the neutral nations should secure, in time of war, an unarmed neutrality.

"Were the neutral nations to associate, under an honorable injunction of fidelity to each other, and publickly declare to the world, that if any belligerent power shall seize or molest any ship or vessel belonging to the citizens or subjects of any of the powers composing that association, that the whole association will shut its ports against the flag of the offending nation, and will not permit any goods, wares, or merchandize, produced or manufactured in the offending nation, or appertaining thereto, to be imported into any of the ports included in the association, until reparation be made to the injured party; the reparation to be three times the value of the vessel and cargo ; and moreover that all remittances in money, goods, and bills of exchange, do cease to be made to the offending nation, until the said reparation be made. Were the neutral nations only to do this, which it is their direct interest to do, England, as a nation depending on the commerce of neutral nations in time of war, dare not molest them, and France would not. But whilst, from want of a common system, they individually permit England to do it, because individually they cannot resist it, they put France under the necessity of doing the same thing. The supreme of all laws, in all cases, is that of self-preservation." ʃ

It is a notable illustration of the wayward course of political evolution, that the English republic—for it is such—grew largely out of the very parts of its constitution once so oppressive. The foreign origin of the royal family helped to form its wholesome timidity about meddling with politics, allowing thus a development of ministerial government. The hereditary character of the throne, which George III.'s half-insane condition associated with the recklessness of irresponsibility, was by his complete insanity made to serve ministerial independence. Regency is timid about claiming power, and childhood cannot exercise it. The decline of royal and aristocratic authority in England secured freedom to commerce, which necessarily gave hostages to peace. The protection of neutral commerce at sea, concerning which Paine wrote so much, ultimately resulted from English naval strength, which formerly scourged the world.

To Paine, England, at the close of 1797, could appear only as a dragon-guarded prison of fair Humanity. The press was paralyzed, thinkers and publishers were in prison, some of the old orators like Erskine were bought up, and the forlorn hope of liberty rested only with Fox and his fifty in Parliament, overborne by a majority made brutal by strength. The groans of imprisoned thought in his native land reached its outlawed representative in Paris. And at the same time the inhuman decree went forth from that country that there should be no peace with France. It had long been his conviction that the readiness of Great Britain to go to war was due to an insular position that kept the horrors at a distance. War never came home to her. This conviction, which we have several times met in these pages, returned to him with new force when England now insisted on more bloodshed. He was convinced that the right course of France would be to make a descent on England, ship the royal family to Hanover, open the political prisons, and secure the people freedom to make a Constitution. These views, freely expressed to his friends of the Directory and Legislature, reached the ears of Napoleon on his triumphal return from Italy.

The great man called upon Paine in his little room, and invited him to dinner. He made the eloquent professions of republicanism so characteristic of Napoleons until they became pretenders. He told Paine that he slept with the " Rights of Man " under his pillow, and that its author ought to have a statue of gold.[1] He consulted Paine about a descent on England, and adopted the plan. He invited the author to accompany the expedition, which was to consist of a thousand gun-boats, with a hundred men each. Paine consented, " as [so he wrote Jefferson] the intention of the expedition was to give the people of England an opportunity of forming a government for themselves, and thereby bring about peace." One of the points to be aimed at was Norfolk, and no doubt Paine indulged a happy vision of standing once more in Thetford and proclaiming liberty throughout the land !

The following letter (December 29, 1797) from Paine to Barras is in the archives of the Directory, with a French translation :

"CITIZEN PRESIDENT,—A very particular friend of mine, who had a passport to go to London upon some family affairs and to return in three months, and whom I had commissioned upon some affairs of my own (for I find that the English government has seized upon a thousand pounds sterling which I had in the hands of a friend), returned two days ago and gave me the memorandum which I enclose :—the first part relates only to my publication on the event of the 18 Fructidor, and to a letter to Erskine (who had been counsel for the prosecution against a former work of mine the 'Age of Reason ') both of which I desired my friend to publish in London. The other part of the memorandum respects the state of affairs in that country, by which I see they have little

[1] Rickman, p. 164.

or no idea of a descent being made upon them ; tant mieux—
,but they will be guarded in Ireland, as they expect a descent
there.

"I expect a printed copy of the letter to Erskine in a day
or two. As this is in English, and on a subject that will be
amusing to the Citizen Revellière Le Peaux, I will send it to
him. The friend of whom I speak was a pupil of Dessault
the surgeon, and whom I once introduced to you at a public
audience in company with Captain Cooper on his plan respecting the Island of Bermuda.—Salut et Respect."

Thus once again did the great hope of a liberated,
peaceful, and republican Europe shine before simple-
hearted Paine. He was rather poor now, but
gathered up all the money he had, and sent it to
the Council of Five Hundred. The accompanying
letter was read by Coupè at the sitting of January
28, 1798 :

"CITIZENS REPRESENTATIVES,—Though it is not convenient
to me, in the present situation of my affairs, to subscribe to the
loan towards the descent upon England, my economy permits
me to make a small patriotic donation. I send a hundred
livres, and with it all the wishes of my heart for the success of
the descent, and a voluntary offer of any service I can render
to promote it.

"There will be no lasting peace for France, nor for the
world, until the tyranny and corruption of the English government be abolished, and England, like Italy, become a sister
republic. As to those men, whether in England, Scotland, or
Ireland, who, like Robespierre in France, are covered with
crimes, they, like him, have no other resource than in committing more. But the mass of the people are the friends of
liberty : tyranny and taxation oppress them, but they deserve
to be free.

"Accept, Citizens Representatives, the congratulations of an
old colleague in the dangers we have passed, and on the happy
prospect before us. Salut et respect.

"THOMAS PAINE."

Coupè added : " The gift which Thomas Paine offers you appears very trifling, when it is com= pared with the revolting injustice which this faithful friend of liberty has experienced from the English government ; but compare it with the state of poverty in which our former colleague finds himself, and you will then think it considerable." He moved that the notice of this gift and Thomas Paine's letter be printed. " Mention honorable et impression," adds the *Moniteur*.

The President of the Directory at this time was Larevéllière-Lépeaux, a friend of the Theophilan- thropic Society. To him Paine gave, in English, which the president understood, a plan for the descent, which was translated into French, and adopted by the Directory. Two hundred and fifty gun-boats were built, and the expedition abandoned. To Jefferson, Paine intimates his suspicion that it was all " only a feint to cover the expedition to Egypt, which was then preparing." He also states that the British descent on Ostend, where some two thousand of them were made prisoners, " was in search of the gun-boats, and to cut the dykes, to prevent their being assembled." This he was told by Vanhuile, of Bruges, who heard it from the British officers.

After the failure of his attempt to return to America with the Monroes, Paine was for a time the guest of Nicolas de Bonneville, in Paris, and the visit ended in an arrangement for his abode with that family. Bonneville was an editor, thirty- seven years of age, and had been one of the five members of Paine's Republican Club, which

placarded Paris with its manifesto after the king's
flight in 1791. An enthusiastic devotee of Paine's
principles from youth, he had advocated them in
his successive journals, *Le Tribun du Peuple*,
Bouche de Fer, and *Bien Informé*. He had
resisted Marat and Robespierre, and suffered imprisonment during the Terror. He spoke English
fluently, and was well known in the world of letters
by some striking poems, also by his translation into
French of German tales, and parts of Shakespeare.
He had set up a printing office at No. 4 Rue du
Théâtre-Français, where he published liberal pamphlets, also his *Bien Informé*. Then, in 1794, he
printed in French the " Age of Reason." He also
published, and probably translated into French,
Paine's letter to the now exiled Camille Jordan,—
" Lettre de Thomas Paine, sur les Cultes." Paine,
unable to converse in French, found with the
Bonnevilles a home he needed. M. and Madame
Bonneville had been married three years, and their
second child had been named after Thomas Paine,
who stood as his godfather. Paine, as we learn
from Rickman, who knew the Bonnevilles, paid
board, but no doubt he aided Bonneville more by
his pen.

With public affairs, either in France or America,
Paine now mingled but little. The election of John
Adams to the presidency he heard of with dismay.
He wrote to Jefferson that since he was not president, he was glad he had accepted the vice-presidency, "for John Adams has such a talent for
blundering and offending, it will be necessary
to keep an eye over him." Finding, by the aban-

donment of a descent on England for one on Egypt, that Napoleon was by no means his ideal missionary of republicanism, he withdrew into his little study, and now remained so quiet that some English papers announced his arrival and cool reception in America. He was, however, fairly bored with visitors from all parts of the world, curious to see the one international republican left. It became necessary for Madame Bonneville, armed with polite prevarications, to defend him from such sight-seers. For what with his visits to and from the Barlows, the Smiths, and his friends of the Directory, Paine had too little time for the inventions in which he was again absorbed,—his "Saints." Among his intimate friends at this time was Robert Fulton, then residing in Paris. Paine's extensive studies of the steam-engine, and his early discovery of its adaptability to navigation, had caused Rumsey to seek him in England, and Fitch to consult him both in America and Paris. Paine's connection with the invention of the steamboat was recognized by Fulton, as indeed by all of his scientific contemporaries.[1] To Fulton he freely gave his ideas, and may perhaps have had some hope that the steamboat might prove a missionary of international republicanism, though Napoleon had failed.

[1] Sir Richard Phillips says: "In 1778 Thomas Paine proposed, in America, this application of steam." ("Million of Facts," p. 776.) As Sir Richard assisted Fulton in his experiments on the Thames, he probably heard from him the fact about Paine, though, indeed, in the controversy between Rumsey and Fitch, Paine's priority to both was conceded. In America, however, the priority really belonged to the eminent mechanician William Henry, of Lancaster, Pa. When Fitch visited Henry, in 1785, he was told by him that he was not the first to devise steam-navigation; that

It will not be forgotten that in the same year in which Paine startled William Henry with a plan for steam-navigation, namely in 1778, he wrote his sublime sentence about the "Religion of Humanity." The steamships, which Emerson described as enormous shuttles weaving the races of men into the woof of humanity, have at length rendered possible that universal human religion which Paine foresaw. In that old Lancaster mansion of the Henrys, which still stands, Paine left his spectacles, now in our National Museum ; they are strong and far-seeing; through them looked eyes held by visions that the world is still steadily following. One cannot suppress some transcendental sentiment in view of the mystical harmony of this man's inventions for human welfare,—mechanical, political, religious. Of his gunpowder motor, mention has already been made (i., p. 240). On this he was engaged about the time that he was answering Bishop Watson's book on the "Age of Reason." The two occupations are related. He could not believe, he said, that the qualities of gunpowder— the small and light grain with maximum of force— were meant only for murder, and his faith in the divine humanity is in the sentence. To supersede

he himself had thought of it in 1776, and mentioned it to Andrew Ellicott ; and that Thomas Paine, while a guest at his house in 1778, had spoken to him on the subject. I am indebted to Mr. John W. Jordan, of the Historical Society of Pennsylvania, for notes from the papers of Henry, his ancestor, showing that Paine's scheme was formed without knowledge of others, and that it contemplated a turbine application of steam to a wheel. Both he and Henry, as they had not published their plans, agreed to leave Fitch the whole credit. Fitch publicly expressed his gratitude to Paine. Thurston adds that Paine, in 1788, proposed that Congress should adopt the whole matter for the national benefit. (" History of the Growth of the Steam Engine," pp. 252, 253.)

destroying gunpowder with beneficent gunpowder,
and to supersede the god of battles with the God
of Love, were kindred aims in Paine's heart.
Through the fiery furnaces of his time he had come
forth with every part of his being welded and
beaten and shaped together for this Human Service.
Patriotism, in the conventional sense, race-pride,
sectarianism, partizanship, had been burnt out of
his nature. The universe could not have wrung
from his tongue approval of a wrong because it
was done by his own country.

It might be supposed that there were no heavier
trials awaiting Paine's political faith than those it
had undergone. But it was becoming evident that
liberty had not the advantage he once ascribed to
truth over error,—"it cannot be unlearned." The
United States had unlearned it as far as to put into
the President's hands a power of arbitrarily crushing political opponents, such as even George III.
hardly aspired to. The British Treaty had begun to
bear its natural fruits. Washington signed the
Treaty to avoid war, and rendered war inevitable
with both France and England. The affair with
France was happily a transient squall, but it was
sufficient to again bring on Paine the offices of an
American Minister in France. Many an American
in that country had occasion to appreciate his
powerful aid and unfailing kindness. Among these
was Captain Rowland Crocker of Massachusetts,
who had sailed with a letter of marque. His vessel
was captured by the French, and its wounded commander brought to Paris, where he was more
agreeably conquered by kindness. Freeman's

" History of Cape Cod" (of which region Crocker
was a native) has the following :

" His [Captain Crocker's] reminiscences of his residence in
that country, during the most extraordinary period of its
history, were of a highly interesting character.   He had taken
the great Napoleon by the hand ; he had familiarly known
Paine, at a time when his society was sought for and was
valuable.   Of this noted individual, we may in passing say,
with his uniform and characteristic kindness, he always spoke
in terms which sounded strange to the ears of a generation
which has been taught, with or without justice, to regard the
author of ' The Age of Reason ' with loathing and abhorrence.
He remembered Paine as a well-dressed and most gentlemanly
man, of sound and orthodox republican principles, of a good
heart, a strong intellect, and a fascinating address."

The *coup d'état* in America, which made President Adams virtual emperor, pretended constitu-
tionality, and was reversible.   That which Napoleon
and Sieyès—who had his way at last—effected in
France (November 9, 1799) was lawless and fatal.
The peaceful Bonneville home was broken up.
Bonneville, in his *Bien Informé*, described Napoleon as " a Cromwell," and was promptly imprisoned.
Paine, either before or soon after this catastrophe,
went to Belgium, on a visit to his old friend Vanhuile, who had shared his cell in the Luxembourg
prison.   Vanhuile was now president of the municipality of Bruges, and Paine got from him information about European affairs.   On his return he
found Bonneville released from prison, but under
severe surveillance, his journal being suppressed.
The family was thus reduced to penury and
anxiety, but there was all the more reason that
Paine should stand by them.   He continued his

abode in their house, now probably supported by drafts on his resources in America, to which country they turned their thoughts.

The European Republic on land having become hopeless, Paine turned his attention to the seas. He wrote a pamphlet on "Maritime Compact," including in it ten articles for the security of neutral commerce, to be signed by the nations entering the "Unarmed Association," which he proposed. This scheme was substantially the same as that already quoted from his letter "To the People of France, and to the French Armies." It was translated by Bonneville, and widely circulated in Europe. Paine sent it in manuscript to Jefferson, who at once had it printed. His accompanying letter to Jefferson (October 1, 1800) is of too much biographical interest to be abridged.

"DEAR SIR,—I wrote to you from Havre by the ship Dublin Packet in the year 1797. It was then my intention to return to America; but there were so many British frigates cruising in sight of the port, and which after a few days knew that I was at Havre waiting to go to America, that I did not think it best to trust myself to their discretion, and the more so, as I had no confidence in the Captain of the Dublin Packet (Clay). I mentioned to you in that letter, which I believe you received thro' the hands of Colonel [Aaron] Burr, that I was glad since you were not President that you had accepted the nomination of Vice President.

"The Commissioners Ellsworth & Co.[1] have been here about eight months, and three more useless mortals never came upon

---

[1] Oliver Ellsworth, William V. Murray, and William R. Davie, were sent by President Adams to France to negotiate a treaty. There is little doubt that the famous letter of Joel Barlow to Washington, October 2, 1798, written in the interest of peace, was composed after consultation with Paine. Adams, on reading the letter, abused Barlow. "Tom Paine," he said, "is

public business. Their presence appears to me to have been
rather an injury than a benefit. They set themselves up for a
faction as soon as they arrived. I was then in Belgia. Upon
my return to Paris I learned they had made a point of not
returning the visits of Mr. Skipwith and Barlow, because, they
said, they had not the confidence of the executive. Every
known republican was treated in the same manner. I learned
from Mr. Miller of Philadelphia, who had occasion to see them
upon business, that they did not intend to return my visit, if I
made one. This I supposed it was intended I should know,
that I might not make one. It had the contrary effect. I
went to see Mr. Ellsworth. I told him, I did not come to see
him as a commissioner, nor to congratulate him upon his mission ;
that I came to see him because I had formerly known him in
Congress. I mean not, said I, to press you with any questions,
or to engage you in any conversation upon the business you
are come upon, but I will nevertheless candidly say that I know
not what expectations the Government or the people of America
may have of your mission, or what expectations you may have
yourselves, but I believe you will find you can do but little.
The treaty with England lies at the threshold of all your business. The American Government never did two more foolish
things than when it signed that Treaty and recalled Mr. Monroe, who was the only man could do them any service. Mr.
Ellsworth put on the dull gravity of a Judge, and was silent.
I added, you may perhaps make a treaty like that you have
made with England, which is a surrender of the rights of the
American flag ; for the principle that neutral ships make
neutral property must be general or not at all. I then changed
the subject, for I had all the talk to myself upon this topic,
and enquired after Sam. Adams, (I asked nothing about John,)
Mr. Jefferson, Mr. Monroe, and others of my friends, and the
melancholy case of the yellow fever,—of which he gave me as
circumstantial an account as if he had been summing up a case
to a Jury. Here my visit ended, and had Mr. Ellsworth been

not a more worthless fellow." But he obeyed the letter. The Commissioners he sent were associated with the anti-French and British party in America,
but peace with America was of too much importance to the new despot of
France for the opportunity to be missed of forming a Treaty.

as cunning as a statesman, or as wise as a Judge, he would have returned my visit that he might appear insensible of the intention of mine.

"I now come to the affairs of this country and of Europe. You will, I suppose, have heard before this arrives to you, of the battle of Marengo in Italy, where the Austrians were defeated—of the armistice in consequence thereof, and the surrender of Milan, Genoa, etc., to the french—of the successes of the french army in Germany—and the extension of the armistice in that quarter—of the preliminaries of peace signed at Paris—of the refusal of the Emperor [of Austria] to ratify these preliminaries—of the breaking of the armistice by the french Government in consequence of that refusal—of the 'gallant' expedition of the Emperor to put himself at the head of his Army—of his pompous arrival there—of his having made his will—of prayers being put in all his churches for the preservation of the life of this Hero—of General Moreau announcing to him, immediately on his arrival at the Army, that hostilities would commence the day after the next at sunrise, unless he signed the treaty or gave security that he would sign within 45 days—of his surrendering up three of the principal keys of Germany (Ulm, Philipsbourg, and Ingolstad), as security that he would sign them. This is the state things [they] are now in, at the time of writing this letter ; but it is proper to add that the refusal of the Emperor to sign the preliminaries was motived upon a note from the King of England to be admitted to the Congress for negociating Peace, which was consented to by the french upon the condition of an armistice at Sea, which England, before knowing of the surrender the Emperor had made, had refused. From all which it appears to me, judging from circumstances, that the Emperor is now so compleatly in the hands of the french, that he has no way of getting out but by a peace. The Congress for the peace is to be held at Luneville, a town in france. Since the affair of Rastadt the french commissioners will not trust themselves within the Emperor's territory.

"I now come to domestic affairs. I know not what the Commissioners have done, but from a paper I enclose to you, which appears to have some authority, it is not much. The paper as you will perceive is considerably prior to this letter. I knew that the Commissioners before this piece appeared intended setting off. It is therefore probable that what they have done is conformable to what this paper mentions, which certainly will not atone for the expence their mission has incurred, neither are they, by all the accounts I hear of them, men fitted for the business.

"But independently of these matters there appears to be a state of circumstances rising, which if it goes on, will render all partial treaties unnecessary. In the first place I doubt if any peace will be made with England; and in the second place, I should not wonder to see a coalition formed against her, to compel her to abandon her insolence on the seas. This brings me to speak of the manuscripts I send you.

"The piece No. 1, without any title, was written in consequence of a question put to me by Bonaparte. As he supposed I knew England and English Politics he sent a person to me to ask, that in case of negociating a Peace with Austria, whether it would be proper to include England. This was when Count St. Julian was in Paris, on the part of the Emperor negociating the preliminaries:—which as I have before said the Emperor refused to sign on the pretence of admitting England.

"The piece No. 2, entitled *On the Jacobinism of the English at Sea*, was written when the English made their insolent and impolitic expedition to Denmark, and is also an auxiliary to the politic of No. 1. I shewed it to a friend [Bonneville] who had it translated into french, and printed in the form of a Pamphlet, and distributed gratis among the foreign Ministers, and persons in the Government. It was immediately copied into several of the french Journals, and into the official Paper, the Moniteur. It appeared in this paper one day before the last dispatch arrived from Egypt; which agreed perfectly with what I had said respecting Egypt. It hit the two cases of Denmark and Egypt in the exact proper moment.

"The piece No. 3, entitled *Compact Maritime*, is the sequel of No. 2 digested in form. It is translating at the time I write this letter, and I am to have a meeting with the Senator Garat upon the subject. The pieces 2 and 3 go off in manuscript to England, by a confidential person, where they will be published.

"By all the news we get from the North there appears to be something meditating against England. It is now given for certain that Paul has embargoed all the English vessels and English property in Russia till some principle be established for protecting the Rights of neutral Nations, and securing the liberty of the Seas. The preparations in Denmark continue, notwithstanding the convention that she has made with England, which leaves the question with respect to the right set up by England to stop and search Neutral vessels undecided. I send you the paragraphs upon the subject.

"The tumults are great in all parts of England on account of the excessive price of corn and bread, which has risen since the harvest. I attribute it more to the abundant increase of paper, and the non-circulation of cash, than to any other cause. People in trade can push the paper off as fast as they receive it, as they did by continental money in America; but as farmers have not this opportunity they endeavor to secure themselves by going considerably in advance.

"I have now given you all the great articles of intelligence, for I trouble not myself with little ones, and consequently not with the Commissioners, nor any thing they are about, nor with John Adams, otherwise than to wish him safe home, and a better and wiser man in his place.

"In the present state of circumstances and the prospects arising from them, it may be proper for America to consider whether it is worth her while to enter into any treaty at this moment, or to wait the event of those circumstances which, if they go on will render partial treaties useless by deranging them. But if, in the mean time, she enters into any treaty it ought to be with a condition to the following purpose : Reserving to herself the right of joining in an association of Nations for the protection of the Rights of Neutral Commerce and the security of the liberty of the Seas.

"The pieces 2, 3, may go to the press. They will make a small pamphlet and the printers are welcome to put my name to it. It is best it should be put from thence; they will get into the newspapers. I know that the faction of John Adams abuses me pretty heartily. They are welcome. It does not disturb me, and they lose their labour; and in return for it I am doing America more service, as a neutral nation, than their expensive Commissioners can do, and she has that service from me for nothing. The piece No. 1 is only for your own amusement and that of your friends.

"I come now to speak confidentially to you on a private subject. When Mr. Ellsworth and Davie return to America, Murray will return to Holland, and in that case there will be nobody in Paris but Mr. Skipwith that has been in the habit of transacting business with the french Government since the revolution began. He is on a good standing with them, and if the chance of the day should place you in the presidency you cannot do better than appoint him for any purpose you may have occasion for in France. He is an honest man and will do his country Justice, and that with civility and good manners to the government he is commissioned to act with ; a faculty which that Northern Bear Timothy Pickering wanted, and which the Bear of that Bear, John Adams, never possessed.

"I know not much of Mr. Murray, otherwise than of his unfriendliness to every American who is not of his faction, but I am sure that Joel Barlow is a much fitter man to be in Holland than Mr. Murray. It is upon the fitness of the man to the place that I speak, for I have not communicated a thought upon the subject to Barlow, neither does he know, at the time of my writing this (for he is at Havre), that I have intention to do it.

"I will now, by way of relief, amuse you with some account of the progress of Iron Bridges. The french revolution and Mr. Burke's attack upon it, drew me off from any pontifical Works. Since my coming from England in '92, an Iron Bridge of a single arch 236 feet span versed sine 34 feet, has been cast at the Iron Works of the Walkers where my model was, and erected over the river Wear at Sunderland in the county of Durham in England. The two members in Parliament for the County, Mr. Bourdon and Mr. Milbank, were the principal subscribers ; but the direction was committed to Mr. Bourdon. A very sincere friend of mine, Sir Robert Smyth, who lives in france, and whom Mr. Monroe well knows, supposing they had taken their plan from my model wrote to Mr.

Milbank upon the subject.   Mr. Milbank answered the letter, which answer I have by me and I give you word for word the part concerning the Bridge : 'With respect to the Bridge over the river Wear at Sunderland it certainly is a Work well deserving admiration both for its structure, durability and utility, and I have good grounds for saying that the first Idea was taken from Mr. Paine's bridge exhibited at Paddington. But with respect to any compensation to Mr. Paine, however desirous of rewarding the labours of an ingenious man, I see not how it is in my power, having had nothing to do with his bridge after the payment of my subscription, Mr. Bourdon being accountable for the whole.   But if you can point out any mode by which I can be instrumental in procuring for Mr. P. any compensation for the advantages which the public may have derived from his ingenious model, from which certainly the outlines of the Bridge at Sunderland was taken, be assured it will afford me very great satisfaction.'

"I have now made two other models, one is pasteboard, five feet span and five inches of height from the cords.   It is in the opinion of every person who has seen it one of the most beautifull objects the eye can behold.   I then cast a model in Metal following the construction of that in pasteboard and of the same dimensions.   The whole was executed in my own Chamber.   It is far superior in strength, elegance, and readiness in execution to the model I made in America, and which you saw in Paris.   I shall bring those Models with me when I come home, which will be as soon as I can pass the seas in safety from the piratical John Bulls.

"I suppose you have seen, or have heard of the Bishop of Landaff's answer to my second part of the Age of reason. As soon as I got a copy of it I began a third part, which served also as an answer to the Bishop ; but as soon as the clerical Society for promoting *Christian Knowledge* knew of my intention to answer the Bishop, they prosecuted, as a Society, the printer of the first and second parts, to prevent that answer appearing.   No other reason than this can be assigned for their prosecuting at the time they did, because the first part had been in circulation above three years and the second part more than one, and they prosecuted immediately on knowing that I was taking up their Champion. The Bishop's answer, like Mr. Burke's attack on the french revolution, served me as a back-ground to bring forward other subjects upon, with more advantage than if the background was not there. This is the motive that induced me to answer him, otherwise I should have gone on without taking any notice of him. I have made and am still making additions to the manuscript, and shall continue to do so till an opportunity arrive for publishing it.

"If any American frigate should come to france, and the direction of it fall to you, I will be glad you would give me the opportunity of returning. The abscess under which I suffered almost two years is entirely healed of itself, and I enjoy exceeding good health. This is the first of October, and Mr. Skipwith has just called to tell me the Commissioners set off for Havre tomorrow. This will go by the frigate but not with the knowledge of the Commissioners. Remember me with much affection to my friends and accept the same to yourself."

As the Commissioners did not leave when they expected, Paine added several other letters to Jefferson, on public affairs. In one (October 1st) he says he has information of increasing aversion in the English people to their government. "It was the hope of conquest, and is now the hope of peace that keeps it [Pitt's administration] up." Pitt is anxious about his paper money. "The credit of Paper is suspicion asleep. When suspicion wakes the credit vanishes as the dream would." "England has a large Navy, and the expense of it leads to her ruin." The English nation is tired of war, longs for peace, "and, calculates upon defeat as it would upon victory." On October 4th, after the Commissioners had concluded a treaty, Paine alludes to an article said to be in it, requiring certain expenditures in France, and says that if he, Jefferson, be "in the chair, and not otherwise," he should offer himself for this business, should an agent be required. " It will serve to defray my expenses until I can return, but I wish it may be with the condition of returning. I am not tired of working for nothing, but I cannot afford it. This appointment will aid me in promoting the object I am now upon of a law of nations for the protection of neutral commerce." On October 6th he reports to Jefferson that at an entertainment given the American envoys, Consul Le Brun gave the toast : " A l'union de l'Amérique avec les puissances du Nord pour faire respecter la liberté des mers." On October 15th the last of his enclosures to Jefferson is written. He says that Napoleon, when asked if there would be more war, replied : " Nous n'aurions plus qu'une guerre d'écritoire." In all of Paine's writing about Napoleon, at this time, he seems as if watching a thundercloud, and trying to make out meteorologically its drift, and where it will strike.

CHAPTER XV.

THE LAST YEAR IN EUROPE.

On July 15, 1801, Napoleon concluded with Pius VII. the Concordat. Naturally, the first victim offered on the restored altar was Theophilanthropy. I have called Paine the founder of this Society, because it arose amid the controversy excited by the publication of " Le Siècle de la Raison," its manual and tracts reproducing his ideas aud language ; and because he gave the inaugural discourse. Theism was little known in France save as iconoclasm, and an assault on the Church : Paine treated it as a Religion. But, as he did not speak French, the practical organization and management of the Society were the work of others, and mainly of a Russian named Hauëy. There had been a good deal of odium incurred at first by a society which satisfied neither the pious nor the freethinkers, but it found a strong friend on the Directory. This was Larévellière-Lépeaux, whose secretary, Antoine Vallée, and young daughter, had become interested in the movement. This statesman never joined the Society, but he had attended one of its meetings, and, when a distribution of religious edifices was made, Theophilanthropy was assigned ten parish churches. It is said that when Larevéllière-

Lépeaux mentioned to Talleyrand his desire for the spread of this Society, the diplomat said : " All you have to do is to get yourself hanged, and revive the third day." Paine, who had pretty nearly fulfilled that requirement, saw the Society spread rapidly, and he had great hopes of its future. But Pius VII. also had an interested eye on it, and though the Concordat did not go into legal operation until 1802, Theophilanthropy was offered as a preliminary sacrifice in October, 1801.

The description of Paine by Walter Savage Landor, and representations of his talk, in the " Imaginary Conversations," so mix up persons, times, and places, that I was at one time inclined to doubt whether the two had met. But Mr. J. M. Wheeler, a valued correspondent in London, writes me : " Landor told my friend Mr. Birch of Florence that he particularly admired Paine, and that he visited him, having first obtained an interview at the house of General Dumouriez. Landor declared that Paine was always called ' Tom,' not out of disrespect, but because he was a jolly good fellow." An interview with Paine at the house of Dumouriez could only have occurred when the General was in Paris, in 1793. This would account for what Landor says of Paine taking refuge from trouble in brandy. There had been, as, Rickman testifies, and as all the facts show, nothing of this kind since that period. It would appear therefore that Landor must have mixed up at least two interviews with Paine, one in the time of Dumouriez, the other in that of Napoleon. Not even such an artist as Landor could invent the language ascribed to Paine concerning the French and Napoleon.

"The whole nation may be made as enthusiastic about a salad as about a constitution ; about the colour of a cockade as about a consul or a king. You will shortly see the real strength and figure of Bonaparte. He is wilful, headstrong, proud, morose, presumptuous ; he will be guided no longer ; he has pulled the pad from his forehead, and will break his nose or bruise his cranium against every table, chair, and brick in the room, until at last he must be sent to the hospital."

Paine prophesies that Napoleon will make himself emperor, and that "by his intemperate use of power and thirst of dominion" he will cause the people to "wish for their old kings, forgetting what beasts they were." Possibly under the name "Mr. Normandy" Landor disguises Thomas Poole, referred to on a preceding page. Normandy's sufferings on account of one of Paine's books are not exaggerated. In Mrs. Sanford's work is printed a letter from Paris, July 20, 1802, in which Poole says: "I called one morning on Thomas Paine. He is an original, amusing fellow. Striking, strong physiognomy. Said a great many quaint things, and read us part of a reply which he intends to publish to Watson's 'Apology.'"

Paine seems to have had no relation with the ruling powers at this time, though an Englishman who visited him is quoted by Rickman (p. 198) as remarking his manliness and fearlessness, and that he spoke as freely as ever after Bonaparte's supremacy. One communication only to any member of the government appears ; this was to the

[1] "Thomas Poole and His Friends," ii., p. 85.

Minister of the Interior concerning a proposed iron bridge over the Seine.[1] Political France and Paine had parted.

Under date of March 18, 1801, President Jefferson informs Paine that he had sent his manuscripts (Maritime Compact) to the printer to be made into a pamphlet, and that the American people had returned from their frenzy against France. He adds :

" You expressed a wish to get a passage to this country in a public vessel. Mr. Dawson is charged with orders to the captain of the Maryland to receive and accommodate you back if you can be ready to depart at such short warning. Rob. R. Livingston is appointed minister plenipotentiary to the republic of France, but will not leave this till we receive the ratification of the convention by Mr. Dawson.[2] I am in hopes you will find us returned generally to sentiments worthy of former times. In these it will be your glory to have steadily labored, and with as much effect as any man living. That you may long live to continue your useful labors and to reap the reward in the thankfulness of nations, is my sincere prayer. Accept assurances of my high esteem and affectionate attachment."

---

[1] " THE MINISTER OF THE INTERIOR TO THOMAS PAINE : I have received, Citizen, the observations that you have been so good as to address to me upon the construction of iron bridges. They will be of the greatest utility to us when the new kind of construction goes to be executed for the first time. With pleasure I assure you, Citizen, that you have rights of more than one kind to the gratitude of nations, and I give you, cordially, the expression of my particular esteem.—CHAPTAL."

It is rather droll, considering the appropriation of his patent in England, and the confiscation of a thousand pounds belonging to him, to find Paine casually mentioning that at this time a person came from London with plans and drawings to consult with him about an iron arch of 600 feet, over the Thames, then under consideration by a committee of the House of Commons.

[2] " Beau Dawson," an eminent Virginia Congressman.

The subjoined notes are from letters of Paine to Jefferson :

Paris, June 9, 1801. " Your very friendly letter by Mr. Dawson gave me the real sensation of happy satisfaction, and what served to increase it was that he brought it to me himself before I knew of his arrival. I congratulate America on your election. There has been no circumstance with respect to America since the times of her revolution that excited so much attention and expectation in France, England, Ireland, and Scotland as the pending election for President of the United States, nor any of which the event has given more general joy :

" I thank you for the opportunity you give me of returning by the Maryland, but I shall wait the return of the vessel that brings Mr. Livingston."

Paris, June 25, 1801. " The Parliamentaire, from America to Havre, was taken in going out, and carried into England. The pretence, as the papers say, was that a Swedish Minister was on board for America. If I had happened to have been there, I suppose they would have made no ceremony in conducting me on shore."

Paris, March 17, 1802. " As it is now Peace, though the definitive Treaty is not yet signed, I shall set off by the first opportunity from Havre or Dieppe, after the equinoctial gales are over. I continue in excellent health, which I know your friendship will be glad to hear of.—Wishing you and America every happiness, I remain your former fellow-labourer and much obliged fellow-citizen.

Paine's determination not to return to America in a national vessel was owing to a paragraph he saw in a Baltimore paper, headed " Out at Last." It stated that Paine had written to the President, expressing a wish to return by a national ship, and that " permission was given." There was here an indication that Jefferson's invitation to Paine by the Hon. John Dawson had become known to the President's enemies, and that Jefferson, on being attacked, had apologized by making the matter appear an act of charity. Paine would not believe that the President was personally responsible for the apologetic paragraph, which seemed inconsistent with the cordiality of the letter brought by Dawson; but, as he afterwards wrote to Jefferson, "it determined me not to come by a national ship."[1]   His request had been made at a time when any other than a national American ship was pretty certain to land him in an English prison. There was evidently no thought of any *éclat* in the matter, but no doubt a regard for economy as well as safety.

The following to the eminent deist lecturer in New York, Elihu Palmer, bears the date, "Paris, February 21, 1802, since the Fable of Christ":

"DEAR FRIEND, I received, by Mr. Livingston, the letter you wrote me, and the excellent work you have published ["The Principles of Nature"].   I see you have thought deeply on the subject, and expressed your thoughts in a strong and clear style. The hinting and intimating manner of writing that was formerly used on subjects of this kind, produced skepticism, but not conviction. It is necessary to be bold. Some people can be reasoned into sense, and others must be shocked into it. Say a bold thing that will stagger them, and they will begin to think.

[1] It was cleared up afterwards. Jefferson had been charged with sending a national ship to France for the sole purpose of bringing Paine home, and Paine himself would have been the first to condemn such an assumption of power. Although the President's adherents thought it right to deny this, Jefferson wrote to Paine that he had nothing to do with the paragraph. "With respect to the letter [offering the ship] I never hesitate to avow and justify it in conversation. In no other way do I trouble myself to contradict anything which is said. At that time, however, there were anomalies in the motions of some of our friends which events have at length reduced to regularity."

"There is an intimate friend of mine, Colonel Joseph Kirkbride of Bordentown, New Jersey, to whom I would wish you to send your work. He is an excellent man, and perfectly in our sentiments. You can send it by the stage that goes partly by land and partly by water, between New York and Philadelphia, and passes through Bordentown.

"I expect to arrive in America in May next. I have a third part of the Age of Reason to publish when I arrive, which, if I mistake not, will make a stronger impression than any thing I have yet published on the subject.

"I write this by an ancient colleague of mine in the French Convention, the citizen Lequinio, who is going [as] Consul to Rhode Island, and who waits while I write.[1] Yours in friendship."

The following, dated July 8, 1802, to Consul Rotch, is the last letter I find written by Paine from Paris:

"My Dear Friend,—The bearer of this is a young man that wishes to go to America. He is willing to do anything on board a ship to lesson the expense of his passage. If you know any captain to whom such a person may be usefull I will be obliged to you to speak to him about it.

"As Mr. Otte was to come to Paris in order to go to America, I wanted to take a passage with him, but as he stays in England to negociate some arrangements of Commerce, I have given up that idea. I wait now for the arrival of a person from England whom I want to see,[2] after which, I shall bid adieu to restless and wretched Europe. I am with affectionate esteem to you and Mrs. Rotch,

"Yours,

"Thomas Paine."

The President's cordial letter had raised a happy vision before the eyes of one sitting amid the ruins

[1] J. M. Lequinio, author of "Prejudices Destroyed," and other rationalistic works, especially dealt with in Priestley's "Letters to the Philosophers of France."
[2] No doubt Clio Rickman.

of his republican world. As he said of Job, he had
"determined, in the midst of accumulating ills, to
impose upon himself the hard duty of contentment."   Of the comrades with whom he began the
struggle for liberty in France but a small circle remained. As he wrote to Lady Smith,—from whom
he must now part,—" I might almost say like Job's
servant, 'and I only am escaped.'"   Of the American and English friends who cared for him when
he came out of prison few remain.

The President's letter came to a poor man in a
small room, furnished only with manuscripts and
models of inventions. Here he was found by an
old friend from England, Henry Redhead Yorke,
who, in 1795, had been tried in England for
sedition.   Yorke has left us a last glimpse of the
author in "wretched and restless Europe." The
"rights of man" had become so antiquated in
Napoleon's France, that Yorke found Paine's
name odious on account of his antislavery writings, the people "ascribing to his espousal of
the rights of the negroes of St. Domingo the
resistance which Leclercq had experienced from
them."   He found Paine in No. 4 Rue du
Théâtre Français.   A "jolly-looking woman" (in
whom we recognize Madame Bonneville) scrutinized Yorke severely, but was smiling enough
on learning that he was Paine's old friend.   He
was ushered into a little room heaped with boxes
of documents, a chaos of pamphlets and journals.
While Yorke was meditating on the contrast
between this habitation of a founder of two
great republics and the mansions of their rulers,

his old friend entered, dressed in a long flannel gown.

"Time seemed to have made dreadful ravages over his whole frame, and a settled melancholy was visible on his countenance. He desired me to be seated, and although he did not recollect me for a considerable time, he conversed with his usual affability. I confess I felt extremely surprised that he should have forgotten me ; but I resolved not to make myself known to him, as long as it could be avoided with propriety. In order to try his memory, I referred to a number of circumstances which had occurred while we were in company, but carefully abstained from hinting that we had ever lived together. He would frequently put his hand to his forehead, and exclaim, 'Ah ! I know that voice, but my recollection fails !' At length I thought it time to remove his suspense, and stated an incident which instantly recalled me to his mind. It is impossible to describe the sudden change which this effected ; his countenance brightened, he pressed me by the hand, and a silent tear stole down his cheek. Nor was I less affected than himself. For some time we sat without a word escaping from our lips. 'Thus are we met once more, Mr. Paine,' I resumed, 'after a long separation of ten years, and after having been both of us severely weather-beaten.' 'Aye,' he replied, 'and who would have thought that we should meet in Paris ?' He then enquired what motive had brought me here, and on my explaining myself, he observed with a smile of contempt, 'They have shed blood enough for liberty, and now they have it in perfection. This is not a country for an honest man to live in ; they do not understand any thing at all of the principles of free government, and the best way is to leave them to themselves. You see they have conquered all Europe, only to make it more miserable than it was before.' Upon this, I remarked that I was surprised to hear him speak in such desponding language of the fortune of mankind, and that I thought much might yet be done for the Republic. 'Republic !' he exclaimed, 'do you call this a Republic ? Why they are worse off than the slaves of Constantinople ; for there, they expect to be bashaws in heaven by submitting to be slaves below, but here they believe neither in heaven nor hell, and yet are slaves by choice. I know of no Republic in the world except America, which is the only country for such men as you and I. It is my intention to get away from this place as soon as possible, and I hope to be off in the autumn ; you are a young man and may see better times, but I have done with Europe, and its slavish politics.'

"I have often been in company with Mr. Paine, since my arrival here, and I was not a little surprised to find him wholly indifferent about the public spirit in England, or the remaining influence of his doctrines among its people. Indeed he seemed to dislike the mention of the subject ; and when, one day, in order to provoke discussion, I told him I had altered my opinions upon many of his principles, he answered, 'You certainly have the right to do so ; but you cannot alter the nature of things ; the French have alarmed all honest men ; but still truth is truth. Though you may not think that my principles are practicable in England, without bringing on a great deal of misery and confusion, you are, I am sure, convinced of their justice.' Here he took occasion to speak in terms of the utmost severity of Mr ——, who had obtained a seat in parliament, and said that 'parsons were always mischievous fellows when they turned politicians.' This gave rise to an observation respecting his 'Age of Reason,' the publication of which I said had lost him the good opinion of numbers of his English advocates. He became uncommonly warm at this remark, and in a tone of singular energy declared that he would not have published it if he had not thought it calculated to 'inspire mankind with a more exalted idea of the Supreme Architect of the Universe, and to put an end to villainous imposture.' He then broke out with the most violent invectives against our received opinions, accompanying them at the same time with some of the most grand and sublime conceptions of an Omnipotent Being, that I ever heard or read of. In the support of his opinion, he avowed himself ready to lay down his life, and said 'the Bishop of Llandaff may roast me in Smithfield if he likes, but human torture cannot shake my conviction.' He reached down a copy of the Bishop's work, interleaved with remarks upon it, which he read me ; after which he admitted the liberality of the

Bishop, and regretted that in all controversies among men a similar temper was not maintained. But in proportion as he appeared listless in politics, he seemed quite a zealot in his religious creed ; of which the following is an instance. An English lady of our acquaintance, not less remarkable for her talents than for elegance of manners, entreated me to contrive that she might have an interview with Mr. Paine. In consequence of this I invited him to dinner on a day when we were to be favoured with her company. But as she is a very rigid Roman Catholic I cautioned Mr. Paine, beforehand, against touching upon religious subjects, assuring him at the same time that she felt much interested to make his acquaintance. With much good nature he promised to be *discreet.* . . . For above four hours he kept every one in astonishment and admiration of his memory, his keen observation of men and manners, his numberless anecdotes of the American Indians, of the American war, of Franklin, Washington, and even of his Majesty, of whom he told several curious facts of humour and benevolence. His remarks on genius and taste can never be forgotten by those present. Thus far everything went on as I could wish ; the sparkling champagne gave a zest to his conversation, and we were all delighted. But alas! alas! an expression relating to his 'Age of Reason' having been mentioned by one of the company, he broke out immediately. He began with Astronomy,—addressing himself to Mrs. Y.,—he declared that the least inspection of the motion of the stars was a convincing proof that Moses was a liar. Nothing could stop him. In vain I attempted to change the subject, by employing every artifice in my power, and even attacking with vehemence his political principles. He returned to the charge with unabated ardour. I called upon him for a song though I never heard him sing in my life. He struck up one of his own composition ; but the instant he had finished it he resumed his favourite topic. I felt extremely mortified, and remarked that he had forgotten his promise, and that it was not fair to wound so deeply the opinions of the ladies. 'Oh! ' said he, 'they 'll come again. What a pity it is that people should be so prejudiced! ' To which I retorted that their prejudices might be virtues. 'If so,' he replied, ' the blossoms may be beautiful to the eye, but the root is weak.' One of the most extraordinary properties belonging to Mr. Paine is his power of retaining everything he has written in the course of his life. It is a fact that he can repeat word for word every sentence in his ' Common Sense,' ' Rights of Man,' etc., etc. The Bible is the only book which he has studied, and there is not a verse in it that is not familiar to him. In shewing me one day the beautiful models of two bridges he had devised he observed that Dr. Franklin once told him that ' books are written to please, houses built for great men, churches for priests, but no bridges for the people.' These models exhibit an extraordinary degree not only of skill but of taste ; and are wrought with extreme delicacy entirely by his own hands. The largest is nearly four feet in length ; the iron works, the chains, and every other article belonging to it, were forged and manufactured by himself. It is intended as the model of a bridge which is to be constructed across the Delaware, extending 480 feet with only one arch. The other is to be erected over a lesser river, whose name I forget, and is likewise a single arch, and of his own workmanship, excepting the chains, which, instead of iron, are cut out of pasteboard, by the fair hand of his correspondent the ' Little Corner of the World,' whose indefatigable perseverance is extraordinary. He was offered £3000 for these models and refused it. The iron bars, which I before mentioned that I noticed in a corner of his room, were also forged by himself, as the model of a crane, of a new description. He put them together, and exhibited the power of the lever to a most surprising degree." [1]

About this time Sir Robert Smith died, and another of the ties to Paris was snapped. His beloved Bonnevilles promised to follow him to the New World. His old friend Rickman has come over to see him off, and observed that " he did not drink spirits, and wine he took moderately ; he even objected to any spirits being laid in as a part of his

---

[1] " Letters from France," etc., London, 1804, 2 vols., 8vo. Thirty-three pages of the last letter are devoted to Paine.

sea-stock." These two friends journeyed together
to Havre, where, on September 1st, the way-worn
man begins his homeward voyage. Poor Rickman,
the perpetually prosecuted, strains his eyes till the
sail is lost, then sits on the beach and writes his
poetical tribute to Jefferson and America for recalling Paine, and a touching farewell to his
friend :

> " Thus smooth be thy waves, and thus gentle the breeze,
>   As thou bearest my Paine far away ;
> O waft him to comfort and regions of ease,
> Each blessing of freedom and friendship to seize,
>   And bright be his setting sun's ray."

Who can imagine the joy of those eyes when
they once more beheld the distant coast of the
New World ! Fifteen years have passed,—years
in which all nightmares became real, and liberty's
sun had turned to blood,—since he saw the happy
land fading behind him. Oh, America, thine old
friend who first claimed thy republican independence, who laid aside his Quaker coat and fought for
thy cause, believing it sacred, is returning to thy
breast ! This is the man of whom Washington
wrote : " His writings certainly had a powerful
effect on the public mind,—ought they not then
to meet an adequate return ? He is poor ! He is
chagrined ! " It is not money he needs now, but
tenderness, sympathy ; for he comes back from an
old world that has plundered, outlawed, imprisoned
him for his love of mankind. He has seen his
dear friends sent to the guillotine, and others are
pining in British prisons for publishing his " Rights
of Man,"—principles pronounced by President

Jefferson and Secretary Madison to be those of the United States. Heartsore, scarred, white-haired, there remains to this veteran of many struggles for humanity but one hope, a kindly welcome, a peaceful haven for his tempest-tossed life. Never for an instant has his faith in the heart of America been shaken. Already he sees his friend Jefferson's arms extended ; he sees his old comrades welcoming him to their hearths ; he sees his own house and sward at Bordentown, and the beautiful Kirkbride mansion beside the Delaware,—river of sacred memories, soon to be spanned by his graceful arch. How the ladies he left girls,—Fanny, Kitty, Sally,—will come with their husbands to greet him ! How will they admire the latest bridge-model, with Lady Smith's delicate chainwork for which (such is his estimate of friendship) he refused three thousand pounds, though it would have made his mean room palatial ! Ah, yes, poor heart, America will soothe your wounds, and pillow your sinking head on her breast ! America, with Jefferson in power, is herself again. They do not hate men in America for not believing in a celestial Robespierre. Thou stricken friend of man, who hast appealed from the god of wrath to the God of Humanity, see in the distance that Maryland coast, which early voyagers called Avalon, and sing again your song when first stepping on that shore twenty-seven years ago :

> " I come to sing that summer is at hand,
>   The summer time of wit, you 'll understand ;
>   Plants, fruits, and flowers, and all the smiling race:
>   That can the orchard or the garden grace ;

The Rose and Lily shall address the fair,
And whisper sweetly out, ' My dears, take care : '
With sterling worth the Plant of Sense shall rise,
And teach the curious to philosophize ! '
The frost returns ?   We 'll garnish out the scenes
With stately rows of Evergreens,
Trees that will bear the frost, and deck their tops
With everlasting flowers, like diamond drops." '

---

[1] " The Snowdrop and Critic," *Pennsylvania Magazine*, 1775. Couplets
are omitted between those given.

CHAPTER XVI.

THE AMERICAN INQUISITION.

On October 30th Paine landed at Baltimore. More than two and a half centuries had elapsed since the Catholic Lord Baltimore appointed a Protestant Governor of Maryland, William Stone, who proclaimed in that province (1648) religious freedom and equality. The Puritans, crowding thither, from regions of oppression, grew strong enough to exterminate the religion of Lord Baltimore who had given them shelter, and imprisoned his Protestant Governor. So, in the New World, passed the Inquisition from Catholic to Protestant hands.

In Paine's first American pamphlet, he had repeated and extolled the principle of that earliest proclamation of religious liberty. "Diversity of religious opinions affords a larger field for Christian kindness." The Christian kindness now consists in a cessation of sectarian strife that they may unite in stretching the author of the "Age of Reason" on their common rack, so far as was possible under a Constitution acknowledging no deity. This persecution began on the victim's arrival.

Soon after landing Paine wrote to President Jefferson: "I arrived here on Saturday from Havre,

after a passage of sixty days. I have several cases
of models, wheels, etc., and as soon as I can get
them from the vessel and put them on board the
packet for Georgetown I shall set off to pay my
respects to you. Your much obliged fellow-citizen,
—THOMAS PAINE."

On reaching Washington City Paine found his
dear friend Monroe starting off to resume his ministry in Paris, and by him wrote to Mr. Este,
banker in Paris (Sir Robert Smith's son-in-law),
enclosing a letter to Rickman, in London. " You
can have no idea," he tells Rickman, " of the agitation which my arrival occasioned." Every paper is
"filled with applause or abuse."

"My property in this country has been taken care of by my
friends, and is now worth six thousand pounds sterling ; which
put in the funds will bring me £400 sterling a year. Remember me in friendship and affection to your wife and family, and
in the circle of our friends. I am but just arrived here, and the
minister sails in a few hours, so that I have just time to write
you this. If he should not sail this tide I will write to my good
friend Col. Bosville, but in any case I request you to wait on
him for me.[1] Yours in friendship."

[1] Paine still had faith in Bosville. He was slow in suspecting any man
who seemed enthusiastic for liberty. In this connection it may be mentioned
that it is painful to find in the " Diary and Letters of Gouverneur Morris,"
(ii., p. 426) a confidential letter to Robert R. Livingston, Minister in France,
which seems to assume that Minister's readiness to receive slanders of Jefferson, who appointed him, and of Paine whose friendship he seemed to value.
Speaking of the President, Morris says : " The employment of and confidence
in adventurers from abroad will sooner or later rouse the pride and indignation of this country." Morris' editor adds : " This was probably an allusion
to Thomas Paine, who had recently returned to America and was supposed
to be an intimate friend of Mr. Jefferson, who, it was said, received him
warmly, dined him at the White House, and could be seen walking arm in
arm with him on the street any fine afternoon." The allusion to " adventurers " was no doubt meant for Paine, but not to his reception by Jefferson,
for Morris' letter was written on August 27th, some two months before

The defeated Federalists had already prepared
their batteries to assail the President for inviting
Paine to return on a national ship, under escort of
a Congressman. It required some skill for these
adherents of John Adams, a Unitarian, to set the
Inquisition in motion. It had to be done, however,
as there was no chance of breaking down Jefferson
but by getting preachers to sink political differences
and hound the President's favorite author. Out of
the North, stronghold of the " British Party," came
this partisan crusade under a pious flag. In Virginia and the South the " Age of Reason " was
fairly discussed, its influence being so great that
Patrick Henry, as we have seen, wrote and burnt a
reply. In Virginia, Deism, though largely prevailing, had not prevented its adherents from supporting the Church as an institution. It had become
their habit to talk of such matters only in private.
Jefferson had not ventured to express his views in
public, and was troubled at finding himself mixed
up with the heresies of Paine.[1] The author on

Paine's arrival. It was probably meant by Morris to damage Paine in Paris,
where it was known that he was intimate with Livingston, who had been introduced by him to influential men, among others to Sir Robert Smith and
Este, bankers. It is to be hoped that Livingston resented Morris' assumption of his treacherous character. Morris, who had shortly before dined at
the White House, tells Livingston that Jefferson "is descending to a condition which I find no decent word to designate." Surely Livingston's descendants should discover his reply to that letter.

[1] To the Rev. Dr. Waterhouse (Unitarian) who had asked permission to
publish a letter of his, Jefferson, with a keen remembrance of Paine's fate,
wrote (July 19, 1822): " No, my dear Sir, not for the world. Into what
a hornet's nest would it thrust my head !—The *genus irritabile vatum*, on
whom argument is lost, and reason is by themselves disdained in matters of
religion. Don Quixote undertook to redress the bodily wrongs of the world,
but the redressment of mental vagaries would be an enterprise more than
Quixotic. I should as soon undertake to bring the crazy skulls of Bedlam to

reaching Lovell's Hotel, Washington, had made known his arrival to the President, and was cordially received ; but as the newspapers came in with their abuse, Jefferson may have been somewhat intimidated.   At any rate Paine so thought. Eager to disembarrass the administration, Paine published a letter in the *National Intelligencer*, which had cordially welcomed him, in which he said that he should not ask or accept any office.[1] He meant to continue writing and bring forward his mechanical projects.   None the less did the " federalist " press use Paine's infidelity to belabor the President, and the author had to write defensive letters from the moment of his arrival.   On October 29th, before Paine had landed, the *National Intelligencer* had printed (from a Lancaster, Pa., journal) a vigorous letter, signed " A Republican," showing that the denunciations of Paine were not religious, but political, as John Adams was also unorthodox.   The " federalists " must often have wished that they had taken this warning,

sound understanding as to inculcate reason into that of an Athanasian.   I am old, and tranquillity is now my *summum bonum*.   Keep me therefore from the fire and faggot of Calvin and his victim Servetus.   Happy in the prospect of a restoration of a primitive Christianity, I must leave to younger athletes to lop off the false branches which have been engrafted into it by the mythologists of the middle and modern ages."—MS. belonging to Dr. Fogg of Boston.

[1] The *National Intelligencer* (Nov. 3d), announcing Paine's arrival at Baltimore, said, among other things : " Be his religious sentiments what they may, it must be their [the American people's] wish that he may live in the undisturbed possession of our common blessings, and enjoy them the more from his active participation in their attainment."   The same paper said, Nov. 10th : " Thomas Paine has arrived in this city [Washington] and has received a cordial reception from the Whigs of Seventy-six, and the republicans of 1800, who have the independence to feel and avow a sentiment of gratitude for his eminent revolutionary services."

for Paine's pen was keener than ever, and the opposition had no writer to meet him. His eight "Letters to the Citizens of the United States" were scathing, eloquent, untrammelled by partisanship, and made a profound impression on the country,—for even the opposition press had to publish them as part of the news of the day.[1]

On Christmas Day Paine wrote the President a suggestion for the purchase of Louisiana. The French, to whom Louisiana had been ceded by Spain, closed New Orleans (November 26th) against foreign ships (including American), and prohibited deposits there by way of the Mississippi. This caused much excitement, and the "federalists" showed eagerness to push the administration into a belligerent attitude toward France. Paine's "common sense" again came to the front, and he sent Jefferson the following paper :

"OF LOUISIANA.

"Spain has ceded Louisiana to france, and france has excluded the Americans from N. Orleans and the navigation of the Mississippi ; the people of the Western Territory have complained of it to their Government, and the governt. is of consequence involved and interested in the affair   The question then is—What is the best step to be taken ?

" The one is to begin by memorial and remonstrance against an infraction of a right. The other is by accommodation, still keeping the right in view, but not making it a groundwork.

"Suppose then the Government begin by making a proposal to france to repurchase the cession, made to her by Spain, of

---

[1] They were published in the *National Intelligencer* of November 15th, 22d, 29th, December 6th, January 25th, and February 2d, 1803. Of the others one appeared in the *Aurora* (Philadelphia), dated from Bordentown, N. J., March 12th, and the last in the Trenton *True American*, dated April 21st.

Louisiana, provided it be with the consent of the people of Louisiana or a majority thereof.

"By beginning on this ground any thing can be said without carrying the appearance of a threat,—the growing power of the western territory can be stated as matter of information, and also the impossibility of restraining them from seizing upon New Orleans, and the equal impossibility of france to prevent it.

"Suppose the proposal attended to, the sum to be given comes next on the carpet. This, on the part of America, will be estimated between the value of the Commerce, and the quantity of revenue that Louisiana will produce.

"The french treasury is not only empty, but the Government has consumed by anticipation a great part of the next year's revenue. A monied proposal will, I believe, be attended to; if it should, the claims upon france can be stipulated as part of the payment, and that sum can be paid here to the claimants.

"——I congratulate you on the *birthday of the New Sun*, now called christmas-day; and I make you a present of a thought on Louisiana.

"T. P"

Jefferson next day told Paine, what was as yet a profound secret, that he was already contemplating the purchase of Louisiana.[1]

[1] "The idea occurred to me," Paine afterwards wrote to the President, "without knowing it had occurred to any other person, and I mentioned it to Dr. Leib who lived in the same house (Lovell's); and, as he appeared pleased with it, I wrote the note and showed it to him before I sent it. The next morning you said to me that measures were already taken in that business. When Leib returned from Congress I told him of it. 'I knew that,' said he. 'Why then,' said I, 'did you not tell me so, because in that case I would not have sent the note.' 'That is the very reason,' said he; 'I would not tell you, because two opinions concurring on a case strengthen it.' I do not, however, like Dr. Leib's motion about Banks. Congress ought to be very cautious how it gives encouragement to this speculating project of banking, for it is now carried to an extreme. It is but another kind of striking paper money. Neither do I like the notion respecting the recession of the territory [District of Columbia.]." Dr. Michael Leib was a representative from Pennsylvania.

The " New Sun " was destined to bring his sun-
strokes on Paine. The pathetic story of his wrongs
in England, his martyrdom in France, was not
generally known, and, in reply to attacks, he had
to tell it himself. He had returned for repose and
found himself a sort of battlefield. One of the
most humiliating circumstances was the discovery
that in this conflict of parties the merits of his religion were of least consideration. The outcry of
the country against him, so far as it was not merely
political, was the mere ignorant echo of pulpit
vituperation. His well-considered theism, fruit of
so much thought, nursed amid glooms of the
dungeon, was called infidelity or atheism. Even
some from whom he might have expected discriminating criticism accepted the vulgar version and
wrote him in deprecation of a work they had not
read. Samuel Adams, his old friend, caught in
this *schwärmerei*, wrote him from Boston (November 30th) that he had " heard " that he had " turned
his mind to a defence of infidelity." Paine copied
for him his creed from the " Age of Reason," and
asked, " My good friend, do you call believing in
God infidelity ? "

This letter to Samuel Adams (January 1, 1803)
has indications that Paine had developed farther
his theistic ideal.

"We cannot serve the Deity in the manner we serve those
who cannot do without that service. He needs no service from
us. We can add nothing to eternity. But it is in our power to
render a service acceptable to him, and that is, not by praying,
but by endeavoring to make his creatures happy. A man does
not serve God by praying, for it is himself he is trying to serve ;

and as to hiring or paying men to pray, as if the Deity needed instruction, it is in my opinion an abomination. I have been exposed to and preserved through many dangers, but instead of buffeting the Deity with prayers, as if I distrusted him, or must dictate to him, I reposed myself on his protection ; and you, my friend, will find, even in your last moments, more consolation in the silence of resignation than in the murmuring wish of a prayer."

Paine must have been especially hurt by a sentence in the letter of Samuel Adams in which he said : " Our friend, the president of the United States, has been calumniated for his liberal sentiments, by men who have attributed that liberality to a latent design to promote the cause of infidelity." To this he did not reply, but it probably led him to feel a deeper disappointment at the postponement of the interviews he had hoped to enjoy with Jefferson after thirteen years of separation. A feeling of this kind no doubt prompted the following note (January 12th) sent to the President :

" I will be obliged to you to send back the Models, as I am packing up to set off for Philadelphia and New York. My intention in bringing them here in preference to sending them from Baltimore to Philadelphia, was to have some conversation with you on those matters and others I have not informed you of. But you have not only shown no disposition towards it, but have, in some measure, by a sort of shyness, as if you stood in fear of federal observation, precluded it. I am not the only one, who makes observations of this kind."

Jefferson at once took care that there should be no misunderstanding as to his regard for Paine. The author was for some days a guest in the President's family, where he again met Maria Jefferson (Mrs. Eppes) whom he had known in Paris. Randall says the devout ladies of the family had been shy of Paine, as was but natural, on account of the President's reputation for rationalism, but "Paine's discourse was weighty, his manners sober and inoffensive ; and he left Mr. Jefferson's mansion the subject of lighter prejudices than he entered it."[1]

Paine's defamers have manifested an eagerness to ascribe his maltreatment to personal faults. This is not the case. For some years after his arrival in the country no one ventured to hint anything disparaging to his personal habits or sobriety. On January 1, 1803, he wrote to Samuel Adams : "I have a good state of health and a happy mind; I take care of both by nourishing the first with temperance, and the latter with abundance." Had not this been true the "federal" press would have noised it abroad. He was neat in his attire. In all portraits, French and American, his dress is in accordance with the fashion. There was not, so far as I can discover, a suggestion while he was at Washington, that he was not a suitable guest for any drawing-room in the capital. On February 23, 1803, probably, was written the following which I find among the Cobbett papers :

From Mr. Paine to Mr. Jefferson, on the occasion of a toast being given at a federal dinner at Washington, of "MAY THEY NEVER KNOW PLEASURE WHO LOVE PAINE."

"I send you, Sir, a tale about some Feds,
    Who, in their wisdom, got to loggerheads.

---

[1] "Life of Jefferson," ii., 642 *seq.* Randall is mistaken in some statements. Paine, as we have seen, did not return on the ship placed at his service by the President ; nor did the President's letter appear until long after his return, when he and Jefferson felt it necessary in order to disabuse the public mind of the most absurd rumors on the subject.

The case was this, they felt so flat and sunk,
They took a glass together and got drunk.
Such things, you know, are neither new nor rare,
For some will hary themselves when in despair.
It was the natal day of Washington,
And that they thought a famous day for fun ;
For with the learned world it is agreed,
The better day the better deed.
They talked away, and as the glass went round
They grew, in point of wisdom, more profound ;
For at the bottom of the bottle lies
That kind of sense we overlook when wise.
Come, here 's a toast, cried one, with roar immense,
May none know pleasure who love Common Sense.
Bravo ! cried some,—no, no ! some others cried,
But left it to the waiter to decide.
I think, said he, the case would be more plain,
To leave out Common Sense, and put in Paine.
On this a mighty noise arose among
This drunken, bawling, senseless throng.
Some said that Common Sense was all a curse,
That making people wiser made them worse ;
It learned them to be careful of their purse,
And not be laid about like babes at nurse,
Nor yet believe in stories upon trust,
Which all mankind, to be well governed must ;
And that the toast was better at the first,
And he that did n't think so might be cursed.
So on they went, till such a fray arose
As all who know what Feds are may suppose."

On his way northward, to his old home in Bordentown, Paine passed many a remembered spot,
but found little or no greeting on his journey.
In Baltimore a " New Jerusalemite," as the Sweden-
borgian was then called, the Rev. Mr. Hargrove,
accosted him with the information that the key to
scripture was found, after being lost 4,000 years.

"Then it must be very rusty," answered Paine.
In Philadelphia his old friend Dr. Benjamin Rush
never came near him. "His principles," wrote
Rush to Cheetham, "avowed in his 'Age of Reason,' were so offensive to me that I did not wish
to renew my intercourse with him." Paine made
arrangements for the reception of his bridge
models at Peale's Museum, but if he met any
old friend there no mention of it appears. Most
of those who had made up the old circle—Franklin,
Rittenhouse, Muhlenberg—were dead, some were
away in Congress; but no doubt Paine saw George
Clymer. However, he did not stay long in Philadelphia, for he was eager to reach the spot he always
regarded as his home, Bordentown. And there,
indeed, his hope, for a time, seemed to be fulfilled.
It need hardly be said that his old friend Colonel
Kirkbride gave him hearty welcome. John Hall,
Paine's bridge mechanician, "never saw him
jollier," and he was full of mechanical "whims and
schemes" they were to pursue together. Jefferson was candidate for the presidency, and Paine
entered heartily into the canvass; which was not
prudent, but he knew nothing of prudence. The
issue not only concerned an old friend, but was
turning on the question of peace with France. On
March 12th he writes against the "federalist"
scheme for violently seizing New Orleans. At a
meeting in April, over which Colonel Kirkbride pre-
sides, Paine drafts a reply to an attack on Jefferson's administration, circulated in New York. On
April 21st he writes the refutation of an attack on
Jefferson, *àpropos* of the national vessel offered for

his return, which had been coupled with a charge that Paine had proposed to the Directory an invasion of America! In June he writes about his bridge models (then at Peale's Museum, Philadelphia), and his hope to span the Delaware and the Schuylkill with iron arches.

Here is a letter written to Jefferson from Bordentown (August 2d) containing suggestions concerning the beginning of government in Louisiana, from which it would appear that Paine's faith in the natural inspiration of *vox populi* was still imperfect :

"I take it for granted that the present inhabitants know little or nothing of election and representation as constituting government. They are therefore not in an immediate condition to exercise those powers, and besides this they are perhaps too much under the influence of their priests to be sufficiently free.

"I should suppose that a Government *provisoire* formed by Congress for three, five, or seven years would be the best mode of beginning. In the meantime they may be initiated into the practice by electing their Municipal government, and after some experience they will be in train to elect their State government. I think it would not only be good policy but right to say, that the people shall have the right of electing their Church Ministers, otherwise their Ministers will hold by authority from the Pope. I do not make it a compulsive article, but to put it in their power to use it when they please. It will serve to hold the priests in a stile of good behavior, and also to give the people an idea of elective rights. Anything, they say, will do to learn upon, and therefore they may as well begin upon priests.

"The present prevailing language is french and spanish, but it will be necessary to establish schools to teach english as the laws ought to be in the language of the Union.

"As soon as you have formed any plan for settling the Lands. I shall be glad to know it. My motive for this is because there are thousands and tens of thousands in England and Ireland and also in Scotland who are friends of mine by principle, and who would gladly change their present country and condition. Many among them, for I have friends in all ranks of life in those countries, are capable of becoming monied purchasers to any amount.

"If you can give me any hints respecting Louisiana, the quantity in square miles, the population, and amount of the present Revenue I will find an opportunity of making some use of it. When the formalities of the cession are compleated, the next thing will be to take possession, and I think it would be very consistent for the President of the United States to do this in person.

"What is Dayton gone to New Orleans for? Is he there as an Agent for the British as Blount was said to be?"

Of the same date is a letter to Senator Breckenridge, of Kentucky, forwarded through Jefferson:

"MY DEAR FRIEND,—Not knowing your place of Residence in Kentucky I send this under cover to the President desiring him to fill up the direction.

"I see by the public papers and the Proclamation for calling Congress, that the cession of Louisiana has been obtained. The papers state the purchase to be 11,250,000 dollars in the six per cents and 3,750,000 dollars to be paid to American claimants who have furnished supplies to France and the french Colonies and are yet unpaid, making on the whole 15,000,000 dollars.

"I observe that the faction of the Feds who last Winter were for going to war to obtain possession of that country and who attached so much importance to it that no expense or risk ought be spared to obtain it, have now altered their tone and say it is not worth having, and that we are better without it than with it. Thus much for their consistency. What follows is for your private consideration.

"The second section of the 2d article of the constitution says, The 'President shall have Power by and with the consent of the senate to make Treaties provided two thirds of the senators present concur.'

"A question may be supposed to arise on the present case, which is, under what character is the cession to be considered and taken up in congress, whether as a treaty, or in some other shape ? I go to examine this point.

"Though the word, Treaty, as a Word, is unlimited in its meaning and application, it must be supposed to have a defined meaning in the constitution. It there means Treaties of alliance or of navigation and commerce—Things which require a more profound deliberation than common acts do, because they entail on the parties a future reciprocal responsibility and become afterwards a supreme law on each of the contracting countries which neither can annull. But the cession of Louisiana to the United States has none of these features in it. It is a sale and purchase. A sole act which when finished, the parties have no more to do with each other than other buyers and sellers have. It has no future reciprocal consequences (which is one of the marked characters of a Treaty) annexed to it ; and the idea of its becoming a supreme law to the parties reciprocally (which is another of the characters of a Treaty) is inapplicable in the present case. There remains nothing for such a law to act upon.

"I love the restriction in the constitution which takes from the Executive the power of making treaties of his own will : and also the clause which requires the consent of two thirds of the Senators, because we cannot be too cautious in involving and entangling ourselves with foreign powers ; but I have an equal objection against extending the same power to the senate in cases to which it is not strictly and constitutionally applicable, because it is giving a nullifying power to a minority. Treaties, as already observed, are to have future consequences and whilst they remain, remain always in execution externally as well as internally, and therefore it is better to run the risk of losing a good treaty for the want of two thirds of the senate than be exposed to the danger of ratifying a bad one by a small majority. But in the present case no operation is to follow but what acts itself within our own Territory and under our own laws. We are the sole power concerned after the cession is accepted and the money paid, and therefore the cession is not a Treaty in the constitutional meaning of the word subject to be rejected by a minority in the senate.

" The question whether the cession shall be accepted and the bargain closed by a grant of money for the purpose, (which I take to be the sole question) is a case equally open to both houses of congress, and if there is any distinction of *formal right*, it ought according to the constitution, as a money transaction, to begin in the house of Representatives.

" I suggest these matters that the senate may not be taken unawares, for I think it not improbable that some Fed, who intends to negative the cession, will move to take it up as if it were a Treaty of Alliance or of Navigation and Commerce.

" The object here is an increase of territory for a valuable consideration. It is altogether a home concern—a matter of domestic policy. The only real ratification is the payment of the money, and as all verbal ratification without this goes for nothing, it would be a waste of time and expense to debate on the verbal ratification distinct from the money ratification. The shortest way, as it appears to me, would be to appoint a committee to bring in a report on the President's Message, and for that committee to report a bill for the payment of the money. The french Government, as the seller of the property, will not consider anything ratification but the payment of the money contracted for.

" There is also another point, necessary to be aware of, which is, to accept it in toto. Any alteration or modification in it, or annexed as a condition is so far fatal, that it puts it in the power of the other party to reject the whole and propose new Terms. There can be no such thing as ratifying in part, or with a condition annexed to it and the ratification to be binding. It is still a continuance of the negociation.

"It ought to be presumed that the American ministers have done to the best of their power and procured the best possible terms, and that being immediately on the spot with the other party they were better Judges of the whole, and of what could, or could not be done, than any person at this distance, and unacquainted with many of the circumstances of the case, can possibly be.

" If a treaty, a contract, or a cession be good upon the whole, it is ill policy to hazard the whole, by an experiment to get some trifle in it altered. The right way of proceeding in such case is to make sure of the whole by ratifying it, and then instruct the minister to propose a clause to be added to the Instrument to obtain the amendment or alteration wished for. This was the method Congress took with respect to the Treaty of Commerce with France in 1778. Congress ratified the whole and proposed two new articles which were agreed to by France and added to the Treaty.

" There is according to newspaper account an article which admits french and spanish vessels on the same terms as American vessels. But this does not make it a commercial Treaty. It is only one of the Items in the payment : and it has this advantage, that it joins Spain with France in making the cession and is an encouragement to commerce and new settlers.

" With respect to the purchase, admitting it to be 15 millions dollars, it is an advantageous purchase. The revenue alone purchased as an annuity or rent roll is worth more—at present I suppose the revenue will pay five per cent for the purchase money.

" I know not if these observations will be of any use to you. I am in a retired village and out of the way of hearing the talk of the great world. But I see that the Feds, at least some of them, are changing their tone and now reprobating the acquisition of Louisiana ; and the only way they can take to lose the affair will be to take it up as they would a Treaty of Commerce and annull it by a Minority ; or entangle it with some condition that will render the ratification of no effect.

" I believe in this state (Jersey) we shall have a majority at the next election. We gain some ground and lose none anywhere. I have half a disposition to visit the Western World next spring and go on to New Orleans. They are a new people and unacquainted with the principles of representative government and I think I could do some good among them.

" As the stage-boat which was to take this letter to the Post-office does not depart till to-morrow, I amuse myself with continuing the subject after I had intended to close it.

" I know little and can learn but little of the extent and present population of Louisiana. After the cession be compleated and the territory annexed to the United States it will, I suppose, be formed into states, one, at least, to begin with.

The people, as I have said, are new to us and we to them and a great deal will depend on a right beginning. As they have been transferred backward and forward several times from one European Government to another it is natural to conclude they have no fixed prejudices with respect to foreign attachments, and this puts them in a fit disposition for their new condition. The established religion is roman ; but in what state it is as to exterior ceremonies (such as processions and celebrations), I know not. Had the cession to france continued with her, religion I suppose would have been put on the same footing as it is in that country, and there no ceremonial of religion can appear on the streets or highways ; and the same regulation is particularly necessary now or there will soon be quarrells and tumults between the old settlers and the new. The Yankees will not move out of the road for a little wooden Jesus stuck on a stick and carried in procession nor kneel in the dirt to a wooden Virgin Mary. As we do not govern the territory as provinces but incorporated as states, religion there must be on the same footing it is here, and Catholics have the same rights as Catholics have with us and no others. As to political condition the Idea proper to be held out is, that we have neither conquered them, nor bought them, but formed a Union with them and they become in consequence of that union a part of the national sovereignty.

" The present Inhabitants and their descendants will be a majority for some time, but new emigrations from the old states and from Europe, and intermarriages, will soon change the first face of things, and it is necessary to have this in mind when the first measures shall be taken. Everything done as an expedient grows worse every day, for in proportion as the mind grows up to the full standard of sight it disclaims the expedient. America had nearly been ruined by expedients in the first stages of the revolution, and perhaps would have been so, had not ' Common Sense ' broken the charm and the Declaration of Independence sent it into banishment.

" Yours in friendship

" remember me in   " THOMAS PAINE.[1]
the circle of your friends."

---

[1] The original is in possession of Mr. William F. Havermeyer, Jr.

Mr. E. M. Woodward, in his account of Borden-town, mentions among the "traditions" of the place, that Paine used to meet a large number of gentlemen at the "Washington House," kept by Debora Applegate, where he conversed freely "with any proper person who approached him."

"Mr. Paine was too much occupied in literary pursuits and writing to spend a great deal of his time here, but he generally paid several visits during the day. His drink was invariably brandy. In walking he was generally absorbed in deep thought, seldom noticed any one as he passed, unless spoken to, and in going from his home to the tavern was frequently ob-served to cross the street several times. It is stated that several members of the church were turned from their faith by him, and on this account, and the general feeling of the com-munity against him for his opinions on religious subjects, he was by the mass of the people held in odium, which feeling to some extent was extended to Col. Kirkbride."

These "traditions" were recorded in 1876. Paine's "great power of conversation" was remem-bered. But among the traditions, even of the religious, there is none of any excess in drinking.

Possibly the turning of several church-members from their faith may not have been so much due to Paine as to the parsons, in showing their "reli-gion" as a gorgon turning hearts to stone against a benefactor of mankind. One day Paine went with Colonel Kirkbride to visit Samuel Rogers, the Colonel's brother-in-law, at Bellevue, across the river. As he entered the door Rogers turned his back, refusing his old friend's hand, because it had written the "Age of Reason." Presently Borden-town was placarded with pictures of the Devil flying away with Paine. The pulpits set up a chorus of vituperation. Why should the victim spare the altar on which he is sacrificed, and justice also? Dogma had chosen to grapple with the old man in its own way. That it was able to break a driven leaf Paine could admit as truly as Job; but he could as bravely say: Withdraw thy hand from me, and I will answer thee, or thou shalt answer me! In Paine too it will be proved that such outrages on truth and friendship, on the rights of thought, proceed from no God, but from the destructive forces once personified as the adversary of man.

Early in March Paine visited New York, to see Monroe before his departure for France. He drove with Kirkbride to Trenton; but so furious was the pious mob, he was refused a seat in the Trenton stage. They dined at Government House, but when starting for Brunswick were hooted. These were the people for whose liberties Paine had marched that same road on foot, musket in hand. At Trenton insults were heaped on the man who by camp-fires had written the *Crisis*, which animated the conquerors of the Hessians at that place, in "the times that tried men's souls." These people he helped to make free,—free to cry *Crucify!*

Paine had just written to Jefferson that the Louisianians were "perhaps too much under the influence of their priests to be sufficiently free." Probably the same thought occurred to him about people nearer home, when he presently heard of Colonel Kirkbride's sudden unpopularity, and death. On October 3d Paine lost this faithful friend.[1]

[1] It should be stated that Burlington County, in which Bordentown is situated, was preponderantly Federalist, and that Trenton was in the hands of a Federalist mob of young well-to-do rowdies. The editor of the *True American*, a Republican paper to which Paine had contributed, having commented on a Fourth of July orgie of those rowdies in a house associated with the revolution, was set upon with bludgeons on July 12th, and suffered serious injuries. The Grand Jury refused to present the Federalist ruffians, though the evidence was clear, and the mob had free course.

The facts of the Paine mob are these : after dining at Government House, Trenton, Kirkbride applied for a seat on the New York stage for Paine. The owner, Voorhis, cursed Paine as "a deist," and said, "I 'll be damned if he shall go in my stage." Another stage-owner also refused, saying, "My stage and horses were once struck by lightning, and I don't want them to suffer again." When Paine and Kirkbride had entered their carriage a mob surrounded them with a drum, playing the "rogue's march." The local reporter (*True American*) says, "Mr. Paine discovered not the least emotion of fear or anger, but calmly observed that such conduct had no tendency to hurt his feelings or injure his fame." The mob then tried to frighten the horse with the drum, and succeeded, but the two gentlemen reached a friend's house in Brunswick in safety. A letter from Trenton had been written to the stage-master there also, to prevent Paine from securing a seat, whether with success does not appear.

CHAPTER XVII.

NEW ROCHELLE AND THE BONNEVILLES.

THE Bonnevilles, with whom Paine had resided in Paris, were completely impoverished after his departure. They resolved to follow Paine to America, depending on his promise of aid should they do so. Foreseeing perils in France, Nicolas, unable himself to leave at once, hurried off his wife and children—Benjamin, Thomas, and Louis. Madame Bonneville would appear to have arrived in August, 1803. I infer this because Paine writes, September 23d, to Jefferson from Stonington, Connecticut; and later letters show that he had been in New York, and afterwards placed Thomas Paine Bonneville with the Rev. Mr. Foster (Universalist) of Stonington for education. Madame Bonneville was placed in his house at Bordentown, where she was to teach French.

At New York, Paine found both religious and political parties sharply divided over him. At Lovett's Hotel, where he stopped, a large dinner was given him, March 18th, seventy being present. One of the active promoters of this dinner was James Cheetham, editor of the *American Citizen*, who, after seriously injuring Paine by his patronage, became his malignant enemy.

In the summer of 1803 the political atmosphere was in a tempestuous condition, owing to the widespread accusation that Aaron Burr had intrigued with the Federalists against Jefferson to gain the presidency. There was a Society in New York called " Republican Greens," who, on Independence Day, had for a toast " Thomas Paine, the Man of the People," and who seem to have had a piece of music called the " Rights of Man." Paine was also apparently the hero of that day at White Plains, where a vast crowd assembled, " over 1,000," among the toasts being : " Thomas Paine—the bold advocate of rational liberty—the People's friend." He probably reached New York again in August. A letter for " Thomas Payne " is in the advertised Letter-list of August 6th, and in the *American Citizen* (August 9th) are printed (and misprinted) " Lines, extempore, by Thomas Paine, July, 1803." [1]

---

[1] " Quick as the lightning's vivid flash
    The poet's eye o'er Europe rolls ;
  Sees battles rage, hears tempests crash,
    And dims at horror's threatening scowls.

" Mark ambition's ruthless king,
    With crimsoned banners scathe the globe ;
  While trailing after conquest's wing,
    Man's festering wounds his demons probe.

" Palléd with streams of reeking gore
    That stain the proud imperial day,
  He turns to view the western shore,
    Where freedom holds her boundless sway.

" 'T is here her sage triumphant sways
    An empire in the people's love ;
  'T is here the sovereign will obeys
    No king but Him who rules above."

The verses, crudely expressing the contrast between President Jefferson and King George—or Napoleon, it is not clear which,—sufficiently show that Paine's genius was not extempore. His reputation as a patriotic minstrel was high; his "Hail, great Republic," to the tune of "Rule Britannia," was the established Fourth-of-July song, and it was even sung at the dinner of the American consul in London (Erving) March 4, 1803, the anniversary of Jefferson's election. Possibly the extempore lines were sung on some Fourth-of-July occasion. I find "Thomas Paine" and the "Rights of Man" favorite toasts at republican celebrations in Virginia also at this time. In New York we may discover Paine's coming and going by rancorous paragraphs concerning him in the *Evening Post*.[1] Perhaps the most malignant wrong done Paine in this paper was the adoption of his signature, "Common Sense," by one of its contributors!

[1] On July 12th the *Evening Post* (edited by William Coleman) tries to unite republicanism and infidelity by stating that Part I. of the "Age of Reason" was sent in MS. to Mr. Fellows of New York, and in the following year Part II. was gratuitously distributed "from what is now the office of the Aurora." On September 24th that paper publishes a poem about Paine, ending :

> "And having spent a lengthy life in evil,
> Return again unto thy parent Devil !"

Another paragraph says that Franklin hired Paine in London to come to America and write in favor of the Revolution,—a remarkable example of federalist heredity from "Toryism." On September 27th the paper prints a letter purporting to have been found by a waiter in Lovett's Hotel after Paine's departure,—a long letter to Paine, by some red-revolutionary friend, of course gloating over the exquisite horrors filling Europe in consequence of the "Rights of Man." The pretended letter is dated "Jan. 12, 1803," and signed "J. Oldney." The paper's correspondent pretends to have found out Oldney, and conversed with him. No doubt many simple people believed the whole thing genuine.

The most learned physician in New York, Dr. Nicholas Romayne, invited Paine to dinner, where he was met by John Pintard, and other eminent citizens. Pintard said to Paine : "I have read and re-read your 'Age of Reason,' and any doubts which I before entertained of the truth of revelation have been removed by your logic. Yes, sir, your very arguments against Christianity have convinced me of its truth." "Well then," answered Paine, "I may return to my couch to-night with the consolation that I have made at least one Christian."[1] This authentic anecdote is significant. John Pintard, thus outdone by Paine in politeness, founded the Tammany Society, and organized the democratic party. When the "Rights of Man" appeared, the book and its author were the main toasts of the Tammany celebrations ; but it was not so after the "Age of Reason" had appeared. For John Pintard was all his life a devotee of Dutch Reformed orthodoxy. Tammany, having begun with the populace, had by this time got up somewhat in society. As a rule the "gentry" were Federalists, though they kept a mob in their back yard to fly at the democrats on occasion. But with Jefferson in the presidential chair, and Clinton vice-president, Tammany was in power. To hold this power Tammany had to court the clergy. So there was no toast to Paine in the Wigwam of 1803.[2]

President Jefferson was very anxious about the constitutional points involved in his purchase

---

[1] Dr. Francis' "Old New York," p. 140.

[2] *The New York Daily Advertiser* published the whole of Part I. of the

of Louisiana, and solicited Paine's views on the whole subject. Paine wrote to him extended communications, among which was the letter of September 23d, from Stonington. The interest of the subject is now hardly sufficient to warrant publication of the whole of this letter, which, however, possesses much interest.

"Your two favours of the 10 and 18 ult. reached me at this place on the 14th inst. ; also one from Mr. Madison. I do not suppose that the framers of the Constitution thought anything about the acquisition of new territory, and even if they did it was prudent to say nothing about it, as it might have suggested to foreign Nations the idea that we contemplated foreign conquest. It appears to me to be one of those cases with which the Constitution had nothing to do, and which can be judged of only by the circumstances of the times when such a case shall occur. The Constitution could not foresee that Spain would cede Louisiana to France or to England, and therefore it could not determine what our conduct should be ín consequence of such an event. The cession makes no alteration in the Constitution ; it only extends the principles of it over a larger territory, and this certainly is within the morality of the Constitution, and not contrary to, nor beyond, the expression or intention of any of its articles . . . Were a question to arise it would apply, not to the Cession, because it violates no article of the Constitution, but to Ross and Morris's motion. The Constitution empowers Congress

"Rights of Man " in 1791 (May 6-27), the editor being then John Pintard. At the end of the publication a poetical tribute to Paine was printed. Four of the lines run :

> "Rous'd by the reason of his manly page,
> Once more shall Paine a listening world engage ;
> From reason's source a bold reform he brings,
> By raising up mankind he pulls down kings."

At the great celebration (October 12, 1792) of the third Centenary of the discovery of America, by the sons of St. Tammany, New York, the first man toasted after Columbus was Paine, and next to Paine " The Rights of Man." They were also extolled in an ode composed for the occasion, and sung.

to *declare* war, but to make war without declaring it is anti-constitutional. It is like attacking an unarmed man in the dark. There is also another reason why no such question should arise. The english Government is but in a tottering condition and if Bonaparte succeeds, that Government will break up. In that case it is not improbable we may obtain Canada, and I think that Bermuda ought to belong to the United States. In its present condition it is a nest for piratical privateers. This is not a subject to be spoken of, but it may be proper to have it in mind.

" The latest news we have from Europe in this place is the insurrection in Dublin. It is a disheartening circumstance to the english Government, as they are now putting arms into the hands of people who but a few weeks before they would have hung had they found a pike in their possession. I think the probability is in favour of the descent [on England by Bonaparte] . . .

" I shall be employed the ensuing Winter in cutting two or three thousand Cords of Wood on my farm at New Rochelle for the New York market distant twenty miles by water. The Wood is worth 3½ dollars per load as it stands. This will furnish me with ready money, and I shall then be ready for whatever may present itself of most importance next spring. I had intended to build myself a house to my own taste, and a workshop for my mechanical operations, and make a collection, as authors say, of my works, which with what I have in manuscript will make four, or five octavo volumes, and publish them by subscription, but the prospects that are now opening with respect to England hold me in suspence.

" It has been customary in a President's discourse to say something about religion. I offer you a thought on this subject. The word, religion, used as a word *en masse* has no application to a country like America. In catholic countries it would mean exclusively the religion of the romish church ; with the Jews, the jewish religion ; in England, the protestant religion or in the sense of the english church, the established religion ; with the Deists it would mean Deism ; with the Turks, Mahometism &c., &c., As well as I recollect it is *Lego*, *Relego*, *Relegio*, *Religion*, that is say, tied or bound by an oath or obligation. The french use the word properly; when a woman enters a convent, she is called a novitiate; when she takes the oath, she is a *religieuse*, that is, she is bound by an oath. Now all that we have to do, as a Government with the word religion, in this country, is with the civil rights of it, and not at all with its *creeds*. Instead therefore of using the word religion, as a word en masse, as if it meant a creed, it would be better to speak only of its civil rights; *that all denominations of religion are equally protected, that none are dominant, none inferior, that the rights of conscience are equal to every denomination and to every individual and that it is the duty of Government to preserve this equality of conscientious rights.* A man cannot be called a hypocrite for defending the civil rights of religion, but he may be suspected of insincerity in defending its creeds.

"I suppose you will find it proper to take notice of the impressment of American seamen by the Captains of British vessels, and procure a list of such captains and report them to their government. This pretence of searching for british seamen is a new pretence for visiting and searching American vessels. . . .

"I am passing some time at this place at the house of a friend till the wood cutting time comes on, and I shall engage some cutters here and then return to New Rochelle. I wrote to Mr. Madison concerning the report that the british Government had cautioned ours not to pay the purchase money for Louisiana, as they intended to take it for themselves. I have received his [negative] answer, and I pray you make him my compliments.

"We are still afflicted with the yellow fever, and the Doctors are disputing whether it is an imported or a domestic disease. Would it not be a good measure to prohibit the arrival of all vessels from the West Indies from the last of June to the middle of October. If this was done this session of Congress, and we escaped the fever next summer, we should always know how to escape it. I question if performing quarantine is a sufficient guard. The disease may be in the cargo, especially that part which is barrelled up, and not in the persons on board, and when that cargo is opened on our wharfs, the hot steaming air in contact with the ground imbibes the infection. I can conceive that infected air can be barrelled up, not in a hogshead

of rum, nor perhaps sucre, but in a barrel of coffee. I am
badly off in this place for pen and Ink, and short of paper. I
heard yesterday from Boston that our old friend S. Adams was
at the point of death. Accept my best wishes."

When Madame Bonneville left France it was
understood that her husband would soon follow.
but he did not come, nor was any letter received
from him.   This was probably the most important
allusion in a letter of Paine, dated New York,
March 1, 1804, to " Citizen Skipwith, Agent Commercial d'Amerique, Paris."

" DEAR FRIEND—I have just a moment to write you a line
by a friend who is on the point of sailing for Bordeaux. The
Republican interest is now compleatly triumphant.   The
change within this last year has been great. We have now
14 States out of 17,—N. Hampshire, Mass. and Connecticut
stand out.   I much question if any person will be started
against Mr. Jefferson. Burr is rejected for the vice-presidency ;
he is now putting up for Governor of N. York.   Mr. Clinton
will be run for vice-president.   Morgan Lewis, Chief Justice
of the State of N. Y. is the Republican candidate for Governor
of that State.

" I have not received a line from Paris, except a letter from
Este, since I left it.   We have now been nearly 80 days without news from Europe. What is Barlow about ? I have not
heard anything from him except that he is *always* coming.
What is Bonneville about ?   Not a line has been received from
him. Respectful compliments to Mr. Livingston and family.
Yours in friendship."

Madame Bonneville, unable to speak English,
found Bordentown dull, and soon turned up in
New York.   She ordered rooms in Wilburn's
boarding-house, where Paine was lodging, and
the author found the situation rather complicated.
The family was absolutely without means of their

own, and Paine, who had given them a comfortable home at Bordentown, was annoyed by their coming on to New York. Anxiety is shown in the following letter written at 16 Gold St., New York, March 24th, to " Mr. Hyer, Bordenton, N. J."

" DEAR SIR,—I received your letter by Mr. Nixon, and also a former letter, but I have been so unwell this winter with a fit of gout, tho' not so bad as I had at Bordenton about twenty years ago, that I could not write, and after I got better I got a fall on the ice in the garden where I lodge that threw me back for above a month. I was obliged to get a person to copy off the letter to the people of England, published in the Aurora, March 7, as I dictated it verbally, for all the time my complaint continued. My health and spirits were as good as ever. It was my intention to have cut a large quantity of wood for the New York market, and in that case you would have had the money directly, but this accident and the gout prevented my doing anything. I shall now have to take up some money upon it, which I shall do by the first of May to put Mrs. Bonneville into business, and I shall then discharge her bill. In the mean time I wish you to receive a quarter's rent due on the 1st of April from Mrs Richardson, at $25 per ann., and to call on Mrs. Read for 40 or 50 dollars, or what you can get, and to give a receipt in my name. Col. Kirkbride should have discharged your bill, it was what he engaged to do. Mrs. Wharton owes for the rent of the house while she lived in it, unless Col. Kirkbride has taken it into his accounts. Samuel Hileyar owes me 84 dollars lent him in hard money. Mr. Nixon spake to me about hiring my house, but as I did not know if Mrs. Richardson intended to stay in it or quit it I could give no positive answer, but said I would write to you about it. Israel Butler also writes me about taking at the same rent as Richardson pays. I will be obliged to you to let the house as you may judge best. I shall make a visit to Bordenton in the spring, and I shall call at your house first.

" There have been several arrivals here in short passages from England. P. Porcupine, I see, is become the panegyrist of Bonaparte. You will see it in the Aurora of March 19, and also the message of Bonaparte to the french legislature. It is a good thing.

"Mrs. Bonneville sends her compliments. She would have wrote, but she cannot yet venture to write in English. I congratulate you on your new appointment.

"Yours in friendship."[1]

Paine's letter alluded to was printed in the *Aurora* with the following note:

"To THE EDITOR.—As the good sense of the people in their elections has now put the affairs of America in a prosperous condition at home and abroad, there is nothing immediately important for the subject of a letter. I therefore send you a piece on another subject."

The piece presently appeared as a pamphlet of sixteen pages with the following title : "Thomas Paine to the People of England, on the Invasion of England. Philadelphia : Printed at the Temple of Reason Press, Arch Street. 1804." Once more the hope had risen in Paine's breast that Napoleon was to turn liberator, and that England was to be set free. "If the invasion succeed I hope Bonaparte will remember that this war has not been provoked by the people. It is altogether the act of the government without their consent or knowledge ; and though the late peace appears to have been insidious from the first, on the part of the government, it was received by the people with a sincerity of joy." He still hopes that the English people may be able to end the trouble peacefully, by compelling Parliament to fulfil the Treaty of Amiens, naïvely informing them that "a Treaty

[1] I am indebted for this letter to the N. Y. Hist. Society, which owns the original.

ought to be fulfilled." The following passages may
be quoted:

" In casting my eye over England and America, and comparing them together, the difference is very striking. The two
countries were created by the same power, and peopled from the
same stock. What then has caused the difference ? Have those
who emigrated to America improved, or those whom they left
behind degenerated ? . . . We see America flourishing in
peace, cultivating friendship with all nations, and reducing her
public debt and taxes, incurred by the revolution. On the
contrary we see England almost perpetually in war, or warlike
disputes, and her debt and taxes continually increasing.
Could we suppose a stranger, who knew nothing of the
origin of the two nations, he would from observation conclude
that America was the old country, experienced and sage,
and England the new, eccentric and wild. Scarcely had England drawn home her troops from America, after the revolutionary war, than she was on the point of plunging herself
into a war with Holland, on account of the Stadtholder ; then
with Russia ; then with Spain on account of the Nootka cat-
skins ; and actually with France to prevent her revolution.
Scarcely had she made peace with France, and before she had
fulfilled her own part of the Treaty, than she declared war
again, to avoid fulfilling the Treaty. In her Treaty of peace
with America, she engaged to evacuate the western posts
within six months ; but, having obtained peace, she refused
to fulfil the conditions, and kept possession of the posts, and
embroiled herself in an Indian war.[1] In her Treaty of peace
with France, she engaged to evacuate Malta within three
months ; but, having obtained peace, she refused to evacuate
Malta, and began a new war."

Paine points out that the failure of the French
Revolution was due to "the provocative interference of foreign powers, of which Pitt was the
principal and vindictive agent," and affirms the

---

[1] Paine's case is not quite sound at this point. The Americans had not,.
on their side, fulfilled the condition of paying their English debts.

success of representative government in the United States after thirty years' trial. "The people of England have now two revolutions before them,— the one as an example, the other as a warning. Their own wisdom will direct them what to choose and what to avoid ; and in everything which regards their happiness, combined with the common good of mankind, I wish them honor and success."

During this summer, Paine wrote a brilliant paper on a memorial sent to Congress from the French inhabitants of Louisiana. They demanded immediate admission to equal Statehood, also the right to continue the importation of negro slaves. Paine reminds the memorialists of the " mischief caused in France by the possession of power before they understood principles." After explaining their position, and the freedom they have acquired by the merits of others, he points out their ignorance of human " rights " as shown in their guilty notion that to enslave others is among them. " Dare you put up a petition to Heaven for such a power, without fearing to be struck from the earth by its justice ? Why, then, do you ask it of man against man ? Do you want to renew in Louisiana the horrors of Domingo ? "

This article (dated September 22d) produced great effect. John Randolph of Roanoke, in a letter to Albert Gallatin (October 14th), advises "the printing of . . . thousand copies of Tom Paine's answer to their remonstrance, and transmitting them by as many thousand troops, who can speak a language perfectly intelligible to the people of Louisiana, whatever that of their governor may be."

Nicolas Bonneville still giving no sign, and Madame being uneconomical in her notions of money, Paine thought it necessary—morally and financially—to let it be known that he was not responsible for her debts. When, therefore, Wilburn applied to him for her board ($35), Paine declined to pay, and was sued. Paine pleaded *non assumpsit*, and, after gaining the case, paid Wilburn the money.

It presently turned out that the surveillance of Nicolas Bonneville did not permit him to leave France, and, as he was not permitted to resume his journal or publications, he could neither join his family nor assist them.

Paine now resolved to reside on his farm. The following note was written to Col. John Fellows. It is dated at New Rochelle, July 9th :

"FELLOW CITIZEN,—As the weather is now getting hot at New York, and the people begin to get out of town, you may as well come up here and help me settle my accounts with the man who lives on the place. You will be able to do this better than I shall, and in the mean time I can go on with my literary works, without having my mind taken off by affairs of a different kind. I have received a packet from Governor Clinton, enclosing what I wrote for. If you come up by the stage you will stop at the post-office, and they will direct you the way to the farm. It is only a pleasant walk. I send a price for the Prospect ; if the plan mentioned in it is pursued, it will open a way to enlarge and give establishment to the deistical church ; but of this and some other things we will talk when you come up, and the sooner the better. Yours in friendship."

Paine was presently enjoying himself on his farm

at New Rochelle, and Madame Bonneville began
to keep house for him.

"It is a pleasant and healthy situation [he wrote to Jefferson somewhat later], commanding a prospect always green and
peaceable, as New Rochelle produces a great deal of grass and
hay.   The farm contains three hundred acres, about one hundred of which is meadow land, one hundred grazing and village
land, and the remainder woodland.   It is an oblong about a
mile and a half in length.   I have sold off sixty-one acres and
a half for four thousand and twenty dollars.   With this money
I shall improve the other part, and build an addition 34 feet
by 32 to the present dwelling."

He goes on into an architectural description,
with drawings, of the arched roof he intends to
build, the present form of roof being "unpleasing
to the eye."   He also draws an oak floor such as
they make in Paris, which he means to imitate.

With a black cook, Rachel Gidney, the family
seemed to be getting on with fair comfort ; but on
Christmas Eve an event occurred which came near
bringing Paine's plans to an abrupt conclusion.
This is related in a letter to William Carver, New
York, dated January 16th, at New Rochelle.

"ESTEEMED FRIEND,—I have recd. two letters from you,
one giving an account of your taking Thomas to Mr. Foster[1]
—the other dated Jany. 12—I did not answer the first because
I hoped to see you the next Saturday or the Saturday after.
What you heard of a gun being fired into the room is true—
Robert and Rachel were both gone out to keep Christmas Eve
and about eight o'clock at Night the gun were fired.   I ran
immediately out, one of Mr. Dean's boys with me, but the
person that had done it was gone.   I directly suspected who
it was, and I hallooed to him by name, that *he was discovered.*
I did this that the party who fired might know I was on the
watch.   I cannot find any ball, but whatever the gun was

---

[1] Thomas Bonneville, Paine's godson, at school in Stonington.

charged with passed through about three or four inches below the window making a hole large enough to a finger to go through—the muzzle must have been very near as the place is black with the powder, and the glass of the window is shattered to pieces. Mr Shute after examining the place and getting what information could be had, issued a warrant to take up Derrick, and after examination committed him.

"He is now on bail (five hundred dollars) to take his trial at the supreme Court in May next. Derrick owes me forty-eight dollars for which I have his note, and he was to work it out in making stone fence which he has not even begun and besides this I have had to pay fortytwo pounds eleven shillings for which I had passed my word for him at Mr. Pelton's store. Derrick borrowed the Gun under pretence of giving Mrs. Bayeaux a Christmas Gun. He was with Purdy about two hours before the attack on the house was made and he came from thence to Dean's half drunk and brought with him a bottle of Rum, and Purdy was with him when he was taken up.

"I am exceedingly well in health and shall always be glad to see you. Hubbs tells me that your horse is getting better. Mrs. Shute sent for the horse and took him when the first snow came but he leaped the fences and came back. Hubbs says there is a bone broke. If this be the case I suppose he has broke or cracked it in leaping a fence when he was lame on the other hind leg, and hung with his hind legs in the fence. I am glad to hear what you tell me of Thomas. He shall not want for anything that is necessary if he be a good boy for he has no friend but me. You have not given me any account about the meeting house. Remember me to our Friends. Yours in friendship." [1]

The window of the room said to have been Paine's study is close to the ground, and it is marvellous that he was not murdered.[2]

[1] I am indebted for this letter to Dr. Clair J. Grece, of England, whose uncle, Daniel Constable, probably got it from Carver.

[2] Derrick (or Dederick) appears by the records at White Plains to have been brought up for trial May 19, 1806, and to have been recognized in the sum of $500 for his appearance at the next Court of Oyer and Terminer and General Gaol Delivery, and in the meantime to keep the peace towards the

The most momentous change which had come over America during Paine's absence was the pro-slavery reaction. This had set in with the first Congress. An effort was made by the Virginia representatives to check the slave traffic by impos-ing a duty of $10 on each negro imported, but was defeated by an alliance of members from more Southern States and professedly antislavery men of the North. The Southern leader in this first victory of slavery in Congress was Major Jackson of Geor-gia, who defended the institution as scriptural and civilizing. The aged Dr. Franklin published (*Fed-eral Gazette*, March 25, 1790) a parody of Jackson's speech, purporting to be a speech uttered in 1687 by a Divan of Algiers in defence of piracy and slavery, against a sect of Erika, or Purists, who had peti-tioned for their suppression. Franklin was now president of the American Antislavery Society, founded in Philadelphia in 1775 five weeks after the appearance of Paine's scheme of emancipation (March 8, 1775). Dr. Rush was also active in the cause, and to him Paine wrote (March 16, 1790) the letter on the subject elsewhere quoted (i., p. 271). This letter was published by Rush (*Co-lumbian Magazine*, vol. ii., p. 318) while the country was still agitated by the debate which was going on in Congress at the time when it was written, on a petition of the Antislavery Society, signed by Franklin, — his last public act. Franklin died

People, and especially towards Thomas Payne (*sic*). Paine, Christopher Hubbs, and Andrew A. Dean were recognized in $50 to appear and give evi-dence against Derrick. Nothing further appears in the records (examined for me by Mr. B. D. Washburn up to 1810). It is pretty certain that Paine did not press the charge.

April 17, 1790, twenty-five days after the close of
the debate, in which he was bitterly denounced by
the proslavery party.   Washington had pronounced
the petition "inopportune,"—his presidential mansion in New York was a few steps from the slave-
market,—Jefferson (now Secretary of State) had no
word to say for it, Madison had smoothed over the
matter by a compromise.   Thenceforth slavery had
become a suppressed subject, and the slave trade,
whenever broached in Congress, had maintained its
immunity.   In 1803, even under Jefferson's administration, the negroes fleeing from oppression in
Domingo were forbidden asylum in America, because it was feared that they would incite servile
insurrections.   That the United States, under
presidency of Jefferson, should stand aloof from
the struggle of the negroes in Domingo for
liberty, cut Paine to the heart.   Unperturbed by
the attempt made on his own life a few days before,
he wrote to Jefferson on New Year's Day, 1805,
(from New Rochelle,) what may be regarded as an
appeal :

   " DEAR SIR,—I have some thoughts of coming to Washington this winter, as I may as well spend a part of it there as
elsewhere.   But lest bad roads or any other circumstance
should prevent me I suggest a thought for your consideration,
and I shall be glad if in this case, as in that of Louisiana, we
may happen to think alike without knowing what each other
had thought of.
   " The affair of Domingo will cause some trouble in either of
the cases in which it now stands.   If armed merchantmen
force their way through the blockading fleet it will embarrass
us with the french Government ; and, on the other hand, if
the people of Domingo think that we show a partiality to the
french injurious to them there is danger they will turn Pirates

upon us, and become more injurious on account of vicinity than the barbary powers, and England will encourage it, as she encourages the Indians. Domingo is lost to France either as to the Government or the possession of it. But if a way could be found out to bring about a peace between france and Domingo through the mediation, and under the guarantee of the United States, it would be beneficial to all parties, and give us a great commercial and political standing, not only with the present people of Domingo but with the West Indies generally. And when we have gained their confidence by acts of justice and friendship, they will listen to our advice in matters of Civilization and Government, and prevent the danger of their becoming pirates, which I think they will be, if driven to desperation.

"The United States is the only power that can undertake a measure of this kind. She is now the Parent of the Western world, and her knowledge of the local circumstances of it gives her an advantage in a matter of this kind superior to any European Nation. She is enabled by situation, and grow[ing] importance to become a guarantee, and to see, as far as her advice and influence can operate, that the conditions on the part of Domingo be fulfilled. It is also a measure that accords with the humanity of her principles, with her policy, and her commercial interest.

"All that Domingo wants of France, is, that France agree to let her alone, and withdraw her forces by sea and land ; and in return for this Domingo to give her a monopoly of her commerce for a term of years,—that is, to import from France all the utensils and manufactures she may have occasion to use or consume (except such as she can more conveniently procure from the manufactories of the United States), and to pay for them in produce. France will gain more by this than she can expect to do even by a conquest of the Island, and the advantage to America will be that she will become the carrier of both, at least during the present war.

"There was considerable dislike in Paris against the Expedition to Domingo ; and the events that have since taken place were then often predicted. The opinion that generally prevailed at that time was that the commerce of the Island was better than the conquest of it,—that the conquest could not be accomplished without destroying the negroes, and in that case the Island would be of no value.

"I think it might be signified to the french Government, yourself is the best judge of the means, that the United States are disposed to undertake an accommodation so as to put an end to this otherwise endless slaughter on both sides, and to procure to France the best advantages in point of commerce that the state of things will admit of. Such an offer, whether accepted or not, cannot but be well received, and may lead to a good end.

"There is now a fine snow, and if it continues I intend to set off for Philadelphia in about eight days, and from thence to Washington. I congratulate your constituents on the success of the election for President and Vice-President.

"Yours in friendship,

"THOMAS PAINE."

The journey to Washington was given up, and Paine had to content himself with his pen. He took in several newspapers, and was as keenly alive as ever to the movements of the world. His chief anxiety was lest some concession might be made to the Louisianians about the slave trade, that region being an emporium of the traffic which grew more enterprising and brutal as its term was at hand. Much was said of the great need of the newly acquired region for more laborers, and it was known that Jefferson was by no means so severe in his opposition to slavery as he was once supposed to be. The President repeatedly invited Paine's views, and they were given fully and freely. The following extracts are from a letter dated New York, January 25, 1805 :

"Mr. Levy Lincoln and Mr. Wingate called on me at N. York, where I happened to be when they arrived on their Journey from Washington to the Eastward : I find by Mr. Lincoln that the Louisiana Memorialists will have to return as they came and the more decisively Congress put an end to this business the better. The Cession of Louisiana is a great acquisition ; but great as it is it would be an incumbrance on the Union were the prayer of the petitioners to be granted, nor would the lands be worth settling if the settlers are to be under a french jurisdiction. . . . When the emigrations from the United States into Louisiana become equal to the number of french inhabitants it may then be proper and right to erect such part where such equality exists into a constitutional state ; but to do it now would be sending the american settlers into exile. . . . For my own part, I wish the name of Louisiana to be lost, and this may in a great measure be done by giving names to the new states that will serve as discriptive of their situation or condition. France lost the names and almost the remembrance of provinces by dividing them into departments with appropriate names.

" Next to the acquisition of the territory and the Government of it is that of settling it. The people of the Eastern States are the best settlers of a new country, and of people from abroad the German Peasantry are the best. The Irish in general are generous and dissolute. The Scotch turn their attention to traffic, and the English to manufactures. These people are more fitted to live in cities than to be cultivators of new lands. I know not if in Virginia they are much acquainted with the importation of German redemptioners, that is, servants indented for a term of years. The best farmers in Pennsylvania are those who came over in this manner or the descendants of them. The price before the war used to be twenty pounds pennsylvania currency for an indented servant for four years, that is, the ship owner, got twenty pounds per head passage money, so that upon two hundred persons he would receive after their arrival four thousand pounds paid by the persons who purchased the time of their indentures which was generally four years. These would be the best people, of foreigners, to bring into Louisiana—because they would grow to be citizens. Whereas bringing poor negroes to work the lands in a state of slavery and wretchedness, is, besides the immorality of it, the certain way of preventing population and consequently of preventing revenue. I question if the revenue arising from ten Negroes in the consumption of imported articles is equal to that of one white citizen. In the articles of dress and of the table it is almost impossible to make a comparison.

" These matters though they do not belong to the class of principles are proper subjects for the consideration of Government ; and it is always fortunate when the interests of Government and that of humanity act unitedly. But I much doubt if the Germans would come to be under a french Jurisdiction. Congress must frame the laws under which they are to serve out their time ; after which Congress might give them a few acres of land to begin with for themselves and they would soon be able to buy more. I am inclined to believe that by adopting this method the Country will be more peopled in about twenty years from the present time than it has been in all the times of the french and Spaniards. Spain, I believe, held it chiefly as a barrier to her dominions in Mexico, and the less it was improved the better it agreed with that policy ; and as to france she never shewed any great disposition or gave any great encouragement to colonizing. It is chiefly small countries, that are straitened for room at home, like Holland and England, that go in quest of foreign settlements. . . .

"I have again seen and talked with the gentleman from Hamburg. He tells me that some Vessels under pretence of shipping persons to America carried them to England to serve as soldiers and sailors. He tells me he has the Edict or Proclamation of the Senate of Hamburg forbidding persons shipping themselves without the consent of the Senate, and that he will give me a copy of it, which if he does soon enough I will send with this letter. He says that the American Consul has been spoken to respecting this kidnapping business under American pretences, but that he says he has no authority to interfere. The German members of Congress, or the Philadelphia merchants or ship-owners who have been in the practice of importing German redemptioners, can give you better information respecting the business of importation than I can. But the redemptioners thus imported must be at the charge of the Captain or ship owner till their time is sold. Some of the quaker Merchants of Philadelphia went a great deal into the importation of German servants or redemptioners. It agreed

with the morality of their principles that of bettering people's
condition, and to put an end to the practice of importing
slaves. I think it not an unreasonable estimation to suppose
that the population of Louisiana may be increased ten thousand
souls every year. What retards the settlement of it is the
want of labourers, and until labourers can be had the sale of
the lands will be slow. Were I twenty years younger, and my
name and reputation as well known in European countries as
it is now, I would contract for a quantity of land in Louisiana
and go to Europe and bring over settlers. . . .

"It is probable that towards the close of the session I may
make an excursion to Washington. The piece on Gouverneur
Morris's Oration on Hamilton and that on the Louisiana
Memorial are the last I have published ; and as every thing of
public affairs is now on a good ground I shall do as I did after
the War, remain a quiet spectator and attend now to my own
affairs.

"I intend making a collection of all the pieces I have published, beginning with Common Sense, and of what I have by
me in manuscript, and publish them by subscription. I have
deferred doing this till the presidential election should be
over, but I believe there was not much occasion for that caution. There is more hypocrisy than bigotry in America.
When I was in Connecticut the summer before last, I fell in
company with some Baptists among whom were three Ministers.
The conversation turned on the election for President, and one
of them who appeared to be a leading man said ' They cry out
against Mr. Jefferson because, they say he is a Deist. Well, a
Deist may be a good man, and if he think it right, it is right
to him. For my own part,' said he, ' I had rather vote for a
Deist than for a blue-skin presbyterian.' ' You judge right,'
said I, ' for a man that is not of any of the sectaries will hold
the balance even between all ; but give power to a bigot of any
sectary and he will use it to the oppression of the rest, as the
blue-skins do in connection.' They all agree in this sentiment, and I have always found it assented to in any company
I have had occasion to use it.

"I judge the collection I speak of will make five volumes
octavo of four hundred pages each at two dollars a volume to
be paid on delivery ; and as they will be delivered separately,

as fast as they can be printed and bound the subscribers may stop when they please. The three first volumes will be political and each piece will be accompanied with an account of the state of affairs at the time it was written, whether in America, france, or England, which will also shew the occasion of writing it. The first expression in the first N°· of the Crisis published the 19th December '76 is ' *These are the times that try men's souls.*' It is therefore necessary as explanatory to the expression in all future times to shew what those times were. The two last volumes will be theological and those who do not chuse to take them may let them alone. They will have the right to do so, by the conditions of the subscription. I shall also make a miscellaneous Volume of correspondence, Essays, and some pieces of Poetry, which I believe will have some claim to originality. . . .

"I find by the Captain [from New Orleans] above mentioned that several Liverpool ships have been at New Orleans. It is chiefly the people of Liverpool that employ themselves in the slave trade and they bring cargoes of those unfortunate Negroes to take back in return the hard money and the produce of the country. Had I the command of the elements I would blast Liverpool with fire and brimstone. It is the Sodom and Gomorrah of brutality. . . .

"I recollect when in France that you spoke of a plan of making the Negroes tenants on a plantation, that is, alotting each Negroe family a quantity of land for which they were to pay to the owner a certain quantity of produce. I think that numbers of our free negroes might be provided for in this manner in Louisiana. The best way that occurs to me is for Congress to give them their passage to New Orleans, then for them to hire themselves out to the planters for one or two years ; they would by this means learn plantation business, after which to place them on a tract of land as before mentioned. A great many good things may now be done ; and I please myself with the idea of suggesting my thoughts to you.

"Old Captain Landais who lives at Brooklyn on Long Island opposite New York calls sometimes to see me. I knew him in Paris. He is a very respectable old man. I wish something had been done for him in Congress on his petition ; for I think something is due to him, nor do I see how the Statute

of limitation can consistently apply to him.   The law in John
Adams's administration, which cut off all commerce and communication with france, cut him off from the chance of coming to America to put in his claim.   I suppose that the claims
of some of our merchants on England, france and Spain is
more than 6 or 7 years standing yet no law of limitation, that
I know of take place between nations or between individuals
of different nations.   I consider a statute of limitation to be a
domestic law, and can only have a domestic opperation.   Dr.
Miller, one of the New York Senators in Congress, knows
Landais and can give you an account of him.

"Concerning my former letter, on Domingo, I intended had I
come to Washington to have talked with Pichon about it—if you
had approved that method, for it can only be brought forward
in an indirect way.   The two *Emperors* are at too great a distance in objects and in colour to have any intercourse but by
Fire and Sword, yet something I think might be done.   It is
time I should close this long epistle.   Yours in friendship."

Paine made but a brief stay in New York (where
he boarded with William Carver).   His next letter
(April 22d) is from New Rochelle, written to John
Fellows, an auctioneer in New York City, one of
his most faithful friends.

· "CITIZEN : I send this by the N. Rochelle boat and have
desired the boatman to call on you with it.   He is to bring up
Bebia and Thomas and I will be obliged to you to see them
safe on board.   The boat will leave N. Y. on friday.

"I have left my pen knife at Carver's.   It is, I believe, in the
writing desk.   It is a small french pen knife that slides into
the handle.   I wish Carver would look behind the chest in the
bed room.   I miss some papers that I suppose are fallen down
there.   The boys will bring up with them one pair of the
blankets Mrs. Bonneville took down and also my best blanket
which is at Carver's.—I send enclosed three dollars for a
ream of writing paper and one dollar for some letter paper,
and porterage to the boat.   I wish you to give the boys some
good advice when you go with them, and tell them that the

better they behave the better it will be for them.   I am now
their only dependance, and they ought to know it.   Yours in
friendship."

"All my Nos. of the Prospect, while I was at Carver's, are
left there.   The boys can bring them.   I have received no No.
since I came to New Rochelle."[1]

The Thomas mentioned in this letter was Paine's
godson, and "Bebia" was Benjamin,—the late
Brigadier-General Bonneville, U. S. A.   The third
son, Louis, had been sent to his father in France.
The *Prospect* was Elihu Palmer's rationalistic paper.

Early in this year a series of charges affecting
Jefferson's public and private character were published by one Hulbert, on the authority of Thomas
Turner of Virginia.   Beginning with an old charge
of cowardice, while Governor (of which Jefferson
had been acquitted by the Legislature of Virginia),
the accusation proceeded to instances of immorality, persons and placed being named.   The following letter from New Rochelle, July 19th, to John
Fellows enclosed Paine's reply, which appeared in
the *American Citizen*, July 23d and 24th :

"CITIZEN—I inclose you two pieces for Cheetham's paper,
which I wish you to give to him yourself.   He may publish one
No. in one daily paper, and the other number in the next
daily paper, and then both in his country paper.   There has
been a great deal of anonimous (*sic*) abuse thrown out in the
federal papers against Mr. Jefferson, but until some names
could be got hold of it was fighting the air to take any notice
of them.   We have now got hold of two names, your townsman
Hulbert, the hypocritical Infidel of Sheffield, and Thomas
Turner of Virginia, his correspondent.   I have already given
Hulbert a basting with my name to it, because he made use of
my name in his speech in the Mass. legislature.   Turner has

[1] This letter is in the possession of Mr. Grenville Kane, Tuxedo, N. Y.

not given me the same cause in the letter he wrote (and evidently) to Hulbert, and which Hulbert, (for it could be no other person) has published in the Repertory to vindicate himself. Turner has detailed his charges against Mr. Jefferson, and I have taken them up one by one, which is the first time the opportunity has offered for doing it ; for before this it was promiscuous abuse. I have not signed it either with my name or signature (Common Sense) because I found myself obliged, in order to made such scoundrels feel a little smart, to go somewhat out of my usual manner of writing, but there are some sentiments and some expressions that will be supposed to be in my stile, and I have no objection to that supposition, but I do not wish Mr. Jefferson to be *obliged* to know it is from me.

"Since receiving your letter, which contained no direct information of any thing I wrote to you about, I have written myself to Mr. Barrett accompanied with a piece for the editor of the Baltimore Evening Post, who is an acquaintance of his, but I have received no answer from Mr. B., neither has the piece been published in the Evening Post. I will be obliged to you to call on him & to inform me about it. You did not tell me if you called upon Foster ; but at any rate do not delay the enclosed.—I do not trouble you with any messages or compliments, for you never deliver any. Your's in friendship."[1]

By a minute comparison of the two alleged specifications of immorality, Paine proved that one was intrinsically absurd, and the other without trustworthy testimony. As for the charge of cowardice, Paine contended that it was the duty of a civil magistrate to move out of danger, as Congress had done in the Revolution. The article was signed "A Spark from the Altar of '76," but the writer was easily recognized. The service thus done Jefferson was greater than can now be easily realized.

[1] I am indebted for this letter to Mr. John M. Robertson, editor of the *National Reformer*, London.

Another paper by Paine was on "Constitutions, Governments, and Charters." It was an argument to prove the unconstitutionality in New York of the power assumed by the legislature to grant charters. This defeated the object of annual elections, by placing the act of one legislature beyond the reach of its successor. He proposes that all matters of "extraordinary legislation," such as those involving grants of land and incorporations of companies, shall be passed only by a legislature succeeding the one in which it was proposed. "Had such an article been originally in the Constitution [of New York] the bribery and corruption employed to seduce and manage the members of the late legislature, in the affair of the Merchants' Bank, could not have taken place. It would not have been worth while to bribe men to do what they had no power of doing."

Madame Bonneville hated country life, and insisted on going to New York. Paine was not sorry to have her leave, as she could not yet talk English, and did not appreciate Paine's idea of plain living and high thinking. She apparently had a notion that Paine had a mint of money, and, like so many others, might have attributed to parsimony efforts the unpaid author was making to save enough to give her children, practically fatherless, some start in life. The philosophic solitude in which he was left at New Rochelle is described in a letter (July 31st) to John Fellows, in New York.

"It is certainly best that Mrs. Bonneville go into some family as a teacher, for she has not the least talent of managing affairs for herself. She may send Bebia up to me. I will

take care of him for his own sake and his father's, but that is
all I have to say. . . . I am master of an empty house, or
nearly so. I have six chairs and a table, a straw-bed, a feather-
bed, and a bag of straw for Thomas, a tea kettle, an iron pot,
an iron baking pan, a frying pan, a gridiron, cups, saucers,
plates and dishes, knives and forks, two candlesticks and a pair
of snuffers. I have a pair of fine oxen and an ox-cart, a good
horse, a Chair, and a one-horse cart; a cow, and a sow and
9 pigs. When you come you must take such fare as you
meet with, for I live upon tea, milk, fruit-pies, plain dumplins,
and a piece of meat when I get it; but I live with that
retirement and quiet that suit me. Mrs. Bonneville was an
encumbrance upon me all the while she was here, for she would
not do anything, not even make an apple dumplin for her own
children. If you cannot make yourself up a straw bed, I can
let you have blankets, and you will have no occasion to go over
to the tavern to sleep.

"As I do not see any federal papers, except by accident, I
know not if they have attempted any remarks or criticisms on
my Eighth Letter, [or] the piece on Constitutional Governments and Charters, the two numbers on Turner's letter, and
also the piece on Hulbert. As to anonymous paragraphs, it is
not worth noticing them. I consider the generality of such
editors only as a part of their press, and let them pass.—I
want to come to Morrisania, and it is probable I may come on
to N. Y., but I wish you to answer this letter first.—Yours in
friendship."

It must not be supposed from what Paine says
of Madame Bonneville that there was anything
acrimonious in their relations. She was thirty-one
years younger than Paine, fond of the world, handsome. The old gentleman, all day occupied with
writing, could give her little companionship, even
if he could have conversed in French. But he
indulged her in every way, gave her more money

---

[1] I am indebted for an exact copy of the letter from which this is extracted
to Dr. Garnett of the British Museum, though it is not in that institution.

than he could afford, devcted his ever decreasing
means to her family.   She had boundless reverence
for him, but, as we have seen, had no taste for
country life.   Probably, too, after Dederick's attempt
on Paine's life she became nervous in the lonely
house.   So she had gone to New York, where she
presently found good occupation as a teacher of
French in several families.   Her sons, however,
were fond of New Rochelle, and of Paine, who had
a knack of amusing children, and never failed to
win their affection.[1]

The spring of 1805 at New Rochelle was a
pleasant one for Paine.   He wrote his last political
pamphlet, which was printed by Duane, Philadelphia, with the title : " Thomas Paine to the Citizens
of Pennsylvania, on the Proposal for Calling a Convention."   It opens with a reference to his former
life and work in Philadelphia.   " Removed as I
now am from the place, and detached from everything of personal party, I address this token to
you on the ground of principle, and in remembrance
of former times and friendships."   He gives an
historical account of the negative or veto-power,
finding it the English Parliament's badge of disgrace under William of Normandy, a defence of
personal prerogative that ought to find no place in
a republic.   He advises that in the new Constitution the principle of arbitration, outside of courts,

---

[1] In the Tarrytown *Argus*, October 18, 1890, appeared an interesting
notice of the Rev. Alexander Davis (Methodist), by C. K. B[uchanan] in
which it is stated that Davis, a native of New Rochelle, remembered the
affection of Paine, who "would bring him round-hearts and hold him
on his knee."   Many such recollections of his little neighbors have been
reported.

should be established.   The governor should possess no power of patronage ; he should make one in
a Council of Appointments.   The Senate is an imitation of the House of Lords.   The Representatives should be divided by lot into two equal parts,
sitting in different chambers.   One half, by not
being entangled in the debate of the other on the
issue submitted, nor committed by voting, would
become silently possessed of the arguments, and be
in a calm position to review the whole.   The votes
of the two houses should be added together, and
the majority decide.   Judges should be removable
by some constitutional mode, without the formality
of impeachment at "stated periods." (In 1807 Paine
wrote to Senator Mitchell of New York suggesting
an amendment to the Constitution of the United
States by which judges of the Supreme Court might
be removed by the President for reasonable cause,
though insufficient for impeachment, on the address
of a majority of both Houses of Congress.)

In this pamphlet was included the paper already
mentioned (on Charters, etc.), addressed to the
people of New York.   The two essays prove that
there was no abatement in Paine's intellect, and
that despite occasional "flings" at the "Feds,"—
retorts on their perpetual naggings,—he was still
occupied with the principles of political philosophy.

At this time Paine had put the two young Bonnevilles at a school in New Rochelle, where they
also boarded.   He had too much solitude in the
house, and too little nourishment for so much work.
So the house was let and he was taken in as a
boarder by Mrs. Bayeaux, in the old Bayeaux

House, which is still standing,[1]—but Paine's pecuniary situation now gave him anxiety. He was earning nothing, his means were found to be far less than he supposed, the needs of the Bonnevilles increasing. Considering the important defensive articles he had written for the President, and their long friendship, he ventured (September 30th) to allude to his situation and to remind him that his State, Virginia, had once proposed to give him a tract of land, but had not done so. He suggests that Congress should remember his services.

"But I wish you to be assured that whatever event this proposal may take it will make no alteration in my principles or my conduct. I have been a volunteer to the world for thirty years without taking profits from anything I have published in America or Europe. I have relinquished all profits that those publications might come cheap among the people for whom they were intended—Yours in friendship."

This was followed by another note (November 14th) asking if it had been received. What answer came from the President does not appear.

About this time Paine published an essay on "The cause of the Yellow Fever, and the means of preventing it in places not yet infected with it. Addressed to the Board of Health in America." The treatise, which he dates June 27th, is noticed by Dr. Francis as timely. Paine points out that the epidemic which almost annually afflicted New York, had been unknown to the Indians; that it began around the wharves, and did not reach the higher

[1] Mrs. Bayeaux is mentioned in Paine's letter about Dederick's attempt on his life.

parts of the city. He does not believe the disease certainly imported from the West Indies, since it is not carried from New York to other places. He thinks that similar filthy conditions of the wharves and the water about them generate the miasma alike in the West Indies and in New York. It would probably be escaped if the wharves were built on stone or iron arches, permitting the tides to cleanse the shore and carry away the accumulations of vegetable and animal matter decaying around every ship and dock. He particularly proposes the use of arches for wharves about to be constructed at Corlder's Hook and on the North River.

Dr. Francis justly remarks, in his "Old New York," that Paine's writings were usually suggested by some occasion. Besides this instance of the essay on the yellow fever, he mentions one on the origin of Freemasonry, there being an agitation in New York concerning that fraternity. But this essay—in which Paine, with ingenuity and learning, traces Freemasonry to the ancient solar mythology also identified with Christian mythology—was not published during his life. It was published by Madame Bonneville with the passages affecting Christianity omitted. The original manuscript was obtained, however, and published with an extended preface, criticizing Paine's theory, the preface being in turn criticized by Paine's editor. The preface was probably written by Colonel Fellows, author of a large work on Freemasonry.

CHAPTER XVIII.

A NEW YORK PROMETHEUS.

WHEN Paine left Bordentown, on March 1st, 1803, driving past placards of the devil flying away with him, and hooted by a pious mob at Trenton, it was with hope of a happy reunion with old friends in more enlightened New York. Col. Few, formerly senator from Georgia, his friend of many years, married Paine's correspondent, Kitty Nicholson, to whom was written the beautiful letter from London (i., p. 247). Col. Few had become a leading man in New York, and his home, and that of the Nicholsons, were of highest social distinction. Paine's arrival at Lovett's Hotel was well known, but not one of those former friends came near him. " They were actively as well as passively religious," says Henry Adams, " and their relations with Paine after his return to America in 1802 were those of compassion only, for his intemperate and offensive habits, and intimacy was impossible." [1] But Mr. Adams will vainly search his materials for any intimation at that time of the intemperate or offensive habits.

The "compassion" is due to those devotees of an idol requiring sacrifice of friendship, loyalty, and

---

[1] " Life of Albert Gallatin." Gallatin continued to visit Paine.

intelligence. What a mistake they made! The old author was as a grand organ from which a cunning hand might bring music to be remembered through the generations. In that brain were stored memories of the great Americans, Frenchmen, Englishmen who acted in the revolutionary dramas, and of whom he loved to talk. What would a diary of interviews with Paine, written by his friend Kitty Few, be now worth ? To intolerance, the least pardonable form of ignorance, must be credited the failure of those former friends, who supposed themselves educated, to make more of Thomas Paine than a scarred monument of an Age of Unreason.

But the ostracism of Paine by the society which, as Henry Adams states, had once courted him " as the greatest literary genius of his day," was not due merely to his religious views, which were those of various statesmen who had incurred no such odium. There was at work a lingering dislike and distrust of the common people. Deism had been rather aristocratic. From the scholastic study, where heresies once written only in Latin were daintily wrapped up in metaphysics, from drawing-rooms where cynical smiles went round at · Methodism, and other forms of " Christianity in earnest," Paine carried heresy to the people. And he brought it as a religion,—as fire from the fervid heaven that orthodoxy had monopolized. The popularity of his writing, the revivalistic earnestness of his protest against dogmas common to all sects, were revolutionary ; and while the vulgar bigots were binding him on their rock of ages, and tearing his vitals, most of the educated, the social leaders, were too prudent to manifest any sympathy they may have felt.[1]

It were unjust to suppose that Paine met with nothing but abuse and maltreatment from ministers of serious orthodoxy in New York. They had warmly opposed his views, even denounced them, but the controversy seems to have died away until he took part in the deistic propaganda of Elihu Palmer.[2] The following to Col. Fellows (July 31st) shows Paine much interested in the "cause":

"I am glad that Palmer and Foster have got together. It will greatly help the cause on. I enclose a letter I received a few days since from Groton, in Connecticut. The letter is well written, and with a good deal of sincere enthusiasm. The publication of it would do good, but there is an impropriety in publishing a man's name to a private letter. You may show the letter to Palmer and Foster. . . . Remember me to my much respected friend Carver and tell him I am sure we shall succeed if we hold on. We have already silenced the clamor of the priests. They act now as if they would say, let us alone and we will let you alone. You do not tell me if the Prospect goes on. As Carver will want pay he may have it from me, and pay when it suits him ; but I expect he will take a ride up some Saturday, and then he can chuse for himself."

The result of this was that Paine passed the winter in New York, where he threw himself

[1] When Paine first reached New York, 1803, he was (March 5th) entertained at supper by John Crauford. For being present Eliakim Ford, a Baptist elder, was furiously denounced, as were others of the company.

[2] An exception was the leading Presbyterian, John Mason, who lived to denounce Channing as "the devil's disciple." Grant Thorburn was psalm-singer in this Scotch preacher's church. Curiosity to see the lion led Thorburn to visit Paine, for which he was "suspended." Thorburn afterwards made amends by fathering Cheetham's slanders of Paine after Cheetham had become too infamous to quote.

warmly into the theistic movement, and no doubt occasionally spoke from Elihu Palmer's platform.

The rationalists who gathered around Elihu Palmer in New York were called the " Columbian Illuminati." The pompous epithet looks like an effort to connect them with the Columbian Order (Tammany) which was supposed to represent Jacobinism and French ideas generally. Their numbers were considerable, but they did not belong to fashionable society. Their lecturer, Elihu Palmer, was a scholarly gentleman of the highest character. A native of Canterbury, Connecticut, (born 1754,) he had graduated at Dartmouth. He was married by the Rev. Mr. Watt to a widow, Mary Powell, in New York (1803), at the time when he was lecturing in the Temple of Reason (Snow's Rooms, Broadway). This suggests that he had not broken with the clergy altogether. Somewhat later he lectured at the Union Hotel, William Street. He had studied divinity, and turned against the creeds what was taught him for their support.

" I have more than once [says Dr. Francis] listened to Palmer ; none could be weary within the sound of his voice ; his diction was classical ; and much of his natural theology attractive by variety of illustration. But admiration of him sank into despondency at his assumption, and his sarcastic assaults on things most holy. His boldest phillippic was his discourse on the title-page of the Bible, in which, with the double shield of jacobinism and infidelity, he warned rising America against confidence in a book authorised by the monarchy of England. Palmer delivered his sermons in the Union Hotel in William Street."

Dr. Francis does not appear to have known Paine personally, but had seen him. Palmer's chief friends in New York were, he says, John Fellows ; Rose, an unfortunate lawyer ; Taylor, a philanthropist ; and Charles Christian. Of Rev. John Foster, another rationalist lecturer, Dr. Francis says he had a noble presence and great eloquence. Foster's exordium was an invocation to the goddess of Liberty. He and Palmer called each other Brother. No doubt Paine completed the Triad.

Col. John Fellows, always the devoted friend of Paine, was an auctioneer, but in later life was a constable in the city courts. He has left three volumes which show considerable literary ability, and industrious research ; but these were unfortunately bestowed on such extinct subjects as Freemasonry, the secret of Junius, and controversies concerning General Putnam. It is much to be regretted that Colonel Fellows should not have left a volume concerning Paine, with whom he was in especial intimacy, during his last years.

Other friends of Paine were Thomas Addis Emmet, Walter Morton, a lawyer, and Judge Hertell, a man of wealth, and a distinguished member of the State Assembly. Fulton also was much in New York, and often called on Paine. Paine was induced to board at the house of William Carver (36 Cedar Street), which proved a grievous mistake. Carver had introduced himself to Paine, saying that he remembered him when he was an exciseman at Lewes, England, he (Carver) being a young farrier there. He made loud professions of deism, and of devotion to Paine. The

farrier of Lewes had become a veterinary prac-
titioner and shopkeeper in New York. Paine supposed that he would be cared for in the house of
this active rationalist, but the man and his family
were illiterate and vulgar. His sojourn at Carver's
probably shortened Paine's life. Carver, to antici-
pate the narrative a little, turned out to be a bad-
hearted man and a traitor.

Paine had accumulated a mass of fragmentary
writings on religious subjects, and had begun publishing them in a journal started in 1804 by Elihu
Palmer,— *The Prospect; or View of the Moral
World.* This succeeded the paper called *The
Temple of Reason.* One of Paine's objects was to
help the new journal, which attracted a good deal
of attention. His first communication (February 18,
1804), was on a sermon by Robert Hall, on " Modern Infidelity," sent him by a gentleman in New
York. The following are some of its trenchant
paragraphs :

" Is it a fact that Jesus Christ died for the sins of the world,
and how is it proved ? If a God he could not die, and as a
man he could not redeem : how then is this redemption proved
to be fact ? It is said that Adam eat of the forbidden fruit, com-
monly called an apple, and thereby subjected himself and all
his posterity forever to eternal damnation. This is worse than
visiting the sins of the fathers upon the children unto the third
and fourth generations. But how was the death of Jesus
Christ to affect or alter the case ? Did God thirst for blood ?
If so, would it not have been better to have crucified Adam
upon the forbidden tree, and made a new man ? "

" Why do not the Christians, to be consistent, make Saints of
Judas and Pontius Pilate, for they were the persons who accomplished the act of salvation. The merit of a sacrifice, if there can

be any merit in it, was never in the thing sacrificed, but in the persons offering up the sacrifice—and therefore Judas and Pilate ought to stand first in the calendar of Saints."

Other contributions to the *Prospect* were : " Of the word Religion "; " Cain and Abel "; " The Tower of Babel"; " Of the religion of Deism compared with the Christian Religion"; "Of the Sabbath Day in Connecticut"; " Of the Old and New Testaments"; " Hints towards forming a Society for inquiring into the truth or falsehood of ancient history, so far as history is connected with systems of religion ancient and modern "; " To the members of the Society styling itself the Missionary Society"; " On Deism, and the writings of Thomas Paine"; " Of the Books of the New Testament." There were several communications without any heading. Passages and sentences from these little essays have long been a familiar currency among freethinkers.

"We admire the wisdom of the ancients, yet they had no bibles, nor books, called revelation. They cultivated the reason that God gave them, studied him in his works, and rose to eminence."

" The Cain and Abel of Genesis appear to be no other than the ancient Egyptian story of Typhon and Osiris, the darkness and the light, which answered very well as allegory without being believed as fact."

" Those who most believe the Bible are those who know least about it."

" Another observation upon the story of Babel is, the inconsistence of it with respect to the opinion that the bible is the word of God given for the information of mankind ; for nothing could so effectually prevent such a word being known by mankind as confounding their language."

" God has not given us reason for the purpose of confounding us."

" Jesus never speaks of Adam, of the Garden of Eden, nor of what is called the fall of man."

" Is not the Bible warfare the same kind of warfare as the Indians themselves carry on ? " [On the presentation of a Bible to some Osage chiefs in New York.]

" The remark of the Emperor Julian is worth observing. ' If,' said he, ' there ever had been or could be a Tree of Knowledge, instead of God forbidding man to eat thereof, it would be that of which he would order him to eat the most.' "

" Do Christians not see that their own religion is founded on a human sacrifice ? Many thousands of human sacrifices have since been offered on the altar of the Christian Religion."

" For several centuries past the dispute has been about doctrines. It is now about fact."

" The Bible has been received by Protestants on the authority of the Church of Rome."

" The same degree of hearsay evidence, and that at third and fourth hand, would not, in a court of justice, give a man title to a cottage, and yet the priests of this profession presumptuously promise their deluded followers the kingdom of Heaven."

" Nobody fears for the safety of a mountain, but a hillock of sand may be washed away. Blow then, O ye priests, " the Trumpet in Zion," for the Hillock is in danger."

The force of Paine's negations was not broken by any weakness for speculations of his own. He constructed no system to invite the missiles of antagonists. It is, indeed, impossible to deny without affirming ; denial that two and two make five affirms that they make four. The basis of Paine's denials being the divine wisdom and benevolence, there was in his use of such expressions an implication of limitation in the divine nature. Wisdom implies the necessity of dealing with difficulties.

and benevolence the effort to make all sentient creatures happy. Neither quality is predicable of an omniscient and omnipotent being, for whom there could be no difficulties or evils to overcome. Paine did not confuse the world with his doubts or with his mere opinions. He stuck to his certainties, that the scriptural deity was not the true one, nor the dogmas called Christian reasonable. But he felt some of the moral difficulties surrounding theism, and these were indicated in his reply to the Bishop of Llandaff.

"The Book of Job belongs either to the ancient Persians, the Chaldeans, or the Egyptians ; because the structure of it is consistent with the dogma they held, that of a good and evil spirit, called in Job *God* and *Satan*, existing as distinct and separate beings, and it is not consistent with any dogma of the Jews. . . . The God of the Jews was the God of everything. All good and evil came from him. According to Exodus it was God, and not the Devil, that hardened Pharaoh's heart. According to the Book of Samuel it was an evil spirit from God that troubled Saul. And Ezekiel makes God say, in speaking of the Jews, 'I gave them statutes that were not good, and judgments by which they should not live.' . . . As to the precepts, principles, and maxims in the Book of Job, they show that the people abusively called the heathen, in the books of the Jews, had the most sublime ideas of the Creator, and the most exalted devotional morality. It was the Jews who dishonored God. It was the Gentiles who glorified him."

Several passages in Paine's works show that he did not believe in a personal devil; just what he did believe was no doubt written in a part of his reply to the Bishop, which, unfortunately, he did not live to carry through the press. In the part that we have he expresses the opinion that the

Serpent of Genesis is an allegory of winter, necessitating the "coats of skins" to keep Adam and
Eve warm, and adds : "Of these things I shall
speak fully when I come in another part to speak
of the ancient religion of the Persians, and compare it with the modern religion of the New
Testament." But this part was never published.
The part published was transcribed by Paine and
given, not long before his death, to the widow of
Elihu Palmer, who published it in the *Theophilanthropist* in 1810. Paine had kept the other part,
no doubt for revision, and it passed with his effects
into the hands of Madame Bonneville, who eventually became a devotee. She either suppressed it
or sold it to some one who destroyed it. We can
therefore only infer from the above extract the
author's belief on this momentous point. It seems
clear that he did not attribute any evil to the divine
Being. In the last article Paine published he
rebukes the "Predestinarians" for dwelling mainly
on God's "physical attribute" of power. "The
Deists, in addition to this, believe in his moral
attributes, those of justice and goodness."

Among Paine's papers was found one entitled
"My private thoughts of a Future State," from
which his editors have dropped important sentences.

"I have said in the first part of the Age of Reason that 'I
hope for happiness after this life.' This hope is comfortable
to me, and I presume not to go beyond the comfortable idea of
hope, with respect to a future state. I consider myself in the
hands of my Creator, and that he will dispose of me after this
life, consistently with his justice and goodness. I leave all
these matters to him as my Creator and friend, and I hold it to

be presumption in man to make an article of faith as to what the Creator will do with us hereafter.   I do not believe, because a man and a woman make a child, that it imposes on the Creator the unavoidable obligation of keeping the being so made in eternal existence hereafter.   It is in his power to do so, or not to do so, and it is not in our power to decide which he will do." [After quoting from Matthew 25th the figure of the sheep and goats he continues :] " The world cannot be thus divided.   The moral world, like the physical world, is composed of numerous degrees of character, running imperceptibly one into the other, in such a manner that no fixed point can be found in either. That point is nowhere, or is everywhere.   The whole world might be divided into two parts numerically, but not as to moral character ; and therefore the metaphor of dividing them, as sheep and goats can be divided, whose difference is marked by their external figure, is absurd.   All sheep are still sheep ; all goats are still goats ; it is their physical nature to be so. But one part of the world are not all good alike, nor the other part all wicked alike.   There are some exceedingly good, others exceedingly wicked.   There is another description of men who cannot be ranked with either the one or the other—they belong neither to the sheep nor the goats.   And there is still another description of them who are so very insignificant, both in character and conduct, as not to be worth the trouble of damning or saving, or of raising from the dead.   My own opinion is, that those whose lives have been spent in doing good, and endeavouring to make their fellow mortals happy, for this is the only way in which we can serve God, will be happy hereafter ; and that the very wicked will meet with some punishment. But those who are neither good nor bad, or are too insignificant for notice, will be dropt entirely.   This is my opinion.   It is consistent with my idea of God's justice, and with the reason that God has given me, and I gratefully know that he has given me a large share of that divine gift."

The closing tribute to his own reason, written in privacy, was, perhaps pardonably, suppressed by the modern editor, and also the reference to the insignificant who "will be dropt entirely."   This

sentiment is not indeed democratic, but it is significant. It seems plain that Paine's conception of
the universe was dualistic. Though he discards
the notion of a devil, I do not find that he ever
ridicules it. No doubt he would, were he now living, incline to a division of nature into organic
and inorganic, and find his deity, as Zoroaster did,
in the living as distinguished from, and sometimes
in antagonism with, the "not-living.". In this belief he would now find himself in harmony with
some of the ablest modern philosophers.[1]

The opening year 1806 found Paine in New Rochelle. By insufficient nourishment in Carver's
house his health was impaired. His means were
getting low, insomuch that to support the Bonnevilles he had to sell the Bordentown house and
property.[2] Elihu Palmer had gone off to Philadelphia for a time; he died there of yellow fever in
1806. The few intelligent people whom Paine
knew were much occupied, and he was almost
without congenial society. His hint to Jefferson
of his impending poverty, and his reminder that
Virginia had not yet given him the honorarium
he and Madison approved, had brought no result.
With all this, and the loss of early friendships, and
the theological hornet-nest he had found in New

---

[1] John Stuart Mill, for instance. See also the Rev. Dr. Abbott's "Ker-
nel and Husk" (London), and the great work of Samuel Laing, "A
Modern Zoroastrian."

[2] It was bought for $300 by his friend John Oliver, whose daughter, still
residing in the house, told me that her father to the end of his life
"thought everything of Paine."   John Oliver, in his old age, visited
Colonel Ingersoll in order to testify against the aspersions on Paine's
character and habits.

York, Paine began to feel that his return to America was a mistake.

The air-castle that had allured him to his beloved land had faded. His little room with the Bonnevilles in Paris, with its chaos of papers, was preferable; for there at least he could enjoy the society of educated persons, free from bigotry. He dwelt a stranger in his Land of Promise.

So he resolved to try and free himself from his depressing environment. He would escape to Europe again. Jefferson had offered him a ship to return in, perhaps he would now help him to get back. So he writes (Jan. 30th) a letter to the President, pointing out the probabilities of a crisis in Europe which must result in either a descent on England by Bonaparte, or in a treaty. In the case that the people of England should be thus liberated from tyranny, he (Paine) desired to share with his friends there the task of framing a republic. Should there be, on the other hand, a treaty of peace, it would be of paramount interest to American shipping that such treaty should include that maritime compact, or safety of the seas for neutral ships, of which Paine had written so much, and which Jefferson himself had caused to be printed in a pamphlet. Both of these were, therefore, Paine's subjects. "I think," he says, "you will find it proper, perhaps necessary, to send a person to France in the event of either a treaty or a descent, and I make you an offer of my services on that occasion to join Mr. Monroe. . . . As I think that the letters of a friend to a friend have some claim to an answer, it will be agreeable to me to receive an answer to this, but without any wish that you should commit yourself, neither can you be a judge of what is proper or necessary to be done till about the month of April or May."

This little dream must also vanish. Paine must face the fact that his career is ended.

It is probable that Elihu Palmer's visit to Philadelphia was connected with some theistic movement in that city. How it was met, and what annoyances Paine had to suffer, are partly intimated in the following letter, printed in the Philadelphia *Commercial Advertiser*, February 10, 1806.

"To JOHN INSKEEP, MAYOR OF THE CITY OF PHILADELPHIA.

"I saw in the *Aurora* of January the 30th a piece addressed to you and signed Isaac Hall. It contains a statement of your malevolent conduct in refusing to let him have Vine-st. Wharf after he had bid fifty dollars more rent for it than another person had offered, and had been unanimously approved of by the Commissioners appointed by law for that purpose. Among the reasons given by you for this refusal, one was, that '*Mr Hall was one of Paine's disciples.*' If those whom you may chuse to call my disciples follow my example in doing good to mankind, they will pass the confines of this world with a happy mind, while the hope of the hypocrite shall perish and delusion sink into despair.

"I do not know who Mr. Inskeep is, for I do not remember the name of Inskeep at Philadelphia in '*the time that tried men's souls.*' He must be some mushroom of modern growth that has started up on the soil which the generous services of Thomas Paine contributed to bless with freedom ; neither do I know what profession of religion he is of, nor do I care, for if he is a man malevolent and unjust, it signifies not to what class or sectary he may hypocritically belong.

"As I set too much value on my time to waste it on a man of so little consequence as yourself, I will close this short address with a declaration that puts hypocrisy and malevolence to defiance. Here it is : My motive and object in all my political works, beginning with Common Sense, the first work I ever published, have been to rescue man from tyranny and false systems and false principles of government, and enable him to be free, and establish government for himself ; and I have borne my share of danger in Europe and in America in every attempt I have made for this purpose. And my motive and object in all my publications on religious subjects, beginning with the first part of the Age of Reason, have been to bring man to a right reason that God has given him ; to impress on him the great principles of divine morality, justice, mercy, and a benevolent disposition to all men and to all creatures ; and to excite in him a spirit of trust, confidence and consolation in his creator, unshackled by the fable and fiction of books, by whatever invented name they may be called. I am happy in the continual contemplation of what I have done, and I thank God that he gave me talents for the purpose and fortitude to do it. It will make the continual consolation of my departing hours, whenever they finally arrive.

"THOMAS PAINE."

" ' *These are the times that try men's souls.*' Crisis No. 1, written while on the retreat with the army from fort Lee to the Delaware and published in Philadelphia in the dark days of 1776 December the 19th, six days before the taking of the Hessians at Trenton."

But the year 1806 had a heavier blow yet to inflict on Paine, and it naturally came, though in a roundabout way, from his old enemy Gouverneur Morris. While at New Rochelle, Paine offered his vote at the election, and it was refused, on the ground that he was not an American citizen ! The supervisor declared that the former American Minister, Gouverneur Morris, had refused to reclaim him from a French prison because he was not an

American, and that Washington had also refused to reclaim him. Gouverneur Morris had just lost his seat in Congress, and was politically defunct, but his ghost thus rose on poor Paine's pathway. The supervisor who disfranchised the author of "Common Sense" had been a "Tory" in the Revolution ; the man he disfranchised was one to whom the President of the United States had written, five years before : " I am in hopes you will find us returned generally to sentiments worthy of former times. In these it will be your glory to have steadily labored, and with as much effect as any man living." There was not any question of Paine's qualification as a voter on other grounds than the supervisor (Elisha Ward) raised. More must presently be said concerning this incident. Paine announced his intention of suing the inspectors, but meanwhile he had to leave the polls in humiliation. It was the fate of this founder of republics to be a monument of their ingratitude.

And now Paine's health began to fail. An intimation of this appears in a letter to Andrew A. Dean, to whom his farm at New Rochelle was let, dated from New York, August, 1806. It is in reply to a letter from Dean on a manuscript which Paine had lent him. [1]

---

[1] " I have read," says Dean, "with good attention your manuscript on Dreams, and Examination of the Prophecies in the Bible. I am now searching the old prophecies, and comparing the same to those said to be quoted in the New Testament. I confess the comparison is a matter worthy of our serious attention ; I know not the result till I finish ; then, if you be living, I shall communicate the same to you. I hope to be with you soon." Paine was now living with Jarvis, the artist. One evening he fell as if by apoplexy, and, as he lay, his first word was (to Jarvis) : " My corporeal functions have ceased ; my intellect is clear; this is a proof of immortality."

" RESPECTED FRIEND : I received your friendly letter, for which I am obliged to you.   It is three weeks ago to day (Sunday, Aug. 15,) that I was struck with a fit of an apoplexy, that deprived me of all sense and motion.   I had neither pulse nor breathing, and the people about me supposed me dead.   I had felt exceedingly well that day, and had just taken a slice of bread and butter for supper, and was going to bed.   The fit took me on the stairs, as suddenly as if I had been shot through the head ; and I got so very much hurt by the fall, that I have not been able to get in and out of bed since that day, otherwise than being lifted out in a blanket, by two persons ; yet all this while my mental faculties have remained as perfect as I ever enjoyed them.   I consider the scene I have passed through as an experiment on dying, and I find death has no terrors for me.   As to the people called Christians, they have no evidence that their religion is true.   There is no more proof that the Bible is the word of God, than that the Koran of Mahomet is the word of God.   It is education makes all the difference. Man, before he begins to think for himself, is as much the child of habit in Creeds as he is in ploughing and sowing.   Yet creeds, like opinions, prove nothing.   Where is the evidence that the person called Jesus Christ is the begotten Son of God ? The case admits not of evidence either to our senses or our mental faculties : neither has God given to man any talent by which such a thing is comprehensible.   It cannot therefore be an object for faith to act upon, for faith is nothing more than an assent the mind gives to something it sees cause to believe is fact.   But priests, preachers, and fanatics, put imagination in the place of faith, and it is the nature of the imagination to believe without evidence.   If Joseph the carpenter dreamed (as the book of Matthew, chapter 1st, says he did,) that his betrothed wife, Mary, was with child by the Holy Ghost, and that an angel told him so, I am not obliged to put faith in his dream ; nor do I put any, for I put no faith in my own dreams, and I should be weak and foolish indeed to put faith in the dreams of others.—The Christian religion is derogatory to the Creator in all its articles.   It puts the Creator in an inferior point of view, and places the Christian Devil above him.   It is he, according to the absurd story in Genesis, that outwits the

Creator, in the garden of Eden, and steals from him his favorite creature, man ; and, at last, obliges him to beget a son, and
put that son to death, to get man back again. And this the
priests of the Christian religion, call redemption.

"Christian authors exclaim against the practice of offering
human sacrifices, which, they say, is done in some countries ;
and those authors make those exclamations without ever reflect-
ing that their own doctrine of salvation is founded on a human
sacrifice. They are saved, they say, by the blood of Christ.
The Christian religion begins with a dream and ends with a
murder.

"As I am well enough to sit up some hours in the day,
though not well enough to get up without help, I employ myself as I have always done, in endeavoring to bring man to the
right use of the reason that God has given him, and to direct
his mind immediately to his Creator, and not to fanciful sec-
ondary beings called mediators, as if God was superannuated
or ferocious.

"As to the book called the Bible, it is blasphemy to call it
the word of God. It is a book of lies and contradictions, and
a history of bad times and bad men. There are but a few good
characters in the whole book. The fable of Christ and his
twelve apostles, which is a parody on the sun and the twelve
signs of the Zodiac, copied from the ancient religions of the
eastern world, is the least hurtful part. Every thing told of
Christ has reference to the sun. His reported resurrection is
at sunrise, and that on the first day of the week ; that is, on
the day anciently dedicated to the sun, and from thence called
Sunday ; in latin Dies Solis, the day of the sun ; as the next
day, Monday, is Moon day. But there is no room in a letter
to explain these things. While man keeps to the belief of one
God, his reason unites with his creed. He is not shocked with
contradictions and horrid stories. His bible is the heavens
and the earth. He beholds his Creator in all his works, and
every thing he beholds inspires him with reverence and gratitude. From the goodness of God to all, he learns his duty to
his fellow-man, and stands self-reproved when he transgresses
it. Such a man is no persecutor. But when he multiplies his
creed with imaginary things, of which he can have neither evi-

dence nor conception, such as the tale of the garden of Eden, the talking serpent, the fall of man, the dreams of Joseph the carpenter, the pretended resurrection and ascension, of which there is even no historical relation, for no historian of those times mentions such a thing, he gets into the pathless region of confusion, and turns either frantic or hypocrite. He forces his mind, and pretends to believe what he does not believe. This is in general the case with the Methodists. Their religion is all creed and no morals.

" I have now my friend given you a fac-simile of my mind on the subject of religion and creeds, and my wish is, that you may make this letter as publicly known as you find opportunities of doing. Yours in friendship."

The " Essay on Dream " was written early in 1806 and printed in May, 1807. It was the last work of importance written by Paine. In the same pamphlet was included a part of his reply to the Bishop of Llandaff, which was written in France : " An Examination of the Passages in the New Testament, quoted from the Old, and called Prophecies of the Coming of Jesus Christ." The Examination is widely known and is among Paine's characteristic works,—a continuation of the " Age of Reason." The " Essay on Dream " is a fine specimen of the author's literary art. Dream is the imagination awake while the judgment is asleep. " Every person is mad once in twenty-four hours ; for were he to act in the day as he dreams in the night, he would be confined for a lunatic." Nathaniel Hawthorne thought spiritualism " a sort of dreaming awake." Paine explained in the same way some of the stories on which popular religion is founded. The incarnation itself rests on what an angel told Joseph in a dream, and others are referred to. "This story of dreams has thrown Europe into a dream for more than a thousand years. All the efforts that nature, reason, and conscience have made to awaken man from it have been ascribed by priestcraft and superstition to the workings of the devil, and had it not been for the American revolution, which by establishing the universal right of conscience, first opened the way to free discussion, and for the French revolution which followed, this religion of dreams had continued to be preached, and that after it had ceased to be believed."

But Paine was to be reminded that the revolution had not made conscience free enough in America to challenge waking dreams without penalties. The following account of his disfranchisement at New Rochelle, was written from Broome St., New York, May 4, 1807, to Vice-President Clinton.

"RESPECTED FRIEND,—Elisha Ward and three or four other Tories who lived within the british lines in the revolutionary war, got in to be inspectors of the election last year at New Rochelle. Ward was supervisor. These men refused my vote at the election, saying to me: 'You are not an American; our minister at Paris, Gouverneur Morris, would not reclaim you when you were emprisoned in the Luxembourg prison at Paris, and General Washington refused to do it.' Upon my telling him that the two cases he stated were falsehoods, and that if he did me injustice I would prosecute him, he got up, and calling for a constable, said to me, 'I will commit you to prison.' He chose, however, to sit down and go no farther with it.

"I have written to Mr. Madison for an attested copy of Mr. Monro's letter to the then Secretary of State Randolph, in which Mr. Monro gives the government an account of his reclaiming me and my liberation in consequence of it; and also for an attested copy of Mr. Randolph's answer, in which he says : 'The President approves what you have done in the case of Mr. Paine.' The matter I believe is, that, as I had not been guillotined, Washington thought best to say what he did. As to Gouverneur Morris, the case is that he did reclaim me ; but his reclamation did me no good, and the probability is, he did not intend it should. Joel Barlow and other Americans in Paris had been in a body to reclaim me, but their application, being unofficial, was not regarded. I then applied to Morris. I shall subpœna Morris, and if I get attested copies from the Secretary of State's office it will prove the lie on the inspectors.

" As it is a new generation that has risen up since the declaration of independence, they know nothing of what the political state of the country was at the time the pamphlet 'Common Sense' appeared ; and besides this there are but few of the old standers left, and none that I know of in this city.

" It may be proper at the trial to bring the mind of the court and the jury back to the times I am speaking of, and if you see no objection in your way, I wish you would write a letter to some person, stating, from your own knowledge, what the condition of those times were, and the effect which the work 'Common Sense,' and the several members of the 'Crisis' had upon the country. It would, I think, be best that the letter should begin directly on the subject in this manner : Being informed that Thomas Paine has been denied his rights of citizenship by certain persons acting as inspectors at an election at New Rochelle, &c.

" I have put the prosecution into the hands of Mr. Riker, district attorney, who can make use of the letter in his address to the Court and Jury. Your handwriting can be sworn to by persons here, if necessary. Had you been on the spot I should have subpœnaed you, unless it had been too inconvenient to you to have attended. Yours in friendship."

To this Clinton replied from Washington, 12th May, 1807 :

" DEAR SIR,—I had the pleasure to receive your letter of the 4th instant, yesterday ; agreeably to your request I have this day written a letter to Richard Riker, Esquire, which he will show you. I doubt much, however, whether the Court will admit it to be read as evidence.

"I am indebted to you for a former letter. I can make no other apology for not acknowledging it before than inability to give you such an answer as I could wish. I constantly keep the subject in mind, and should any favorable change take place in the sentiments of the Legislature, I will apprize you of it.

"I am, with great esteem, your sincere friend."

In the letter to Madison Paine tells the same story. At the end he says that Morris' reclamation was not out of any good will to him. "I know not what he wrote to the french minister; whatever it was he concealed it from me." He also says Morris could hardly keep himself out of prison.[1]

A letter was also written to Joel Barlow, at Washington, dated Broome Street, New York, May 4th. He says in this:

"I have prosecuted the Board of Inspectors for disfranchising me. You and other Americans in Paris went in a body to the Convention to reclaim me, and I want a certificate from you, properly attested, of this fact. If you consult with Gov. Clinton he will in friendship inform you who to address it to.

"Having now done with business I come to meums and tuums. What are you about? You sometimes hear of me but I never hear of you. It seems as if I had got to be master of the feds and the priests. The former do not attack my political publications; they rather try to keep them out of sight by silence. And as to the priests, they act as if they would say, let us alone and we will let you alone. My Examination of the passages called prophecies is printed, and will be published next week. I have prepared it with the Essay on Dream. I do not believe that the priests will attack it, for it is not a book of opinions but of facts. Had the Christian Religion done any good in the world I would not have exposed it, how-

[1] The letter is in Mr. Frederick McGuire's collection of Madison papers.

ever fabulous I might believe it to be.   But the delusive idea
of having a friend at court whom they call a redeemer, who
pays all their scores, is an encouragement to wickedness.

"What is Fulton about ?   Is he taming a whale to draw his
submarine boat ?   I wish you would desire Mr. Smith to send
me his country National Intelligencer.   It is printed twice a
week without advertisement.   I am somewhat at a loss for
want of authentic intelligence.   Yours in friendship."

It will be seen that Paine was still in ignorance
of the conspiracy which had thrown him in prison,
nor did he suspect that Washington had been
deceived by Gouverneur Morris, and that his private letter to Washington might have been suppressed by Pickering.[1]   It will be seen, by Madame

---

[1] It has been already surmised (ii., p. 174), that Washington's Secretary of State might have kept Paine's letter from the President, and thus
prevented an answer, which might have led to an explanation.   I had not
then observed a reference to that letter by Madison, in writing to Monroe
(April 7, 1796), which proves that Paine's communication to Washington
had been read by Pickering.   Monroe was anxious lest some attack on
the President should be written by Paine while under his roof,—an impropriety avoided by Paine as we have seen,—and had written to Madison on
the subject.   Madison answers: "I have given the explanation you desired
to F. A. M[uhlenberg], who has not received any letter as yet, and has promised to pay due regard to your request.   It is proper you should know that
Thomas Paine wrote some time ago a severe letter to the President which
Pickering mentioned to me in harsh terms when I delivered a note from
Thomas Paine to the Secretary of State, inclosed by T. P. in a letter to
me.   Nothing passed, however, that betrayed the least association of your
patronage or attention to Thomas Paine with the circumstance ; nor am I
apprehensive that any real suspicion can exist of your countenancing or even
knowing the steps taken by T. P. under the influence of his personal feelings or political principles.   At the same time the caution you observe is
by no means to be disapproved.   Be so good as to let T. P. know that I
have received his letter and handed his note to the Secretary of State, which
requested copies of such letters as might have been written hence in his behalf.
The note did not require any answer either to me or through me, and I have
heard nothing of it since I handed it to Pickering."   At this time the Secretary of State's office contained the President's official recognition of Paine's
citizenship ; but this application for the papers relating to his imprisonment
by a foreign power received no reply, though it was evidently couched in

Bonneville's and Jarvis' statements elsewhere, that Paine lost his case against Elisha Ward, on what ground it is difficult to imagine. The records of the Supreme Court, at Albany, and the Clerk's office at White Plains, have been vainly searched for any trace of this trial. Mr. John H. Riker, son of Paine's counsel, has examined the remaining papers of Richard Riker (many were accidentally destroyed) without finding anything related to the matter. It is so terrible to think that with Jefferson, Clinton, and Madison at the head of the government, and the facts so clear, the federalist Elisha Ward could vindicate his insult to Thomas Paine, that it may be hoped the publication of these facts will bring others to light that may put a better face on the matter.[1] Madame Bonneville may have mis-

respectful terms ; as the letter was open for the eye of Madison, who would not have conveyed it otherwise. It is impossible that Washington could have sanctioned such an outrage on one he had recognized as an American citizen. There is thus reason to believe that Timothy Pickering, as he had kept back a letter in the case of Randolph, intercepted that of Paine to Washington (Sept. 20, 1795), whose silence brought on him the public letter.

[1] Gilbert Vale relates an anecdote which suggests that a reaction may have occurred in Elisha Ward's family : "At the time of Mr. Paine's residence at his farm, Mr. Ward, now a coffee-roaster in Gold Street, New York, and an assistant alderman, was then a little boy and residing at New Rochelle. He remembers the impressions his mother and some religious people made on him by speaking of *Tom* Paine, so that he concluded that *Tom* Paine must be a very bad and brutal man. Some of his elder companions proposed going into Mr. Paine's orchard to obtain some fruit, and he, out of fear, kept at a distance behind, till he beheld, with surprise, Mr. Paine come out and assist the boys in getting apples, patting one on the head and caressing another, and directing them where to get the best. He then advanced and received his share of encouragement, and the impression this kindness made on him determined him at a very early period to examine his writings. His mother at first took the books from him, but at a later period restored them to him, observing that he was then of an age to judge for himself ; perhaps she had herself been gradually undeceived, both as to his character and writings."

understood the procedure for which she had to pay costs, as Paine's legatee. Whether an ultimate decision was reached or not, the sufficiently shameful fact remains that Thomas Paine was practically disfranchised in the country to which he had rendered services pronounced pre-eminent by Congress, by Washington, and by every soldier and statesman of the Revolution.

Paine had in New York the most formidable of enemies,—an enemy with a newspaper. This was James Cheetham, of whom something has been said in the preface to this work (p. xvi.). In addition to what is there stated, it may be mentioned that Paine had observed, soon after he came to New York, the shifty course of this man's paper, *The American Citizen.* But it was the only republican paper in New York, supported Governor Clinton, for which it had reason, since it had the State printing,—and Colonel Fellows advised that Cheetham should not be attacked. Cheetham had been an attendant on Elihu Palmer's lectures, and after his participation in the dinner to Paine, his federalist opponent, the *Evening Post,* alluded to his being at Palmer's. Thereupon Cheetham declared that he had not heard Palmer for two years. In the winter of 1804 he casually spoke of Paine's "mischievous doctrines." In the following year, when Paine wrote the defence of Jefferson's personal character already alluded to, Cheetham omitted a reference in it to Alexander Hamilton's pamphlet, by which he escaped accusation of official defalcation by confessing an amorous intrigue.[1]

[1] " I see that Cheetham has left out the part respecting Hamilton and

Cheetham having been wont to write of Hamilton as "the gallant of Mrs. Reynolds," Paine did not give much credit to the pretext of respect for the dead, on which the suppression was justified. He was prepared to admit that his allusion might be fairly suppressed, but perceived that the omission was made merely to give Cheetham a chance for vaunting his superior delicacy, and casting a suspicion on Paine. "Cheetham," wrote Paine, "might as well have put the part in, as put in the reasons for which he left it out. Those reasons leave people to suspect that the part suppressed related to some new discovered immorality in Hamilton worse than the old story."

About the same time with Paine, an Irishman came to America, and, after travelling about the country a good deal, established a paper in New York called *The People's Friend.* This paper began a furious onslaught on the French, professed to have advices that Napoleon meant to retake New Orleans, and urged an offensive alliance of the United States with England against France and Spain. These articles appeared in the early autumn of 1806, when, as we have seen, Paine was especially beset by personal worries. They made him frantic. His denunciations, merited as they

Mrs. Reynolds, but for my own part I wish it had been in. Had the story never been publicly told I would not have been the first to tell it ; but Hamilton had told it himself, and therefore it was no secret ; but my motive in introducing it was because it was applicable to the subject I was upon, and to show the revilers of Mr. Jefferson that while they are affecting a morality of horror at an unproved and unfounded story about Mr. Jefferson, they had better look at home and give vent to their horror, if they had any, at a real case of their own Dagon (*sic*) and his Delilah."—Paine to Colonel Fellows, July 31, 1805.

were, of this assailant of France reveal the unstrung condition of the old author's nerves. Duane, of the Philadelphia *Aurora*, recognized in Carpenter a man he had seen in Calcutta, where he bore the name of Cullen. It was then found that he had on his arrival in America borne the *alias* of Maccullen. Paine declared that he was an "emissary" sent to this country by Windham, and indeed most persons were at length satisfied that such was the case. Paine insisted that loyalty to our French alliance demanded Cullen's expulsion. His exposures of "the emissary Cullen" (who disappeared) were printed in a new republican paper in New York, *The Public Advertiser*, edited by Mr. Frank. The combat drew public attention to the new paper, and Cheetham was probably enraged by Paine's transfer of his pen to Frank. In 1807, Paine had a large following in New York, his friends being none the less influential among the masses because not in the fashionable world. Moreover, the very popular Mayor of New York, De Witt Clinton, was a hearty admirer of Paine. So Cheetham's paper suffered sadly, and he opened his guns on Paine, declaring that in the Revolution he (Paine) "had stuck very correctly to his pen in a safe retreat," that his "Rights of Man" merely repeated Locke, and so forth. He also began to denounce France and applaud England, which led to the belief that, having lost republican patronage, Cheetham was aiming to get that of England.

In a "Reply to Cheetham" (August 21st), Paine met personalities in kind. "Mr. Cheetham, in his rage for attacking everybody and everything that is not his own (for he is an ugly-tempered man, and he carries the evidence of it in the vulgarity and forbiddingness of his countenance—God has set a mark upon Cain), has attacked me, etc." In reply to further attacks, Paine printed a piece headed "Cheetham and his Tory Paper." He said that Cheetham was discovering symptoms of being the successor of Cullen, *alias* Carpenter. "Like him he is seeking to involve the United States in a quarrel with France for the benefit of England." This article caused a duel between the rival editors, Cheetham and Frank, which seems to have been harmless. Paine wrote a letter to the *Evening Post*, saying that he had entreated Frank to answer Cheetham's challenge by declaring that he (Paine) had written the article and was the man to be called to account. In company Paine mentioned an opinion expressed by the President in a letter just received. This got into the papers, and Cheetham declared that the President could not have so written, and that Paine was intoxicated when he said so. For this Paine instituted a suit against Cheetham for slander, but died before any trial.

Paine had prevailed with his pen, but a terrible revenge was plotted against his good name. The farrier William Carver, in whose house he had lived, turned Judas, and concocted with Cheetham the libels against Paine that have passed as history.

CHAPTER XIX.

PERSONAL TRAITS.

On July 1, 1806, two young English gentlemen, Daniel and William Constable, arrived in New York, and for some years travelled about the country. The Diary kept by Daniel Constable has been shown me by his nephew, Clair J. Grece, LL.D. It contains interesting allusions to Paine, to whom they brought an introduction from Rickman.

"July 1. To the Globe, in Maiden Lane, to dine. Mr. Segar at the Globe offered to send for Mr. Paine, who lived only a few doors off : He seemed a true Painite.

" 3d. William and I went to see Thomas Paine. When we first called he was taking a nap. . . . Back to Mr. Paine's about 5 o'clock, sat about an hour with him. . . . I meant to have had T. Paine in a carriage with me to-morrow, and went to inquire for one. The price was $1 per hour, but when I proposed it to T. P. he declined it on account of his health.

" 4th. Friday. Fine clear day. The annual Festival of Independence. We were up by five o'clock, and on the battery saw the cannons fired, in commemoration of liberty, which had been employed by the English against the sacred cause. The people seemed to enter into the spirit of the day : stores &c. were generally shut. . . . In the fore part of the day I had the honour of walking with T. Paine along the Broadway. The day finished peaceably, and we saw no scenes of quarreling or drunkenness.

" 14. A very hot day. Evening, met T. Paine in the Broadway and walked with him to his house.

"Oct. 29 [on returning from a journey]. Called to see T. Paine, who was walking about Carver's shop."

"Nov. 1. Changed snuff-boxes with T. Paine at his lodgings.[1] The old philosopher, in bed at 4 o'clock afternoon, seems as talkative and well as when we saw him in the summer."

In a letter written jointly by the brothers to their parents, dated July 6th, they say that Paine "begins to feel the effects of age. The print I left at Horley is a very strong likeness. He lives with a small family who came from Lewes [Carvers] quite retired, and but ʾlittle known or noticed." They here also speak of "the honour of walking with our old friend T. Paine in the midst of the bustle on Independence Day." There is no suggestion, either here or in the Diary, that these gentlemen of culture and position observed anything in the appearance or habits of Paine that diminished the pleasure of meeting him. In November they travelled down the Mississippi, and on their return to New York, nine months later, they heard (July 20, 1807) foul charges against Paine from Carver. "Paine has left his house, and they have had a violent disagreement. Carver charges Paine with many foul vices, as debauchery, lying, ingratitude, and a total want of common honour in all his actions, says that he drinks regularly a quart of brandy per day." But next day they call on Paine, in "the Bowery road," and William Constable writes :

"He looks better than last year. He read us an essay on national defence, comparing the different expenses and powers

[1] Dr. Grece showed me Paine's papier-maché snuff-box, which his uncle had fitted with silver plate, inscription, decorative eagle, and banner of "Liberty, Equality." It is kept in a jewel-box with an engraving of Paine on the lid.

of gunboats and ships of war and batteries in protecting a
sea coast ; and gave D. C. [Daniel Constable] a copy of his
Examination of the texts of scriptures called prophecies, etc.,
which he published a short time since. He says that this
work is of too high a cut for the priests and that they will
not touch it."

These brothers Constable met Fulton, " a friend
of Paine's," just then experimenting with his steamboat on the Hudson. They also found that a
scandal had been caused by a report brought to
the British Consul that thirty passengers on the ship
by which they (the Constables) came, had " the
Bible bound up with the ' Age of Reason,' and
that they spoke in very disrespectful terms of the
mother country." Paine had left his farm at New
Rochelle, at which place the travellers heard stories
of his slovenliness, also that he was penurious,
though nothing was said of intemperance.

Inquiry among aged residents of New Rochelle
has been made from time to time for a great many
years. The Hon. J. B. Stallo, late U. S. Minister
to Italy, told me that in early life he visited the
place and saw persons who had known Paine, and
declared that Paine resided there without fault.
Paine lived for a time with Mr. Staple, brother of
the influential Captain Pelton, and the adoption
of Paine's religious views by some of these persons
caused the odium.[1] Paine sometimes preached at
New Rochelle.

---

[1] Mr. Burger, Pelton's clerk, used to drive Paine about daily. Vale says :
" He [Burger] describes Mr. Paine as really abstemious, and when pressed
to drink by those on whom he called during his rides, he usually refused with
great firmness, but politely. In one of these rides .he was met by De Witt
Clinton, and their mutual greetings were extremely hearty. Mr. Paine at

Cheetham publishes a correspondence purporting to have passed between Paine and Carver, in November, 1806, in which the former repudiates the latter's bill for board (though paying it), saying he was badly and dishonestly treated in Carver's house, and had taken him out of his Will. To this a reply is printed, signed by Carver, which he certainly never wrote ; specimens of his composition, now before me, prove him hardly able to spell a word correctly or to frame a sentence.[1] The letter in Cheetham shows a practised hand, and was evidently written for Carver by the "biographer." This ungenuineness of Carver's letter, and expressions not characteristic in that of Paine render the correspondence mythical. Although Carver passed many penitential years hanging about Paine celebrations, deploring the wrong he had done Paine, he could not squarely repudiate the correspondence,

this time was the reverse of morose, and though careless of his dress and prodigal of his snuff, he was always clean and well clothed. Mr. Burger describes him as familiar with children and humane to animals, playing with the neighboring children, and communicating a friendly pat even to a passing dog." Our frontispiece shows Paine's dress in 1803.

[1] In the Concord (Mass.) Public Library there is a copy of Cheetham's book, which belonged to Carver, by whom it was filled with notes. He says : "Cheetham was a hypocrate turned Tory," "Paine was not Drunk when he wrote the thre pedlars for me, I sold them to a gentleman, a Jew for a dollar—Cheetham knew that he told a lie saying Paine was drunk—any person reading Cheetham's life of Paine that [sic] his pen was guided by prejudice that was brought on by Cheetham's altering a peice that Paine had writen as an answer to a peice that had apeared in his paper, I had careyd the peice to Cheetham, the next Day the answer was printed with the alteration, Paine was angry, sent me to call Cheetham I then asked how he undertook to mutilate the peice, if aney thing was rong he knew ware to find him & sad he never permitted a printer to alter what he had wrote, that the sence of the peice was spoiled—by this means their freind ship was broken up through life——" (The marginalia in this volume have been copied for me with exactness by Miss E. G. Crowell, of Concord.)

to which Cheetham had compelled him to swear in court. He used to declare that Cheetham had obtained under false pretences and printed without authority letters written in anger. But thrice in his letter to Paine Carver says he means to publish it. Its closing words are : " There may be many grammatical errours in this letter. To you I have no apologies to make ; but I hope a candid and impartial public will not view them 'with a critick's eye.'" This is artful ; besides the fling at Paine's faulty grammar, which Carver could not discover, there is a pretence to faults in his own letter which do not exist, but certainly would have existed had he written it. The style throughout is transparently Cheetham's.

In the book at Concord the unassisted Carver writes : " The libel for wich [*sic*] he [Cheetham] was sued was contained in the letter I wrote to Paine." This was the libel on Madame Bonneville, Carver's antipathy to whom arose from his hopes of Paine's property. In reply to Paine's information, that he was excluded from his Will, Carver says : " I likewise have to inform you, that I totally disregard the power of your mind and pen ; for should you, by your conduct, permit this letter to appear in public, in vain may you attempt to print or publish any thing afterwards." This is plainly an attempt at blackmail. Carver's letter is dated December 2, 1806. It was not published during Paine's life, for the farrier hoped to get back into the Will by frightening Madame Bonneville and other friends of Paine with the stories he meant to tell. About a year before Paine's death he made another blackmailing attempt. He raked up the scandalous stories published by " Oldys " concerning Paine's domestic troubles in Lewes, pretending that he knew the facts personally. " Of these facts Mr. Carver has offered me an affidavit," says Cheetham. " He stated them all to Paine in a private letter which he wrote to him a year before his death ; to which no answer was returned. Mr. Carver showed me the letter soon after it was written." On this plain evidence of long con- spiracy with Cheetham, and attempt to blackmail Paine when he was sinking in mortal illness, Carver never made any comment. When Paine was known to be near his end Carver made an effort at concili- ation. " I think it a pity," he wrote, " that you or myself should depart this life with envy in our hearts against each other—and I firmly believe that no difference would have taken place between us, had not some of your pretended friends endeavored to have caused a separation of friendship between us." [1] But abjectness was not more effectual than blackmail. The property went to the Bonnevilles, and Carver, who had flattered Paine's " great mind," in the letter just quoted, proceeded to write a mean one about the dead author for Cheetham's projected biography. He did not, however, expect Cheetham to publish his slanderous letter about Paine and Madame Bonneville, which he meant merely for extortion ; nor could Cheetham have got the letter had he not written it. All of Cheet- ham's libels on Paine's life in New York are ampli- fications of Carver's insinuations. In describing

[1] " A Bone to Gnaw for Grant Thorburn." By W. Carver (1836).

Cheetham as " an abominable liar," Carver passes sentence on himself. On this blackmailer, this confessed libeller, rest originally and fundamentally the charges relating to Paine's last years.

It has already been stated that Paine boarded for a time in the Bayeaux mansion. With Mrs. Bayeaux lived her daughter, Mrs. Badeau. In 1891 I visited, at New Rochelle, Mr. Albert Badeau, son of the lady last named, finding him, as I hope he still is, in good health and memory. Seated in the arm-chair given him by his mother, as that in which Paine used to sit by their fireside, I took down for publication some words of his. " My mother would never tolerate the aspersions on Mr. Paine. She declared steadfastly to the end of her life that he was a perfect gentleman, and a most faithful friend, amiable, gentle, never intemperate in eating or drinking. My mother declared that my grandmother equally pronounced the disparaging reports about Mr. Paine slanders. I never remember to have seen my mother angry except when she heard such calumnies of Mr. Paine, when she would almost insult those who uttered them. My mother and grandmother were very religious, members of the Episcopal Church." What Mr. Albert Badeau's religious opinions are I do not know, but no one acquainted with that venerable gentleman could for an instant doubt his exactness and truthfulness. It certainly was not until some years after his return to America that any slovenliness could be observed about Paine, and the contrary was often remarked in former times.[1] After he had come to New York,

[1] " He dined at my table," said Aaron Burr. " I always considered Mr.

and was neglected by the pious ladies and gentlemen with whom he had once associated, he neglected his personal appearance. " Let those dress who need it," he said to a friend.

Paine was prodigal of snuff, but used tobacco in no other form. He had aversion to profanity, and never told or listened to indecent anecdotes.

With regard to the charges of excessive drinking made against Paine, I have sifted a vast mass of contrarious testimonies, and arrived at the following conclusions. In earlier life Paine drank spirits, as was the custom in England and America ; and he unfortunately selected brandy, which causes alcoholic indigestion, and may have partly produced the oft-quoted witness against him—his somewhat red nose. His nose was prominent, and began to be red when he was fifty-five. That was just after he had been dining a good deal with rich people in England, and at public dinners. During his early life in England (1737–1774) no instance of excess was known, and Paine expressly pointed the Excise Office to his record. " No complaint of the least dishonesty or intemperance has ever appeared against me." His career in America (1774–1787) was free from any suspicion of intemperance. John Hall's daily diary while working with Paine for months is minute, mentioning everything, but

Paine a gentleman, a pleasant companion, and a good-natured and intelligent man ; decidedly temperate, with a proper regard for his personal appearance, whenever I have seen him." (Quoted in *The Beacon*, No. 30, May, 1837.) " In his dress." says Joel Barlow, " he was generally very cleanly, though careless, and wore his hair queued with side curls, and powdered, like a gentleman of the old French School. His manners were easy and gracious, his knowledge universal."

in no case is a word said of Paine's drinking. This was in 1785–7. Paine's enemy, Chalmers (" Oldys "), raked up in 1791 every charge he could against Paine, but intemperance is not included. Paine told Rickman that in Paris, when borne down by public and private affliction, he had been driven to excess. That period I have identified on a former page (ii., p. 59) as a few weeks in 1793, when his dearest friends were on their way to the guillotine, whither he daily expected to follow them. After that Paine abstained altogether from spirits, and drank wine in moderation. Mr. Lovett, who kept the City Hotel, New York, where Paine stopped in 1803 and 1804 for some weeks, wrote a note to Caleb Bingham, of Boston, in which he says that Paine drank less than any of his boarders. Gilbert Vale, in preparing his biography, questioned D. Burger, the clerk of Pelton's store at New Rochelle, and found that Paine's liquor supply while there was one quart of rum per week. Brandy he had entirely discarded. He also questioned Jarvis, the artist, in whose house Paine resided in New York (Church Street) five months, who declared that what Cheetham had reported about Paine and himself was entirely false. Paine, he said, " did not and could not drink much." In July, 1809, just after Paine's death, Cheetham wrote Barlow for information concerning Paine, " useful in illustrating his character," and said : " He was a great drunkard here, and Mr. M., a merchant of this city, who lived with him when he was arrested by order of Robespierre, tells me he was intoxicated when that event happened." Barlow, recently returned from

Europe, was living just out of Washington; he could know nothing of Cheetham's treachery, and fell into his trap; he refuted the story of " Mr. M.," of course, but took it for granted that a supposed republican editor would tell the truth about Paine in New York, and wrote of the dead author as having "a mind, though strong enough to bear him up and to rise elastic under the heaviest hand of oppression, yet unable to endure the contempt of his former friends and fellow-laborers, the rulers of the country that had received his first and greatest services; a mind incapable of looking down with serene compassion, as it ought, on the rude scoffs of their imitators, a new generation that knows him not; a mind that shrinks from their society, and unhappily seeks refuge in low company, or looks for consolation in the sordid, solitary bottle, etc."[1] Barlow, misled as he was, well knew Paine's nature, and that if he drank to excess it was not from appetite, but because of ingratitude and wrong. The man was not a stock or a stone. If any can find satisfaction in the belief that Paine found no Christian in America so merciful as rum, they may perhaps discover some grounds for it in a brief period of his sixty-ninth year. While living in the house of Carver, Paine was seized with an illness that threatened to be mortal, and from which he never fully recovered. It is probable that he was kept alive for a time by spirits during the terrible time, but this ceased when in the latter part of 1806 he left Carver's to live with Jarvis. In the

[1] Todd's "Joel Barlow," p. 236. The "Mr. M." was one Murray, an English speculator in France, where he never resided with Paine at all.

spring of 1808 he resided in the house of Mr. Hitt, a baker, in Broome Street, and there remained ten months. Mr. Hitt reports that Paine's weekly supply then—his seventy-second year, and his last— was three quarts of rum per week.

After Paine had left Carver's he became acquainted with more people. The late Judge Tabor's recollections have been sent me by his son, Mr. Stephen Tabor, of Independence, Iowa.

"I was an associate editor of the *New York Beacon* with Col. John Fellows, then (1836) advanced in years, but retaining all the vigor and fire of his manhood. He was a ripe scholar, a most agreeable companion, and had been the correspondent and friend of Jefferson, Madison, Monroe and John Quincy Adams, under all of whom he held a responsible office. One of his productions was dedicated, by permission, to [J. Q.] Adams, and was republished and favorably received in England. Col. Fellows was the soul of honor and inflexible in his adherence to truth. He was intimate with Paine during the whole time he lived after returning to this country, and boarded for a year in the same house with him.

"I also was acquainted with Judge Hertell, of New York City, a man of wealth and position, being a member of the New York Legislature, both in the Senate and Assembly, and serving likewise on the judicial bench. Like Col. Fellows, he was an author, and a man of unblemished life and irreproachable character.

"These men assured me of their own knowledge derived from constant personal intercourse during the last seven years of Paine's life, that he never kept any company but what was entirely respectable, and that all accusations of drunkenness were grossly untrue. They saw him under all circumstances and *knew* that he was never intoxicated. Nay, more, they said, for that day, he was even abstemious. That was a drinking age and Paine, like Jefferson, could "bear but little spirit," so that he was constitutionally temperate.

"Cheetham refers to William Carver and the portrait painter

Jarvis. I visited Carver, in company with Col. Fellows, and naturally conversed with the old man about Paine. He said that the allegation that Paine was a drunkard was altogether without foundation. In speaking of his letter to Paine which Cheetham published, Carver said that he was angry when he wrote it and that he wrote unwisely, as angry men generally do ; that Cheetham obtained the letter under false pretenses and printed it without authority.

"Col. Fellows and Judge Hertell visited Paine throughout the whole course of his last illness. They repeatedly conversed with him on religious topics and they declared that he died serenely, philosophically and resignedly. This information I had directly from their own lips, and their characters were so spotless, and their integrity so unquestioned, that more reliable testimony it would be impossible to give."

During Paine's life the world heard no hint of sexual immorality connected with him, but after his death Cheetham published the following : " Paine brought with him from Paris, and from her husband in whose house he had lived, Margaret Brazier Bonneville, and her three sons. *Thomas* has the features, countenance, and temper of Paine." Madame Bonneville promptly sued Cheetham for slander. Cheetham had betrayed his "pal," Carver, by printing the letter concocted to blackmail Paine, for whose composition the farrier no doubt supposed he had paid the editor with stories borrowed from " Oldys," or not actionable. Cheetham probably recognized, when he saw Madame Bonneville in court, that he too had been deceived, and that any illicit relation between the accused lady and Paine, thirty years her senior, was preposterous. Cheetham's lawyer (Griffin) insinuated terrible things that his witnesses were to prove, but they all dissolved into Carver. Mrs.

Ryder, with whom Paine had boarded, admitted
trying to make Paine smile by saying Thomas was
like him, but vehemently repudiated the slander.
" Mrs. Bonneville often came to visit him. She
never saw but decency with Mrs. Bonneville. She
never staid there but one night, when Paine was
very sick." Mrs. Dean was summoned to support
one of Carver's lies that Madame Bonneville tried
to cheat Paine, but denied the whole story (which
has unfortunately been credited by Vale and other
writers). The Rev. Mr. Foster, who had a claim
against Paine's estate for tuition of the Bonnevilles, was summoned. " Mrs. Bonneville," he testified, "might possibly have said as much as that
but for Paine she would not have come here, and
that he was under special obligations to provide for
her children." A Westchester witness, Peter Underhill, testified that " he one day told Mrs. Bonneville that her child resembled Paine, and Mrs.
Bonneville said it was Paine's child." But, apart
from the intrinsic incredibility of this statement
(unless she meant "god-son"), Underhill's character
broke down under the testimony of his neighbors,
Judge Sommerville and Captain Pelton. Cheetham
had thus no dependence but Carver, who actually
tried to support his slanders from the dead lips of
Paine ! But in doing so he ruined Cheetham's case
by saying that Paine told him Madame Bonneville
was never the wife of M. Bonneville ; the charge
being that she was seduced from her husband. It
was extorted from Carver that Madame Bonneville, having seen his scurrilous letter to Paine,
threatened to prosecute him ; also that he had

taken his wife to visit Madame Bonneville. Then it became plain to Carver that Cheetham's case was lost, and he deserted it on the witness-stand; declaring that "he had never seen the slightest indication of any meretricious or illicit commerce between Paine and Mrs. Bonneville, that they never were alone together, and that all the three children were alike the objects of Paine's care." Counsellor Sampson (no friend to Paine) perceived that Paine's Will was at the bottom of the business. "That is the key to this mysterious league of apostolic slanderers, mortified expectants and disappointed speculators." Sampson's invective was terrific; Cheetham rose and claimed protection of the court, hinting at a duel. Sampson took a pinch of snuff, and pointing his finger at the defendant, said:

"If he complains of personalities, he who is hardened in every gross abuse, he who lives reviling and reviled, who might construct himself a monument with no other materials but those records to which he is a party, and in which he stands enrolled as an offender [1]: if he cannot sit still to hear his accusation, but calls for the protection of the court against a counsel whose duty it is to make his crimes appear, how does *she* deserve protection, whom he has driven to the sad necessity of coming here to vindicate her honor, from those personalities he has lavished on her?"

The editor of Counsellor Sampson's speech says that the jury "although composed of men of different political sentiments, returned in a few minutes a verdict of guilty." It is added:

[1] Cheetham was at the moment a defendant in nine or ten cases for libel.

"The court, however, when the libeller came up the next day to receive his sentence, highly commended the book which contained the libellous publication, declared that it tended to serve the cause of religion, and imposed no other punishment on the libeller than the payment of $150, with a direction that the costs be taken out of it. It is fit to remark, lest foreigners who are unacquainted with our political condition should receive erroneous impressions, that Mr. Recorder Hoffman does not belong to the Republican party in America, but has been elevated to office by men in hostility to it, who obtained a temporary ascendency in the councils of state." [1]

Madame Bonneville had in court eminent witnesses to her character,—Thomas Addis Emmet, Fulton, Jarvis, and ladies whose children she had taught French. Yet the scandal was too tempting an illustration of the "Age of Reason" to disappear with Cheetham's defeat. Americans in their peaceful habitations were easily made suspicious of a French woman who had left her husband in Paris and followed Paine; they could little realize the complications into which ten tempestuous years had thrown thousands of families in France, and how such poor radicals as the Bonnevilles had to live as they could. The scandal branched into variants. Twenty-five years later pious Grant Thorburn promulgated that Paine had run off from Paris with the wife of a tailor named Palmer. "Paine made no scruples of living with this woman openly." (Mrs. Elihu Palmer, in her penury, was employed by Paine to attend to his rooms, etc.,

[1] "Speech of Counsellor Sampson ; with an Introduction to the Trial of James Cheetham, Esq., for a libel on Margaret Brazier Bonneville, in his Memoirs of Thomas Paine. Philadelphia : Printed by John Sweeny, No. 357 Arch Street, 1810." I am indebted for the use of this rare pamphlet, and for other information, to the industrious collector of *causes célèbres*, Mr. E. B. Wynn, of Watertown, N. Y.

during a few months of illness.) As to Madame
Bonneville, whose name Grant Thorburn seems
not to have heard, she was turned into a roman-
tic figure. Thorburn says that Paine escaped the
guillotine by the execution of another man in his
place.

"The man who suffered death for Paine, left a widow, with
two young children in poor circumstances. Paine brought
them all to this country, supported them while he lived, and, it
is said, left most of his property to them when he died. The
widow and children lived in apartments up town by themselves. He then boarded with Carver. I believe his conduct
was disinterested and honorable to the widow. She appeared
to be about thirty years of age, and was far from being handsome." [1]

Grant Thorburn was afterwards led to doubt
whether this woman was the widow of the man
guillotined, but declares that when "Paine first
brought her out, he and his friends passed her off
as such." As a myth of the time (1834), and an
indication that Paine's generosity to the Bonneville family was well known in New York, the
story is worth quoting. But the Bonnevilles never
escaped from the scandal. Long years afterward,
when the late Gen. Bonneville was residing in St.
Louis, it was whispered about that he was the
natural son of Thomas Paine, though he was born
before Paine ever met Madame Bonneville. Of
course it has gone into the religious encyclopædias. The best of them, that of McClintock
and Strong, says: "One of the women he supported [in France] followed him to this country."
After the fall of Napoleon, Nicholas Bonneville,

[1] "Forty Years' Residence in America."

relieved of his surveillance, hastened to New York, where he and his family were reunited, and enjoyed the happiness provided by Paine's self-sacrificing economy.

The present writer, having perused some thousands of documents concerning Paine, is convinced that no charge of sensuality could have been brought against him by any one acquainted with the facts, except out of malice. Had Paine held, or practised, any latitudinarian theory of sexual liberty, it would be recorded here, and his reasons for the same given. I have no disposition to suppress anything. Paine was conservative in such matters. And as to his sacrificing the happiness of a home to his own pleasure, nothing could be more inconceivable.

Above all, Paine was a profoundly religious man, —one of the few in our revolutionary era of whom it can be said that his delight was in the law of his Lord, and in that law did he meditate day and night. Consequently, he could not escape the immemorial fate of the great believers, to be persecuted for unbelief—by unbelievers.

CHAPTER XX.

DEATH AND RESURRECTION.

THE blow that Paine received by the refusal of his vote at New Rochelle was heavy. Elisha Ward, a Tory in the Revolution, had dexterously gained power enough to give his old patrons a good revenge on the first advocate of independence. The blow came at a time when his means were low, and Paine resolved to apply to Congress for payment of an old debt. The response would at once relieve him, and overwhelm those who were insulting him in New York. This led to a further humiliation, and one or two letters to Congress, of which Paine's enemies did not fail to make the most.[1]

[1] Paine had always felt that Congress was in his debt for his voyage to France for supplies with Col. Laurens (i., p. 171). In a letter (Feb. 20, 1782) to Robert Morris, Paine mentions that when Col. Laurens proposed that he should accompany him, as secretary, he was on the point of establishing a newspaper. He had purchased twenty reams of paper, and Mr. Izard had sent to St. Eustatia for seventy more. This scheme, which could hardly fail of success, was relinquished for the voyage. It was undertaken at the urgent solicitation of Laurens, and Paine certainly regarded it as official. He had ninety dollars when he started, in bills of exchange ; when Col. Laurens left him, after their return, he had but two louis d'or. The Memorial sent by Paine to Congress (Jan. 21, 1808) recapitulated facts known to my reader. It was presented by the Hon. George Clinton, Jr., February 4, and referred to the Committee of Claims. On February 14th Paine wroth a statement concerning the $3,000 given him (1785) by Congress, which he maintained was an indemnity for injustice done him in the Deane case. Laurens had long been dead. The Committee consulted the

The letters are those of a broken-hearted man, and it seems marvellous that Jefferson, Madison, and the Clintons did not intervene and see that some recognition of Paine's former services, by those who should not have forgotten them, was made without the ill-judged memorial.   While they were enjoying their grandeur the man who, as Jefferson wrote, " steadily laboured, and with as much effect as any man living," to secure America freedom, was living—or rather dying—in a miserable lodging-house, 63 Partition Street.   He had gone there for economy; for he was exhibiting that morbid apprehension about his means which is a well-known symptom of decline in those who have suffered poverty in early life.   Washington, with 40,000 acres, wrote in his last year as if facing ruin.   Paine had only a little farm at New Rochelle.   He had for some time suffered from want of income, and at last had to sell the farm he meant for the Bonnevilles for $10,000 ; but the purchaser died, and at his widow's appeal the contract was cancelled.   It was at this time that he appealed to Congress.   It appears, however,

President, whose reply I know not. Vice-President Clinton wrote (March 23, 1808) that " from the information I received at the time I have reason to believe that Mr. Paine accompanied Col. Laurens on his mission to France in the course of our revolutionary war, for the purpose of negotiating a loan, and that he acted as his secretary on that occasion ; but although I have no doubt of the truth of this fact, I cannot assert it from my own actual knowledge." There was nothing found on the journals of Congress to show Paine's connection with the mission. The old author was completely upset by his longing to hear the fate of his memorial, and he wrote two complaints of the delay, showing that his nerves were shattered. " If," he says, March 7th, " my memorial was referred to the Committee of Claims for the purpose of losing it, it is unmanly policy. After so many years of service my heart grows cold towards America."

that Paine was not anxious for himself, but for the family of Madame Bonneville, whose statement on this point is important.

The last letter that I can find of Paine's was written to Jefferson, July 8, 1808 :

" The british Ministry have out-schemed themselves. It is not difficult to see what the motive and object of that Ministry were in issuing the orders of Council. They expected those orders would force all the commerce of the United States to England, and then, by giving permission to such cargoes as they did not want for themselves to depart for the Continent of Europe, to raise a revenue out of those countries and America. But instead of this they have lost revenue ; that is, they have lost the revenue they used to receive from American imports, and instead of gaining all the commerce they have lost it all.

"This being the case with the british Ministry it is natural to suppose they would be glad to tread back their steps, if they could do it without too much exposing their ignorance and obstinacy. The Embargo law empowers the President to suspend its operation whenever he shall be satisfied that our ships can pass in safety. It therefore includes the idea of empowering him to use means for arriving at that event. Suppose the President were to authorise Mr. Pinckney to propose to the british Ministry that the United States would negociate with France for rescinding the Milan Decree, on condition the English Ministry would rescind their orders of Council ; and in that case the United States would recall their Embargo. France and England stand now at such a distance that neither can propose any thing to the other, neither are there any neutral powers to act as mediators. The U. S. is the only power that can act.

"Perhaps the british Ministry if they listen to the proposal will want to add to it the Berlin decree, which excludes english commerce from the continent of Europe; but this we have nothing to do with, neither has it any thing to do with the Embargo. The british Orders of Council and the Milan decree are parallel cases, and the cause of the Embargo. Yours in friendship."

Paine's last letters to the President are characteristic. One pleads for American intervention to stay
the hand of French oppression among the negroes
in St. Domingo; for the colonization of Louisiana
with free negro laborers; and his very last letter is
an appeal for mediation between France and England for the sake of peace.

Nothing came of these pleadings of Paine; but
perhaps on his last stroll along the Hudson, with
his friend Fulton, to watch the little steamer, he
may have recognized the real mediator beginning
its labors for the federation of the world.

Early in July, 1808, Paine removed to a comfortable abode, that of Mrs. Ryder, near which
Madame Bonneville and her two sons resided. The
house was on Herring Street (afterwards 293
Bleecker), and not far, he might be pleased to find,
from " Reason Street." Here he made one more
attempt to wield his pen,—the result being a brief
letter " To the Federal Faction," which he warns
that they are endangering American commerce by
abusing France and Bonaparte, provoking them to
establish a navigation act that will exclude American ships from Europe. " The United States have
flourished, unrivalled in commerce, fifteen or sixteen
years. But it is not a permanent state of things. It
arose from the circumstances of the war, and most
probably will change at the close of the present war.
The Federalists give provocation enough to promote it."

Apparently this is the last letter Paine ever sent
to the printer. The year passed peacefully away;
indeed there is reason to believe that from the middle of July, 1808, to the end of January, 1809, he

fairly enjoyed existence. During this time he made acquaintance with the worthy Willett Hicks, watchmaker, who was a Quaker preacher. His conversations with Willett Hicks — whose cousin, Elias Hicks, became such an important figure in the Quaker Society twenty years later—were fruitful.

Seven serene months then passed away. Towards the latter part of January, 1809, Paine was very feeble. On the 18th he wrote and signed his Will, in which he reaffirms his theistic faith. On February 1st the Committee of Claims reported unfavorably on his memorial, while recording, "That Mr. Paine rendered great and eminent services to the United States during their struggle for liberty and independence cannot be doubted by any person acquainted with his labours in the cause, and attached to the principles of the contest." On February 25th he had some fever, and a doctor was sent for. Mrs. Ryder attributed the attack to Paine's having stopped taking stimulants, and their resumption was prescribed. About a fortnight later symptoms of dropsy appeared. Towards the end of April Paine was removed to a house on the spot now occupied by No. 59 Grove Street, Madame Bonneville taking up her abode under the same roof. The owner was William A. Thompson, once a law partner of Aaron Burr, whose wife, *née* Maria Holdron, was a niece of Elihu Palmer. The whole of the back part of the house (which was in a lot, no street being then cut) was given up to Paine.[1] Reports of neglect of Paine by Madame Bonneville

---

[1] The topographical facts were investigated by John Randel, Jr., Civil Engineer, at the request of David C. Valentine, Clerk of the Common Council, New York, his report being rendered April 6, 1864.

have been credited by some, but are unfounded.
She gave all the time she could to the sufferer, and
did her best for him.   Willett Hicks sometimes
called, and his daughter (afterwards Mrs. Cheese-
man) used to take Paine delicacies.   The only pro-
curable nurse was a woman named Hedden, who
combined piety and artfulness.   Paine's physician
was the most distinguished in New York, Dr. Romaine, but nurse Hedden managed to get into the
house one Dr. Manly, who turned out to be Cheetham's   spy.   Manly   afterwards   contributed   to
Cheetham's book a lying letter, in which he claimed
to have been Paine's physician.   It will be seen,
however, by Madame Bonneville's narrative to Cobbett, that Paine was under the care of his friend, Dr.
Romaine.   As Manly, assuming that he called as
many did, never saw Paine alone, he was unable to
assert that Paine recanted, but he converted the exclamations of the sufferer into prayers to Christ.[1]

The god of wrath who ruled in New York a
hundred years, through the ministerial prerogatives,
was guarded by a Cerberean legend.   The three
alternatives of the heretic were, recantation, special
judgment, terrible death.   Before Paine's arrival

[1] Another claimant to have been Paine's physician has been cited. In
1876 (*N. Y. Observer*, Feb. 17th) Rev. Dr. Wickham reported from a late
Dr. Matson Smith, of New Rochelle, that he had been Paine's physician,
and witnessed his drunkenness. Unfortunately for Wickham he makes
Smith say it was on his farm where Paine "spent his latter days." Paine
was not on his farm for two years before his death. Smith could never have
attended Paine unless in 1803, when he had a slight trouble with his hands,
—the only illness he ever had at New Rochelle,—while the guest of a neighbor, who attests his sobriety. Finally, a friend of Dr. Smith is living, Mr.
Albert Willcox, who writes me his recollection of what Smith told him of
Paine. Neither drunkenness, nor any item of Wickham's report is mentioned. He said Paine was afraid of death, but could only have heard it.

in America, the excitement on his approach had
tempted a canny Scot, Donald Fraser, to write
an anticipated "Recantation" for him, the title-
page being cunningly devised so as to imply that
there had been an actual recantation. On his
arrival in New York, Paine found it necessary to
call Fraser to account. The Scotchman pleaded
that he had vainly tried to earn a living as fencing-
master, preacher, and school-teacher, but had got
eighty dollars for writing the "Recantation."
Paine said : " I am glad you found the expedient a
successful shift for your needy family; but write no
more concerning Thomas Paine. I am satisfied
with your acknowledgment—try something more
worthy of a man." [1] The second mouth of Cer-
berus was noisy throughout the land ; revivalists
were describing in New Jersey how some "infidel"
had been struck blind in Virginia, and in Virginia
how one was struck dumb in New Jersey. But
here was the very head and front of what they
called " infidelity," Thomas Paine, who ought to
have gathered in his side a sheaf of thunderbolts,
preserved by more marvellous "providences" than
any sectarian saint. Out of one hundred and sixty
carried to the guillotine from his prison, he alone
was saved, by the accident of a chalk mark
affixed to the wrong side of his cell door. On
two ships he prepared to return to America, but
was prevented ; one sank at sea, the other was
searched by the British for him particularly. And
at the very moment when New Rochelle disciples
were calling down fire on his head, Christopher

[1] Dr. Francis' "Old New York," p. 139.

Dederick tried vainly to answer the imprecation; within a few feet of Paine, his gun only shattered the window at which the author sat. "Providence must be as bad as Thomas Paine," wrote the old deist. This amounted to a sort of contest like that of old between the prophets of Baal and those of Jehovah. The deists were crying to their antagonists : "Perchance he sleepeth." It seemed a test case. If Paine was spared, what heretic need tremble ? But he reached his threescore years and ten in comfort; and the placard of Satan flying off with him represented a last hope.

Skepticism and rationalism were not understood by pious people a hundred years ago. In some regions they are not understood yet. Renan thinks he will have his legend in France modelled after Judas. But no educated Christian conceives of a recantation or extraordinary death-bed for a Darwin, a Parker, an Emerson. The late Mr. Bradlaugh had some fear that he might be a posthumous victim of the "infidel's legend." In 1875, when he was ill in St. Luke's Hospital, New York, he desired me to question the physicians and nurses, that I might, if necessary, testify to his fearlessness and fidelity to his views in the presence of death. But he has died without the "legend," whose decline dates from Paine's case ; that was its crucial challenge.

The whole nation had recently been thrown into a wild excitement by the fall of Alexander Hamilton in a duel with Aaron Burr. Hamilton's worldliness had been notorious, but the clergymen (Bishop Moore and the Presbyterian John Mason) reported his dying words of unctuous piety and orthodoxy. In a public letter to the Rev. John Mason, Paine said :

"Between you and your rival in communion ceremonies, Dr. Moore of the Episcopal church, you have, in order to make yourselves appear of some importance, reduced General Hamilton's character to that of a feeble-minded man, who in going out of the world wanted a passport from a priest. Which of you was first applied to for this purpose is a matter of no consequence. The man, sir, who puts his trust and confidence in God, that leads a just and moral life, and endeavors to do good, does not trouble himself about priests when his hour of departure comes, nor permit priests to trouble themselves about him."

The words were widely commented on, and both sides looked forward, almost as if to a prize-fight, to the hour when the man who had unmade thrones, whether in earth or heaven, must face the King of Terrors. Since Michael and Satan had their legendary combat for the body of Moses, there was nothing like it. In view of the pious raids on Paine's death-bed, freethinkers have not been quite fair. To my own mind, some respect is due to those humble fanatics, who really believed that Paine was approaching eternal fires, and had a frantic desire to save him.[1]

Paine had no fear of death ; Madame Bonne-ville's narrative shows that his fear was rather of

[1] Nor should it be forgotten that several liberal Christians, like Hicks, were friendly towards Paine at the close of his life, whereas his most malignant enemies were of his own " Painite " household, Carver and Cheetham. Mr. William Erving tells me that he remembers an English clergyman in New York, named Cunningham, who used to visit his (Erving's) father. He heard him say that Paine and he were friends ; and that "the whole fault was that people hectored Paine, and made him say things he would never say to those who treated him as a gentleman."

living too long. But he had some such fear as that of Voltaire when entering his house at Fernay after it began to lighten. He was not afraid of the lightning, he said, but of what the neighboring priest would make of it should he be struck. Paine had some reason to fear that the zealots who had placarded the devil flying away with him might fulfil their prediction by body-snatching. His unwillingness to be left alone, ascribed to superstitious terror, was due to efforts to get a recantation from him, so determined that he dare not be without witnesses. He had foreseen this. While living with Jarvis, two years before, he desired him to bear witness that he maintained his theistic convictions to the last. Jarvis merrily proposed that he should make a sensation by a mock recantation, but the author said, "Tom Paine never told a lie." When he knew that his illness was mortal he solemnly reaffirmed these opinions in the presence of Madame Bonneville, Dr. Romaine, Mr. Haskin, Captain Pelton, and Thomas Nixon.[1] The nurse Hedden, if the Catholic Bishop of Boston (Fenwick) remembered accurately thirty-seven years later, must have conspired to get him into the patient's room, from which, of course, he was stormily expelled. But the Bishop's story is so like a pious novelette that, in the absence of any mention of his visit by Madame Bonneville, herself a Catholic, one cannot be sure that the interview he waited so long to report did not take place in some slumberous episcopal chamber in Boston.[2]

[1] See the certificate of Nixon and Pelton to Cobbett (Vale, p. 177).

[2] Bishop Fenwick's narrative (*U. S. Catholic Magazine*, 1846) is quoted in the *N. Y. Observer*, September 27, 1877. (Extremes become friends when a freethinker is to be crucified.)

It was rumored that Paine's adherents were keeping him under the influence of liquor in order that he might not recant,—so convinced, at heart, or enamoured of Calvinism was this martyr of Theism, who had published his "Age of Reason" from the prison where he awaited the guillotine.[1]

Of what his principles had cost him Paine had near his end a reminder that cut him to the heart. Albert Gallatin had remained his friend, but his connections, the Fews and Nicholsons, had ignored the author they once idolized. The woman for whom he had the deepest affection, in America, had been Kitty Nicholson, now Mrs. Few. Henry Adams, in his biography of Gallatin, says: "When confined to his bed with his last illness he [Paine] sent for Mrs. Few, who came to see him, and when they parted she spoke some words of comfort and religious hope. Poor Paine only turned his face to the wall, and kept silence." What is Mr. Adams' authority for this? According to Rickman, Sherwin, and Vale, Mr. and Mrs. Few came of their own accord, and "Mrs. Few expressed a wish to renew their former friendship." Paine said to her, "very impressively, 'You have neglected me, and I beg that you will leave the room.' Mrs. Few went into the garden and wept bitterly." I doubt this tradition also, but it was cruelly tantali-

---

[1] Engineer Randel (orthodox), in his topographical report to the Clerk of the City Council (1864), mentions that the "very worthy mechanic," Amasa Wordsworth, who saw Paine daily, told him "there was no truth in such report, and that Thomas Paine had declined saying anything on that subject [religion]." "Paine," testifies Dr. Francis, "clung to his infidelity to the last moment of his natural life." Dr. Francis (orthodox) heard that Paine yielded to King Alcohol, but says Cheetham wrote with "settled malignity," and suspects "sinister motives" in his "strictures on the fruits. of unbelief in the degradation of the wretched Paine."

zing for his early friend, after ignoring him six
years, to return with Death.

If, amid tortures of this kind, the annoyance of
fanatics and the "Painites" who came to watch
them, and the paroxysms of pain, the sufferer
found relief in stimulants, the present writer can
only reflect with satisfaction that such resource
existed. For some time no food would stay on his
stomach. In such weakness and helplessness he
was for a week or so almost as miserable as the
Christian spies could desire, and his truest friends
were not sorrowful when the peace of death
approached. After the years in which the stories
of Paine's wretched end have been accumulating,
now appears the testimony of the Catholic lady,—
persons who remember Madame Bonneville assure
me that she was a perfect lady,—that Paine's mind
was active to the last, that shortly before death
he made a humorous retort to Dr. Romaine, that
he died after a tranquil night.

Paine died at eight o'clock on the morning of
June 8, 1809. Shortly before, two clergymen had
invaded his room, and so soon as they spoke about
his opinions Paine said: "Let me alone; good
morning!" Madame Bonneville asked if he was
satisfied with the treatment he had received in her
house, and he said "Oh yes." These were the last
words of Thomas Paine.

On June 10th Paine's friends assembled to look
on his face for the last time. Madame Bonneville
took a rose from her breast and laid it on that of
her dead benefactor. His adherents were busy
men, and mostly poor; they could not undertake

the then difficult journey (nearly twenty-five miles) to the grave beyond New Rochelle. Of the *cortége* that followed Paine a contemptuous account was printed (Aug. 7th) in the London *Packet:*

"Extract of a letter dated June 20th, Philadelphia, written by a gentleman lately returned from a tour: 'On my return from my journey, when I arrived near Harlem, on York island, I met the funeral of Tom Paine on the road. It was going on to East Chester. The followers were two negroes, the next a carriage with six drunken Irishmen, then a riding chair with two men in it, one of whom was asleep, and then an Irish Quaker on horseback. I stopped my sulkey to ask the Quaker what funeral it was; he said it was Paine, and that his friends as well as his enemies were all glad that he was gone, for he had tired his friends out by his intemperance and frailties. I told him that Paine had done a great deal of mischief in the world, and that, if there was any purgatory, he certainly would have a good share of it before the devil would let him go. The Quaker replied, he would sooner take his chance with Paine than any man in New York, on that score. He then put his horse on a trot, and left me.' "

The funeral was going to West Chester; one of the vehicles contained Madame Bonneville and her children; and the Quaker was not an Irishman. I have ascertained that a Quaker did follow Paine, and that it was Willett Hicks. Hicks, who has left us his testimony that Paine was "a good man, and an honest man," may have said that Paine's friends were glad that he was gone, for it was only humane to so feel, but all said about "intemperance and frailties" is doubtless a gloss of the correspondent, like the "drunken Irishmen" substituted for Madame Bonneville and her family.

Could the gentleman of the sulky have appreciated the historic dignity of that little *cortége* he would have turned his horse's head and followed it.   Those two negroes, travelling twenty-five miles on foot, represented the homage of a race for whose deliverance Paine had pleaded from his first essay written in America to his recent entreaty for the President's intervention in behalf of the slaughtered negroes of Domingo.[1]   One of those vehicles bore the wife of an oppressed French author, and her sons, one of whom was to do gallant service to this country in the War of 1812, the other to explore the unknown West.   Behind the Quaker preacher, who would rather take his chance in the next world with Paine than with any man in New York, was following invisibly another of his family and name, who presently built up Hicksite Quakerism, the real monument of Paine, to whom unfriendly Friends refused a grave.

The grand people of America were not there, the clergy were not there; but beside the negroes stood the Quaker preacher and the French Catholic woman.   Madame Bonneville placed her son Benjamin—afterwards General in the United States army—at one end of the grave, and standing herself at the other end, cried, as the earth fell on the coffin : " Oh, Mr. Paine, my son stands here as testimony of the gratitude of America, and I for France ! "[2]

[1] " On the last day men shall wear
      On their heads the dust,
   As ensign and as ornament
      Of their lowly trust."—*Hafiz.*

[2] No sooner was Paine dead than the ghoul sat gloating upon him.   I found in the Rush papers a letter from Cheetham (July 31st) to Benjamin Rush : " Since Mr. Paine's arrival in this city from Washington, when on his way you very properly avoided him, his life, keeping the lowest com-

The day of Paine's death was a day of judgment. He had not been struck blind or dumb ; Satan had not carried him off ; he had lived beyond his three-score years and ten and died peacefully in his bed. The self-appointed messengers of Zeus had managed to vex this Prometheus who brought fire to men, but could not persuade him to whine for mercy, nor did the predicted thunderbolts come. This immunity of Thomas Paine brought the deity of dogma into a dilemma. It could be explained only on the the theory of an apology made and accepted by the said deity. Plainly there had to be a recantation somewhere. Either Paine had to recant or Dogma had to recant.

The excitement was particularly strong among

pany, has been an uninterrupted scene of filth, vulgarity, and drunkenness. As to the reports, that on his deathbed he had something like compunctious visitings of conscience with regard to his deistical writings and opinions, they are altogether groundless. He resisted very angrily, and with a sort of triumphant and obstinate pride, all attempts to draw him from those doc-trines. Much as you must have seen in the course of your professional practice of everything that is offensive in the poorest and most depraved of the species, perhaps you have met with nothing excelling the miserable con-dition of Mr. Paine. He had scarcely any visitants. It may indeed be said that he was totally neglected and forgotten. Even Mrs. Bournville [*sic*], a woman, I cannot say a Lady, whom he brought with him from Paris, the wife of a Parisian of that name, seemed desirous of hastening his death. He died at Greenwich, in a small room he had hired in a very obscure house. He was hurried to his grave with hardly an attending person. An ill-natured epitaph, written on him in 1796, when it was supposed he was dead, very correctly describes the latter end of his life. He

> " Blasphemes the Almighty, lives in filth like a hog,
> Is abandoned in death and interr'd like a dog."

The object of this letter was to obtain from Rush, for publication, some abuse of Paine ; but the answer honored Paine, save for his heresy, and is quoted by freethinkers as a tribute.

Within a year the grave opened for Cheetham also, and he sank into it branded by the law as the slanderer of a woman's honor, and scourged by the community as a traitor in public life.

the Quakers, who regarded Paine as an apostate Quaker, and perhaps felt compromised by his desire to be buried among them.   Willett Hicks told Gilbert Vale that he had been beset by pleading questions.   " Did thee never hear him call on Christ ? " " As for money," said Hicks, " I could have had any sum."   There was found, later on, a Quakeress, formerly a servant in the family of Willett Hicks, not proof against such temptations.   She pretended that she was sent to carry some delicacy to Paine, and heard him cry " Lord Jesus have mercy upon me " ; she also heard him declare " if the Devil has ever had any agency in any work he has had it in my writing that book [the ' Age of Reason ']." [1] Few souls are now so belated as to credit such stories ; but my readers may form some conception of the mental condition of the community in which Paine died from the fact that such absurdities were printed, believed, spread through the world. The Quaker servant became a heroine, as the one divinely appointed witness of Tom Paine's recantation.

[1] " Life and Gospel Labors of Stephen Grellet."   This " valuable young Friend," as Stephen Grellet calls her, had married a Quaker named Hinsdale. Grellet, a native of France, convert from Voltaire, led the anti-Hicksites, and was led by his partisanship to declare that Elias promised him to suppress his opinions !   The cant of the time was that " deism might do to live by but not to die by."   But it had been announced in Paine's obituaries that " some days previous to his demise he had an interview with some Quaker gentlemen on the subject [of burial in their graveyard] but as he declined a renunciation of his deistical opinions his anxious wishes were not complied with."   But ten years later, when Hick's deism was spreading, death-bed terrors seemed desirable, and Mary (Roscoe) Hinsdale, formerly Grellet's servant also, came forward to testify that the recantation refused by Paine to the " Quaker gentlemen," even for a much desired end, had been previously confided to her for no object at all !   The story was published by one Charles Collins, a Quaker, who afterwards admitted to Gilbert Vale his doubts of its truth, adding " some of our *friends* believe she indulges in opiates " (Vale, p. 186).

But in the end it was that same Mary that hastened the resurrection of Thomas Paine. The controversy as to whether Mary was or was not a calumniator ; whether orthodoxy was so irresistible that Paine must needs surrender at last to a servant-girl who told him she had thrown his book into the fire ; whether she was to be believed against her employer, who declared she never saw Paine at all ; all this kept Paine alive. Such boiling up from the abysses, of vulgar credulity, grotesque superstition, such commanding illustrations of the Age of Un-reason, disgusted thoughtful Christians.[1]

Such was the religion which was supposed by some to have won Paine's heart at last, but which, when mirrored in the controversy over his death, led to a tremendous reaction. The division in the

[1] The excitement of the time was well illustrated in a notable caricature by the brilliant artist John Wesley Jarvis. Paine is seen dead, his pillow "Common Sense," his hand holding a manuscript, "A rap on the knuckles for John Mason." On his arm is the label, "Answer to Bishop Watson." Under him is written : "A man who devoted his whole life to the attain-ment of two objects—rights of man and freedom of conscience—had his vote denied when living, and was denied a grave when dead !" The Catholic Father O'Brian (a notorious drunkard), with very red nose, kneels over Paine, exclaiming, "Oh you ugly drunken beast !" The Rev. John Mason (Presbyterian) stamps on Paine, exclaiming, "Ah, Tom ! Tom ! thou 'lt get thy frying in hell ; they 'll roast thee like a herring.

> " They 'll put thee in the furnace hot,
>   And on thee bar the door :
>   How the devils all will laugh
>   To hear thee burst and roar ! "

The Rev. Dr. Livingston kicks at Paine's head, exclaiming, " How are the mighty fallen, Right fol-de-riddle-lol !" Bishop Hobart kicks the feet, singing :

> " Right fol-de-rol, let 's dance and sing,
>   Tom is dead, God save the king—
>   The infidel now low doth lie—
>   Sing Hallelujah—hallelujah ! "

A Quaker turns away with a shovel, saying, " I 'll not bury thee."

Quaker Society swiftly developed. In December, 1826, there was an afternoon meeting of Quakers of a critical kind, some results of which led directly to the separation. The chief speaker was Elias Hicks, but it is also recorded that "Willet Hicks was there, and had a short testimony, which seemed to be impressive on the meeting." He had stood in silence beside the grave of the man whose chances in the next world he had rather take than those of any man in New York; but now the silence is broken.[1]

I told Walt Whitman, himself partly a product of Hicksite Quakerism, of the conclusion to which I had been steadily drawn, that Thomas Paine rose again in Elias Hicks, and was in some sort the origin of our one American religion. I said my visit was mainly to get his "testimony" on the subject for my book, as he was born in Hicks' region, and mentions in "Specimen Days" his acquaintance with Paine's friend, Colonel Fellows. Walt said, for I took down his words at the time:

"In my childhood a great deal was said of Paine in our neighborhood, in Long Island. My father, Walter Whitman, was

---

[1] Curiously enough, Mary (Roscoe) Hinsdale turned up again. She had broken down under the cross-examination of William Cobbett, but he had long been out of the country when the Quaker separation took place. Mary now reported that a distinguished member of the Hicksite Society, Mary Lockwood, had recanted in the same way as Paine. This being proved false, the hysterical Mary sank and remained in oblivion, from which she is recalled only by the Rev. Rip Van Winkle. It was the unique sentence on Paine to recant and yet be damned. This honor belies the indifference expressed in the rune taught children sixty years ago:

> "Poor Tom Paine! there he lies:
> Nobody laughs and nobody cries:
> Where he has gone or how he fares,
> Nobody knows and nobody cares!"

rather favorable to Paine. I remember hearing Elias Hicks preach ; and his look, slender figure, earnestness, made an impression on me, though I was only about eleven. He died in 1830. He is well represented in the bust there, one of my treasures. I was a young man when I enjoyed the friendship of Col. Fellows,—then a constable of the courts ; tall, with ruddy face, blue eyes, snowy hair, and a fine voice ; neat in dress, an old-school gentleman, with a military air, who used to awe the crowd by his looks ; they used to call him 'Aristides.' I used to chat with him in Tammany Hall. It was a time when, in religion, there was as yet no philosophical middle-ground ; people were very strong on one side or the other ; there was a good deal of lying, and the liars were often well paid for their work. Paine and his principles made the great issue. Paine was double-damnably lied about. Col. Fellows was a man of perfect truth and exactness ; he assured me that the stories disparaging to Paine personally were quite false. Paine was neither drunken nor filthy ; he drank as other people did, and was a high-minded gentleman. I incline to think you right in supposing a connection between the Paine excitement and the Hicksite movement. Paine left a deep, clear-cut impression on the public mind. Col. Fellows told me that while Paine was in New York he had a much larger following than was generally supposed. After his death a reaction in his favor appeared among many who had opposed him, and this reaction became exceedingly strong between 1820 and 1830, when the division among the Quakers developed. Probably William Cobbett's conversion to Paine had something to do with it. Cobbett lived in the neighborhood of Elias Hicks, in Long Island, and probably knew him. Hicks was a fair-minded man, and no doubt read Paine's books carefully and honestly. I am very glad you are writing the Life of Paine. Such a book has long been needed. Paine was among the best and truest of men."

Paine's risen soul went marching on in England also. The pretended recantation proclaimed there was exploded by William Cobbett, and the whole controversy over Paine's works renewed. One after another deist was sent to prison for publishing

Paine's works, the last being Richard Carlile and his wife. In 1819, the year in which William Cobbett carried Paine's bones to England, Richard Carlile and his wife, solely for this offence, were sent to prison,—he for three years, with fine of £1,500, she for two years, with fine of £500.[1] This was a suicidal victory for bigotry. When these two came out of prison they found that wealthy gentlemen had provided for them an establishment in Fleet Street, where these books were thenceforth sold unmolested. Mrs. Carlile's petition to the House of Commons awakened that body and the whole country. When Richard Carlile entered prison it was as a captive deist ; when he came out the freethinkers of England were generally atheists.

But what was this atheism ? Merely another Declaration of Independence. Common sense and common justice were entering into religion as they were entering into government. Such epithets as " atheism," " infidelity," were but labels of outlawry which the priesthood of all denominations

---

[1] I have before me an old fly-leaf picture, issued by Carlile in the same year. It shows Paine in his chariot advancing against Superstition. Superstition is a snaky-haired demoness, with poison-cup in one hand and dagger in the other, surrounded by instruments of torture, and treading on a youth. Behind her are priests, with mask, crucifix, and dagger. Burning faggots surround them with a cloud, behind which are worshippers around an idol, with a priest near by, upholding a crucifix before a man burning at the stake. Attended by fair genii, who uphold a banner inscribed, " Moral Rectitude." Paine advances, uplifting in one hand the mirror of Truth, in the other his " Age of Reason." There are ten stanzas describing the conflict, Superstition being described as holding

> " in vassalage a doating World,
> Till Paine and Reason burst upon the mind,
> And Truth and Deism their flag unfurled."

pronounced upon men who threatened their throne, precisely as "sedition" was the label of outlawry fixed by Pitt on all hostility to George III. In England, atheism was an insurrection of justice against any deity diabolical enough to establish the reign of terror in that country or any deity worshipped by a church which imprisoned men for their opinions. Paine was a theist, but he arose legitimately in his admirer Shelley, who was punished for atheism. Knightly service was done by Shelley in the struggle for the Englishman's right to read Paine. If any enlightened religious man of to-day had to choose between the godlessness of Shelley and the godliness that imprisoned good men for their opinions, he would hardly select the latter. The genius of Paine was in every word of Shelley's letter to Lord Ellenborough on the punishment of Eaton for publishing the "Age of Reason." [1]

In America "atheism" was never anything but the besom which again and again has cleared the

[1] "Whence is any right derived, but that which power confers, for persecution? Do you think to convert Mr. Eaton to your religion by embittering his existence? You might force him by torture to profess your tenets, but he could not believe them except you should make them credible, which perhaps exceeds your power. Do you think to please the God you worship by this exhibition of your zeal? If so the demon to whom some nations offer human hecatombs is less barbarous than the Deity of civilized society. . . . Does the Christian God, whom his followers eulogize as the deity of humility and peace—he, the regenerator of the world, the meek reformer—authorise one man to rise against another, and, because lictors are at his beck, to chain and torture him as an infidel? When the Apostles went abroad to convert the nations, were they enjoined to stab and poison all who disbelieved the divinity of Christ's mission? . . . The time is rapidly approaching—I hope that you, my Lord, may live to behold its arrival—when the Mahometan, the Jew, the Christian, the Deist, and the Atheist will live together in one community, equally sharing the benefits which arrive from its association, and united in the bonds of charity and brotherly love."

human mind of phantasms represented in outrages on honest thinkers. In Paine's time the
phantasm which was called Jehovah represented a
grossly ignorant interpretation of the Bible; the
revelation of its monstrous character, represented
in the hatred, slander, falsehood, meanness, and
superstition, which Jarvis represented as crows and
vultures hovering near the preachers kicking
Paine's dead body, necessarily destroyed the phantasm, whose pretended power was proved nothing
more than that of certain men to injure a man who
out-reasoned them. Paine's fidelity to his un-
answered argument was fatal to the consecrated
phantasm. It was confessed to be ruling without
reason, right, or humanity, like the King from
whom "Common Sense," mainly, had freed
America, and not by any "Grace of God" at all,
but through certain reverend Lord Norths and
Lord Howes. Paine's peaceful death, the benevolent distribution of his property by a will affirming
his Theism, represented a posthumous and potent
conclusion to the "Age of Reason."

Paine had aimed to form in New York a Society
for Religious Inquiry, also a Society of Theophilanthropy. The latter was formed, and his posthumous works first began to appear, shortly after
his death, in an organ called *The Theophilanthropist.* But his movement was too cosmopolitan to
be contained in any local organization. "Thomas
Paine," said President Andrew Jackson to Judge
Hertell, "Thomas Paine needs no monument
made by hands; he has erected a monument in
the hearts of all lovers of liberty." The like may

be said of his religion : Theophilanthropy, under a hundred translations and forms, is now the fruitful branch of every religion and every sect. The real cultivators of skepticism,—those who ascribe to deity biblical barbarism, and the savagery of nature,—have had their day.

The removal and mystery of Paine's bones appear like some page of Mosaic 'mythology.[1] An English caricature pictured Cobbett seated on Paine's coffin, in a boat named RIGHTS OF MAN, rowed by NEGRO SLAVES.

"A singular coincidence [says Dr. Francis] led me to pay a visit to Cobbett at his country seat, within a couple of miles of the city, on the island, on the very day that he had exhumed the bones of Paine, and shipped them for England. I will here repeat the words which Cobbett gave utterance to at the friendly interview our party had with him. 'I have just performed a duty, gentlemen, which has been too long delayed : you have neglected too long the remains of Thomas Paine. I have done myself the honor to disinter his bones. I have removed them from New Rochelle. I have dug them up ; they are now on their way to England. When I myself return, I shall cause them to speak the common sense of the

[1] The bones of Thomas Paine were landed in Liverpool November 21, 1819. The monument contemplated by Cobbett was never raised. There was much parliamentary and municipal excitement. A Bolton town-crier was imprisoned nine weeks for proclaiming the arrival. In 1836 the bones passed with Cobbett's effects into the hands of a Receiver (West). The Lord Chancellor refusing to regard them as an asset, they were kept by an old day-laborer until 1844, when they passed to B. Tilley, 13 Bedford Square, London, a furniture dealer. In 1849 the empty coffin was in possession of J. Chennell, Guildford. The silver plate bore the inscription "Thomas Paine, died June 8, 1809, aged 72." In 1854, Rev. R. Ainslie (Unitarian) told E. Truelove that he owned "the skull and the right hand of Thomas Paine," but evaded subsequent inquiries. The removal caused excitement in America. Of Paine's gravestone the last fragment was preserved by his friends of the Bayeaux family, and framed on their wall. In November, 1839, the present marble monument at New Rochelle was erected.

great man ; I shall gather together the people of Liverpool and Manchester in one assembly with those of London, and those bones will effect the reformation of England in Church and State.' "

Mr. Badeau, of New Rochelle, remembers standing near Cobbett's workmen while they were digging up the bones, about dawn. There is a legend that Paine's little finger was left in America, a fable, perhaps, of his once small movement, now stronger than the loins of the bigotry that refused him a vote or a grave in the land he so greatly served. As to his bones, no man knows the place of their rest to this day. His principles rest not. His thoughts, untraceable like his dust, are blown about the world which he held in his heart. For a hundred years no human being has been born in the civilized world without some spiritual tincture from that heart whose every pulse was for humanity, whose last beat broke a fetter of fear, and fell on the throne of thrones.

APPENDIX A.

In the autumn of 1792 William Cobbett arrived in America. Among the papers preserved by the family of Thomas Jefferson is a letter from Cobbett, enclosing an introduction from Mr. Short, U. S. Secretary of Legation at Paris. In this letter, dated at Wilmington, Delaware, November 2, 1792, the young Englishman writes: "Ambitious to become the citizen of a free state I have left my native country, England, for America. I bring with me youth, a small family, a few useful literary talents, and that is all."

Cobbett had been married in the same year, on February 5th, and visited Paris, perhaps with an intention of remaining, but becoming disgusted with the revolution he left for America. He had conceived a dislike of the French revolutionary leaders, among whom he included Paine. He thus became an easy victim of the libellous Life of Paine, by George Chalmers, which had not been reprinted in America, and reproduced the statements of that work in a brief biographical sketch published in Philadelphia, 1796. In later life Cobbett became convinced that he had been deceived into giving fresh currency to a tissue of slanders.

In the very year of this publication, afterwards much lamented, Paine published in Europe a work that filled Cobbett with admiration. This was "The Decline and Fall of the English System of Finance," which predicted the suspension of gold payments by the Bank of England that followed the next year. The pamphlet became Cobbett's text-book, and his *Register* was eloquent in Paine's praise, the more earnestly, he confessed, because he had "been one of his most violent assailants." "Old age having laid his hand upon this truly great man, this truly philosophical politician, at his expiring flambeau I lighted my taper."

A sketch of Thomas Paine and some related papers of Cobbett are generously confided to me by his daughter, Eleanor Cobbett, through her nephew, William Cobbett, Jr., of Woodlands, near Manchester, England. The public announcement (1818) by Cobbett, then in America, of his intention to write a Life of Paine, led to his negotiation with Madame Bonneville, who, with her husband, resided in New York. Madame Bonneville had been disposing of some of Paine's manuscripts, such as that on "Freemasonry," and the reply to Bishop Watson, printed in *The Theophilanthropist* (1810). She had also been preparing, with her husband's assistance, notes for a biography of Paine, because of the "unjust efforts to tarnish the memory of Mr. Paine"; adding, "*Et l'indignation m'a fait prendre la plume.*" Cobbett agreed to give her a thousand dollars for the manuscript, which was to contain important letters from and to eminent men. She stated (September 30,

1819) her conditions, that it should be published in England, without any addition, and separate from any other writings. I suppose it was one or all of these conditions that caused the non-completion of the bargain. Cobbett re-wrote the whole thing, and it is now all in his writing except a few passages by Madame Bonneville, which I indicate by brackets, and two or three by his son, J. P. Cobbett. Although Madame Bonneville gave some revision to Cobbett's manuscript, most of the letters to be supplied are merely indicated. No trace of them exists among the Cobbett papers. Soon afterward the Bonnevilles went to Paris, where they kept a small book shop. Nicolas died in 1828. His biography in Michaud's Dictionary is annotated by the widow, and states that in 1829 she had begun to edit for publication the Life and posthumous papers of Thomas Paine. From this it would appear that she had retained the manuscript, and the original letters. In 1833 Madame Bonneville emigrated to St. Louis, where her son, the late General Bonneville, lived. Her Catholicism became, I believe, devout with advancing years, and to that cause, probably also to a fear of reviving the old scandal Cheetham had raised, may be due the suppression of the papers, with the result mentioned in the introduction to this work. She died in St. Louis, October 30, 1846, at the age of 79. Probably William Cobbett did not feel entitled to publish the manuscript obtained under such conditions, or he might have waited for the important documents that were never sent. He died in 1835.

The recollections are those of both M. and

Madame Bonneville. The reader will find no difficulty in making out the parts that represent Madame's personal knowledge and reminiscences, as Cobbett has preserved her speech in the first person, and, with characteristic literary acumen, her expressions in such important points. His manuscript is perfect, and I have little editing to do beyond occasional correction of a date, supplying one or two letters indicated, which I have found, and omitting a few letters, extracts, etc., already printed in the body of this work, where unaccompanied by any comment or addition from either Cobbett or the Bonnevilles.

At the time when this Cobbett-Bonneville sketch was written New York was still a provincial place. Nicolas Bonneville, as Irving describes him, seated under trees at the Battery, absorbed in his classics, might have been regarded with suspicion had it been known that his long separation from his family was due to detention by the police. Madame Bonneville is reserved on that point. The following incident, besides illustrating the characters of Paine and Bonneville, may suggest a cause for the rigor of Bonneville's surveillance. In 1797, while Paine and Bonneville were editing the *Bien In-formé*, a "suspect" sought asylum with them. This was Count Barruel-Beauvert, an author whose writings alone had caused his denunciation as a royalist. He had escaped from the Terror, and now wandered back in disguise, a pauper Count, who knew well the magnanimity of the two men whose protection he asked. He remained, as proof-reader, in the Bonneville house for some time, safely; but when the conspiracy of 18 Fructidor (September 4, 1797) exasperated the Republic against royalists, the Count feared that he might be the means of compromising his benefactors, and disappeared. When the royalist conspiracy against Bonaparte was discovered, Barruel-Beauvert was again hunted, and arrested (1802). His trial probably brought to the knowledge of the police his former sojourn with Paine and Bonneville. Bonaparte sent by Fouché a warning to Paine that the eye of the police was upon him, and that "on the first complaint he would be sent to his own country, America." Whether this, and the closer surveillance on Bonneville, were connected with the Count, who also suffered for a time, or whether due to their anti-slavery writings on Domingo, remains conjectural. Towards the close of life Bonneville received a pension, which was continued to his widow. So much even a monarchy with an established church could do for a republican author, and a freethinker; for Bonneville had published heresies like those of Paine.

THOMAS PAINE.

A SKETCH OF HIS LIFE AND CHARACTER.

[More exactly than any other author Thomas Paine delineates every Circumstantial Events, private or Public in his Writings; nevertheless, since many pretended Histories of the Life of T. P. have been published, tracing him back to the day of his][1] birth, we shall shortly observe, that, as was never

---

[1] The bracketed words, Madame Bonneville's, are on a separate slip. An opening paragraph by Cobbett is crossed out by her pen : " The early years of the life of a Great Man are of little consequence to the world. Whether Paine made stays or gauged barrels before he became a public character, is

denied by himself, he was born at Thetford, in the County of Norfolk, England on the 29. January, in the year 1737; that his father Joseph Paine was a stay-maker, and by religion a Quaker; that his mother was the daughter of a country-attorney, and that she belonged to the Church of England; but, it appears, that she also afterwards became a Quaker; for these parents both belonged to the Meeting in 1787, as appears from a letter of the father to the son. The above-mentioned histories relate (and the correctness of the statement has not been denied by him), that Paine was educated at the free-school of Thetford; that he left it in 1752, when he was fifteen years of age, and then worked for some time with his father: that in a year afterwards, he went to London: that from London he went to Dover: that about this time he was on the eve of becoming a sailor: that he afterwards did embark on board a privateer: that, between the years 1759 and 1774 he was a staymaker, an excise officer, a grocer, and an usher to a school; and that, during the period he was twice married, and seperated by mutual consent, from his second wife.[1]

In this year 1774 and in the month of September, Paine sailed from England for Philadelphia, where he arrived safe; and now we *begin* his history; for here we have him in connection with his literary labours.

It being an essential part of our plan to let Thomas Paine speak in his own words, and explain himself the reason for his actions, whenever we find written papers in his own hand, though in incomplete notes or fragments, we shall insert such, in order to enable the reader to judge for himself, and to estimate the slightest circumstances. *Souvent d'un grand dessin un mot nous fait juger.* "A word often enables us to judge of a great design."

of no more importance to us than whether he was swaddled with woollen or with linen. It is the man, in conjunction with those labours which have produced so much effect in the world, whom we are to follow and contemplate. Nevertheless, since many pretended histories of the life of Paine have been published, etc."

[1] The dates given by Cobbett from contemporary histories require revision by the light of the careful researches made by myself and others, as given at the beginning of this biography.

"I happened to come to America a few months before the breaking out of hostilities. I found the disposition of the people such that they might have been led by a thread and governed by a reed. Their suspicion was quick and penetrating, but their attachment to Britain was obstinate, and it was at that time a kind of treason to speak against it. They disliked the Ministry, but they esteemed the Nation. Their idea of grievance operated without resentment, and their single object was reconciliation. Bad as I believed the Ministry to be, I never conceived them capable of a measure so rash and wicked as the commencing of hostilities ; much less did I imagine the Nation would encourage it. I viewed the dispute as a kind of law-suit, in which I supposed the parties would find a way either to decide or settle it. I had no thoughts of independence or of arms. The world could not then have persuaded me that I should be either a soldier or an author. If I had any talents for either they were buried in me, and might ever have continued so had not the necessity of the times dragged and driven them into action. I had formed my plan of life, and conceiving myself happy wished everybody else so. But when the country, into which I had just set my foot, was set on fire about my ears, it was time to stir. It was time for every man to stir." [1]

His first intention at Philadelphia was to establish an Academy for young ladies, who were to be taught many branches of learning then little known in the education of young American ladies. But, in 1775, he undertook the management of the Pennsylvania Magazine.

About this time he published, in Bradford's journal, an essay on the slavery of the negroes, which was universally well received ; and also stanzas on the death of General Wolfe.

In 1776, January 10, he published Common Sense. In the same year he joined the army as aid-de-camp to General Greene. Gordon, in his history of the Independence of the United States (vol. ii. p. 78), says : [*Wanting*.]—Ramsay (Lond. ed. i. p. 336) says : [*Wanting*.] Anecdote of Dr. Franklin

---

[1] From *Crisis vii.*, dated Philadelphia, November 21, 1778. In Cobbett's MS. the extract is only indicated.

preserved by Thomas Paine : [*Wanting, but no doubt one else-where given, in the Hall manuscripts.*]

When Washington had made his retreat from New York Thomas Paine published the first number of the *Crisis*, which was read to every corporal's guard in the camp. It revived the army, reunited the members of the [New York] Convention, when despair had reduced them to nine in number, while the militia were abandoning their standards and flying in all directions. The success of the army at Trenton was, in some degree, owing to this first number of the Crisis. In 1778 he discovered the robberies of Silas Deane, an agent of the United States in France. He gave in his resignation as Secretary, which was accepted by the Congress. In 1779 he was appointed Clerk to the General Assembly of Pennsylvania, which office he retained until 1780. In 1780 he departed for France with Col. John Laurens, commissioned especially by the Congress to the Court at Versailles to obtain the aid that was wanted. (See Gordon's Hist., v. iii., p. 154.) After his return from France he received the following letter from Col. Laurens :

" CAROLINA, April 18, 1782.—I received the letter wherein you mention my horse and trunk, (the latter of which was left at Providence). The misery which the former has suffered at different times, by mismanagement, has greatly distressed me. He was wounded in service, and I am much attached to him. If he can be of any service to you, I entreat your acceptance of him, more especially if you will make use of him in bringing you to a country (Carolina) where you will be received with open arms, and all that affection and respect which our citizens are anxious to testify to the author of Common Sense, and the Crisis.

"Adieu ! I wish you to regard this part of America (Carolina) as your particular home—and everything that I can command in it to be in common between us."

On the 10th of April, 1783, the definitive treaty of peace was received and published. Here insert the letter from Gen. Nathaniel Greene :

" ASHLEY-RIVES (Carolina), Nov. 18, 1782.—Many people wish to get you into this country.

" I see you are determined to follow your genius and not your fortune. I have always been in hopes that Congress would have made some handsome acknowledgement to you for past services. I must confess that I think you have been shamefully neglected ; and that America is indebted to few characters more than to you. But as your passion leads to fame, and not to wealth, your mortification will be the less. Your fame for your writings, will be immortal. At present my expenses are great ; nevertheless, if you are not conveniently situated, I shall take a pride and pleasure in contributing all in my power to render your situation happy." [1]

Then letter from his father.—" Dear Son, &c." [*Lost.*]

The following letter from William Livingston (Trenton, 4 November, 1784) will show that Thomas Paine was not only honored with the esteem of the most famous persons, but that they were all convinced that he had been useful to the country.[2]

At this time Thomas Paine was living with Colonel Kirkbride, Bordentown, where he remained till his departure for France. He had bought a house [in], and five acres of marshy land over against, Bordentown, near the Delaware, which overflowed it frequently. He sold the land in 1787.

Congress gave an order for three thousand dollars, which Thomas Paine received in the same month.

Early in 1787 he departed for France. He carried with him the model of a bridge of his own invention and construction, which he submitted, in a drawing, to the French Academy, by whom it was approved. From Paris he went to London on the 3 September 1787 ; and in the same month he went to Thetford, where he found his father was dead, from the small-pox ; and where he settled an allowance on his mother of 9 shillings a week.

A part of 1788 he passed in Rotherham, in Yorkshire, where his bridge was cast and erected, chiefly at the expense of the ingenious Mr. Walker. The experiment, however, cost Thomas Paine a considerable sum.

When Burke published his *Reflexions on the French Rev-*

---

[1] This and the preceding letter supplied by the author.
[2] Not found. Referred to in this work, vol. i., p. 200.

olution, Thomas Paine answered him in his *First Part of the Rights of Man.* In January, 1792, appeared the *Second Part of the Rights of Man.* The sale of the *Rights of Man* was prodigious, amounting in the course of one year to about a hundred thousand copies.

In 1792 he was prosecuted for his Rights of Man by the Attorney General, McDonald, and was defended by Mr. Erskine, and found guilty of libel. But he was now in France, and could not be brought up for judgment.

Each district of France sent electors to the principal seat of the Department, where the Deputies to the National Assembly were chosen. Two Departments appointed Thomas Paine their Deputy, those of *Oise* and of *Pas de Calais*, of which he accepted the latter. He received the following letter from the President of the National Assembly, Hérault de Séchelles :

" To THOMAS PAINE :

" France calls you, Sir, to its bosom, to perform one of the most useful and most honorable functions, that of contributing, by wise legislation, to the happiness of a people, whose destinies interest all who think and are united with the welfare of all who suffer in the world.

" It becomes the nation that has proclaimed the *Rights of Man*, to desire among her legislators him who first dared to estimate the consequences of those Rights, and who has developed their principles with that *Common Sense*, which is the only genius inwardly felt by all men, and the conception of which springs forth from nature and truth.

" The National Assembly gave you the title of Citizen, and had seen with pleasure that its decree was sanctioned by the only legitimate authority, that of the people, who had already claimed you, even before you were nominated.

" Come, Sir, and enjoy in France the most interesting of scenes for an observer and a philosopher,—that of a confiding and generous people who, infamously betrayed for three years, and wishing at last to end the struggle between slavery and liberty, between sincerity and perfidy, at length arises in its resolute and gigantic force, gives up to the sword of the law those guilty crowned things who betrayed them, resists the barbarians whom they raised up to destroy the nation. Her citizens turned soldiers, her territory into camp and fortress, she yet calls and collects in congress the lights scattered through the universe. Men of genius, the most capable for their wisdom and virtue, she now calls to give to her people a government the most proper to insure their liberty and happiness.

"The Electoral Assembly of the Department of Oise, anxious to be the first to elect you, has been so fortunate as to insure to itself that honour ; and when many of my fellow citizens desired me to inform you of your election, I remembered, with infinite pleasure, having seen you at Mr. Jefferson's, and I congratulated myself on having had the pleasure of knowing you.

"HÉRAULT,

"President of the National Assembly."

At the trial of Louis XVI. before the National Convention Thomas Paine at the Tribune, with the deputy Bancal for translator and interpreter, gave his opinion, written, on the capital sentence on Louis :—That, though a Deputy of the National Convention of France, he could not forget, that, previous to his being that, he was a citizen of the United States of America, which owed their liberty to Louis, and that gratitude would not allow him to vote for the death of the benefactor of America. On the 21st of January, 1793, Louis XVI was beheaded in the Square of Louis XV. (Letter to Marat. Letter to Marat.) [1]

Thomas Paine was named by the Assembly as one of the Committee of Legislation, and, as he could not discuss article by article without the aid of an interpreter, he drew out a plan of a constitution.[2]

The reign of terror began on the night of the 10th of March 1793, when the greatest number and the best part of the real friends to freedom had retired [from the Convention]. But, as the intention of the conspiracy against the Assembly had been suspected, as the greatest part of the Deputies they wished to

[1] Both missing. Possibly the second should be to Danton. See ii., p. 53.
[2] See ii., p. 37 *seq.*, of this work.

sacrifice had been informed of the threatening danger, as, moreover, a mutual fear [existed] of the cunning tyrany of some usurper, the conspirators, alarmed, could not this night consummate their horrible machinations. They therefore, for this time, confined themselves to single degrees of accusation and arrestation against the most valuable part of the National Convention. Robespiere had placed himself at the head of a conspiring Common-Hall, which dared to dictate *laws of blood* and proscription to the Convention. All those whom he could not make bend under a Dictatorship, which a certain number of anti-revolutionists feigned to grant him, as a tool which they could destroy at pleasure, were guilty of being suspected, and secretly destined to disappear from among the living. Thomas Paine, as his marked enemy and rival, by favour of the *decree on the suspected* was classed among the *suspected*, and, as a *foreigner*, was imprisoned in the Luxembourg in December 1793. (See Letter to Washington.) [1]

From this document it will be seen, that, while in the prison, he was, for a month, afflicted with an illness that deprived him of his memory. It was during this illness of Thomas Paine that the fall of Robespierre took place. Mr. Monroe, who arrived at Paris some days afterwards, wrote to Mr. Paine, assuring him of his friendship, as appears from the letter to Washington. Fifteen days afterwards Thomas Paine received a letter from Peter Whiteside. [2] In consequence of this letter Thomas Paine wrote a memorial to Mr. Monroe. Mr. Monroe now claimed Thomas Paine, and he *came out of the prison on the 6th of November, 1794, after ten months of imprisonment.* He went to live with Mr. Monroe, who had cordially offered him his house. In a short time after, the Convention called him to take his seat in that Assembly ; which he did, for the reasons he alleges in his letter to Washington.

The following two pieces Thomas Paine wrote while in Prison : " Essay on Aristocracy." " Essay on the character of Robespierre." [*Both missing.*]

---

[1] This is the bitter letter of which when it appeared Cobbett had written such a scathing review.

[2] The letter telling him of the allegations made by some against his American citizenship.

Thomas Paine received the following letter from Madame Lafayette, whose husband was then a prisoner of war in Austria :

"19 BRUMAIRE, PARIS.—I was this morning so much agitated by the kind visit from Mr. Monroe, that I could hardly find words to speak ; but, however, I was, my dear Sir, desirous to tell you, that the news of your being set at liberty, which I this morning learnt from General Kilmaine, who arrived here at the same time with me, has given me a moment's consolation in the midst of this abyss of misery, where I shall all my life remain plunged. Gen. Kilmaine has told me that you recollected me, and have taken great interest in my situation ; for which I am exceedingly grateful.

"Accept, along with Mr. Monroe, my congratulations upon your being restored to each other, and the assurances of these sentiments from her who is proud to proclaim them, and who well deserved the title of citizen of *that* second country, though I have assuredly never failed, nor shall ever fail, to the former. Salut and friendship.

"With all sincerity of my heart,
"N. LAFAYETTE."

On the 27 January, 1794, Thomas Paine published in Paris, the First Part of the "Age of Reason."

Seeing the state of things in America, Thomas Paine wrote a letter to Gen. Washington 22 February 1795. Mr. Monroe entreated him not to send it, and, accordingly it was not sent to Washington ; but it was afterwards published.

A few months after his going out of prison, he had a violent fever. Mrs. Monroe showed him all possible kindness and attention. She provided him with an excellent nurse, who had for him all the anxiety and assiduity of a sister. She neglected nothing to afford him ease and comfort, when he was totally unable to help himself. He was in the state of a helpless child who has its face and hands washed by its mother. The surgeon was the famous Dessault, who cured him of an abscess which he had in his side. After the horrible 13 Brumaire, a friend of Thomas Paine being very sick, he, who was in the house, went to bring his own excellent nurse to take care of his sick friend : a fact of little account in itself, but a sure evidence of ardent and active friendship and kindness.

The Convention being occupied with a discussion of the question of what Constitution ought to be adopted, that of 1791 or that of 1793, Thomas Paine made a speech (July 7, 1795) as a member of the [original] Committee [on the Constitution] and Lanthénas translated it and read it in the Tribune. This speech has been translated into English, and published in London ; but, the language of the author has been changed by the two translations. It is now given as written by the author. [*Missing.*]

In April, 1796, he wrote his *Decline and Fall of the British System of Finance ;* and, on the 30th of July of that year he sent his letter to Washington off for America by Mr. ———— who sent it to Mr. Bache, a newspaper printer of Philadelphia, to be published, and it was published the same year. The name of the gentleman who conveyed the letter, and who wrote the following to Thomas Paine, is not essential and therefore we suppress it. [*Missing.*]

We here insert a letter from Talleyrand, the Minister of Foreign Affairs, to show that Thomas Paine was always active and attentive in doing every thing which would be useful to America. [*Missing.*]

Thomas Paine after he came out of prison and had re-entered the Convention wrote the following letter. [*Missing.*]

The following is essentially connected with the foregoing : " Paris, October 4, 1796." [*Missing.*]

In October, 1796, Thomas Paine published the *Second Part of the Age of Reason.*

This year Mr. Monroe departed from France, and soon after Thomas Paine went to Havre de Grace, to embark for the United States. But, he did not, upon inquiry, think it prudent to go, on account of the great number of English vessels then cruizing in the Channel. He therefore came back to Paris ; but, while at Havre, wrote the following letter, 13 April 1797, to a friend at Paris. [*Missing.*]

The following letter will not, we hope, seem indifferent to the reader : " Dear Sir, I wrote to you etc." [*Missing.*]

At this time it was that Thomas Paine took up his abode

at Mr. Bonneville's, who had known him at the Minister Roland's, and as Mr. B. spoke English, Thomas Paine addressed himself to him in a more familiar and friendly manner than to any other persons of the society. It was a reception of Hospitality which was here given to Thomas Paine for a week or a fortnight; but, the visit lasted till 1802, when he and Mr. Bonneville parted,—alas never to meet again !

Our House was at No. 4 Rue du Théâtre François. All the first floor was occupied as a printing office. The whole house was pretty well filled ; and Mr. Bonneville gave up his study, which was not a large one, and a bed-chamber to Thomas Paine. He was always in his apartments excepting at meal times. He rose late. He then used to read the newspapers, from which, though he understood but little of the French language when spoken, he did not fail to collect all the material information relating to politics, in which subject he took most delight. When he had his morning's reading, he used to carry back the journals to Mr. Bonneville, and they had a chat upon the topicks of the day.

If he had a short jaunt to take, as for instance, to Puteaux just by the bridge of Neuilly, where Mr. Skipwith lived, he always went on foot, after suitable preparations for the journey in that way. I do not believe he ever hired a coach to go out on pleasure during the whole of his stay in Paris. He laughed at those who, depriving themselves of a wholesome exercise, could make no other excuse for the want of it than that they were able to take it whenever they pleased. He was never idle in the house. If not writing he was busily employed on some mechanical invention, or else entertaining his visitors. Not a day escaped without his receiving many visits. Mr. Barlow, Mr. Fulton, Mr. Smith [Sir Robert] came very often to see him. Many travellers also called on him ; and, often, having no other affair, talked to him only of his great reputation and their admiration of his works. He treated such visitors with civility, but with little ceremony, and, when their conversation was mere chit-chat, and he found they had nothing particular to say to him, he used to retire to his own pursuits, leaving them to entertain themselves with their own ideas.

He sometimes spent his evenings at Mr. Barlow's, where

Mr. Fulton lived, or at Mr. Smith's [Sir Robert], and sometimes at an Irish Coffee-house in Condé Street, where Irish,
English, and American people met.   He here learnt the state
of politics in England and America.   He never went out after
dinner without first taking a nap, which was always of two or
three hours length.   And, when he went out to a dinner of
parade, he often came home for the purpose of taking his
accustomed sleep.   It was seldom he went into the society of
French people ; except when, by seeing some one in office or
power, he could obtain some favour for his countrymen who
might be in need of his good offices.   These he always performed with pleasure, and he never failed to adopt the most
likely means to secure success.   But in one instance he failed.
He wrote as follows to Lord Cornwallis ; but, he did not save
Napper Tandy. Letter to Lord Cornwallis. Letter 27 Brumaire,
4 year.   Letter 23 Germinal 4 year.   [*The three letters missing*.]

C. Jourdan made a report to the Convention on the re-
establishment of *Bells*, which had been suppressed, and, in great
part melted.   Paine published, on this occasion, a letter to C.
Jourdan.[1]

He had brought with him from America, as we have seen, a
model of a bridge of his own construction and invention, which
model had been adopted in England *for building bridges* under
his own direction. He employed part of his time, while at our
house, in bringing this model to high perfection, and this he
accomplished to his wishes. He afterwards, and according to
the model, made a bridge of lead, which he accomplished by
moulding different blocks of lead, which, when joined together,
made the form that he required. This was most pleasant
amusement for him.   Though he fully relied on the strength
of his new bridge, and would produce arguments enough in
proof of its infallible strength, he often demonstrated the
proof by blows of the sledge-hammer, not leaving anyone in
doubt on the subject.   One night he took off the scaffold of
his bridge and seeing that it stood firm under the repeated
strokes of hammer, he was so ravished that an enjoyment so
great was not to be sufficiently felt if confined to his own

[1] The words "which will find a place in the Appendix" are here crossed
out by Madame Bonneville. See ii., p. 258 concerning Jourdan.

bosom. He was not satisfied without admirers of his success. One night we had just gone to bed, and were surprised at hearing repeated strokes of the hammer. Paine went into Mr. Bonneville's room and besought him to go and see his bridge : come and look, said he, it bears all my blows and stands like a rock. Mr. Bonneville arose, as well to please himself by seeing a happy man as to please him by looking at his bridge. Nothing would do, unless I saw the sight as well as Mr. Bonneville. After much exultation : "nothing, in the world," said he, "is so fine as my bridge"; and, seeing me standing by without uttering a word, he added, "*except a woman!*" which happy compliment to the sex he seemed to think, a full compensation for the trouble caused by this nocturnal visit to the bridge.

A machine for planing boards was his next invention, which machine he had executed partly by one blacksmith and partly by another. The machine being put together by him, he placed it on the floor, and with it planed boards to any number that he required, to make some models of *wheels*. Mr. Bonneville has two of these wheels now. There is a specification of the wheels, given by Mr. Paine himself. This specification, together with a drawing of the model, made by Mr. Fulton, were deposited at Washington, in February 1811 ; and the other documents necessary to obtain a patent as an invention of Thomas Paine, for the benefit of Madam Bonneville. To be presented to the Directory of France, a memorial on the progress and construction of iron bridges. On this subject the two pieces here subjoined will throw sufficient light. (Memoir upon Bridges.—Upon Iron Bridges.—To the Directory.— Memoir on the Progress and Construction &c.)

Preparations were made, real or simulated, for a Descent upon England. Thomas Paine was consulted by B. 8. who was then in the house of Talma, and he wrote the following notes and instructions. Letter at Brussells.—The Ça-ira of America.—To the Consul Lépeaux.[1]

---

[1] This paragraph is in the writing of Madame Bonneville. "B. 8." means Bonaparte, and seems to be some cipher. All of the pieces by Paine mentioned are missing ; also that addressed "To the Directory," for the answer to which see p. 296 of this volume.

Chancellor Livingston, after his arrival in France, came a few times to see Paine.   One morning we had him at breakfast, Dupuis, the author of the Origin of Worship, being of the party ; and Mr. Livingston, when he got up to go away, said to Mr. Paine smiling, " Make your Will ; leave the mechanics, the iron bridge, the wheels, etc. to America, and your religion to France."

Thomas Paine, while at our house, published in Mr. Bonneville's journal (the *Bien Informé*) several articles on passing events.[1]

A few days before his departure for America, he said, at Mr. Smith's [Sir Robert] that he had nothing to detain him in France ; for that he was neither in love, debt, nor difficulty.   Some lady observed, that it was not, in the company of ladies, gallant to say he was not in love.   Upon this occasion he wrote the *New Covenant*, from the *Castle in the Air* to the *Little Corner of the World*, in three stanzas, and sent it with the following words : " As the ladies are better judges of gallantry than the men are, I will thank you to tell me, whether the enclosed be gallantry.   If it be, it is truly original ; and the merit of it belongs to the person who inspired it."   The following was the answer of Mrs. Smith. " If the usual style of gallantry was as clever as your new covenant, many a fair ladies heart would be in danger, but the *Little Corner of the World* receives it from the Castle in the Air ; it is agreeable to her as being the elegant fancy of a friend.—C. SMITH."   [*Stanzas missing.*]

At this time, 1802, public spirit was at end in France.   The real republicans were harrassed by eternal prosecutions. Paine was a truly grateful man : his friendship was active and warm, and steady.   During the six years that he lived in our house, he frequently pressed us to go to America, offering us all that he should be able to do for us, and saying that he would bequeath his property to our children.   Some affairs of great consequence made it impracticable for Mr. Bonneville to quit France ; but, foreseeing a new revolution, that would strike, personally, many of the Republicans, it was re-

---

[1] The following words are here crossed out : " Also several pieces of poetry, which will be published hereafter, with his miscellaneous prose."

solved, soon after the departure of Mr. Paine for America, that I should go thither with my children, relying fully on the good offices of Mr. Paine, whose conduct in America justified that reliance.

In 1802 Paine left France, regretted by all who knew him. He embarked at Havre de Grace on board a stout ship, belonging to Mr. Patterson, of Baltimore, he being the only passenger. After a very stormy passage, he landed at Baltimore on the 30th of October, 1812. He remained there but a few days, and then went to Washington, where he published his Letters to the Americans.

A few months afterwards, he went to Bordentown, to his friend Col. Kirkbride, who had invited him, on his return, by the following letter of 12 November 1802. [*Missing.*]

He staid at Bordentown about two months, and then went to New York, where a great number of patriots gave him a splendid dinner at the City Hotel. In June, 1803, he went to Stonington, New England, to see some friends ; and in the autumn he went to his farm at New Rochelle. (The letter of Thomas Paine to Mr. Bonneville, 20 Nov., 1803.) [*Missing.*]

An inhabitant of this village offered him an apartment, of which he accepted, and while here he was taken ill. His complaint was a sort of paralytic affection, which took away the use of his hands. He had had the same while at Mr. Monroe's in Paris, after he was released from prison. Being better, he went to his farm, where he remained a part of the winter, and he came to New York to spend the rest of it ; but in the spring (1804) he went back to his farm. The farmer who had had his farm for 17 or 18 years, instead of paying his rent, brought Mr. Paine a bill for fencing, which made Paine his debtor ! They had a law-suit by which Paine got nothing but the right of paying the law-expenses ! This and other necessary expenses compelled him to sell sixty acres of his land. He then gave the honest farmer notice to quit the next April (1805).

Upon taking possession of the farm himself, he hired *Christopher Derrick* to cultivate it for him. He soon found that Derrick was not fit for his place, and he, therefore, discharged him. This was in the summer ; and, on Christmas Eve ensuing, about six o'clock, Mr. Paine being in his room, on the ground floor, reading, a gun was fired a few yards from the window. The contents of the gun struck the bottom part of the window, and all the charge, which was of small shot, lodged, as was next day discovered, in the window sill and wall. The shooter, in firing the gun, *fell ;* and the barrel of the gun had entered the ground where he fell, and left an impression, which Thomas Paine observed the next morning. Thomas Paine went immediately to the house of a neighboring farmer, and there (seeing a gun, he took hold of it, and perceived that the muzzle of the gun was filled with fresh earth. And then he heard that Christopher Derick had borrowed the gun about five o'clock the evening before, and had returned it again before six o'clock the same evening. Derick was arrested, and Purdy, his brother farmer, became immediately and voluntarily his bail. The cause was brought forward at New Rochelle ; and Derick was acquitted.[1]

In 1806 Thomas Paine offered to vote at New Rochelle for the election. But his vote was not admitted ; on the pretence only of his not being a citizen of America ; whereon he wrote the following letters. [*The letters are here missing, but no doubt the same as those on pp.* 379–80 *of this volume.*]

This case was pleaded before the Supreme Court of New York by Mr. Riker, then Attorney General, and, though Paine *lost his cause,* I as his legatee, did not lose the having to *pay for it.* It is however, an undoubted fact, that Mr. Paine was an American Citizen.

He remained at New Rochelle till June 1807 ; till disgust of every kind, occasioned by the gross and brutal conduct of some of the people there, made him resolve to go and live at New York.

On the 4th of April, 1807, he wrote the following letter to Mr. Bonneville [in Paris] :

" MY DEAR BONNEVILLE : Why don't you come to America Your wife and two boys, Benjamin and Thomas, are here, and in good health. They all speak English very well ; but Thomas has forgot his French. I intend to provide for the

---

[1] See p. 343 of this volume. Several paragraphs here are in the writing of J. P. Cobbett, then with his father in New York.

boys, but, I wish to see you here. We heard of you by letters by Madget and Captain Hailey. Mrs. Bonneville, and Mrs. Thomas, an English woman, keep an academy for young ladies.

"I send this by a friend, Mrs. Champlin, who will call on Mercier at the Institute, to know where you are. Your affectionate friend."

And some time after the following letter :

"My dear Bonneville : I received your letter by Mrs. Champlin, and also the letter for Mrs. Bonneville, and one from her sister. I have written to the American Minister in Paris, Mr. Armstrong, desiring him to interest himself to have your *surveillance* taken off *on condition of your coming to join your family in the United States.*

"This letter, with Mrs. Bonneville's, come to you under cover to the American Minister from Mr. Madison, Secretary of State. As soon as you receive it I advise you to call on General Armstrong and inform him of the proper method to have your surveillance taken off. Mr. Champagny, who succeeds Talleyrand, is, I suppose, the same who was Minister of the Interior, from whom I received a handsome friendly letter, respecting the iron bridge. I think you once went with me to see him.

"Call on Mr Skipwith with my compliments. He will inform you what vessels will sail for New York and where from. Bordeaux will be the best place to sail from. I believe Mr. Lee is American Consul at Bordeaux. When you arrive there, call on him, with my compliments. You may contrive to arrive at New York in April or May. The passages, in the Spring, are generally short ; seldom more than five weeks, and often less.

"Present my respects to Mercier, Bernardin St. Pierre, Dupuis, Grégoire.—When you come, I intend publishing all my works, and those I have yet in manuscript, by subscription. They will make 4 or 5 vol. 4°, or 5 vol. 8°, about 400 pages each. Yours in friendship.—T. P." [1]

---

[1] This letter is entirely in the writing of Madame Bonneville. Beneath it is written : " The above is a true copy of the original ; I have compared the two together. James P. Cobbett." The allusion to Champagny is either a slip of Madame's pen or Paine's memory. The minister who wrote him

While Paine was one day taking his usual after-dinner nap, an old woman called, and, asking for Mr. Paine, said she had something of great importance to communicate to him. She was shown into his bed-chamber ; and Paine, raising himself on his elbow, and turning towards the woman, said : " What do you want with me ? " " I came," said she, " from God, to tell you, that if you don't repent, and believe in Christ, you 'll be dammed." " Poh, poh, it 's not true," said Paine ; " you are not sent with such an impertinent message. Send her away. Pshaw ! God would not send such a foolish ugly old woman as you. Turn this messenger out. Get away ; be off : shut the door." And so the old woman packed herself off.

After his arrival Paine published several articles in the newspapers of New York and Philadelphia. Subsequent to a short illness which he had in 1807, he could not walk without pain, and the difficulty of walking increased every day. On the 21st of January, 1808, he addressed a memorial to the Congress of the United States, asking remuneration for his services ; and, on the 14th of February, the same year, another on the same subject. These documents and his letter to the Speaker are as follows.[1]

The Committee of Claims, to which the memorial had been submitted, passed the following resolution : " Resolved, that Thomas Paine has leave to withdraw his memorial and the papers accompanying the same." He was deeply grieved at this refusal ; some have blamed him for exposing himself to it. But, it should be recollected, that his expenses were greatly augmented by his illness, and he saw his means daily diminish, while he feared a total palsy ; and while he expected to live to a very great age, as his ancestors had before him. His money yielded no interest, always having been unwilling to place money out in that way.

He had made his will in 1807, during the short illness already noticed. But three months later, he assembled his

about his bridge was Chaptal. See ii., p. 296. The names in the last paragraph show what an attractive literary circle Paine had left in France, for a country unable to appreciate him.

[1] "Are as follows " in Madame B.'s writing, after striking out Cobbett's words, " will be found in the Appendix." The documents and letters are not given, but they are well known. See ii., p. 405.

friends, and read to them another will ; saying that he had believed such and such one to be his friend, and that now having altered his belief in them, he had also altered his will. From motives of the same kind, he, three months before his death, made another will, which he sealed up and directed *to me*, and gave it me to keep, observing to me, that I was more interested in it than any body else.

He wished to be buried in the Quaker burying ground, and sent for a member of the committee [Willett Hicks] who lived in the neighborhood. The interview took place on the 19th of March, 1809. Paine said, when we were looking out for another lodging, we had to put in order the affairs of our present abode. This was precisely the case with him ; all his affairs were settled, and he had only to provide his burying-ground ; his father had been a Quaker, and he hoped they would not refuse him a grave ; " I will," added he, " pay for the digging of it."

The committee of the Quakers refused to receive his body, at which he seemed deeply moved, and observed to me, who was present at the interview, that their refusal was foolish. "You will," said I, "be buried on your *farm*." " I have no objection to that," said he " but the farm will be sold, and they will dig my bones up before they be half rotten." " Mr. Paine," I replied, " have confidence in your friends. I assure you, that the place where you will be buried, shall never be sold." He seemed satisfied ; and never spoke upon this subject again. I have been as good as my word.

Last December [1818] the land of the farm having been divided between my children, I gave fifty dollars to keep apart and to myself, the place whereon the grave was.

Paine, doubtless, considered me and my children as strangers in America. His affection for us was, at any rate, great and sincere. He anxiously recommended us to the protection of Mr. Emmet, saying to him, " when I am dead, Madam Bonneville will have no friend here." And a little time after, obliged to draw money from the Bank, he said, with an air of sorrow, " you will have nothing left." [1]

[1] Paine's Will appoints Thomas Addis Emmet, Walter Morton (with $200 each), and Madame Bonneville executors ; gives a small bequest to the widow of Elihu Palmer, and a considerable one to Rickman of London, who was to

He was now become extremely weak. His strength and appetite daily departed from him ; and in the day-time only he was able, when not in bed, to sit up in his arm-chair to read the newspapers, and sometimes write. When he could no longer quit his bed, he made some one read the newspapers to him. His mind was always active. He wrote nothing for the press after writing his last will, but he would converse, and took great interest in politics. The vigour of his mind, which had always so strongly characterized him, did not leave him to the last moment. He never complained of his bodily suf- ferings, though they became excessive. His constitution was strong. The want of exercise alone was the cause of his suf- ferings. Notwithstanding the great inconveniences he was obliged to sustain during his illness, in a carman's house

---

divide with Nicholas Bonneville proceeds of the sale of the North part of his farm. To Madame Bonneville went his manuscripts, movable effects, stock in the N. Y. Phœnix Insurance Company estimated at $1500, and money in hand. The South part of the New Rochelle farm, over 100 acres, were given Madame Bonneville in trust for her children, Benjamin and Thomas, "their education and maintenance, until they come to the age of twenty-one years, in order that she may bring them well up, give them good and useful learning, and instruct them in their duty to God, and the practice of morality." At majority they were to share and share alike in fee simple. He desires to be buried in the Quaker ground,—"my father belonged to that profession, and I was partly brought up in it,"—but if this is not permitted, to be buried on his farm. "The place where I am to be buried to be a square of twelve feet, to be enclosed with rows of trees, and a stone or post and railed fence, with a head-stone with my name and age engraved upon it, author of "Common Sense." He confides Mrs. Bonneville and her children to the care of Emmet and Morton. "Thus placing confidence in their friendship, I herewith take my final leave of them and of the world. I have lived an honest and useful life to mankind ; my time has been spent in doing good ; and I die in perfect composure and resignation to the will of my Creator God." The Will, dated January 18, 1809, opens with the words, "The last Will and Testament of me, the subscriber, Thomas Paine, repos- ing confidence in my Creator God, and in no other being, for I know of no other, and I believe in no other."

Mr. William Fayel, to whom I am indebted for much information concern- ing the Bonnevilles in St. Louis, writes me that so little is known of Paine's benefactions, that "an ex-senator of the United States recently asserted that Gen. Bonneville was brought over by Jefferson and a French lady ; and a French lady, who was intimate with the Bonnevilles, assured me that General Bonneville was sent to West Point by Lafayette."

[Ryder's], in a small village [Greenwich], without any bosom friend in whom he could repose confidence, without any society he liked, he still did not complain of his sufferings. I indeed, went regularly to see him twice a week ; but, he said to me one day : " I am here alone, for all these people are nothing to me, day after day, week after week, month after month, and you don't come to see me."

In a conversation between him and Mr. [Albert] Gallatin, about this time, I recollect his using these words : " *I am very sorry that I ever returned to this country.*" As he was thus situated and paying a high price for his lodgings [1] he expressed a wish to come to my house. This must be a great inconvenience to me from the frequent visits to Mr. Thomas Paine ; but, I, at last, consented ; and hired a house in the neighborhood, in May 1809, to which he was carried in an arm-chair, after which he seemed calm and satisfied, and gave himself no trouble about anything. He had no disease that required a Doctor, though Dr. Romaine came to visit him twice a week. The swelling, which had commenced at his feet, had now reached his body, and some one had been so officious as to tell him that he ought to be *tapped*. He asked me if this was necessary. I told him, that I did not know ; but, that, unless he was likely to derive great good from it, it should not be done. The next [day] Doctor Romaine came and brought a physician with him, and they resolved that the tapping need not take place.

He now grew weaker and weaker very fast. A very few days before his death, Dr. Romaine said to me, " I don't think he can live till night." Paine, hearing some one speak, opens his eyes, and said : " 'T is you Doctor : what news ? " " Mr. such an one is gone to France on such business." " He will do nothing there," said Paine. " Your belly diminishes," said the Doctor. " And yours augments," said Paine.

When he was near his end, two American clergymen came to see him, and to talk with him on religious matters. " Let me alone," said he ; " good morning." He desired they should be admitted no more. One of his friends came to New York ; a person for whom he had a great esteem, and whom

---

[1] The sentence thus far is struck out by Madame Bonneville.

he had not seen for a long while. He was overjoyed at seeing him ; but, this person began to speak upon religion, and Paine turned his head on the other side, and remained silent, even to the adieu of the person.[1]

Seeing his end fast approaching, I asked him, in presence of a friend, if he felt satisfied with the treatment he had received at our house, upon which he could only exclaim, *O ! yes !* He added other words, but they were incoherent. It was impossible for me not to exert myself to the utmost in taking care of a person to whom I and my children owed so much. He now appeared to have lost all kind of feeling. He spent the night in tranquillity, and expired in the morning at eight o'clock, after a short oppression, at my house in Greenwich, about two miles from the city of New York. Mr. Jarvis, a Painter, who had formerly made a portrait of him, moulded his head in plaster, from which a bust was executed.

He was, according to the American custom, deposited in a mahogany coffin, with his name and age engraved on a silver-plate, put on the coffin. His corpse was dressed in a shirt, a muslin gown tied at neck and wrists with black ribbon, stockings, drawers ; and a cap was put under his head as a pillow. (He never slept in a night-cap.) Before the coffin was placed on the carriage, I went to see him ; and having a rose in my bosom, I took it out, and placed on his breast. Death had not disfigured him. Though very thin, his bones were not protuberant. He was not wrinkled, and had lost very little hair.

His voice was very strong even to his last moments. He often exclaimed, oh, lord help me ! An exclamation the involuntary effect of pain. He groaned deeply, and when a question was put to him, calling him by his name, he opened his eyes, as if waking from a dream. He never answered the question, but asked one himself ; as, what is it o'clock, &c.

On the ninth of June my son and I, and a few of Thomas Paine's friends, set off with the corpse to New Rochelle, a place 22 miles from New York. It was my intention to have him buried in the Orchard of his own farm ; but the farmer who lived there at that time said, that Thomas Paine, walk-

---

[1] Cobbett's words erased : " and Paine could no longer bear the sight of him."

ing with him one day, said, pointing to another part of the land, he was desirous of being buried there. "Then," said I, "that shall be the place of his burial." And, my instructions were accordingly put in execution. The head-stone was put up about a week afterwards with the following inscription : " Thomas Paine, Author of " Common Sense," died the eighth of June, 1809, aged 72 years." According to his will, a wall twelve feet square was erected round his tomb. Four trees have been planted outside the wall, two weeping willows and two cypresses. Many persons have taken away pieces of the tombstone and of the trees, in memory of the deceased ; foreigners especially have been eager to obtain these memorials, some of which have been sent to England.[1] They have been put in frames and preserved. Verses in honor of Paine have been written on the head stone. The grave is situated at the angle of the farm, by the entrance to it.

This interment was a scene to affect and to wound any sensible heart. Contemplating who it was, what man it was, that we were committing to an obscure grave on an open and disregarded bit of land, I could not help feeling most acutely. Before the earth was thrown down upon the coffin, I, placing myself at the east end of the grave, said to my son Benjamin, " stand you there, at the other end, as a witness for grateful America." Looking round me, and beholding the small group of spectators, I exclaimed, as the earth was tumbled into the grave, " Oh ! Mr. Paine ! My son stands here as testimony of the gratitude of America, and I, for France ! " This was the funeral ceremony of this great politician and philosopher ![2]

[1] The breaking of the original gravestone has been traditionally ascribed to pious hatred. A fragment of it, now in New York, is sometimes shown at celebrations of Paine's birthday as a witness of the ferocity vented on Paine's grave. It is satisfactory to find another interpretation.

[2] Paine's friends, as we have said, were too poor to leave their work in the city, which had refused Paine a grave. The Rev. Robert Bolton, in his History of Westchester County, introduces Cheetham's slanders of Paine with the words : " as his own biographer remarks." His own ! But even Cheetham does not lie enough for Bolton, who says : " His [Paine's] body was brought up from New York in a hearse used for carrying the dead to Potter's Field ; a white man drove the vehicle, accompanied by a negro to dig the grave." The whole Judas legend is in that allusion to Potter's Field. Such is history, where Paine is concerned !

The eighty-eight acres of the north part were sold at 25 dollars an acre. The half of the south (the share of Thomas de Bonneville) has been sold for the total sum of 1425 dollars. The other part of the south, which was left to Benjamin de Bonneville, has just (1819) been sold in lots, reserving the spot in which Thomas Paine was buried, being a piece of land 45 feet square.

Thomas Paine's posthumous works. He left the manuscript of his answer to Bishop Watson ; the Third Part of his Age of Reason ; several pieces on Religious subjects, prose and verse. The great part of his posthumous political works will be found in the Appendix. Some correspondences cannot be, as yet, published.[1]

In *Mechanics* he has left two models of wheels for carriages, and of a machine to plane boards. Of the two models of bridges, left at the Philadelphia Museum, only one has been preserved, and that in great disorder, one side being taken entirely off. But, I must say here, that it was then out of the hands of Mr. Peale.[2]

Though it is difficult, at present, to make some people believe that, instead of being looked on as a *deist* and a *drunkard*, Paine ought to be viewed as a philosopher and a truly benevolent man, future generations will make amends for the errors of their forefathers, by regarding him as a most worthy man, and by estimating his talents and character according to their real worth.

Thomas Paine was about five feet nine inches high, English measure, and about five feet six French measure. His bust was well proportioned ; and his face oblong. Reflexion was the great expression of his face ; in which was always seen the calm proceeding from a conscience void of reproach. His eye, which was black, was lively and piercing, and told us that he saw into the very heart of hearts [of any one who wished to deceive him].[3] A most benignant smile expressed what he

---

[1] All except the first two MSS., of which fragments exist, and some poems, were no doubt consumed at St. Louis, as stated in the Introduction to this work.

[2] I have vainly searched in Philadelphia for some relic of Paine's bridges.

[3] Bracketed words marked out. In this paragraph and some that follow the hand of Nicolas Bonneville is, I think, discernible.

felt upon receiving an affectionate salutation, or praise delicately conveyed. His leg and foot were elegant, and he stood and walked upright, without stiffness or affectation. [He never wore a sword nor cane], but often walked with his hat in one hand and with his other hand behind his back. His countenance, when walking, was generally thoughtful. In receiving salutations he bowed very gracefully, and, if from an acquaintance, he did not begin with "how d' ye do ? "but, with a "what news ?" If they had none, he gave them his. His beard, his lips, his head, the motion of his eye-brow, all aided in developing his mind.

Was he where he got at the English or American newspapers, he hastened to over-run them all, like those who read to make extracts for their paper. His first glance was for the funds, which, in spite of jobbing and the tricks of government, he always looked on as the sure thermometer of public affairs. Parliamentary Debates, the Bills, concealing a true or sham opposition of such or such orators, the secret pay and violent theatrical declamation, or the revelations of public or private meetings at the taverns ; these interested him so much that he longed for an ear and a heart to pour forth all his soul. When he added that he knew the Republican or the hypocrite, he would affirm, beforehand, that such or such a bill, such or such a measure, would take place ; and very seldom, in such a case, the cunning politic or the clear-sighted observer was mistaken in his assertions ; for they were not for him mere conjectures. He spoke of a future event as of a thing past and consummated. In a country where the slightest steps are expanded to open day, where the feeblest connexions are known from their beginning, and with all the views of ambition, of interest or rivalship, it is almost impossible to escape the eye of such an observer as Thomas Paine, whom no private interest could blind or bewitch, as was said by the clear-sighted Michael Montaigne.

His writings are generally perspicuous and full of light, and often they discover the sardonic and sharp smile of Voltaire. One may see that he wishes to wound to the quick ; and that he hugs himself in his success. But Voltaire all at once over-runs an immense space and resumes his vehement and dramatic step : Paine stops you, and points to the place where you ought to smile with him at the ingenious traits ; a gift to envy and stupidity.

Thomas Paine did not like to be questioned. He used to say, that he thought nothing more impertinent, than to say to any body : "What do you think of that ?" On his arrival at New York, he went to see General Gates. After the usual words of salutation, the General said : "I have always had it in mind, if I ever saw you again, to ask you whether you were married, as people have said." Paine not answering, the General went on : "Tell me how it is." "I never," said Paine, "answer impertinent questions."

Seemingly insensible and hard to himself, he was not so to the just wailings of the unhappy. Without any vehement expression of his sorrow, you might see him calling up all his powers, walking silently, thinking of the best means of consoling the unfortunate applicant ; and never did they go from him without some rays of hope. And as his will was firm and settled, his efforts were always successful. The man hardened in vice and in courts [of law], yields more easily than one imagines to the manly entreaties of a disinterested benefactor.

Thomas Paine loved his friends with sincere and tender affection. His simplicity of heart and that happy kind of openness, or rather, carelessness, which charms our hearts in reading the fables of the good Lafontaine, made him extremely amiable. If little children were near him he patted them, searched his pockets for the store of cakes, biscuits, sugar-plums, pieces of sugar, of which he used to take possession as of a treasure belonging to them, and the distribution of which belonged to him.[1] His conversation was unaffectedly simple and frank ; his language natural ; always abounding in curious anecdotes. He justly and fully seized the characters of all those of whom he related any singular traits. For his conversation was satyrick, instructive, full of witticisms. If he related an anecdote a second time, it was always in the same words and the same tone, like a comic actor who knows the place where he is to be applauded. He neither cut the tale short nor told it too circumstantially. It was real conversa-

---

[1] At this point are the words : "Barlow's letter [i. e. to Cheetham] we agreed to suppress."

tion, enlivened by digressions well brought in. The vivacity of his mind, and the numerous scenes of which he had been a spectator, or in which he had been an actor, rendered his narrations the more animated, his conversation more endearing. His memory was admirable. Politics were his favorite subject. He never spoke on religious subjects, unless pressed to it, and never disputed about such matters. He could not speak French : he could understand it tolerably well when spoken to him, and he understood it when on paper perfectly well. He never went to the theatre : never spoke on dramatic subjects. He rather delighted in ridiculing poetry. He did not like it : he said it was not a serious thing, but a sport of the mind, which often had not common sense. His common reading was the affairs of the day ; not a single newspaper escaped him ; not a political discussion : he knew how to strike while the iron was hot ; and, as he was always on the watch, he was always ready to write. Hence all his pamphlets have been popular and powerful. He wrote with composure and steadiness, as if under the guidance of a tutelary genius. If, for an instant, he stopped, it was always in the attitude of a man who listens. The Saint Jerome of Raphael would give a perfect idea of his contemplative recollection, to listen to the voice from on high which makes itself heard in the heart.

[It will be proper, I believe, to say here, that shortly after the Death of Thomas Paine a book appeared, under the *Title* of : *The Life of Thomas Paine*, by *Cheetham*. In this libel my character was calumniated. I cited the Author before the Criminal Court of New York. He was tried and in spite of all his manœuvres, he was found *guilty*.—M. B. de Bonneville.]

This last paragraph, in brackets, is in the writing of Madame Bonneville.

APPENDIX B.

THE HALL MANUSCRIPTS.

IN 1785, John Hall, an able mechanician and admirable man, emigrated from Leicester, England, to Philadelphia. He carried letters to Paine, who found him a man after his own heart. I am indebted to his relatives, Dr. Dutton Steele of Philadelphia and the Misses Steele, for Hall's journals, which extend over many years. It will be seen that the papers are of historical importance apart from their records concerning Paine. Hall's entries of his daily intercourse with Paine, which he never dreamed would see the light, represent a portraiture such as has rarely been secured of any character in history. The extent already reached by this work compels me to omit much that would impress the reader with the excellent work of John Hall himself, who largely advanced ironwork in New Jersey, and whose grave at Flemmington, surrounded by those of the relatives that followed him, and near the library and workshop he left, merits a noble monument.

Letter. Philadelphia, August 30, 1785.

"I went a day or two past with the Captain and his lady to see the exhibition of patriotic paintings. Paine the author of Common Sense is amongst them. He went from England (had been usher to a school) on board the same vessel that our Captain [Coltman] went in last time ; their acquaintance then commenced and has continued ever since. He resides now in Bordentown in the Jerseys, and it is probable that I may see him before it be long as when he comes to town the Captain says he is sure to call on him. It is supposed the various States have made his circumstances easy—General Washington, said if they did not provide for him he would himself. I think his services were as useful as the sword."

Journal, 1785.

Nov. 16th. Received a Letter from Mr. Pain by his Boy, informing us of his coming this day. Between 3 and 4 Mr. Pain, Col. Kerbright [Kirkbride], and another gentleman came to our door in a waggon.

17th. At dinner Mr. Pain told us a tale of the Indians, he being at a meeting of them with others to settle some affairs in 1776. The Doctor visited Mr. Pain.

19th. Performed a trifling operation for Mr. Pain.

22d. A remark of Mr. Pain's—not to give a deciding opinion between two persons you are in friendship with, lest you lose one by it ; whilst doing that between two persons, your supposed enemies, may make one your friend.

24th. This evening pulled Mr. Pain's Boy a tooth out.

Dec. 12. With much pain drawd the Board in at Hanna's chamber window to work Mr. Pain's bridge on. I pinned 6 more arches together which makes the whole 9. I sweat at it ; Mr. Pain gives me some wine and water as I was very dry. Past 9 o'clock Dr. Hutchinson called in on Mr. Paine.

[The December journal is mainly occupied with mention of Paine's visitors Franklin, Gouverneur Morris, Dr. Rush, Tench Francis, Robert Morris, Rittenhouse, Redman. A rubber of whist in which Paine won is mentioned.]

Sunday Jan. 1st 1786. Mr. Paine went to dine with Dr. Franklin today ; staid till after tea in the evening. They tried the burning of our candles by blowing a gentle current through them. It greatly improved the light. The draught of air is prevented by passing through a cold tube of tallow. The tin of the new lamp by internal reflections is heated and causes a constant current. This is the Doctor's conjecture. [Concerning Paine's candle see i., p. 214.]

Feb. 25th. Mr. Paine not returned. We sent to all the places we could suppose him to be at and no tidings of him. We became very unhappy fearing his political enemies should have shown him foul play. Went to bed at 10 o.c, and about 2 o.c. a knocking at the door proves Mr. Paine.

March 10th. Before 7 o'c a brother saint-maker came with a model of machine to drive boats against stream.[1] He had communicated his scheme to H. who had made alterations and a company had taken it and refused saint-maker partnership. He would fain have given it to Mr. Paine or me, but I a stranger refused and Mr. Paine had enough hobbys of his own. Mr. Paine pointed out a mode to simplify his apparatus greatly. He gave him 5s. to send him one of his maps.

April 15th. Mr. Paine asked me to go and see Indian Chiefs of Sennaka Nation, I gladly assented. They have an interpreter. Mr. Paine wished to see him and made himself known to him by past remembrance as Common Sense, and was introduced into the room, addressed them as "brothers" and shook hands cordially Mr. Paine treated them with 2s. bowl of punch.

Bordentown Letter, May 28. Colonel Kirkbride is the gentleman in whose family I am. My patron [Paine] is likewise a boarder and makes his home here I am diligently employed in Saint making, now in Iron that I had before finished in wood, with some improvements, but you may come and see what it is

Letter, June 4. Skepticism and Credulity are as general here as elsewhere, for what I see. In this town is a Quaker meeting and one of another class—I suppose of the Baptist cast—And a person in town a Tailor by trade that goes about a-soulmending on Sundays to various places, as most necessary, or I suppose advantageous, to himself; for by one trade or the other he has built himself a very elegant frame house

---

[1] Hall calls inventions "saints." This saint-maker is John Fitch, the "H." being Henry of Lancaster. This entry is of much interest. (See ii., p. 281.) The first steamer seems to have gone begging!

in this town. This man's way to Heaven is somewhat different to the other. I am informed he makes publick dippings &c. My Employer has *Common Sense enough* to disbelieve most of the Common Systematic Theories of Divinity but does not seem to establish any for himself. The Colonel [Kirkbride] is as Free as John Coltman.

[Under date of New York, July 31st, Hall writes an account of a journey with Paine to Morrisania, to visit Gen. Morris, and afterwards to the farm at New Rochelle, of which he gives particulars already known to my reader.]

Letter of Paine to John Hall, at Capt. Coltman's, in Letitia Court, Market St, between Front and Second St. Philadelphia :

" Bordentown, Sep. 22, 1786.—Old Friend : In the first place I have settled with Mr. Gordon for the time he has been in the house—in the second I have put Mrs. Read who, you know has part of our house Col. Kirkbride's but is at this time at Lancaster, in possession by putting part of her goods into it.[1] By this means we shall have room at our house (Col. Kirkbride) for carrying on our operations. As Philadelphia is so injurious to your health and as apartments at Wm. Foulke's would not be convenient to you, we can now conveniently make room for you here. Mrs. Kirkbride mentioned this to me herself and it is by the choice of both her and Col. K. that I write it to you. I wish you could come up to-morrow (Sunday) and bring the iron with you. I shall be backward and forward between here and Philadelphia pretty often until the elections are over, but we can make a beginning here and what more iron we may want we can get at the Delaware Works. and if you should want to go to Mount hope you can more conveniently go from here than from Philadelphia—thus you see I have done your business since I have been up. The enclosed letter is for Mr. Henry who is member for Lancaster County. I do not know where he lodges, but if William will be so good as to give it to the door keeper or Clerk of the Assembly it will be safe. Bring up the walnut strips with you. Your coming here will give an opportunity to Joseph to get

---

[1] Mrs. Read was thus transferred to Paine's own house. Her husband died next year and Paine declined to receive any rent.

acquainted with Col. K. who will very freely give any information in his power. Compts. in the family. Your friend and Hbl. servt."

Undated letter of Paine to John Hall, in Philadelphia :

"Fryday Noon.—Old Friend : Inclosed (as the man said by the horse) I send you the battau, as I wish to present it as neat and clean as can be done ; I commit it to your care. The sooner it is got on Board the vessel the better. I shall set off from here on Monday and expect to be in New York on Tuesday. I shall take all the tools that are here with me, and wish you would take some with you, that if we should get on a working fit we may have some to work with. Let me hear from you by the Sunday's boat and send me the name of the vessel and Captain you go with and what owners they belong to at New York, or what merchants they go to. I wrote to you by the last boat, and Peter tells me he gave the letter to Capt. Haines, but Joe says that he enquired for letters and was told there was none—wishing you an agreeable voyage and meeting at New York, I am your friend, and humble servant. Present my compliments to Capt. and Mrs. Coltman and William. Col. and Mrs. Kirkbride's and Polly's compt."

Note of Hall, dated Oct. 3 [1786] " Dashwood Park, of Captain Roberts : On Thursday morning early Sept. 28th I took the stage wagon for Trenton. Jo had gone up by water the day before to a sale of land and a very capital iron works and nailing with a large corn mill. It was a fair sale there was a forge and rolling and slitting mill upon an extensive scale the man has failed—The works with about 60 or 70 acres of land were sold for £9000 currency. Then was put up about 400 acres of land and sold for £2700 currency and I believe a good bargain ; and bought by a friend of mine called Common Sense—Who I believe had no idea of purchasing it when he came there. He took Jo to Bordentown with him that night and they came to look at it the next day ; then Jo went into the Jerseys to find a countryman named Burges but was disappointed   Came back to Bordentown and on Saturday looked all over Mr. Paine's purchase along with him and believes it bought well worth money.

Nov. 21st. Mr. Paine told us an anecdote of a French noble's applying to Dr. Franklin, as the Americans had put away their King, and that nation having formerly chosen a King from Normandy, he offered his service and wished him to lay his letter before Congress. Mr. Paine observed that Britain is the most expensive government in the world. She gives a King a million a year and falls down and worships him. I put on Mr. Paine's hose yesterday. Last night he brought me in my room a pair of warm cloth overshoes as feel very comfortable this morning Had a wooden pot stove stand betwixt my feet by Mr. Paine's desire and found it kept my feet warm.

November 24. As soon as breakfast was over mounted Button [Paine's horse] and set off for Philadelphia. I brought Mr. Paine $120 in gold and silver.

Bordentown 27th, Monday. Day was devoted to rivetting the bars, and punching the upper bar for the bannisters [of the bridge]. Mr. Kirkbride and Polly went to hear a David Jones preach a rhodomontade sermon about the Devil, Mary Magdalen, and against deists, etc.

December 14. This day employed in raising and putting on the abutments again and fitting them. The smith made the nuts of screws to go easier. Then set the ribs at proper distance, and after dinner I and Jackaway [?] put on some temporary pieces on the frame of wood to hold it straight, and when Mr. Pain came they then tied it on its wooden frame with strong cords. I then saw that it had bulged full on one side and hollow on the other. I told him of it, and he said it was done by me—I denied that and words rose high. I at length swore by God that it was straight when I left it, he replied as positively the contrary, and I think myself ill used in this affair.

Philadelphia. Dec. 22nd. Bridge packed and tied on the sled. We arrived in town about 5 o.clock took our bags to Capt. Coltmans, and then went down to Dr. Franklin's, and helped unload the bridge. Mr. Paine called on me ; gave us an anecdote of Dr. Franklin. On Mr. Paine asking him of the value of any new European publication ; he had not been informed of any of importance. There were some religious posthumous anecdotes of Doctor Johnson, of resolves he had made and broken though he had prayed for power and strength to keep them; which showed the Doctor said that he had not much interest there. And such things had better be suppressed as nobody had anything to do betwixt God and man.

December 26. Went with Glentworth to see the Bridge at Dr. Franklin's. Coming from thence met Mr. Pain and Mr. Rittenhouse; returned with them and helped move it for all three to stand upon, and then turned it to examine. Mr. Rittenhouse has no doubt of its strength and sufficiency for the Schuylkill, but wished to know what quantity of iron [it would require,] as he seemed to think it too expensive.

December 27. Walk to the State House. The Bank bill called but postponed until tomorrow. Mr. Pain's letter read, and leave given to exhibit the Bridge at the State House to be viewed by the members. Left the House and met Mr. Pain, who told me Donnalson had been to see and [stand] upon his Bridge, and admitted its strength and powers. Then took a walk beyond Vine street, and passed by the shop where the steamboat apparatus is. Mr. Pain at our house, and talking on the Bank affair brought on a dispute between Mr. Pain and the Captain [Coltman] in which words were very high. A reflection from Captain C. on publications in favour of the Bank having lost them considerable, he [Paine] instantly took that as a reflection on himself, and swore by G—d, let who would, it was a lie. I then left the room and went up stairs. They quarrelled a considerable time, but at length parted tolerably coolly. Dinner being ready I went down; but the Captain continued talking about politics and the Bank, and what he thought the misconduct of Mr. Pain in his being out and in with the several parties. I endeavoured to excuse Mr. Pain in some things relating thereto, by saying it was good sense in changing his ground when any party was going wrong,—and that he seemed to delight in difficulties, in Mechanics particularly, and was pleased in them. The Captain grew warm, and said he knew now he could not eat his dinner. [Here followed a sharp personal quarrel between Hall and Coltman.] In the evening Mr. Paine came in and wished me to be assisting in carrying the model to the State House. We went to Dr. Franklin's and fetched the Bridge to the Committee Room.

1787. Jan. 1. Our Saint I have assisted in moving to the State House and there placed in their Committee room, as by a letter addressed to this Speaker they admitted. And by the desire of my patron (who is not an early riser) I attended to give any information to inquiries until he came. And then I was present when the Assembly with their Speaker inspected it and many other persons as philosophers, Mechanics Statesmen and even Tailors. I observed their sentiments and opinions of it were as different as their features. The philosopher said it would add new light to the great utility. And the tailor (for it is an absolute truth) remarked it cut a pretty figure. It is yet to be laid (or by the by stand) before the Council of State. Then the Philosophical Society and all the other Learned Bodies in this city. And then to be canonised by an Act of State which is solicited to incorporate a body of men to adopt and realise or Brobdinag this our Lilliputian handywork, that is now 13 feet long on a Scale of one to 24. And then will be added another to the world's present Wonders.

January 4. Mr. Pain called in and left me the intended Act of Assembly for a Bridge Company, who are to subscribe $33,330$$, and then are to be put in possession of the present Bridge and premises to answer the interest of their money until they erect a new one ; and after they have erected a new one, and the money arising from it amounts to more than pays interest, it is to become a fund to pay off the principal stockholders, and then the Bridge to become free. Mr. Pain called in ; I gave him my Bill—told him I had charged one day's work and a pair of gloves.

March 15th Mr. Paine's boy called on time to [inquire] of the money spent. Mr. Paine called this evening ; told me of his being with Dr. Franklin and about the chess player, or Automaton, and that the Dr. had no idea of the mode of communication. Mr. Paine has had several visitors, as Mr. Jowel, Rev. Dr. Logan, &c.

Sunday April 16th Prepared to attend Mr. Paine up to Bordentown. Mr. Paine's horse and chair came, mounted and drove through a barren sandy country arrived at Bordentown at half past one-o'clock for dinner. This is the pleasantest situation I have seen in this country.

TRENTON, April 20. Sitting in the house saw a chair pass
down the street with a red coat on, and going out after it believed it to be Mr. Paine, so followed him up to Collins's,
where he was enquiring where I boarded. I just then called to
him, and went with him to Whight's Tavern, and there he paid
me the money I had laid down for him. He is now going for
England by way of France in the French packet which sails
the 25th instant. He asked me to take a ride, and as the stage
was not come in and he going the road I gladly took the
opportunity, as I could return on meeting the stage. On the
journey he told me of the Committee's proceedings on Bridges
and Sewers ; anecdotes of Dr. Franklin, who had sent a letter
by him to the president, or some person, to communicate to
the Society of Civil Architects, who superintend solely over
bridges in France. The model is packed up to go with him.
The Doctor, though full of employ from the Vice President
being ill, and the numerous visitors on State business, and
others that his fame justly procures him, could hardly be
supposed to pay great attention to trifles ; but as he consideres
Mr. Paine his adopted political Son he would endeavor to
write by him to his friends, though Mr. Paine did not press, for
reasons above. In 2 or 3 days he sent him up to Bordentown
no less than a dozen letters to his acquaintance in France.—
He told me many anecdotes of the Doctor, relating to national
and political concerns, and observations of many aged and
sensible men of his acquaintance in that country. And the
treaty that he the Doctor made with the late King of Prussia
by adding an article that, should war ever break out, (though
never a probability of it) Commerce should be left free. The
Doctor said he showed it to the French minister, Vergennes,
who said it met his idea, and was such as he would make even
with England, though he knew they would not,—they were so
fond of robbing and plundering. And the Doctor had gathered
a hint from a Du Quesney that no nation could properly expect to gain by endeavoring to suppress his neighbor, for
riches were to be gained from amongst the rich and not from
poor neighbors ; and a National reciprocity was as much necessary as a domestic one, or [inter] national trade as necessary to
be free as amongst the people of a country. Such and

many more hints passed in riding 2 or 3 miles, until we met the stage. I then shook hands and wished him a good voyage and parted.

Letter from Flemmington, N. J., May 16, 1788, to John Coltman, Leicester, England :

" FRIEND JOHN : Tell that disbelieving sceptical Infidel thy Father that he has wounded my honor, What! Bought the Coat at a rag shop—does he think I would palm such a falsity both upon Gray and Green heads! did not I send you word it was General Washington's. And does he think I shall slanderously brook such a slanderous indignity—No ! I tell him the first Ink that meanders from my pen, which shall be instantly on my setting foot on Brittains Isle, shall be to call him to account. I 'll haul out his Callous Leaden soul with its brother !

"In the late revolution the provincial army lying near Princeton New Jersey one Sunday General Washington and Common Sense each in their chairs rode down there to Meeting Common Sense put up his at a friend's one Mrs. Morgan's and pulling off his great coat put it in the care of a servant man, and as I remember he was of the pure Irish Extraction ; he walked then to meeting and then slipped off with said great coat and some plate of Mr. Morgan. On their return they found what had been done in their absence and relating it to the General his answer was it was necessary to watch as well as pray—but told him he had two and would lend or give him one —and that is the Coat I sent and the fact as related to me and others in public by said [Common Sense.] Nor do I believe that Rome or the whole Romish Church has a better attested miracle in her whole Catalogue than the above—though I dont wish to deem it a miracle, nor do I believe there is any miracle upon record for these 18 hundred years so true as that being General Washington's great coat.—I, labouring hard for said Common Sense at Bordentown, the said coat was hung up to keep snow out of the room. I often told him I should expect that for my pains, but he never would say I should ; but having a chest there I took care and locked it up when I had finished my work, and sent it to you. So far are these historical facts— Maybe sometime hence I may collect dates and periods to them—But why should they be disputed ? has not the world adopted as true a-many affairs without date and of less moment than this, and even pay what is called a holy regard to them ?

" If you communicate this to your Father and he feels a compunction for the above crime and will signify the same by letter, he will find I strictly adhere to the precepts of Christianity and shall forgive.—If not——

" My best wishes to you all.

"JOHN HALL."

Letter of Paine, London, Nov. 25, 1791, to " Mr. John Hall, at Mr. John Coltman's, Shambles Lane, Leicester, England."

" MY OLD FRIEND : I am very happy to see a letter from you, and to hear that our Friends on the other side the water are well. The Bridge has been put up, but being on wood butments they yielded, and it is now taken down. The first rib as an experiment was erected between two steel furnaces which supported it firmly ; it contained not quite three tons of iron, was ninety feet span, height of the arch five feet ; it was loaded with six tons of iron, which remained upon it a twelve month. At present I am engaged on my political Bridge. I shall bring out a new work (Second part of the Rights of Man) soon after New Year. It will produce something one way or other. I see the tide is yet the wrong way, but there is a change of sentiment beginning. I have so far got the ear of John Bull that he will read what I write—which is more than ever was done before to the same extent. Rights of Man has had the greatest run of anything ever published in this country, at least of late years—almost sixteen thousand has gone off—and in Ireland above forty thousand—besides the above numbers one thousand printed cheap are now gone to Scotland by desire from some of the [friends] there. I have been applied to from Birmingham for leave to print ten thousand copies, but I intend, after the next work has had its run among those who will have handsome printed books and fine paper, to print an hundred thousand copies of each work and distribute them at sixpence a-piece ; but this I do not at present talk of, because it will alarm the wise mad folks at St. James's. I have received a letter from Mr. Jefferson who mentioned the great run it has had there. It has been attacked by John Adams, who has brought an host about his ears from all parts of the Continent.   Mr. Jefferson has sent me twenty five different answers to Adams who wrote under the signature of Publicola.   A letter is somewhere in the city for me from Mr. Laurens of S. Carolina.   I hope to receive it in a few days.   I shall be glad at all times to see, or hear from you.   Write to me (under cover) to Gordon, Booksellers N : 166 Fleet Street, before you leave Leicester.   How far is it from thence to Rotherham?   Yours sincerely.

" P. S.   I have done you the compliment of answering your favor the inst. I rec'd. it which is more than I have done by any other—were I to ans. all the letters I receive—I should require half a dozen clerks."

Extracts from John Hall's letters from London, England :

LONDON, January 1792   Burke's publication has produced one way or other near 50 different answers and publications. Nothing of late ever has been so read as Paine's answer. Sometime shortly he will publish a second part of the Rights of Man.   His first part was scrutinized by the Privy Council held on purpose and through fear of making him *more popular* deemed too contemptible for Government notice.   The sale of it for a day or two was rather retarded or not publickly disposed of until it was known by the printers that it would not be noticed by Government.

John Hall to a friend in England :

· " LONDON, Nov. 6, 1792. I dined yesterday with the Revolution Society at the London Tavern.   A very large company assembled and after dinner many truly noble and patriotic toasts were drank.   The most prominent were—The Rights of Man—with 3 times &c.—The Revolution of France—The Revolution of the World—May all the armies of tyrants learn the Brunswick March—May the tree of Liberty be planted in every tyrant city, and may it be an evergreen.   The utmost unanimity prevailed through the company, and several very excellent songs in favor of Liberty were sung.   Every bosom felt the divine glow of patriotism and love of universal freedom. I wish you had been there.   For my part I was transported at the scene.   It happened that a company of Aristocratic french and Spanish merchants were met in the very room under, and

Horne Tooke got up and sarcastically requested the company not to wound the tender feelings of the gentlemen by too much festivity. This sarcasm was followed by such a burst of applause as I never before heard."

From J. Redman, London, Tuesday Dec. 18, 5 p. m. to John Hall, Leicester, England : " Mr. Paine's trial is this instant over. Erskine shone like the morning-Star. Johnson was there. The instant Erskine closed his speech the venal jury interrupted the Attorney General, who was about to make a reply, and without waiting for any answer, or any summing up by the Judge, pronounced him guilty. Such an instance of infernal corruption is scarcely upon record. I have not time to express my indignant feelings on this occasion. At this moment, while I write, the mob is drawing Erskine's carriage home, he riding in triumph—his horses led by another party. Riots at Cambridge, Manchester, Bridport Dorset &c. &c. O England, how art thou fallen ! I am just now told that press warrants are issued today. February, make haste. Mrs R's respects and mine. Yours truly."

[John Hall's London Journal (1792) records frequent meetings there with Paine. " March 5. Met Mr. Paine going to dress on an invitation to dine with the Athenians. He leaves town for a few days to see his aunt." " April 20. Mr. Paine goes out of town tomorrow to compose what I call Burke's Funeral Sermon." " Aug. 5. Mr. Paine looking well and in high spirits." " Sept. 6. Mr. Paine called in a short time. Does not seem to talk much, rather on a reserve, of the prospect of political affairs. He had a letter from G. Washington and Jefferson by the ambassador [Pinckney]." The majority of entries merely mention meeting Paine, whose name, by the way, after the prosecution was instituted, Hall prudently writes " P——n." He also tells the story of Burke's pension.]

" April 19, 1803. Had a ride to Bordentown to see Mr. Paine at Mr. Kirkbride's. He was well and appeared jollyer than I had ever known him. He is full of whims and schemes and mechanical inventions, and is to build a place or shop to carry them into execution, and wants my help."

APPENDIX C.

AT the age of thirty Paine was somewhat stout, and very athletic ; but after his arrival in America (1774) he was rather slender. His height was five feet, nine inches. He had a prominent nose, somewhat like that of Ralph Waldo Emerson. It may have impressed Bonaparte, who insisted, it is said, that a marshal must have a large nose. Paine's mouth was delicate, his chin also ; he wore no whiskers or beard until too feeble with age to shave. His forehead was lofty and unfurrowed ; his head long, the occiput feeble. His complexion was ruddy,—thoroughly English. Charles Lee, during the American revolution, described him as " the man who has genius in his eyes ; " Carlyle quotes from Foster an observation on the brilliancy of Paine's eyes, as he sat in the French Convention. His figure, as given in an early French portrait, is shapely ; its elegance was often remarked. A year or so after his return to America he is shown in a contemporary picture as somewhat stout again, if one may judge by the face. This was probably a result of insufficient exercise, on which he much depended. He was an expert horseman, and, in health, an unwearied walker. He loved music, and could join well in a chorus.

There are eleven original portraits of Thomas Paine, besides a death-mask, a bust, and the profile copied in this work from a seal used on the release at Lewes, elsewhere cited (i., p. 33). That gives some idea of the head and face at the age of thirty-five. I have a picture said to be that of Paine in his youth, but the dress is an anachronism. The earliest portrait of Paine was painted by Charles Willson Peale, in Philadelphia, probably in some early year of the American Revolution, for Thomas Brand Hollis, of London,—the benefactor of Harvard University, one of whose halls bears his name. The same artist painted another portrait of Paine, now badly placed in Independence Hall. There must have been an early engraving from one of Peale's pictures, for John Hall writes October 31, 1786: "A print of Common Sense, if any of my friends want one, may be had by sending to the printshops in London, but they have put a wrong name to it, his being Thomas." [1] The Hollis portrait was engraved in London, 1791, underlined "by Peel [*sic*] of Philadelphia," and published, July 25th, by J. Ridgway, York Street, St. James's Square. Paine holds an open book bearing the words, "Rights of Man," where Peale probably had "Common Sense." On a table with inkstand and pens rests Paine's right elbow, the hand supporting

---

[1] This is puzzling. The only engraving I have found with "Tom" was published in London in 1800. Can there be a portrait lost under some other name?

his chin. The full face appears—young, handsome, gay; the wig is frizzed, a bit of the queue visible. In all of the original portraits of Paine his dress is neat and in accordance with fashion, but in this Hollis picture it is rather fine: the loose sleeves are ornamentally corded, and large wristbands of white lace fall on the cuffs.

While Paine and Jefferson were together in Paris (1787) Paine wrote him a note, August 18th, in which he says: "The second part of your letter, concerning taking my picture, I must feel as an honor done to me, not as a favor asked of me—but in this, as in other matters, I am at the disposal of your friendship." As Jefferson does not appear to have possessed such a portrait, the request was probably made through him. I incline to identify this portrait with an extremely interesting one, now in this country, by an unknown artist. It is one of twelve symmetrical portraits of revolutionary leaders,—the others being Marat, Robespierre, Lafayette, Mirabeau, Danton, Brissot, Pétion, Camille Desmoulins, Billaud de Varennes, Gensonné, Clermont Tonnère. These pictures were reproduced in cheap woodcuts and distributed about France during the Revolution. The originals were secured by Col. Lowry, of South Carolina, and brought to Charleston during the Revolution. At the beginning of the civil war they were buried in leaden cases at Williamstown, South Carolina. At the end of the war they were conveyed to Charleston, where they remained, in the possession of a Mrs. Cole, until purchased by their present owner, Mr. Alfred Ames Howlett, of

Syracuse, New York. As Mirabeau is included, the series must have been begun at an early phase of the revolutionary agitation. The face of Paine here strongly resembles that in Independence Hall. The picture is about two feet high; the whole figure is given, and is dressed in an elegant statesmanlike fashion, with fine cravat and silk stockings from the knee. The table and room indicate official position, but it is the same room as in nine of the other portraits. It is to be hoped that further light may be obtained concerning these portraits.

Well-dressed also, but notably unlike the preceding, is the " Bonneville Paine," one of a celebrated series of two hundred engraved portraits, the publication of which in quarto volumes was begun in Paris in 1796. " F. Bonneville del. et sculpsit " is its whole history. Paine is described in it as " Ex Député à la Convention Nationale," which would mean strictly some time between his expulsion from that assembly in December, 1793, and his recall to it a year later. It could not, however, have been then taken, on account of Paine's imprisonment and illness. It was probably made by F. Bonneville when Paine had gone to reside with Nicolas Bonneville in the spring of 1797. It is an admirable picture in every way, but especially in bringing out the large and expressive eyes. The hair is here free and flowing ; the dress identical with that of the portrait by Jarvis in this work.

The best-known picture of Paine is that painted by his friend George Romney, in 1792. I have inquired through London *Notes and Queries* after the original, which long ago disappeared, and a claimant turned up in Birmingham, England; but in this the hand holds a book, and Sharp's engraving shows no hand. The face was probably copied from the Romney. The large engraving by W. Sharp was published April 20, 1793, and the smaller in 1794. A reproduction by Illman were a fit frontispiece for Cheetham (what satirical things names are sometimes), but ought not to have got into Gilbert Vale's popular biography of Paine. That and a reproduction by Wright in the Mendum edition of Paine's works, have spread through this country something little better than a caricature; and one Sweden has subjected Truelove's edition, in England, to a like misfortune. Paine's friends, Rickman, Constable, and others, were satisfied by the Romney picture, and I have seen in G. J. Holyoake's library a proof of the large engraving, with an inscription on the back by Paine, who presented it to Rickman. It is the English Paine, in all his vigor, and in the thick of his conflict with Burke, but, noble as it is, has not the gentler and more poetic expression which Bonneville found in the liberated prisoner surrounded by affectionate friends. Romney and Sharp were both well acquainted with Paine.

A picturesque Paine is one engraved for Baxter's "History of England," and published by Symonds, July 2, 1796. Dressed with great elegance, Paine stands pointing to a scroll in his left hand, inscribed "Rights of Man." Above his head, on a frame design, a pen lies on a roll marked "Equality." The face is handsome and the likeness good.

A miniature by H. Richards is known to me only as engraved by K. Mackenzie, and published March 31, 1800, by G. Gawthorne, British Library, Strand, London. It is the only portrait that has beneath it " Tom Paine." It represents Paine as rather stout, and the face broad. It is powerful, but the least pleasing of the portraits. The picture in Vale resembles this more than the Romney it professes to copy.

I have in my possession a wood engraving of Paine, which gives no trace of its source or period. It is a vigorous profile, which might have been made in London during the excitement over the " Rights of Man," for popular distribution. It has no wig, and shows the head extraordinarily long, and without much occiput. It is pre-eminently the English radical leader.

Before speaking of Jarvis' great portrait of Paine, I mention a later one by him which Mr. William Erving, of New York, has added to my collection. It would appear to have been circulated at the time of his death. The lettering beneath, following a facsimile autograph, is: " J. W. Jarvis, pinx. 1805. J. R. Ames, del.—L'HOMME DES DEUX MONDES. Born at Thetford, England, Jan. 29, (O. S.) 1737. Died at Greenwich, New York, June 8, 1809." Above the cheap wood-cut is: " A tribute to Paine." On the right, at the top, is a globe, showing the outlines of the Americas, France, England, and Africa. It is supported by the wing of a dove with large olive-branch. On the left upper corner is an open book inscribed: " RIGHTS OF MAN. COMMON SENSE. CRISIS ": supported by a scroll with "DOING JUSTICE, LOVING MERCY. AGE OF REASON." From this book rays break out and illumine the globe opposite. A lower corner shows the balances, and the liberty-cap on a pole, the left being occupied by the United States flag and that of France. Beneath are the broken chain, crown, sword, and other emblems of oppression. A frame rises showing a plumb line, at the top of which the key of the Bastille is crossed by a pen, on Paine's breast. The portrait is surrounded by a "Freedom's Wreath" in which are traceable the floral emblems of all nations. The wreath is bound with a fascia, on which appear, by twos, the following names: "Washington, Monroe; Jefferson, Franklin; J. Stewart, E. Palmer; Barlow, Rush; M. Wollstonecraft, M. B. Bonneville; Clio Rickman, J. Horne Tooke; Lafayette, Brissot."

The portrait of Paine represents him with an unusually full face, as compared with earlier pictures, and a most noble and benevolent expression. The white cravat and dress are elegant. What has become of the original of this second picture by the elder Jarvis? It might easily have fallen to some person who might not recognize it as meant for Paine, though to one who has studied his countenance it conveys the impression of what he probably would have been at sixty-eight. About two years later a drawing was made of Paine by William Constable, which I saw at the house of his nephew, Dr. Clair J. Grece, Redhill, England. It reveals the ravages of age, but conveys a vivid impression of the man's power.

After Paine's death Jarvis took a cast of his face. Mr. Laurence Hutton has had for many years this death-mask which was formerly in the establishment of Fowler and Wells, the phrenologists, and probably used by George Combe in his lectures. This mask has not the large nose of the bust; but that is known to have been added afterwards. The bust is in the New York Historical Society's rooms. In an article on Paine in the *Atlantic Monthly* (1856) it was stated that this bust had to be hidden by the Historical Society to prevent its injury by haters of Paine. This has been quoted by Mr. Robertson, of London, in his "Thomas Paine, an Investigation." I am assured by Mr. Kelby, of that Society, that the statement is unfounded. The Society has not room to exhibit its entire collection, and the bust of Paine was for some time out of sight, but from no such reason as that stated, still less from any prejudice. The face is that of Paine in extreme dilapidation, and would be a dismal misrepresentation if shown in a public place.

Before me are examples of all the portraits I have mentioned (except that in Birmingham), and I have observed contemporary representations of Paine in caricatures or in apotheosis of fly-leaves. Comparative studies convince me that the truest portrait of Paine is that painted by John Wesley Jarvis in 1803, and now in possession of Mr. J. H. Johnston, of New York. The picture from which our frontispiece is taken appeared to be a replica, of somewhat later date, the colors being fresher, but an inscription on the back says "Charles W.

Jarvis, pinxit, July, 1857." From this perfect dupli-
cate Clark Mills made his portrait-bust of Paine
now in the National Museum at Washington, but
it has not hitherto been engraved. Alas, that no
art can send out to the world what colors only can
convey,—the sensibility, the candor, the spiritu-
ality, transfusing the strong features of Thomas
Paine. As I have sat at my long task, now drawn
to a close, the face there on the wall has seemed to
be alive, now flushed with hope, now shadowed
with care, the eyes greeting me daily, the firm
mouth assigning some password—Truth, Justice.

APPENDIX D.

BRIEF LIST OF PAINE'S WORKS.

Case of the Officers of Excise. Written 1772 ; pub. Lond. 1793.

Penn'a Magazine. Edited by Paine, Jan. 1775 — Aug. 1776. Articles enumerated in i. ch. iv. of this biography.

Penn'a Journal. 1775, Jan. 4, Dialogue bet. Wolfe and Gage. March 8, paper signed "Justice and Humanity." Oct. 18, paper sig. "Humanus." 1776. Letters signed "The Forester."

Common Sense, Jan. 10, 1776. Phil. Lond.

Epistle to the People called Quakers. Phil. 1776.

Dialogue between Gen. Montgomery and an American Delegate. Phil. 1776.

The Crisis. 13 Nos. and several supernumerary. 1776—1783.

Preamble to Pa. Act of Emancipation, March 1, 1780.

Public Good. Phil. 1780.

Letter to Abbé Raynal. Phil. 1782.

Thoughts on the Peace. Phil. 1783.

Dissertation on Government, the Bank, etc. Phil. 1786.

Prospects on the Rubicon. Lond. 1787. (2d ed. corrected 1793.)

Letter to Sir G. Staunton. Iron Bridges. London. 1788.

Rights of Man. Lond. 1791. Trs. French, 1791 ; Swedish, 1792.

Address of the "Société Républicaine." Paris, 1791.

Letter to Le Républicain. Paris. July 1791.

Address of Friends of Peace and Liberty. Lond. Aug. 20, 1791.

Rights of Man. Part ii. Lond. 1792. French Tr., 1792.

Letter to Sheriff of Sussex, June 30, 1792.

Letter to the Abbé Sieyès, 1792. Paris and Lond.

Letters to Henry Dundas, June 6 and Sep. 15, 1792. Lond.

Letters to Lord Onslow, June 17 and 21, 1792. Lond.

Address to the Addressers. Lond. Sep. 1792.

Letter to the People of France. Paris. Sep. 25, 1792.

Letter to the Attorney General of England. Nov. 11, 1792. Lond.

Speech in French Convention on bringing Louis Capet to Trial, Nov. 20, 1792. Paris. French ; printed by order of the Convention.

Reasons for preserving the life of Louis Capet. Jan. 1793.

Project of a Constitution. Reported 1793. (Pub. in works of Condorcet.)

Le Siècle de la Raison (essay suppressed by translator). Paris. 1793.

Letter to Danton, 1793. Durand's Documents. New York. 1889.

Age of Reason. Part i. Paris, New York, and London, 1794.

Letter to French Convention (from prison) Aug. 8, 1794.

Mémoire à M. Monroe. Sep. 1794. Paris.

Dissertation on the first principles of Government. Paris. 1795.

Speech in Convention on the proposed Constitution. 1795.

Age of Reason. Part ii. Paris and Lond. 1796.

Decline and Fall of the English System of Finance. (Pub. in all European languages.) 1796.

Letter to George Washington. Phil. 1796.

Agrarian Justice (À la Législature et au Directoire, ou la Justice Agraire.) 1797.

Letter to Erskine. Lond. 1797.

Letter to People and Armies of France. Paris. 1797.

Discourse to the Theophilanthropists. Paris and Lond. 1797.

Letter to Camille Jourdan, on Bells, etc. (Lettre de Thomas Payne sur les Cultes). 1797.

Maritime Compact. The Rights of Neutrals at Sea. 1801.

Letter to Samuel Adams. 1802.

Letters to the Citizens of the United States written 1802. Ed. Lond. 1817.

Letter to the People of England. 1804.

To the French Inhabitants of Louisiana. 1804.

To the Citizens of Pennsylvania (on Convention). Phil. 1805.

On the Cause of the Yellow Fever. New York. 1805.

On Constitutions, Governments, and Charters. New York 1805.

Contributions pub. in The Prospect, N. Y. 1804–5.

Letter to Andrew A. Dean. New York, 1806.

Observations on Gunboats, etc. 1806.

On the Polit. and Military Affairs of Europe, 1806.

To the People of New York. (Fortifications.) 1807.

On Governor Lewis's Speech. 1807.

On Mr. Hale's Resolutions. 1807.

Three Letters to Morgan Lewis. 1807.

On the question, Will there be War? 1807.

Essay on Dream. Examination of the Prophecies. New York, 1807.

Reply to the Bishop of Llandaff. New York. 1810.

Origin of Freemasonry. New York. 1811.

Miscellaneous Poems. By Thomas Paine. London : R. Carlile. 1819.

Paine's principal works have been translated into French and German, and some of them into other European languages.

INDEX.